By Kris Tualla:

A Woman of Choice

A Prince of Norway

A Matter of Principle

Loving the Norseman

Loving the Knight

A Primer for
Beginning Authors

Becoming an
Authorpreneur

Loving
the
Norseman

Kris Tualla

Nannette —
I could not do
this without
you!
♡ Kris

Goodnight Publishing
http://www.GoodnightPublishing.com

Loving the Norseman is a work of fiction. Names, characters, places and incidents are products of the author's imagination or are used fictitiously and are not to be construed as real. Any resemblance to actual events, locales, organizations, or persons, living or dead, is entirely coincidental.

Goodnight Publishing
www.GoodnightPublishing.com

info@GoodnightPublishing.com

Cover Model: Lance Rumsey
StarMaker Models/Talent & Casting
www.starsusa.com

Goodnight Publishing and its Logo are Registered Trademarks.

ISBN-10: 1456562118
EAN-13: 978-1456562113

*This book is dedicated to my writing sisters
at my Arizona RWA Chapters:
Desert Rose, Valley of the Sun, and Saguaro-Tucson.*

*Their constant encouragement with my
unconventional heroes and settings
has been priceless.*

Thank you, ladies.

Chapter One

Balnakeil Bay, Scotland
May 13, 1354

A flash of blinding light wasn't enough warning before the slap of thunder knocked Grier to her knees. Sea wind tried to hold her down and huge raindrops clouted her. The castle grounds were already soaked as Grier struggled to her feet and stumbled back inside the keep.

Never mind the chickens. We'll make do with dried venison for supper.

Lightning chased through pewter clouds. Thunder bellowed, drowning the crash of waves shattering against the rocky shore. Salt spray and rain beat against the keep's narrow leaded windows.

Safely ensconced, Grier flinched, though she knew the thick diamond-shaped glass protected her. Isolated on Scotland's northernmost coast, little Durness Castle had weathered tempests from this bluff for two centuries. It would weather this gale as well.

"It's a bad one," Logan murmured over her shoulder. His breath fogged the chilled panes, in spite of the healthy fire that bathed the kitchen in orange between the storm's flashes of blue.

"Aye." Grier squinted against the violent light and used her woolen sleeve to wipe the window. "What's that?" She nudged her younger cousin.

He canted his head. "Where?"

"Out there, see? Is that a boat?" Through the undulating shroud of rain, a dark object appeared. Sodden, black, tapered and rough, it rocked crazily in the throes of the storm.

"I've never seen a boat the likes of that one." Logan squinted. "Can you see the mast pole? Broke right off, it is!"

Grier and Logan watched the craft as it hurtled toward landfall. No one seemed to be in control of the vessel—or the vessel was already damaged beyond control.

"She'll founder for sure." Logan pressed closer to the glass. "I wonder if anyone's still aboard."

"I'm going down in case there is!" Grier stepped away and glanced around.

Logan faced her, incredulous. "Have ye lost your mind, woman?"

"Not my mind, only my cloak."

Logan snorted and returned his attention to the window. He wiped the glass. "Oh, Lord."

"What?" Grier swooped her woolen cloak from behind a bench and leaned against Logan's broad shoulders.

The wooden craft was pinned against a rock. As the cousins watched, the next swell snapped the hull in half like a pod of summer peas.

"Are ye coming?" She dragged open the kitchen door of the keep, leaving Logan little say in the matter.

Grier gasped as shards of salty water stung her face. Pulling her hood lower against the driven rain, she left through the castle gate, crossed the wood-plank bridge over the dry moat, and stumbled down the embankment until she reached the saturated sand. The sated sea was already discarding shattered timbers.

Before Logan reached her, she saw the first body.

"There!" she shouted, pointing at a tumbling splash of fabric. Roistering wind and water stole her voice; Logan couldn't hear her. She waved and gestured, then threw off her cloak and waded barefoot into the wrestling waves. Logan pushed past her and grabbed the body. Together, they dragged the limp sailor from the thrashing sea. The man's blond head flopped oddly onto his shoulder.

Too late. His neck's broken.

Logan helped her haul him beyond the grasp of the waves and lay him on the sand. Grier made the sign of the cross and felt through her soaked woolen gown for the crucifix she always wore. She squinted as rain ran into her eyes.

"Grier!"

The urgency in Logan's voice bade her to turn. Another figure was washing closer. She ran into the sea, up to her waist, her teeth chattering in the frigid brine. She fought the aggressive advance of water and the suction of its retreat as she and Logan struggled to reach the second body.

But the sea was jealous of its prize and pushed her down. Grier thrashed to regain her footing. She gagged on salt water. She rose defiantly, sand sucking at her ankles, and flung her heavy, wet hair away from her face with her forearm. She gulped air and rain, and curled her toes to gain hold in the shifting underwater ground.

The body bumped hard against her.

Grier twisted and her fingers clenched, but his shirt tore from her grip. On the next surge, she dug her nails past shirt into flesh. Logan appeared beside her and they dragged the second man out of the waves. Logan laid him by his shipmate.

"Is he—" Before Logan could finish, the man shuddered. Grier pushed him onto his side and he vomited seawater on the wet sand.

"Might ye get him inside?" Grier asked, retrieving her cloak with numbed hands. Wind snapped her tangled curls, stinging her eyes and cheeks.

"Aye. I'll manage." Logan squatted and pulled the limp form onto his broad back. The stranger was substantially longer than Logan's nearly six-foot frame but much leaner. Grier saw the angles of his shoulder blades through the tattered skin of his shirt.

"Are there others, do ye think?" Grier asked. Her gaze skimmed the churning waves. She shivered and clenched her jaw to stop her teeth from chattering.

"I don't see anyone, but I'll come back and look." Logan grunted as he shifted the dead weight on his shoulders. He swiped dripping brown hair from his eyes. "For now let's see to this one, and he's alive yet."

Grier ran ahead and clambered up the rise toward the stone

keep. Leaving the kitchen door ajar for Logan, she dragged an unused cot into that room, set it by the fire, and went in search of blankets. When she returned, Logan was inside with the sailor.

"Put him on the cot." Grier shrugged off her wrap and hung it by the blazing hearth. Steam rose from it, filling the space with the dank smell of wet wool.

Logan lowered the man onto the pallet that proved shorter than he by several inches. The sailor moaned, but didn't regain his senses. A gash on his cheek bled freely.

"Undress him. I must see what else needs tending." Grier reached for a linen towel. "Cover his lisk with this."

"That's no' proper!" Logan protested. "You're no' married!"

Grier lifted one eyebrow. "And do you forget all the bodies I prepared for burial when the dying first began? The Black Death was no' particular about that situation, either!"

Logan groused that those persons were beyond caring about modesty, but did as he was bid even so.

Grier went up to her sleeping chamber on the second level of the keep. She lifted a dry kirtle and chemise from her kist, changed into them quickly, and left her wet clothes in a heap on the floor. She grabbed some clean linen rags and hurried back downstairs to the warm kitchen.

The puny afternoon light was weakening outside of the thick, leaded windows. Grier pulled her basket of healing supplies from a shelf and, fresh candle in hand, approached the stranger, now lying naked but for the linen towel.

"His leg's broke. See, there? Hold this." She handed Logan the candle. He paled a little as she prodded the man's shin. "'Tis a clean break, and only the one bone. That's good."

Her experienced hands skimmed over the stranger's mortally cold skin. The left side of his chest was already darkening.

"His ribs are bruised, might be cracked. But nothing's loose." Grier punctuated that assessment with a nod of her head. "A sharp bit o' broken rib can poke a man's lungs, so he's lucky again."

Logan glanced at her. "If he's lucky, I would mislike seeing him on a bad day."

Grier grunted and lifted his arm. "This wrist is swalt. I can no' tell if it's broke, but the bones are where they belong."

"Lucky?"

Her lips twitched. "Aye."

Blood pooled under the man's left eye, most likely from a knot on his forehead. Though his body was marked with random scars, that seemed the extent of his new injuries.

"Stitches or burning?" she mused, not really asking.

"What?" Logan's brown eyes widened.

"The gash on his face. How might I close it." Grier lifted her basket. "I'll do that first, afore he comes sensible. That's *if* he comes sensible."

The cousins considered the limp form stretched naked by the fire. He was far too thin. Grier had no trouble feeling his bones through pale blue skin.

"Stitches. It'll take more time, but will scar him less," Grier decided, and pulled out a needle and thread.

"I'll take that wee look at the water." Logan backed away. "To be sure, ye ken?"

"Aye. Go on then," Grier muttered and threaded her implement.

By the time Logan returned, the gash was closed. Grier dressed it with honey and a strip torn from a linen rag.

"None else washed ashore," Logan confirmed and pushed a stool close to the fire. He sat and pulled his soaked doublet and shirt off over his head. "I'll wrap the other'n and prepare his cairn in the yard when the storm blows over."

Grier nodded her agreement and pointed at the man's left heel. "Will you pull a bit there?"

Logan blanched and turned to face the patient. He gingerly grasped the man's heel and swallowed audibly. "Here?" he asked.

"Aye. Hold it just so." She leaned over the man's leg and listened to his bones as she pressed them into alignment. "Do no' move!"

She laid wool wadding over the break and wrapped a layer of linen around his calf. After a quick perusal of the kitchen, Grier selected two long-handled wood spoons. She laid them along either side of the man's leg with the bowls of the spoons cupping his ankle and wrapped the shafts with strips of linen until his leg was secure.

"Might I move now?" Logan whispered.

"Aye. So long as his leg does no'!" Grier arched her back and stretched.

After she extended the pallet with a wooden box to support the stranger's legs and feet, she covered him in blankets and added peat to the fire. Logan went to put on dry clothes. Outside the sky darkened as, somewhere beyond the storm, the sun made her daily departure.

ᚱᛀ

Supper finished, Grier sat by the fire sipping a cup of warmed mead and watching the man. Fever came on him, and he alternately shivered and sweated. There was naught else she could do for him but pray that he recover. Again, she felt for the crucifix that lived on a thick gold chain around her neck.

It was the only thing she had left of her mother. Her beloved Mam died of consumption ten years ago when Grier was but sixteen. Her grief clung to her, a physical presence both harsh and persistent, and she believed that to be the worst event that could ever befall her.

Until the Black Death.

For six years they lived in terror, watching friends and family fall with no apparent pattern. Over half the people in Durness died, including her beloved Da and his only brother, Logan's da. She and Logan were all that survived. Together they oversaw the castle estate, its small keep, and surviving tenants. Eighteen months had passed since the last death, and Grier dared hope those fearsome days were behind them at last.

She set her mug down and considered the man before her. His long hair, dried by the fire, was matted and salt crusted. It seemed to be light brown. The straggled beard furring his cheeks and throat was a bit darker. She wondered what color eyes he had.

Her gaze wandered to his large frame, now hidden under the blankets, and she pictured how he looked nearly naked. 'Sinewy' was the word that came to her mind. Muscular, he might be, had he enough weight on him. Meals had been sparse for this one. She pondered if it was deprivation on the journey that wasted him, or if deprivation was the cause of his journey. Either way, if he woke, she needed to feed him well.

Logan agreed to sit watch later in the night while Grier rested, but when she returned in the morning he was asleep in his chair.

"Ach! Foolish boy." Grier stoked the dying fire. Then she set about making breakfast, slamming pots on the wood table and hacking slices of bacon with a heavy cleaver. They gave off a tantalizing sizzle when she laid them in the hot pan.

"He spoke last night," Logan mumbled, rubbing sleep from his face.

Grier whirled to face her cousin. "Why did you no' come fetch me?"

"It was no' but gibberish."

"Still!"

Logan shrugged. "It sounded like Norse."

Her brows pulled together. "And how might you know Norse?"

"Malise had family in the Shetlands. They've come to live here now."

"In Durness?" Grier dumped oats into boiling water. She looked for a wooden spoon to stir with afore she remembered what she'd done with them. She used the cleaver instead.

"Aye." Logan made a face at the improvised utensil. "Will the parritch taste like bacon now?"

Grier ignored the query, wondering what other information her cousin withheld concerning the girl he hoped to court. "Who came? And why?"

"It's two old aunts. They're alone since the sickness. Malise's mam said they could live here and help out."

"I wonder how much help a pair of old aunts might be."

"Aye. One's thirty-six. The other's already forty!"

Grier jabbed the cleaver into the oats. "Already forty! And are you thinking that be old?"

"It's twice my age!" Logan looked hurt. "Why are ye mad?"

Grier's jaw tensed and she fought back tears. At the advanced age of twenty-six she was very much alone, having buried one suitor after another in the six years of plague. "Never mind."

"I'll never ken how a woman thinks," he grumbled.

Grier clomped outside to the keep's well, a solid wood bucket banging satisfactorily against her leg. Still chilly in mid-May, the world was scrubbed clean by yesterday's storm; only a few clouds stayed to polish the azure sky. She usually loved the smell of the earth after rain because it was so hopeful. Grier could use a wee bit of hope in her life, but she wasn't holding her breath waiting for it.

She determinedly changed the subject when she reentered the

kitchen. "So you're thinking he's Norse?" she asked, pouring the water into a pot over the fire.

Logan shrugged. "Aye, he could be. From the Shetlands? Or the Orkneys?"

A grunt from the cot swung their heads around. Grier's entire world was swallowed by a pair of pale green eyes the color of newly sprouting thistle leaves. They glowed, bewitching her from beneath the long thatch of twisted, light-brown locks. Something stirred deep inside her and she forgot to breathe.

Those eyes shifted devastatingly away from hers to the pot of water, then returned and blessed her once again.

"Ye—ye must be thirsty," she spoke aloud to break their pull. She hurried to dip a cup into the pot and then knelt beside the cot. "Easy, now. No' too much."

His hand rested over hers and the eyes disappeared for a moment, taking all the world's light with them. Cracked lips caressed the edge of the cup and the clear liquid dribbled between them. When the cup was emptied the eyes reappeared, claimed her soul, and his hand squeezed hers.

"Aye, a bit more shouldn't hurt." Grier lifted a second cup and the man seemed to relax then. When it was drained, he dissolved back into sleep.

Grier remained on her knees by the cot, shaken to her core. Who was this man? And why did his mere gaze seem to alter her life's path? She damped down that daft bit of foolishness. She had indeed been alone far too long if she experienced such fanciful imaginings.

Pushing herself to stand, Grier returned to her cooking. She refused to look in her patient's direction while she finished preparing their breakfast. But the image of his eyes focused on hers remained in her thoughts.

The day progressed in much the same manner: the stranger woke, Grier gave him water, cider or broth, and he collapsed once more into slumber. She was gratified to note that his fever lessened. Given the night shift again, Grier bade Logan to help the man relieve himself, should he be present when the man was awake.

"And call me this time," she chided.

Chapter Two

May 15, 1354

The next morning when Grier came in with the well water, the sailor was awake. Those impossibly pale green eyes reached out to her, wide and intense.

"Orkney?" he rasped, his raw voice painful to hear. The man's eyebrows raised and he patted the edge of the cot with one huge hand. "*Er denne* Orkney?"

"Nay, you're no' in Orkney! You're by Durness. Balnakeil Bay. Scotland."

He managed to slump somehow, considering he was already lying down. "*Skottland.*" His hand crumpled to a fist and he pounded the cot. "*Jeg er ikke ennå hjem.*"

"Hh-yem? Home?" Grier guessed.

Eyes darkening to moss shifted to meet hers from under a lowering brow though no other part of him moved. Grier's gut clenched. His anger was clear, but its direction was not. She set the bucket down and faced him with what she hoped he saw as confident kindness.

"This is my home. My..." She placed her palm against her chest. Then she held her hands over her head like a roof. "Home."

"My home," he mumbled, his voice rough and joyless as his expression.

"Nay, no' your home!" Grier swallowed her trepidation and knelt by the cot. She kept her eyes focused on his. She grasped the man's large hand; it was warm and dry, jaggedly calloused, with long, lean fingers and torn nails. She pressed his palm against his chest. He didn't resist.

"My," she said quietly. He dipped a wee nod. She pointed at him. "Your."

His countenance brightened a tiny bit. He pointed at Grier. "Your?"

She nodded as well. "Aye."

He sighed and swallowed. "*Her er* your home."

"Aye, I believe." She pointed at him and asked, "Your home?"

He looked away from her and shook his head. "*Som jeg leter etter mitt hjem,*" he growled.

Grier laid her knuckles against his weathered cheek. It was warm, but no longer too warm, and held some healthy color at last. She wished she could understand his words. More than her accustomed call to heal, something about this man made her ache to give him comfort. Perhaps it was the lost look in his pale eyes, or the complete lack of a smile lifting his beard-matted cheeks. She sensed he might be as alone—and hopeless—as she.

His gaze jumped to hers then darted around the room, wide and panicked. What little color he had gained, drained from his face.

"*Den andre mannen?*" he croaked. "*Hvor er den andre mannen?*"

"*Mannen?*" Grier startled. Her heart thumped painfully, but she spoke past the pummeling dread. "Other man?"

"*Min venn?*" He clasped his hands together then pantomimed a ship rolling over waves. He pointed at Grier. "*Du*—your—*finner?*"

'Venn' sounded like friend, and she would have bet the castle that 'finner' meant find. Her throat closed up and she could only manage a tiny nod, and then a slow shake of her head.

He sucked a quick breath and winced with pain. Hand on his left side, he exhaled a moan, low and ragged. A tear rolled out the corner of his eye and trickled into his tangled mane.

"*Jeg er til å skylde.*" His cobbled fist pummeled the cot. Again. And again.

And again.

Grier allowed him to grieve for a pace, helpless to soften his anguish. She knew grief far too well; it shredded one's insides until death was preferable. But life most often went onward. She would help his body heal, but the loss of his friend was his to cope with alone.

After several long minutes, she gently turned his face toward her. His skin flushed crimson above the beard, whether with pain or embarrassment she couldn't discern. Downcast eyes, rimmed in red, staggered up her face until they met hers.

Her mouth opened to speak, but she was silenced by his pain. She swallowed thickly and attempted a small, empathetic smile.

"I'm sorry," she whispered.

His lips twitched in acknowledgement. He looked away, closed and wiped his eyes. Grier waited until he looked back to her.

"I," she pointed at her chest, "am Grier MacInnes."

"Gree-er?"

She nodded.

One corner of his mouth curved briefly. "Rydar Martin Petter-Edvard Hansen."

She did smile softly at that. "Ry-dar?" Her tongue rolled the 'r' bookends of his name.

"*Ja*. Rydar Hansen." He rubbed his left side, still wincing a bit.

Grier held out her hand. To her surprise, Rydar pressed it to his lips. They were firm and warm. His voice was low, rough, and achingly tender.

"*Takk du*, Grier."

"You're welcome," she murmured, submerged deliciously in the green sea of his gaze.

When Logan tumbled into the kitchen, Grier jerked her hand from Rydar's and lurched to her feet. She whirled to face her younger cousin.

"Logan! This is Rydar. Rydar Hansen," she blurted. Why was her face growing hot? Nothing inappropriate had transpired between her and the Norse sailor.

"Aye. I ken." Logan nodded his greeting to the man and lifted the lid from a pot over the fire. He made a face when he found only water. "Is there no parritch, then?"

"Ye ken? How?" Grier hurried over to the cabinet, her cheeks tight with embarrassment. She concentrated on the bucket of oats, grabbing the new wooden spoon that she procured yesterday afternoon.

"When you're holding a man's yard for him, it helps to know his name. Might you put milk in the parritch this morn?" Logan swiped a finger through the honey pot and stuck it in his mouth like a wee child, not the grown man that he was.

Grier gave her back to the two men. "That depends on whether the goat's been milked!" she snapped.

"Are ye wroth?" Logan leaned over to see her face, his soft brown eyes searching hers.

"Do we have milk or don't we?" she countered.

"I'll get it," Logan said, his tone more petulant than was suitable for a twenty-year-old laird.

"And when you've done so, I'll put it in the parritch." Grier dumped the oats into the boiling water. "So go."

"And I'll bring eggs as well, aye?" Logan offered before he clomped out of the kitchen.

Sucking air through his teeth, Rydar pushed himself to a sitting position and grimaced. He hummed the breath out slowly and continued to rub the dark bruise on his left side. Tugging the blankets close around his narrow hips, he swung his long legs to the floor with a grunt.

"Go easy, Rydar!" Grier stopped stirring the oats and moved to push her sewing basket under his broken limb. "Ye do no' want to knock it out of place!"

Rydar pulled up the edge of the blanket until he could see the wood spoons strapped to his calf. The astonished look on his face was so unexpected that Grier burst out laughing. She clapped her hand over her mouth, suddenly afraid she might offend. Puzzled eyes lifted to hers above a weak lopsided smile. She lowered her hand and gave a small shrug.

"Did ye always smile like that? Or is it since ye were hurt?" Grier touched the dressing over the stitches in his cheek. Rydar's fingers followed hers and explored the wound. She noticed his pale skin puckering with cold.

"I washed and fixed your clothes," she continued, retrieving his shirt, braies, and hose from a stool by the fire. "Your doublet was gone, but I bade Logan to bring down one of his. I'll find you a new one as soon as I'm able."

Rydar accepted the garments and slipped the repaired shirt over his head. Grier turned back to her cooking while he struggled into the braies and hose. His snorted chuckle beckoned the return of her attention.

Though a big enough man, Logan was shorter and stockier than Rydar. The fabric of his doublet strained at the sailor's broad shoulders, but gaped loose around Rydar's middle. The sleeves ended halfway below his elbows. The skirt of the tunic, which should have reached mid-thigh, barely covered his groin.

Rydar grinned sheepishly at Grier, revealing a slightly crooked front tooth. He extended his arms straight out in from of him. "*Jeg er en kjempe*."

"I've no idea what a 'kyem-pa' is, but you look like a giant!" Grier laughed again.

Logan re-appeared with a bucket of milk, still steaming in the crisp morning air. Three eggs nested in his broad hand. He stopped when he saw Rydar wearing his doublet.

"It's no' the best fit, aye?" Logan handed the eggs to Grier and set the bucket of milk on the table. "We can no' make you shorter, but Grier's cooking will fill you out!"

Rydar's stomach growled loudly in response. Bits of his face not covered by his tangled beard suffused scarlet.

Grier lifted the pot of oat parritch to the table. "Go on then, eat up! I'll cook the eggs."

Logan spooned generous portions into two bowls, and added milk and honey to both. He handed one bowl to Rydar. Rydar scooped up a large bite, blew on it, then put it in his mouth. His eyes closed and he paused.

"*Mmm. Det er god*," he sighed.

"Good?" Logan guessed.

Rydar nodded and scooped another large bite. "Good," he repeated. By the time the eggs were cooked, his bowl was scraped clean.

"Do ye want more?" Grier divided the eggs between the two men, giving the larger portion to Rydar.

"*Mere? Ja. Takk du.*"

"You're welcome." Grier watched while Rydar devoured his portion of eggs in three bites, and then finished another large bowl of oat parritch. When had he eaten last? She suspected it was several days before he shipwrecked. She poured a generous mug of ale for each of the men.

Logan set his empty bowl on the table and gulped the ale. "I'll be off now. The storm set things back a bit and I've more'n a day's work to do." He stood and nodded to Rydar. "I'll see you later, then." The man nodded solemnly in return and Logan headed out of the keep.

Rydar pointed at Logan's disappearing back, then at Grier. He clasped his hands together, eyebrows raised. "Your *mann?*"

The question was reasonable since Logan looked nothing like her. Grier wasn't particularly tall; only three or four inches over five feet. And with her tumultuous orange hair and blue eyes, she favored her mother's family, not her father's.

"What? No. No! He's no' my husband! He's my—" How could she explain 'cousin'? She held both hands, palm down, on either side of her head. "My father and mother."

"Farther, morther? *Far og mor?*" Rydar spoke hesitantly. "*Pappa og mamma?*"

"Yes! My papa and mama!" She stepped to one side, hands still up. "Logan's papa and mama. Do ye ken?"

Rydar nodded, his brow plowed with a puzzled frown.

She clasped hands, miming the connection. "My papa and Logan's papa were brothers."

"Brorthers?" Rydar mimicked, then understanding relaxed his features. "*Brødre! Ja.*"

"*Ja!*" Grier nodded. "We are no' married. I have no husband. No *mann.*"

Rydar leaned back and his clear green eyes swept over her in obvious surprise. "No *mann?*" he repeated. He cocked his head and spread his hands in question.

Grier's smile evaporated. "Twas the Black Death."

"No ken 'black death'," Rydar managed.

"Black. Like this." Grier pointed at the pot hanging over the fire. "And death." She mimicked someone dying.

Rydar shook his head, looking contrite. "No ken. *Jeg er trist.*"

Grier took a deep breath, and faced down the ugly memories. "People died. Lots of people." She held up four fingers and pulled down two. "Dead."

"*Død. Ja?*" He held up five fingers and pulled down two.

"No." Grier sat on the cot beside him and pulled down one more. Rydar held up ten, and she pulled down six.

He looked stunned. "*All er død? Å min Gud!*"

"Aye. All are dead. Most times I wondered if 'mine God' was

anywhere to be found."

Grier rubbed her stinging eyes before any futile tears could fall. Crying would not bring anyone back so there was no point in succumbing. She spoke slowly, clearly, using her hands.

"I buried my papa first, and then Logan's papa. I feared it would never stop until we all…"

Willful tears now pushed their way past her lashes, prodded by the devastation that left her bereft of everyone she loved. Swept forward, she struggled to keep her words ahead of the wave of pain that threatened to swamp her.

"For six years they died."

"*Seks år. Ja,*" Rydar said softly.

Grier stared at the fire and wiped her cheeks on her sleeve. Since the Death her future stretched before her as bleak and endless as a stormy winter sky over the North Sea.

She looked back at Rydar and whispered, "Now there's no one left."

Chapter Three

When Moira pulled open the kitchen's outside door, Grier leapt from Rydar's cot as if it was on fire. That was the second time this morn that she was startled away from the big man. What about this exotic stranger made her feel so intimately connected? That when none but words and kindness passed between them, she was embarrassed to be found doing so?

Moira's wide brown eyes hopped from Grier to the big raggedy sailor and back again. She clutched a freckled hand to her throat.

"Is aught amiss?" she squeaked.

"No! No, come in." Grier rubbed her eyes. "Are ye well, then?"

"Aye. No fever since yesterday. And no spots of any sort, ever." Moira stared at Rydar. "What might he be?" Moira had grown over-familiar, now that she was the only surviving maid still serving the cousins' needs in the small keep.

"You mean 'who,' do you no'?" Grier frowned her discipline at the presumptuous girl. Moira shrugged one shoulder, her gaze still glued.

"This is Rydar Martin Petter-Edvard Hansen. His boat sank in the storm and he washed up on the chyngell. He appears to be Norse."

Rydar grinned weakly when Grier said his complete name. He nodded to Moira. She lowered her eyes.

"Does he speak our language?" she whispered.

"No. No' yet." Grier looked over her shoulder at Rydar. "But I'm teaching him."

"He's rather coarse-looking, isn't he?" Moira sniffed and turned half away. Her auburn braid fell over her shoulder. "Where would ye wish me to start today?"

"The Great Hall. Make it presentable for Sir Hansen. I'll make that his apartment while he bides with us."

"The Hall?" Moira now looked at Rydar with a bit of awe. "Why? Is he noble?"

"I don't think so, by the looks of him. But his leg's broke so he can no' manage the steps to the sleep chambers, and the Hall has a door for his privacy."

Grier swung the water pot over the fire, and glanced around the kitchen. She retrieved a small hatchet and waved it at Moira while she rattled her instructions. "Make certain there's a piss pot for him, and plenty of peat for the fire. And a pitcher of fresh water. And towels for him to wash. I'll see to the noon meal."

"He requires a bit more than a mere pitcher o' water," Moira grumbled.

"Do as I bid, Moira. Your tongue is no' required."

"Aye, my lady." Her narrowed eyes slid to Rydar before she followed Grier outside to fill her wash bucket at the well.

Grier entered the hen's coop and expertly grabbed one victim by the feet. Outside, she used the hatchet to neatly dispose of its head. She turned to leave when a vision of Rydar gulping his parritch caused her to return and grab a second bird. Grier carried dinner to the keep, draining blood along the way. In the kitchen, she plunged the chicken carcasses into boiling water to loosen their feathers and then plopped them on the table.

"My—*hjelp*—your," Rydar spoke from his cot. He wiggled his fingers toward the blanched birds.

"It's no' mens' work," Grier protested.

Rydar obviously did not understand her, but now he jabbed a finger at the table. "My *hjelp* your!" he insisted in his oddly thick accent.

He spoke with such intent that Grier relented. "Aye. You," she pointed at Rydar, "help me." She patted her chest.

He struggled to stand on one leg and Grier hurried to support him. She tucked under his arm, close to his side. It was a surprisingly nice fit, though—even hunched over—he towered above her. Beneath her palm, lean muscle flexed and snaked across his ribs. The thigh of his uninjured leg bunched and shifted under the knit hose. Together, they shuffled him to the table and into a chair. Grier moved her basket to re-prop the splinted limb. Rydar pulled the chickens close and began to pluck them.

"My help you," he nodded.

"I," Grier pointed at her chest. "I help you."

"I help you. *Ja*."

"Aye."

"Aye. *Takk du*."

"Thank you."

"Thank you?" Rydar repeated.

"Aye. Takk du. Thank you."

"*Ja*. Thank you."

"Aye."

Slack-jawed, the two stared at each other for a moment while understanding caught up with their cryptic verbal exchange. Then they burst into shared laughter. Rydar alternately laughed and moaned, grasping his battered ribs and thus setting them off again. Grier wiped her eyes, watering now from this unexpected—but very welcomed—moment of shared silliness.

"Chicken!" she shouted, hefting a headless carcass.

"Chicken!" Rydar answered. "*Kylling!*"

"Table!" Grier pounded on the tabletop.

"*Tabell!*"

"That was easy! I wonder what else? Fire!"

"*Fyr!*"

"Door!"

"*Dør!*"

"Window!"

"*Vindu!*"

Grier smiled into Rydar's expressive green eyes. "This may no' be so hard," she posited.

"No hard." He shook his head. "I *lærer* your *språk* good."

Grier turned her back. *Perhaps I'll learn your 'speak' as well.*

She made bread in contented silence while Rydar cleaned the chickens. When he asked for a '*kniv*' Grier watched, fascinated, as he cleanly butchered the birds. In one iron pan, she piled turnips, onions and herbs, then snuggled the chickens into a second pan. She pushed both pans and the bread into carved-out ovens on either side of the kitchen's huge fireplace.

"Thank you for your help, Rydar," she murmured. The warming intimacy of both the cozy kitchen and sharing her labors with this man in easy quiet filled Grier with a peace she had not felt for a very long time. She turned to smile at him and found him staring at her. His pale eyes searched, questioned. Her shoulders lifted a wee bit and fell. He gave a faint nod and looked away.

Logan returned late in the morning with the news that he had dug out the burial space for the other sailor. He set some of their tenants to the tasks of wrapping the body and gathering stones for the cairn.

"The priest will come from town this afternoon," he informed, leaning over to sniff the hot bread. "What name should we put on the cross?"

Grier turned to Rydar. His squinting eyes remained focused on their lips. "Your—*venn*? Logan dug his grave."

"*Grav?* Aye. *Er det en prest?*" He made the sign of the cross.

"Aye. The priest will come."

"*Presten vil komme.*" He sighed heavily. Grief dug deepening lines through his beard and pressed down his shoulders. His brow twitched and he sniffed a couple times.

"Rydar? What was his name?"

"Name? *Navn, ja?* Arne Jorgensen." He swallowed audibly and shook his head. He closed his eyes and whispered, "*Jeg er trist,* Arne."

The trio's somber midday meal lacked conversation. Logan simply ate, his appreciation of the fare expressed in periodic grunts. Grier picked at her food, distracted by the presence of the ragged male enigma facing her. She considered Rydar from under her lashes and pondered what losses he might be grieving other than his friend. Something had set them adrift in that little boat, risking both their lives. How far had they come? Where were they headed?

And why?

Rydar ate what he obviously considered a polite portion, but Grier saw the longing in his gaze. She heaped his platter a second time without asking. He tried to object, but she would have none of it.

"You're as thin as thread! And I mean to see you filled out." She pushed the platter back towards him and poured another brimming mug of golden ale. "You eat all of that, ye hear?"

While he may not know her words, he clearly got her meaning. With a nod of gratitude, he tackled the victuals, all but licking the platter clean.

ᚱᚺ

Logan fashioned a crutch for Rydar from a forked tree branch and a wad of wool, and Grier helped the man negotiate the keep's worn stone steps. The morning's stuttering clouds had thickened and grayed the afternoon, and a cool, musty breeze tangled her skirt around her legs. Crumbled shells on the path crunched under their feet, the only dirge lamenting the dead sailor.

The priest waited, prayer book and rosary in hand, by a pile of rocks squeezed into the outer edge of the castle's overfilled cemetery. In a fresh ditch lay Arne's shrouded corpse.

Rydar stopped in his awkward process and stared. His stoic countenance paled and the bruises on his face darkened in contrast. Grier saw his jaw clench repeatedly; his chest heaved in jerky breaths. Rydar hobbled forward, leaning heavily on the crutch, his gaze never moving from the still figure wrapped in ivory linen.

When he reached the body, Rydar struggled to lower his considerable length to the ground beside it. His outreached hand trembled over his friend, then lowered to rest on the cloth, fingers twitching, grasping. His shoulders began to shake. He clutched his left side, slumping prostrate alongside his companion. Low, sorrowful moans caused the priest to pause in the sacrament.

Grier moved without thinking. She knelt on the cold, damp ground beside Rydar and gently lifted his head into her lap. Closing her eyes, she tried to sop up the sorrow that spilled from him. She stroked his long, matted hair, rubbed one hunched and shaking shoulder, and hummed tunelessly.

Feeling him relax a wee bit under her touch, she opened her eyes and nodded to the priest to continue. She was surprised to hear Rydar speak Latin along with the cleric.

He must be devout. She crossed herself and felt for her crucifix.

At the conclusion of the rites, Rydar pushed himself upright and scooted back on his arse, watching somberly while the corpse was covered with rocks.

"*Tilg meg*, Arne. *Jeg er slik trist*," he whispered over and over.

When Logan pounded the wood cross labeled 'Arne Jorgensen' at the head of the cairn, Rydar gasped and wiped his reddened eyes. Then Logan walked toward the cemetery gate with the priest, but Grier stayed beside Rydar. She needed to keep touching him, stroking his back or his arm, until finally he pushed her away. He pointed to the keep.

"I *vil komme*," he rasped. She didn't move. "I *vil komme!*" he said again.

Grier stood slowly and smoothed her gown, unwilling to leave him alone but apparently unwelcome to stay. "Aye, then," she murmured. "Do no' stay too long. It's chilling."

He shook his head as if he understood.

The day aged. The sun snuck beneath the clouds and hovered over the water's northwestern horizon. Copper highlights briefly burnished the waves of Balnakeil Bay before Rydar hobbled back into the keep. Grier heard his uneven steps in the hallway and hurried to intercept him.

"There ye be. I'm so sorry about your friend," she said quietly and squeezed his arm.

He nodded, reddened lids lowered, beard-tangled cheeks hollowed out.

"Come, I've something to show you." Grier gestured for him to follow her into the Hall.

He paused inside the door, pale gaze wide and touching everything. Moira had moved the cot and made a bed for him near the fire. On a polished table were a glazed pitcher of water and a stack of folded towels. A less elegant pot waited by the hearth.

The room was well-appointed, having been used for all types of gatherings during the happier days in Grier's memory. Ornately carved chairs and small tables were scattered around. A cabinet rested against the far wall. The fireplace nestled between two tall leaded-glass windows. Woven tapestries on the outer walls depicted both religious icons and scenes from Scotch life.

One large piece illustrated a Viking longship landing on Scottish shores to a welcome of arrows and swords. Rydar tilted his head toward it and gave Grier a puzzling little smile.

Then he spied the mirror.

Chapter Four

The gilt-framed mirror hung opposite the hearth in the formal hall. Pushed by curiosity Rydar hobbled toward it, his pulse thrumming with trepidation. Both his brow and jaw dropped when he saw his reflection. He turned startled eyes to Grier, and then looked back at the polished silver surface. He bent closer and tried to comb his fingers through the matted hair that hung below his shoulders. He pulled at his half-a-foot of tangled beard and turned aside to see the stitched gash. His shoulders slumped.

"Å *min Gud*," he groaned.

"It's no' all that bad." He didn't understand her words, but Grier's tone sounded encouraging. "A bath would help. And a bit o' barbering."

"Barbering! Aye." He knew that word. His grateful grin made a half-hearted appearance; it was the best he could manage right now.

"I'll have Logan give ye a hand this eventide."

"Logan. Aye. *Takk du.*" He stared again, disbelieving his reflection, stunned by its multiple revelations. The man in the mirror was a complete stranger. He never would have imagined that he looked like this. This battered. This thin. This old.

How old was he? His birthday was at the summer solstice; he thought he'd be twenty-seven or twenty-eight. But his father died at the young age of forty-three, and the reflection facing him now looked exactly like his memory of his father. The past years were much harder on him than he realized.

Rydar clenched his jaw, fighting an oppressive sense of failure that threatened to snuff what life still clung to him. The urgency of his journey wrapped its crushing tendrils around his beaten ribs. One thing was undeniable: he must continue on as soon as possible. He had already lost too many years. But the merciless storm had eaten his boat and killed his friend.

And now he had to begin again. Alone.

How might he continue? He lost everything. He had not one thing left on this earth to call his own.

God in Heaven, please save me.

Rydar glanced at Grier's reflection behind him.

Again, he added guiltily.

ᚱᚾ

After yet another of Grier's generous meals, Rydar struggled into the copper tub of steaming water that waited in his adopted chamber. Clumsy because of his splinted leg, his face warmed with keen irritation and unaccustomed embarrassment. Logan pushed a chair near the tub to support Rydar's left foot and keep the dressing dry. Then he said something about 'barbering' and left the room.

Once in the water, Rydar felt his body begin to relax in its embracing heat. He leaned his head back and relished the pleasurable sensation. This relief was better than Valhalla. A very welcome bit of civilization in a life that had been completely devoid of such for nearly two decades.

Rydar contemplated his injuries. The left side of his chest was a dark purple, but already yellowing around the edges. He unwrapped his right wrist, bent too far when the mast broke off his boat the morning of the wreck. The swelling had receded and it hurt less to flex than it had. So the bruises and sprain weren't bad—he'd endured much worse in Grønnland—but the broken leg did throb, the ache relentless in the damp chill of the north Scotland clime. He could not recall the moment it broke but that was of no matter.

It'll mend, he told himself. She's done a fine job with the splint.

Made of spoons.

He chuckled a little in spite of the day's sad events.

Eyes closed, he concentrated on the water's healing warmth, inhaled its steam, and savored every undulating ripple over his puckering skin. He cast his thoughts back, trying to remember the last stone building he had been inside. It had to be in Arendal, before his father moved the family from Norway to Grønnland. All the buildings in that God-forsaken place were made of sod and wood. Mostly sod. Trees were as rare as mermaids there.

How old was he then? Ten or eleven. Not yet a man. Young enough to anticipate adventure and too young to fully understand the hellish existence they landed in. It took but a quarter of the next score of years for him to figure out that the remote arctic settlement—and those Norsemen struggling to eke out a living in it—were irrevocably dying.

He was glad to be alone just now. He felt like crying again. That particular emotion had swamped him more since leaving Grønnland than in all his previous years of life; even when his parents died one after the other, the spark beaten out of them by the harsh reality of a miserable and hopeless existence. But he was a grown man, and grown men didn't cry over mere disappointment.

Guilt poked him hard at this moment of selfish relief. Blessed, welcome relief in the form of safety, food and warmth. Relief that tempered the excitement, terror, and desperation that had dogged him since the decision was first made to build the boat.

It was entirely his idea to build the vessel and sail east for Norway; Arne had never been there. Born in the Grønnland settlement, Arne's only contact with their shared homeland had been the ships that brought both supplies and a few more desperate souls anxious to start new lives. Rydar spun tales of castles and kings and beautiful women, carried by a young adolescent's view of the world. He succeeded in convincing his best friend to join his enterprise when the ships stopped coming.

It may be that the last ship was five or six years ago.

I wonder if this 'Black Death' Grier spoke of reached Norway? Is that the reason the ships didn't come?

And if it was, would he find half of his family dead when he returned? Because he would indeed return; his situation here was merely a delay. Whatever was required of him, he vowed to walk into Hansen Hall at Arendal and reclaim what was his. He couldn't allow anything—or anyone—to stop him. If he did, all of his life to this point would be wasted.

The hall door opened and Logan re-entered, razor and soap in hand. He handed the chunk of soap to Rydar who accepted the soft, pungent substance as if he had been handed an ingot of pure gold. Rydar held his breath and dipped under the water. He scrubbed his hair and beard with the soap, careful of the gash in his cheek. Then he surfaced and soaped his body. He smiled when he handed the slippery bar back to Logan.

"*Det lukter som blomster.*" The soap smelled of flowers.

Logan said something back. Rydar shrugged and shook his head. Then Logan held up the razor and Rydar understood his meaning. He sat up in the tub and presented his chin.

Logan was quite skilled at barbering. He shaved Rydar well, skimming close to the stitches on the left cheek, but not cutting the threads. When he finished, Rydar rinsed himself again in the cooling water, then Logan helped him from the tub. Without thinking, Rydar put his left leg down. A hot spike of pain shot up his shin, causing him to cry out, and he nearly fell.

Logan caught him.

"Have a care, man! It's still broken!" he chided.

Rydar couldn't match any of those words with Norse or any of the other tongues he knew, but was fairly certain what was intended. He jerked a nod, growing increasingly angry that he couldn't understand their particular language. He was unaccustomed to feeling weak and his frustration threatened his ability to remain polite to his saviors. He dried himself, the towel taking the brunt of his irritation, and then dressed again, careful not to rip his repaired shirt.

When Logan handed him a comb he stared at it, momentarily transported. Carved from bone, the brace was wrapped in tooled silver. His mother had one very much like it. Odd. He remembered her comb, but her face was beyond his reach.

It took some work to get the comb through his tangled hair but Rydar eventually accomplished the task. Logan lifted the razor again, this time in question. Then he mimed cutting his own locks, which were chin length. Rydar nodded. He watched tufts of his hair fall to the stone floor before Logan swept them into the fire. They were much darker than he thought. The honeyed blond of his youth had given way to maturity in a world with little sun to lighten it.

"You look good," Logan complimented.

"Good?" he raised one brow, skeptical.

"Aye. If I do say so." Logan grinned and gathered his barbering tools.

"*Takk du.*" Rydar reached out for his crutch and Logan obliged. I need to talk with Grier, he thought. I understand her.

ᚱᚺ

Grier stood in the passageway outside the sleeping chambers. She gripped a brass candlestick tightly in one hand. Her other hand trembled on the rusted latch securing an iron-banded wood door. She drew multiple breathes in an unsuccessful attempt to slow her pulse. She hadn't been in this room since the day her father died.

"It's nigh four years past," she said aloud. "And now it's needful."

She drew a deep breath and held it.

The latch balked, and then yielded with the squawk of aggravated metal. Grier stepped inside. Candlelight flickered across bare walls. Dust coated everything in a gray snowscape of neglect. She moved toward a large cedarwood kist at the foot of the bed.

When Grier had to breathe again, it was not as she feared. The room smelled stale, but the reek of death was gone. Voided bowels, blood, pungent medicines of no value, all of which filled the air on that horrible day had failed to leave a lasting legacy. A wee bit of her trepidation faded. She set the candlestick on the floor and lifted the lid of the kist. The bite of cedar washed away the remembrance.

Her father's clothes were still neatly folded in the coffer. He was a tall man, not quite so tall as Rydar, but taller than Logan. Grier lifted a blue velvet doublet, pleated with pearls. She pressed it to her lips, eyes closed.

"I miss you, Da," she whispered thickly. Her eyes stung with denied tears and her breath warmed the fabric, releasing more of the purging cedar aroma. She remembered the last time she saw her father in this garment. It was her betrothal dinner with Fergus and his parents.

The world was different then, but it was already slipping inexorably into hell.

Grier set the doublet on her lap with a rough sigh and began to dig through the chest. She added a burgundy brocade doublet and one of pale green wool that matched Rydar's eyes. She also gathered up three pair of braies, three pair of hose and four linen shirts.

"Boots!" she gasped. She reached for a soft leather pair and one with wooden soles for outdoor work. She had no idea if either would fit.

Before she left the room, she paused and looked around. Someday soon this chamber would be Logan's. He would marry and bring his bride here. They would sleep in her parents' bed. They would consummate their marriage and birth their children on the same bed she was born in. Her father's land, her father's castle, and her father's keep were now Logan's. Refusing to consider her fate any further, Grier left the bedchamber and shut the latch solidly behind her.

"I'm no' replaced yet!" she stated firmly, and stalked to the top of the stone staircase.

Grier was descending the stairs with the clothing in her arms when Rydar opened the door to his new accommodations. He hobbled out, leaning on the crutch, and turned to look up at her.

She froze mid-step.

Cropped light brown hair swung around his chin, shining like melted gold in the candlelight. Logan's barbering around the stitched gash revealed an expressive face with classic Nordic structure: a high brow, prominent cheekbones and a strong jaw. Deeply set and intense, his pale-jade eyes were framed with crinkled lines and straight brown brows.

Rydar smiled a little, the uninjured cheek lifting higher than the other. His strong features were far beyond Grier's expectations; there had been no hint of the bonny countenance hiding behind the unkempt beard. Her heart thumped as if to push her toward him.

"Good *aften*, Grier," he said in a deep voice that somehow floated up to her.

"G-good eventide, Rydar," she stuttered. Running her elbow along the wall to keep her equilibrium in the presence of this unexpectedly compelling man, Grier continued her descent until she stood before him. Somehow he was taller than she realized. Six-and-a-half feet, she guessed. The incongruent scent of rose soap wafted from this towering, masculine, creature.

Grier tugged at his ill-fitting doublet to draw his attention away from her face, which was suddenly quite hot.

"*Ja*. I giant," he shrugged.

A surprised laugh burst from her.

Rydar's brow dipped. "Giant? Aye?"

"Aye," she assured him. She wagged a finger. "And you're a smart one, ye are. I'll have to keep my eye on you, and that's sure."

Confusion twisted Rydar's expression. His mouth opened and closed, but he frowned and didn't speak. His gaze dropped to the clothes draped over her arm.

"Oh! These are for you!" Grier lifted the bundle.

"For my?" Rydar turned and hobbled back inside the Hall. He stopped beside his pallet and laid the crutch down. Balanced on one foot, he pulled Logan's doublet over his head while Grier set the clothing on the cot beside the crutch. Rydar selected the pale green tunic and slipped it over his oft-repaired shirt. Grier blinked.

It did match his eyes. And somehow, they grew greener.

Rydar looked down at the length of the skirt and sleeves. "Good!" he blurted. "My good!"

"Aye." Grier walked around him. Though his wide shoulders still stretched the fabric a wee bit, the fit was much improved. "It's bonny good."

"You!" Rydar pointed his finger at her. "You good, Grier. *Takk du*."

His words thawed a small corner of her grief. Grier felt it melt away, carrying with it a scrap of her pain. She smiled at the beautiful, gaunt giant and murmured, "You're welcome."

Chapter Five

May 16, 1354

The front door to the keep slammed open.

"Grier? Rydar?" Logan called out. "Are ye about?"

"In here!" she called from the kitchen. Rydar turned from the fish he was cleaning for supper.

Logan's breadth filled the room's narrow entry. "I've brought guests. Might we greet them in another chamber?"

"We can no' use the Hall, Rydar has it. I expect the dining room might do." Grier untied her apron. "Who've you got?"

"Malise and her old aunts."

She frowned at the uncomplimentary designation. "The ones from the Shetlands?"

"Aye! And the same!" Logan disappeared.

"Shetlands?" Rydar's eyes lit with interest. Grier would not have counted it possible that they might glow so intently with their color so pale. But they did, for a moment stealing her intent.

"Um... Aye." she beckoned him. "Come with me."

Rydar wiped his hands on a towel, sniffed them, and made a face. Then he wiped them again, stood on one leg and tucked his crutch under his arm.

"Aye. Come with you," he said in his strange guttural lilt. He repeated everything she said and was quickly gaining simple language. He hobbled after her to the more formal room.

"Ach, I forgot! Sit. I'll be right back!" Grier pointed at the heavy carved chairs arranged around the polished table.

"Forgot. Sit. Be *rett* back. Aye," Rydar said, and sat. A faint grin brushed his confused countenance. His eyes never wavered from hers as though he could absorb her meaning if he only stared at her hard enough. So many times in the days since they rescued him, she would turn unaware and catch his pale gaze. It always made her belly flutter.

Grier hurried back to the kitchen. She procured a tray, six mugs and a pitcher of cooled beer. She was on her way to the dining room when the front door opened and Logan ushered in his young love and her old aunts. At the least, that's who she assumed they must be. Bright sunlight poured in behind them and obscured their features.

"Welcome to Durness Castle!" She dipped her chin; a bow was impossible with the laden tray. "Logan? Might you escort our guests to the dining room?"

"Yes! Of course!" He took Malise by the arm and led her forward. The aunts followed.

Grier placed the tray on the table and Rydar rose on one leg to serve the ale. When she objected, he placed his huge hand over hers.

"I *hjelp* you, aye?"

His touch was warm and firm and looking into his eyes so closely made her forget what it was she meant to say. She blinked and managed, "Aye. Thank you."

He winked at her and her chest tingled in a very unexpected and pleasant manner. What on God's good earth was that about? With more effort than was seemly, she dragged her attention away from Rydar and turned to greet her guests.

Her smile turned to stone. She resolved at that moment to murder Logan rather violently in his bed at the earliest possible opportunity.

Logan's love interest, Malise, was an attractive fifteen-year old with thick chestnut hair and warm hazel eyes. She was shorter and curvier than Grier, but no doubt a good fit for Logan. The aunts, however, were an entirely different story.

Perhaps a hand taller than Grier, the statuesque sisters were garbed in high-waisted gowns of soft, expensive wool, one in deep blue, the other in heather green. Both had blue-gray eyes and pale golden hair, though one's locks were streaked with silver. In defiance of their ages, both women were beautiful by anyone's accounting.

Grier straightened, agonizingly aware of the tattered gray kirtle she wore. She wondered if Rydar would heed the difference in their apparel. But even if he didn't, the aunts were women and they surely would. She smoothed her untamable curly hair from her brow noting that—even after the breezy journey from town—neither of the aunts' hair was disheveled.

She would kill Logan slowly. Torture was most certainly called for.

"Logan?" Grier prompted, forcing her tone to remain as pleasant as she could in the midst of her uncomfortable humiliation and his looming dismemberment.

The young man pulled his eyes from the beaming Malise. "Oh, aye. Might I present Madam Hanne Larsen and the Lady Margoh Henriksen, recently of the Shetland Islands."

Grier now managed a proper bow without the encumbrance of the tray. The aunts' eyes passed over her from tresses to toes. Flickers of confusion and surprise passed between them.

"My cousin, the Lady Grier MacInnes," Logan continued.

Margoh frowned. "You are the lady of the castle?"

"I am, Lady Henriksen." Grier stretched her cheeks wide, hoping her grimace passed for a polite smile. She couldn't stop herself from fingering the nubby fabric of her worn dress.

"Have we come at an inopportune time?" Hanne's tone was frosty.

"No, Madam. I was cooking—it's a turn that pleases me—and did no' wish to sully a decent gown. We are quite happy to have you." Grier faced her cousin. "Logan will you please continue the introductions?"

All eyes shifted to the young man. While Logan gestured toward the sailor, Rydar's gaze bounced from mouth to mouth.

"Aye, of course. May I present our guest, Rydar Hansen of..." A blank look claimed Logan's visage.

"Rydar? You're from Orkney, are ye no'?" Grier assumed.

"Orkney? I? No." Rydar frowned, obviously puzzled. "I come *fra Grønnland*."

"Greenland!" Grier blurted. "You sailed all the way here from Greenland?"

"Aye. Sailed all way here." Rydar turned to the guests, bowed and placed a lingering kiss the back of each of the older women's hands. *"Det er min fornøyelse, fru."*

The women's eyes widened.

"Du taler Norse!" Margoh exclaimed. *"Hvordan er dette mulig?"*

"Er jeg Norsk!" Rydar responded, smiling.

"Please make yourselves comfortable, will you?" Grier interrupted, flustered by the animated exchange she didn't understand. "Might you care for a drink?"

"Thank you," said Madam Larsen, the older aunt. Straight-backed and regal, she lowered into a chair and frowned up at Rydar.

"Lady Henriksen?" Grier held up a mug in question. Her distracted mind juggled shock at both the impossible distance Rydar covered in that small boat, and bewilderment over the odd yearning sparked by the harsh melody of his language.

"Yes, thank you." Lady Henriksen's gaze was locked on the tall Norseman. This sister was definitely not frowning.

"Please sit, Lady." Grier placed the woman's serving of ale in front of a chair. Rydar pulled the chair away from the table.

"Takk du," Margoh murmured and sank seductively into the proffered seat.

"You're welcome," Grier and Rydar responded in unison.

Grier felt her face flame and Rydar gave her a wee grin. Determined to be a proper hostess in spite of the awkward situation, she pressed forward. "What brings you and your sister to Durness, Madam Larsen, if you don't mind my asking?"

"Plague," was the succinct response.

"Now, Hanne! There's no cause to be rude," Margoh scolded. She fluttered her lashes at Rydar and gave an apologetic little shrug.

Grier disguised a derisive snort as a cough. Rydar's amused gaze briefly touched hers.

"Why else would we leave our home, then?" Hanne retorted.

"To join our youngest sister, of course!" Margoh tossed Rydar a brilliant smile. Grier was certain he caught it. Her mood dipped unaccountably.

Grier turned to face Hanne. "I lost my Da. Logan did as well."

"I lost my husband and both my sons." Hanne glared at Grier, challenging her level of grief.

"I, too, lost a husband. But it was no great burden," Margoh added. She turned her profile to Rydar and smoothed her hair, drawing his gaze to the graceful movement of her soft white fingers. "Are you married, Lady MacInnes?"

Grier was so fascinated by the woman's skillful trifling that it took her a moment to realize Margoh now addressed her. She looked down at her work-reddened hands, knotted in her lap. The only way this encounter could be any more uncomfortable was if she were naked.

And her hair on fire.

"No, Madam. I was betrothed thrice. Plague took them all afore the vows were spoken."

"Pity," Hanne responded, her voice flat.

Grier pressed her lips together and considered the older sister. Had she always been so bitter? Of course, the horrors of the Death might certainly turn a person previously disposed to a happier constitution.

Even me, she realized with a start.

Logan ceased whispering with Malise and entered the conversation. "I was of a mind that, since Lady Margoh and Madam Larsen speak both languages, they might tutor Sir Hansen."

"Oh!" Grier forced a polite smile. After that suggestion, Logan might not live long enough to even see his bed. She cleared her throat, stalling. "What a bonny idea."

"My sister has no interest, but I'm willing," Margoh offered. She blinked at Rydar and rested her fingertips against her throat. "Quite."

"Have you asked Rydar?" Grier demanded of the grinning Logan. Unexplained irritation jabbed her toward rudeness.

He frowned. "No. And there's no reason, then, is there? Why would he no' wish to learn?"

Rydar leaned forward when his name was mentioned. "*Hva er deg sir?*"

"*Jeg vil lære du Scots Engelsk.*" Margoh cooed.

"Scots English," Grier injected. Then more softly she added, "Learn my speak."

"Aye," Rydar agreed. He leaned back, satisfaction sculpting his expression. "Good."

Grier challenged Margoh. "You'll have to come here to do it."

"Here?" The woman scowled. "Why?"

"He's got a broken leg, hasn't he? He can no' be walking the mile into Durness, then, can he?" Grier explained to the obviously stupid woman.

"I suppose not." Margoh made a pouty face, but then she turned to Logan and her voice became honey. "Will you fetch me?"

"Fetch you?" Grier yelped, incredulous. "Your leg is no' broken!"

Margoh pointedly ignored her and pressed her case with Logan. "It would be a great boon if ye might be willing, Logan."

Logan glanced at Rydar, then Malise. The girl smiled and dipped her chin, gazing at him from beneath long, auburn lashes. He grinned.

"I shall be very pleased to do so," he answered.

ᚱᚺ

Grier violently scrubbed the pottery mugs hardly caring if she broke one. The aunts' unexpected visit was ghastly. Why hadn't Logan told her what he meant to do? That he was bringing the aunts to the keep today? That he expected them to tutor Rydar? That, far from being old, they were poised and beautiful and dearly dressed and neatly coiffed and Norse-speaking and, and—available? And not just available, but the younger one seemed outright eager for male company. And Rydar's company at that!

The kitchen door opened and Logan strode in on a damp evening sea breeze. He stared at her, his brow lowering.

"Why are ye so wroth?" he chided. He dropped an armload of wood by the hearth. "Atween the two of us, it's I who has reason to be wroth! A laird should no' be required to carry his own firewood!"

"Then hire a manservant, why don't you?" Grier snapped.

"Ye ken as well as I that there are no suitable prospects!" Logan retorted. "They're all dead!"

Grier spun to face him, pushed beyond furious. Her cousin had aptly named her hopeless estate, and yet he had no idea.

"Aye! Open your damned eyes, Logan!" she shouted. "The suitable prospects *are* all dead!" She threw the sopping dish towel hard at his face and ran from the kitchen.

Passing Rydar in the hallway without acknowledgement, Grier

hiked her skirt to her knees and took the stairs two at a time. She slammed the door on her sleep chamber and dove onto her four-poster bed, smashing her face into a feather pillow. She screamed against the cushion without words. She screamed until her abused throat burned so badly she was forced to stop. Then she cried, heartbroken and overwhelmed by loneliness.

When the Death surrounded her, she thought a merciful God might take her as well.

But no, He left her here.

Here to help others through their losses, bury their dead, and keep on living. Here to watch over her father's erstwhile estate until Logan brought home a wife to supplant her. Here to rescue errant sailors who washed up on her chyngell in dire need of her skills.

Here to host old aunts, apparently, while they tutored her errant sailor.

"The 'old aunts' my sweet white arse!" Grier sobbed and punched her pillow. "The younger one just about swived him right there on the table! And now she'll be with him regular, teaching him Scots English." That prospect rested in her gut like a wave-roughened boulder covered with barnacles.

The room darkened as the day died. Her ire dissipated with the fading light. Keeping it alive simply wasn't worth the effort required.

At least the lessons will be here in the castle, she devised. *I might learn Norse in the process, should I like.*

She threw the pillow aside and sat up straight.

That was the answer! Learn Rydar's language! Not that the blond cow would likely invite her to join them. But she couldn't be rude enough to ask Grier to leave, considering it was Grier's home and hospitality that the she-snake was enjoying.

Her jaw dropped open.

Cow?

She-snake?

Grier flopped onto her back with an exasperated groan. *What, in God's good name, is wrong with me?*

Chapter Six

R ydar lay on his pallet in the dark hall and watched a thinning log until it collapsed in two pieces. All that remained in the fireplace was a rough heap of glowing orange and red chunks supported by black skeletons; discarded bones of the satiated fire.

The death of the fire was of no concern to him. Since awakening in this keep, he hadn't experienced hunger or cold. Was he truly in heaven? He was, if Grønnland had been hell.

He shivered at the thought of the windswept wasteland of his adopted home. Jagged peaks stared down on uninhabited meadows of coarse grasses; food that was nearly indigestible to the bony cattle and bleating sheep who spent their short lives searching for sustenance there. When the miserable animals succumbed to the land they were butchered, but their scant flesh was tough and lean.

Then the dark winter came, half the year long. Windy, iced and unforgiving, it forced even the livestock into their longhouses. After lying down for months inside, the animals had to be carried outdoors when the snow melted. With his pampered youth spent in a castle in Arendal, Norway, Rydar never became accustomed to the smell and filth of sharing his roof with his food. There was a time he believed he would never be clean or warm again.

Or his hunger satisfied. Growing tall and lanky and outstripping his family's supplies, Rydar's teen years encompassed a constant search for meat. He hunted with a bow, killing arctic hares or an occasional fox.

Sometimes, his forages took him close to the *skraeling*.

Like those before him, he didn't deign to speak to the squat, dark people who had slits for eyes, but he watched them at times. He followed their example and fashioned a tethered spear with a sharp boned point. Rydar practiced purposefully until he could stab a silver glint deep underwater and pull up a fat cod. On good days, he caught breeding salmon.

Rydar rolled onto his back and stretched, his limbs reaching far beyond the boundaries of the small cot. Still wide awake, the recollection of fresh salmon eggs made his mouth water in spite of the large meal he demolished just two hours before.

He taught his best friend Arne to hunt, and while they traipsed the tundra together he told stories of his childhood in Norway. He used those tales to convince Arne to build the boat with him.

The last Norse ship to reach them rested on the rocky shore, caved in on one side. The two men stripped it of anything usable. It required two summers to cobble together a sea-worthy craft from scavenged lumber, tar and hoof-glue.

Poor Arne. So trusting and hopeful. Arne's life in the Grønnland settlement had been an endless string of cool, dry summers and increasingly brutal winters. He said so many times that he ached for something interesting to happen. To learn a trade of value. To swive a beautiful woman. To see a different land. So when the weather turned and the storm threatened their little boat, Arne climbed the mast and screamed challenges in its face.

"My God, Rydar! I've never felt more alive!" he bellowed, red-faced and grinning madly. He may have been truly mad by then, pushed by hunger and thirst. He died without achieving his goals, but he died fully alive.

And not in Grønnland.

Rydar turned to his side away from the hearth, and punched his pillow until it supported his head. He needed to push these unpleasant memories from his mind. Sleep required more palatable fodder. Fodder the likes of Grier.

Now there was a subject worth pondering.

Rydar had never seen anyone with hair the color of hers. Deep russet shot through by a summer's sunset of orange and gold, those untamed curls were alive with color. He liked candlelight on it best. So far.

And her eyes? They were the same shade as the North Sea on a sunny day. Dark, clear, blue. They were as changing as the waves, and reflected light in shifting momentary glints. Enchanting. Compelling. Beautiful.

Grier wasn't as tall as Norse women. Rydar looked at his palm, and decided she was less than one hand's width taller than five feet. She was sturdy, though, and strong. He liked that. Pale, puny women always died in Grønnland. He had no need for that sort.

Rydar chuckled; from what he recalled of Norway, she was not the most ladylike of women. Those who owned a castle did not do the cooking as well. Nor butcher hens. Nor practice healing.

Nor take the stairs two at a time.

Rydar recalled the vision of her slippered feet and shapely calves under her hiked-up kirtle. Her arse swayed with each double step and her fiery hair blazed down her back. He didn't know what angered her nor why she remained in her chamber for the remainder of the evening. But when she brushed past him, cheeks flushed and eyes like blue flames, he was captivated. For that moment, she owned him.

His eyelids drooped. What might it be like to kiss her? He imagined her full lips against his, moist and slightly parted. Though unmarried—and most likely a virgin—might she kiss with the same passion he saw in her tonight? Did she know of such things? And dare he attempt to find out?

Quit these thoughts and now, Hansen, before they cause you trouble. You've not reached your home. You've got more journey ahead of you, and no visible way to make it!

And no one—not a beautiful flirtatious widow, nor an intriguing high-spirited healer—could be allowed to stop him.

Rydar's resigned sigh became a snore.

May 20, 1354

Rydar roused in the midst of strange dreams in which he was bound against his will. He was back at Hansen Hall in Arendal and the room was his father's, though it didn't appear as it had when he saw it last. He struggled, desperate to free himself, certain that if he could just reach the fireplace, all would be set right.

My chamber behind the mantle.

After a decade, his father's dying utterance still haunted his only son.

When he heard those words, Rydar tore apart the fireplace in their Grønnland longhouse, glad his mother was already gone and wouldn't fight him about it. But there was nothing to be found save stones, crumbling mortar and dust. In his consuming anger, Rydar refused to rebuild it. He preferred to live with an open fire pit rather than put one more mite of effort into that hated, God-forsaken place.

Rydar opened his eyes, releasing himself from the dream's night and forcing himself into the keep's day.

"I need to free myself," he said aloud. Remaining indoors was grating on a soul so accustomed to open sky and vast horizons. "I must get out of the keep and work to get strong again so I can continue my journey. That's what the dream was about."

That determined, he washed, dressed, and crutched his way outside.

The dawn was damp and misty, glowing pinkish in the morning sun. Foggy clouds slowly stepped away, allowing the sun purchase. Rydar paused and looked around the castle grounds, getting his bearings. On his first gray day here when Arne was buried he hadn't been capable of noticing anything beyond his own pain.

The solid oak-and-iron front door of the keep was tucked between the jutting Great Hall on his left, and a taller circular tower on his right. He hopped forward and descended the five granite steps to the ground. The keep faced south, away from the sea.

Sloping like a wide skirt, the grassy yard was laced with crushed-shell pathways. An uneven stone wall, ranging between what Rydar guessed was fifteen and twenty feet in height, surrounded the large yard with strong rectangular arms. A variety of two-story craftsmen's buildings were scattered around the perimeter of the wall and tenants were already about their work. A gate in the south wall stood open to a wooden bridge and forested land beyond. If he remembered rightly, the graveyard was on the east side of the keep. He knew the kitchen door opened to the west.

Rydar followed the raucous clucking of chickens to a low wooden building sheltered against the northwestern outer wall. On the way he passed a substantial vegetable and herb garden outside the kitchen, near the well. That explained why Grier's cooking tasted so good.

"Oh my Lord! Rydar!" She took a quick step backward into the noisy henhouse juggling several eggs in her apron. She managed to keep all but one of them from splattering on the ground.

Rydar lifted a hand in supplication. "Sorry, Grier!"

He hadn't intended to frighten her; though it did bring delightful color to her cheeks and turned her eyes into flashing sapphires. Thus distracted Rydar paused, trying to recall what he should say.

Remembering, he pointed at the broken egg. "I—I much sorry."

She nodded and flipped her abundant rust-colored curls over her shoulder. Rydar wondered what those fascinating curls might feel like if he ran his fingers through them.

Stop it.

"What are you about, then?" she asked.

Rydar shrugged. He created a sentence he hoped made sense. "I come out today morning. See all, aye?"

Her countenance softened with understanding. "Aye. I suppose being cooped up inside would grate on a soul."

He didn't know all her words, but he knew her tone and he knew she understood him. She stepped around him and called to Moira.

"Take these eggs to the kitchen, will you?" she asked.

Moira set her bucket beside the well and edged toward Grier to accept the eggs. Her gaze ran up and down Rydar's frame, and she hurried away once she had the eggs tucked in her own apron. A full week in his presence now and the maid was still unaccountably skittish around him.

"If you're of a mind, I could show you around a bit," Grier offered.

Rydar watched her lips and shrugged; his adopted response when he didn't understand.

She smiled gently. "Come with me."

Those words he knew. "Aye. Thank you."

She turned and walked toward the stable, set against the opposite wall. He noticed that she set a pace he could manage with the crutch. It seemed that was her habit—looking out for others, offering herself in even the smallest manner. Comforting in ways that truly helped. But she was not a rug to be walked on; he'd seen her temper.

A smile tugged his uninjured cheek.

The morning bloomed. Spring's encroaching warmth and last week's rainstorm conspired to coax flowers from beneath the sandy soil. Snippets of color edged the buildings and ran along the bottom of the castle's outer walls. Castle tenants greeted Grier and cast curious glances at him, the limping stranger by her side.

Rydar paused when they passed the cemetery. He squinted at the fresh pile of stones snugged against the far wall, trying not to see it and hoping it wasn't there; but of course it was. He pulled a deep breath, attempting to quell the deep ache of grief, and crossed himself with a silent, *God take his soul.*

Arne was never far from his conscious thoughts. His determination to continue on his journey to reach Norway was, in part, to give Arne's death a purpose. He suddenly decided that if he ever had a son, he'd name the boy Arne. Arne Jorgensen Hansen. Yes, he would. If ever.

Grier tugged at the thick gold chain around her neck until her crucifix topped her neckline.

"Did you have one of these?" She held it toward him.

Rydar reached for the icon, warm from lying against her skin, and lifted it reverently. Even to his eyes it appeared unexpectedly delicate in his large, voyage-roughened hand. He stared at it, examining the intricate gold handiwork. He'd seen things like this as a boy. Then he lifted it to his lips, closed his eyes, and kissed it.

"*Velsignet* Jesus," he whispered.

"It was my Mam's." Grier slipped the crucifix back inside her kirtle.

Rydar watched it fall inside her gown and swallowed thickly, his mouth gone dry. The desire to reach inside her dress in pursuit of the cross, and nestle his hand between her warm, rounded breasts, jabbed him in a very responsive spot.

He twisted his hips away from Grier so she wouldn't notice. His face heated. *Skitt.* Was he no more than a lusty teen? Growing hard at the mere thought of caressing a pair of tits?

Mercifully, Grier walked again. Rydar followed, staying behind her until his inconvenient arousal eased.

As they approached the stable, a groom led out a pair of well-conformed coursers, a bay mare and a black gelding, and tied them to a rail. Rydar crutched forward and looked over his shoulder at Grier, then back at the horses. He hadn't seen a horse since Norway.

His heart thumped its encouragement.

"Do you ride?" Grier asked.

"Ride?" Rydar scrubbed his face with one hand, rasping his four-day-old whiskers. He assumed her meaning—it matched the root of his name, after all—and tucked the easy word into his rapidly growing vocabulary. "Norway, aye. Grønnland, no."

Dare he try to mount one of them? He was pulled to do so even though he hadn't ridden in so many years.

"You lived in Norway?" Grier looked confused. "I thought ye were from Greenland."

"No." Rydar shook his head and moved cautiously, inexorably, toward the big animals. He remembered to hold out his fist for them to sniff. He sidled up to the mare and rubbed her neck. He flashed Grier his most encouraging grin.

"Good?"

"Aye, she's a fine mount. Why do ye ask?"

All Rydar heard was 'aye' before he dropped his crutch and rested both hands on the mare's back. He jumped up with his right leg, supporting his weight on his straightened arms, and threw that leg over the horse's rump before he could be tumbled by her startled side-step. He hitched himself forward, his long legs dangling on either side of the animal.

Rydar patted the mare's neck, murmured Norse caresses in her ear, and leaned forward to grab her tether. Tugging on it, he indicated with his chin for Grier to loose it from the rail.

"Are ye daft?" she responded. "Your leg's broke! And I'll no' be responsible for you losing it, and you hurt it further!"

A bubbling well of mirth surged through him and spilled into the morning, in spite of the constant throbbing in his shin. Rydar laughed with the joy of being off his feet and away from his crutch. Sitting astride the mare felt so good, it was worth any incumbent risk.

"Come, Grier. I ride, aye?" he asked, grinning.

Grier grumbled several more words he didn't catch and with quite a bit of chiding emphasis. But she untied the leather strap and handed it to him. He turned the mare's fine-boned head and tapped her side with his right heel. The horse snorted at the unaccustomed weight and sidled nervously away from the stable into the grassy courtyard.

ᛉᚾ

Fascinated, Grier watched as Rydar tested Salle, her favorite mare, with increasing confidence. He walked her in circles, trotted her in figure eights, and then urged her to an easy canter. Sitting tall, he held himself on Salle's bare back with his knees. Grier could see his thighs tense and flex through the close-fitting knit hose as he urged the mare to do his bidding. His splinted shin rested loose along her belly.

Rydar rode in the yard of the castle for near half an hour. As he did, the anxious lines in his face eased and grew into a relaxed grin. His cropped hair blew around his cheeks. His pale eyes glowed in the slanted morning sunshine. He was so completely different when he was free of his injury's constraints. He was strong. He was in control.

He was magnificent.

The unheralded image of his thighs gripping her hips—the way they gripped the mare—set Grier's cheeks on fire. Long-denied need ached behind her breastbone and spread downward to her thighs. She wrapped her arms around her waist and breathed slowly, trying to calm her rebellious heart. No good could come of such unbridled thoughts. Even so, Grier could not pull her gaze away from the Norseman.

"Breakfast!" she blurted.

Rydar reined the mare and nudged her toward Grier. "Aye?" he asked.

"I need to make breakfast. Are ye no' hungry?" She patted her stomach.

Rydar nodded emphatically. "Make breakfast. Hungry. Aye!" He pointed to his crutch.

Grier retrieved it for him. Rydar swung his right leg over Salle's neck and slid from her back, dropping to the ground on one foot. He almost fell and grabbed Grier for support. She gripped his waist and steadied him. Scowling up at him, she intended to scold but stopped when their eyes met. He looked so happy.

"*Takk du*, Grier! That good! ...Thank you."

His eyes dropped to her lips. They felt his perusal and parted.

"I ride more, aye?"

"Whene'er you wish," she breathed.

Rydar stared at her. His gaze traveled over her features like the fingers of a blind man; she swore she could feel them. She leaned closer without thinking.

"Hungry," he murmured.

Grier yanked her hands from his waist and stepped away.

"Aye!" She thrust the crutch toward him, then whirled and ran toward the keep, not daring to look back.

Chapter Seven

May 21, 1354

Lady Grier?" the puppy whispered. It sat up on its haunches and waved its two front paws in supplication. "Lady Grier? Will you wake up?"

She blinked open her eyes, slowly separating from the dream.

Moira's pale face floated in the dark doorway above the flame of a single candle. "Lady Grier?"

Grier mumbled, "What is it?"

"There's a woman. Says her husband's hurt his back. Says he's in a lot of pain."

"Who is she?" Grier asked, severing her dreams from reality.

"She said they're but passing through. I've never laid eyes on her."

Grier rubbed the remnants of sleep from her eyes. "Aye. I'll come."

"Yes, my lady." The candle moved away, leaving a trail of dancing shadow-shards in its wake.

Grier tossed back her blanket and reached for the blue wool kirtle she left draped over the foot of her bed. She pulled it over her shift and nudged around for her tall leather boots. She plaited her hair on the way down the stairs.

The woman was middle-aged and shabbily dressed, and candlelight deepened the soiled valleys of her face. Grier wondered if the woman worried that her man might die. Or perhaps, the odd thought occurred to her, she worried that he might yet live.

"I'll get my cloak and my basket," Grier said.

"Thank you, m'lady." The woman's voice was as flat as her expression.

The night was cool and moonless, but the sky was twilit gray. The summer solstice was only a month away; the sky would not go dark at all then. The two women walked through the silent castle yard without need of a lantern or rush light.

"Where do you bide?" Grier asked.

"Outside the castle wall, in one of the abandoned huts," she mumbled. "At least, we believed it abandoned."

"Aye." Grier nodded. When their men and sons fell to the Death, many of the poorest families built lean-to hovels from what wood they could find, seeking the protection of the little castle's solid outer walls. They begged and scavenged until either they fell as well, or an opportunity arose and they moved on.

The two women left the castle yard, crossed over the dry moat, and turned west. A fire glowed in one of the ramshackle huts about a hundred yards from the gate. When they reached it, the peasant woman stepped forward and pulled back a canvas drape that covered one side. The man inside moaned.

Grier bent over and went in. The woman followed.

"Is this the healer?" the man rasped. "Have you the poppy medicine for my pain?" His wrinkled face was unevenly flushed. Cropped white hair stuck wildly in all directions like a newly hatched chick. The air reeked of unwashed bodies.

"Aye, I've got that. Might you tell me what happened?" Grier set her basket down. "How were ye hurt?"

The man was trembling, sweating. His countenance twisted with suffering. His eyes jumped to his woman's then back to Grier.

"A cart. It ran over me."

"A cart?" Grier queried. She knelt by the man. "Where? In Durness?"

"Aye."

"Did you no' consider staying put while ye healed?"

"Uh… We hadn't money for lodging."

Grier rested her hand on his shoulder. The man's unwashed stench filled her nostrils and she breathed through her mouth. "Show me. I might be able to do more for you."

"I—I only need the medicine," he stammered. His jaw clenched and he glared a warning at his companion. She backed away, into the low corner of the lean-to.

"If you've broken ribs, you're in danger of puncturing a lung," Grier kept her voice quiet and calm. Her hand remained on the man's shoulder. "I should examine you."

"No!" he blurted. His voice grew louder. "I've no need but the medicine! Can ye no' see I'm in pain?"

Grier offered a comforting smile. "Aye, and yet—"

The man knocked Grier's hand from his shoulder and grabbed her wrist. His bony fingers circled like talons and his nails stabbed her skin. The unexpected strength of his grip belied his condition.

Grier pulled back, disbelieving what was happening. The man yanked on her arm and jerked her off balance. His other fist swung around and pounded into her face. Lightning exploded through her vision. She cried out in pain.

He shoved her violently away from him and scrambled for her basket. She fell to her side on the dirt floor, stunned and trying desperately not to faint.

"Where is it?" he shrieked. "The poppy medicine? Where?"

Grier collected her determination and lifted her head. Her cheek stung like a dozen angry bees had abused it. Everything she saw through that eye looked red and blurred. Her neck hurt, twisted suddenly by the blow.

The man's woman cowered in the slanted corner, hands over her face, whimpering.

"Hush you auld fool!" the man barked. He had the basket open and he pawed through Grier's healing supplies. "WHERE?"

Through the disabling haze of pain, Grier shouted with every mote of authority she could manage. "Careful or ye'll spill it!"

The man froze. His head swiveled to face her. His haggard features twitched. Dark eyes shone unnaturally in the dim lamplight. Sweat sheened his flushed skin.

The terror of realization shot white-hot through Grier. This man was a slave to the poppies and his need would push him to do anything necessary to get more.

Grier slowly pushed up from the dirt and crawled awkwardly toward him. Her cheek throbbed. Her neck stiffened. The force of his attack made her unsure of her balance. She made herself to look at the man and hold her gaze steady. She stretched out one shaky hand.

"G-give me the basket."

He didn't loosen his grip. His gaze ricocheted between her and his prize.

"I've poisons in there, as well," she warned.

Still, he held on. He squinted as if to discern her honesty. The woman in the corner fell silent.

Grier pressed her point. "If ye wish to try your luck go ahead. But I'll no' take responsibility for your death, and ye choose wrong." She tried her best to look stern and not succumb to the tears of panic clutching her throat.

"Will ye be a fool, Grif?" the woman snapped.

"Shut up!" he bellowed over his shoulder.

"Go ahead. Be a fool, Grif!" Grier taunted, stalling to bolster her senses. Her heart slammed so hard against her ribs, she feared they might crack. She couldn't catch her breath.

Grif glared at her, uncertain. His fingers moved spastically over the basket's handle. Grier could smell the rancid breath that panted between his remaining teeth. She parried her advantage.

"Guess which is the poison, Grif, and which is the poppies." She tried to cock one brow, but her face was numb. She spoke her challenge instead. "I'll wait."

With a grunt, the man shoved the basket toward her. "Hurry up, then. I've another fist and you've another cheek."

Grier pulled her feet under her and steadied herself on the basket's handle. She made a show of looking through the contents until she was sure of her balance.

Then she reached deep inside, finding the edge of the false bottom. She wound her fingers around the handle of the knife hidden there, and slid them snug against the steel hilt. She squeezed the bone handle, hard.

Then she drew a deep breath, finally.

"Ah, there it is…" she murmured. She locked her gaze on Grif.

That was her mistake. He snarled like a mad cur, eyes glinting red in the dim light. Then he lunged at her, his outstretched hands curved into claws.

With one desperately smooth motion, Grier pulled the knife from the basket and slashed it across Grif's face. She caught the blade in his open mouth and cut through his cheek, extending his evil grin by several gory inches. Grif's scream raged through the hovel. His fingers clawed at the jagged opening. Blood covered his hands and ran down his throat.

Using the basket handle for leverage, Grier pushed up from the ground and stumbled out of the hut, basket in one hand and bloodied knife in the other.

She didn't look back.

Grier ran unevenly, stumbling with shock and blinded by her swelling eye. She didn't slow when she crossed the dry moat into the castle yard. The crunch of her boots on the crushed-shell path alerted a dog who barked a frantic warning. Was there another set of footfalls? Was he chasing her?

Grier panted up to the closed door of the keep. She dropped the knife and basket and wrestled the door open. When she grabbed the basket, she threw a look toward the moat, but saw nothing.

Yet.

Inside, she tossed her basket on the floor and leaned on the heavy portal to close it. Then she dropped the crossbar into place. Surely he wouldn't be fool enough to follow her.

Grier stood shaking and sweating in the cool keep. She tried unsuccessfully to catch her breath. Her knees felt like wet stalks of barley. Her blood roared in her ears. Her shoulders convulsed with dry sobs.

She felt her way unsteadily down the darkened hall to the kitchen. Once there, she determinedly applied herself to necessary motions. Motions that required no thought, but would occupy her trembling hands.

First she lit a piece of tinder in the banked fire. She used the tinder to light a candle. By its feeble light, she retrieved her basket from where it landed in the hallway.

Grier returned to the kitchen. She pulled out a linen rag. She soaked it in vinegar. She used it to clean her face. Mercifully, the skin wasn't broken, but she would have quite a black eye in the morning. And a very stiff neck.

"Shite!" she swore.

She was angry that she had been attacked, true. But she was much angrier still that she walked into the trap. Her mother warned her with stories of men—and women—who craved the poppy medicine. It was powerful stuff, to be sure. Even so Grier was shocked by Grif's desperation; she had never before seen anyone in that condition. She prayed she never would again.

But a more sinister warning echoed in the night's events: the goodwill she experienced during the Death had passed. Once the treasured and protected daughter of a respected laird, she was now just a common healer. And an unmarried one at that. Without the protection of a husband, she most likely would be robbed; or even violated.

Or named a witch if her skills were mistrusted.

A soft moan escaped her. After losing everything else, would she now lose the last purpose left to her in this life?

A thump at the keep's door sent a shock through her as powerful as lightning. She stilled, and listened, trying to hear past the thunder of her heart.

Footsteps in the hallway. Unsteady footsteps.

Blow out the candle.

The footsteps halted.

"Grier?"

Rydar. A tide of relief.

Answer him.

"I—I'm in the kitchen."

"You are good?" Unsteady shuffling came closer.

"I'm fine!" she lied and hoped her voice did not betray her. "I was called out to a healing." Grier moved to the kitchen door. "Do no' hurt your leg!"

"I'm fine," Rydar mimicked.

Grier stepped into the dark hallway. Rydar was right in front of her. She saw his shape in the light seeping around her from the kitchen's banked fire. Tall, lean, masculine, left knee bent and one hand resting against the wall for balance. She looked up instinctively and saw the faint glimmer of his eyes. He smelled of warm linen and wine.

"The door?" she whispered.

He nodded. "Barred?"

She heard the question in his tone, but didn't acknowledge it. "Good."

Why couldn't she move? It must be a reaction to the attack; her limbs were heavy and unresponsive. She felt light-headed. She was glad Rydar couldn't see her face. Tomorrow she would answer questions. Tonight she only wanted to crawl back into the safety and warmth of her bed and cry herself to sleep. Why couldn't she move?

"Grier?" he whispered.

"Aye?" she answered in kind.

He seemed to be considering something. Then he backed away. "Sleep good."

"Yes. You, too."

He turned and hobbled away from her. She felt his absence in a cold wash of loneliness.

ᚱᚺ

Rydar crutched stiffly down the hall to the kitchen. Grier wasn't there, but a pot of parritch steamed on the table. Beside it rested a loaf of yesterday's bread and four boiled eggs. Thick bacon sizzled in a pan.

Rydar lowered himself gingerly to a chair, his face screwed into a silent display of misery. He served himself some oat parritch, ate it alone, and wondered why it was so.

Something happened to Grier last night. She slammed the door and barred it, though the tiny, isolated keep had not been locked since he arrived. She was frightened by his footfalls and blew out her candle. She clearly thought someone was after her. That was worrisome. Who might it have been?

But then in the hallway, when he stood close to her, he wanted to—what? Protect her? Kiss her? Hold her? Swive her? *Skitt!* He didn't belong here and he had no intention of remaining. So, obviously, he couldn't afford to act on any of those desires. The consequences would be disastrous.

The back door opened with a gust of salty air and Grier stepped into the kitchen. Her glorious red hair hung loose like a veil and hid her face.

"Good morn," she mumbled, glancing sideways at him.

"Good morn, Grier. You sleep good?"

"Aye. Thank you." One ocean-blue eye appeared. "Have you seen Logan?"

"Logan? No." Rydar considered Grier more closely. "Why you ask?"

"He went out last night and…" her voice faltered.

He narrowed his eyes. "And?"

"And I did no' hear him come in." Grier gave Rydar her back. She fidgeted with crockery in the cabinet.

"Door is barred," he pointed out.

"Oh!" Grier whirled, one hand to her temple, and rushed out. Rydar heard the barricade clank to the stone floor. A shaft of blue morning light illuminated the hallway for a brief bit before Grier trudged back into the kitchen carrying a knife crusted with dried blood.

"Grier, what's bad?" Rydar asked.

"I don't know where Logan is," she answered without looking at him.

Worried, Rydar reached out his hand and circled her wrist.

Grier shrieked unexpectedly. She yanked away from his grasp and spun to face him, bloody knife at the ready. Panic almost dominated her countenance, only slightly surpassed by dark purple bruises around one swollen eye.

"Å min Gud…" Rydar rose on one leg and reached toward her. "Grier? Logan do that?"

"Logan? No!" She shook her head awkwardly, and then put a hand over her injured eye. The knife lowered. "Not Logan. It was the man who asked for healing. In the middle of the night. He wanted my poppy medicine."

Rydar pushed copper waves from her face and tucked them behind her ear. He calmly planned to kill whoever did this to her. He understood man, healing, middle and night.

"Poppy medicine?" he asked.

"For pain. A body can come to crave it. Ye ken?" One brilliant blue eye met his.

No, he didn't ken, but that wasn't important. Rydar's gaze ran over her body, searching for other signs. "He hurt you more?"

"No more." She held up the crusted knife. "I hurt him."

Rydar's brows arched. "Dead?" he asked, hopeful on the one hand, though denied his own desire for revenge on the other.

"No." She mimed slashing her cheek.

Rydar smiled a little. Apparently this beautiful woman was capable of more than quick words. Quick actions were useful as well; especially fearless ones. "I no' want you hurt. You help me.

You good woman, Grier."

Her face flushed an attractive shade of pink, enhancing the blue of her uncovered eye.

"Thank you," she whispered. She returned to the meal's preparation and spoke over one shoulder. "I wonder where Logan is, then."

"I no' see him," Rydar offered quietly.

Her shoulders slumped and she faced him again. The naked fear in her expression tore at his gut and he wished he could ease it somehow. Her words crept across the room, carried on her experiences from the night past.

"I pray he's safe."

Chapter Eight

Logan appeared while Rydar ate the last boiled egg.

"And where have ye been?" Grier demanded. She was riven between relief that he was safe and fury at him for frightening her. "I was worrit sick for you!"

"No' so loud, cousin. My head's about to knock off my own shoulders," Logan moaned. He slumped into a chair, rubbing his eyes. "The McKay wine flowed far too freely."

Grier's fists jammed onto her hips. "You got plaistert last night? I hope ye did no' do anything foolish!"

Logan winced. He still hadn't looked at her. "No."

Rydar coughed, his face alarmingly red. He concentrated on the last bit of boiled egg and didn't acknowledge her irritated sideways regard.

Grier turned and stabbed the fire, venting her anger. "So what were ye about, then?"

"'Twas in my honor." Logan slit one eye open. "Might you pour me ale? My tongue's dry as the chyngell."

"Ach!" Grier grunted then moved to do so, casting a dubious glance at the younger man.

"Your honor?" Rydar ventured. He seemed able to follow the conversation.

"Aye."

Grier handed Logan the mug of ale, bumping it against his hand. He accepted it and downed a long pull, ending with a loud belch. He lifted the half-empty mug in toast toward Rydar.

"I'm now formally courting the beautiful Malise McKay, with her father's full blessing," he announced.

"And the wine sealed the deal, did it?" Grier forced a stiff smile for Logan, even though his announcement brought her a very large step closer to ruin. "She's a bonny lass. Congratulations."

Logan downed the last of the ale. Both eyes slammed wide when he saw Grier's face.

"Good Lord, Grier! What happened to you?" He threw a long glance at Rydar, then regarded her again. "Who did that to you?"

Grier lifted the empty egg bowl from the table and told him about her terrifying experience the night before.

"Are ye—did he—I mean, were ye hurt any other ways?" he stammered.

Grier's entire body flushed with keen embarrassment when she realized that was what Rydar had tried to ask her. "No!"

"Aye, well, that's good, then..." He jerked a nod, then winced.

She fixed Logan with a hard stare. "So you understand why I was worrit when you did no' come home!"

"Sorry," he mumbled. "It was no' my intent."

"I wanted you to arrest the man," she prodded.

"And I will."

Grier turned her back, still angry. "He's long gone by now, and I'll wager."

Logan mumbled something unintelligible into his ale mug before draining the last drops.

"You marry?" Rydar asked between bites of thick brown bread covered with honey. He already finished most of the parritch and all of the eggs. He couldn't have gone hungry for days now, but it seemed to Grier he hadn't been full yet, either.

"One step at a time, Rydar!" Logan managed a pained grin. "There's no cause to rush."

"You stayed the night with her family, then?" Grier gave the last of the parritch to Logan along with a pitcher of milk.

"I had need to. I could no' walk across the room, not to speak of a mile home in the twilight!"

"Good," Rydar approved. "Smart do."

"Yes." Logan took a bite of the cold congealed parritch. His eyes rolled and he leapt from the table.

He barely made it out the back door before his stomach began to repay him for yester eve's abuse. Rydar's lips twitched and he lifted his gaze to Grier. His obvious mirth softened her irritation. With a shake of her head, she consented to chuckle her response.

Logan reappeared after the retching stopped, pale and red-eyed. He stumbled back to the table and finished his breakfast under Grier's bemused gaze.

"I'll be going to bed now," Logan murmured. "Wake me if I die."

Grier nodded absently, too distracted by his good news. His depressing, dire, dismal and disheartening good news. The beginning-of-the-end-of-her-life good news.

Logan's announcement of his official courtship would soon lead to a marriage contract. Once the terms were agreed on, Grier would begin handing control of the keep—her own father's keep, awarded to his father by none other than King Robert Bruce himself—to fifteen-year-old Malise McKay. Grier would be third in line then, until their children displaced her even further. It would be up to Malise whether or not she might continue to live here.

As she watched Logan stumble from the room, Grier pressed down the other, more immediate problem with his absence: she and Rydar had been alone in the keep all night without a chaperone. Moira must not have noticed. She crossed herself and said a quick prayer that no one else would find out. If they did, her reputation would be ruined and her nearly solidified spinsterhood irrevocably carved in rough Scotch granite.

ᚱᚾ

Grier trudged through the castle yard later that day. Her wood clogs scuffed the shell path and her basket of healing supplies bumped against her tired calf with every step. She was returning from a mid-day call to a fevered sickbed. While she constantly worried that the Death might reappear, this proved only a childhood illness. She crossed herself, this time in gratitude.

Yesterday's sunny glory was shrouded in mist and interred behind a cloudy cairn. Winds keened across Balnakeil Bay and through the castle ramparts. Heavy and wet, the cool afternoon air pushed against her as if trying to hold her back.

The keep's front door gaped open. Was aught amiss? She

forced her exhausted limbs to stretch a bit farther with each step, hurrying until Rydar appeared in the door's frame. His countenance brightened when their eyes met, and he waved her forward.

"Come, Grier! Good you here now."

"Is everything well?" she called to him.

"Good, all is good." He waited at the doorway, vibrating with impatience. When she reached the steps, he disappeared inside the dusky hallway leaving Grier to follow, unenlightened.

Lady Margoh Henriksen was in the dining room. Grier's hand went to her battered cheek in a self-conscious reflex. It was bad enough that she felt short and overly rounded beside the tall, slim blond. Worse, Margoh was always perfectly groomed while Grier wore gowns suitable for her work. If the 'old aunt' was invited to Durness to help out, why didn't she ever seem to do so?

Rydar set his crutch aside and lowered himself, wincing, into a chair.

"Are ye hurt?" Grier inquired. She set her basket on the floor and circled the table to kneel at his side.

"No." He waved dismissively. "I no' ride long time. Yesterday I ride." His lopsided grin appeared. "Long time."

"Oh! Are ye sore?" Grier rested her palm lightly on Rydar's firmly muscled thigh. "Here?"

Rydar's cheek twitched. "Aye." His eyes flicked to hers. Their pale intensity pinned her.

"I—I have a balm," she stuttered. The heat of his thigh burned past her hand and flowed throughout her frame. Startled, she pulled away, stood and turned aside. "I have it with me. In my basket."

"Are you going to rub it on him here?" Margoh's voice intruded.

"Of course not!" Grier welcomed the older woman's taunt; it cut a path through the confusion that Rydar's heat generated in her. She dug out a pot of salve and set it on the table.

Rydar reached for it, uncorked it, and sniffed. His nose wrinkled and after two swift inhalations, he loosed a thunderous sneeze.

Grier smiled a bit. "It's strong." She flexed her arms to help him understand.

"Aye!" Rydar re-corked the little jug. He set it on the table and rubbed his fingers under his nose. Then he pushed the noxious ointment further away, toward the table's center.

Margoh leaned forward and frowned at Grier. "What happened to you?"

Grier's hand went to her temple. "A man tried to take my poppy medicine."

"How much did he get?"

"None!" she spat, fiercely irritated by Margoh's assumption.

Margoh leaned back. "So you... fought him off?" she asked, her obvious disbelief a banner flying through the room's already tense atmosphere.

"I knifed him off!" Grier declared.

Rydar snorted. Grier turned to glare at him. His face was bright red and he bit his lips together in an unsuccessful attempt to dam his mirth. Grier's irritation slowly dissipated. She grinned at him then, taking the wind out of Margoh's flag of superiority.

After a deliberate pause, Grier considered the older woman. "What occurrence requires that I be here?"

"He has questions." Margoh gripped her hands together on the table and sighed her blatant irritation.

"Questions?" Grier sank into a chair and glanced between the two. Her stomach clenched; this could prove to be a very awkward session. "About what?"

"I'll ask." Margoh turned to Rydar. After a brief exchange in Norse, she faced Grier again. "He wants to know why you were so wroth when Logan stayed away for a night."

"Oh!" Grier felt her cheeks grow hot. She prayed Margoh would not realize what that absence meant for her reputation; she needed to deflect the conversation and quickly. "I was worrit, is all. After what happened to me, especially. Too many ruffians about."

Margoh spoke with Rydar again. Then, "Explain about the ruffians."

Grier shifted her gaze to Rydar. He stared at her, intent and focused. She spoke slowly so Margoh might translate.

"Since the Death, bands of reivers lived off what goods they could scavenge from abandoned crofts. Many died of the plague themselves, sickened by the booty they pilfered. But some survived and grew accustomed to that way of life. The pickings grew slim, though, once the deaths stopped. And the reivers are no' willing to live honorably. They've become bold, attacking travelers at times."

While Grier talked about the bands of robbers, Rydar's brow lowered. He listened to Margoh's translations, but watched Grier with a hard emerald gaze.

"You go today alone," he accused.

"It was no' far. And it was daylight," Grier defended.

"After," Rydar pointed at her cheek, his gesture finishing the statement. "Why you go alone?"

Margoh raised one haughty brow. "I certainly would not have. You invited disaster by doing so, didn't you? Was that intentional?" She tilted her head the tiniest bit toward Rydar.

"No!" Grier bristled at the silent insinuation that she was vying for the Norseman's attention. "My skills have always been available to my tenants."

"Your tenants?" Margoh scoffed. "More rightly stated they're Logan's tenants."

Her barb landed true, piercing Grier's façade of confidence. But before she could shoot back, Rydar stood and looked around the room, drawing both women's slack-jawed notice.

"*Hvor er din våpen?*"

Margoh translated: "He wants to know where your weapons are."

The shift confused Grier for the moment. "Why?"

It was Rydar's turn to startle. He smacked one palm against his chest. "I here, now. I—help Logan. I help you!" His deep accented words bounced through the stone-walled room. "You, woman. I, man. I…" He paused, then a connection was made. His eyes lit with understanding. "I strong. Aye?" He flexed his arms in imitation of Grier.

He looked strong, Grier realized. Eight days of regular meals and ample rest had already changed him. What might the next weeks bring?

"Aye, you're healing quite well," she ventured.

Rydar spoke to Margoh.

"Weapons," she replied.

Rydar fixed Grier with his stare, glowing green embers in the afternoon dusk. "Weapons, Grier. Your weapons. I help you safe. You help me and now I help you."

She had no reason to deny him. Truth be told, his declamation warmed and soothed her. For a moment, she allowed herself to rest in this amazing stranger's promise. For a moment she didn't have to be the one in control. For a brief moment, her way of life was secured.

"Aye. I'll show you the armory before supper, then," she replied.

Rydar relaxed some and sat back down in his chair. "You show me—ar-moh-ree—before supper. Aye. Good." Punctuating the statement with a quick nod, he turned to Margoh. "I learn more speak now."

ᚱᚾ

Rydar concentrated on the language lessons, thankful that *this* borrowed doublet was long enough to cover his sudden response to Grier's hand on his thigh. He hadn't expected her to notice how sore he was and he certainly hadn't expected her to touch him. Most of all, he hadn't expected the thrill that snaked through him when she did.

He wasn't an inexperienced boy after all; he was a fully grown man. He had bedded women many times, though not for several years past. But he hadn't reacted so quickly—or powerfully—since he was fourteen and he touched Gjertrud's hot, heavy breasts for the first time.

His reaction was very unsettling. He wasn't the sort of man to seduce a virgin and then sail away to another land. And indeed he would sail away, as soon as he determined how. He needed to get home to Arendal. Nothing else mattered, not even his beautiful, passionate savior.

Enough. He wrestled his concentration back to Margoh and his language lesson.

When Margoh left, Rydar followed Grier to an iron-banded wooden door. Snugged in a corner of the keep's entry, it opened to the circular tower. Inside the ancient broch, stone steps twisted upward along its walls.

And on those walls hung an array of mortal implements: pikes, axes, swords, arrows. Their lethal steel caught the dim light from above. They gleamed through a layer of dust, poised and eager.

There were wooden longbows measuring six feet from tip to tip, and quivers of barbed iron-tipped arrows. Rydar felt them balance in his tingling palms even before he was close enough to touch them.

He blew a long, low whistle.

"We've not been attacked in my lifetime so they've no' been used for a while. Of course they were of no use against the Death. And the 'ruffians' are a recent danger. I suppose Logan has been too overdone to care for them as he should have," Grier explained.

Rydar watched her lips and caught about half of her words. Enough to understand that the weapons had not been recently needed. That was a relief.

She blew dust from an axe handle and scooped her fingers through a cobweb. "I'll gather these for my basket." She left the tower's enclosure.

Rydar limped to the stone steps and tried to climb upward. He balanced his weight on the crutch, rested one steadying hand against the stones, and put his right foot on the first step. He straightened his leg and pondered how to replicate the sequence considering the narrowness of the steps.

He managed, and got as far as the fourth step before a balance-stealing wobble caused him to grab for the stone walls, tearing his nails and bloodying his fingertips.

"Enough of that," he muttered. He tossed the crutch to the floor below. Its sharp clatter echoed up the curved walls. He lowered himself, grunting over his abused thighs, to sit on a stone step. Pushing with his right leg, Rydar scooted backwards up the staircase on his arse.

The collection of weaponry impressed him. He lifted a longbow from its wall hook, tested it and found the sheepgut had gone hard and brittle. He unstrung the curved wooden stave and dropped it to the tower floor; there was no point in leaving an unusable weapon at the ready. He tested three more and threw two of them after the first.

Reaching higher, he gripped a battle axe. He slipped its leather thong over his wrist and held the violent implement in his right hand. He hefted the handle until it settled, balanced and gleaming with the urge to kill. A steel axe meant death to those it cleaved. There was absolutely no ambiguity in its purpose.

Rydar felt the steel's power vibrate through his arm. His brow lowered and his breath came faster. He swung it through the empty space in the center of the tower. Again. And again. He lifted it near his face and stared at the razor edge.

"We shall be allies," he whispered. "Equal partners, eh? Should the need arise." Rydar scooted down the steps and set the axe at the bottom.

Then he saw the sword.

It leaned, inconspicuous, against the wall behind the door, robed in a scabbard of ornately tooled leather. Above the sheath, brass quillions curved around a walnut handle edged in more brass. His eyes never left the weapon as he fumbled for his crutch and hobbled across the room. He touched it reverently. It held a warmth he couldn't explain.

Rydar received his first sword in Grønnland when he was fourteen, but the steel was mismade. As the winters grew ever colder, it became brittle. He nearly lost his life when it snapped in half; fortunately for him, the impaled wolf died with the sword's pointed half buried in it's chest.

His next sword was crafted from much less elegant iron. Now it lay rusting on the bottom of Balnakeil Bay.

Rydar lifted the leather sheath in his left hand and wrapped his palm around the hilt of this sword. He pulled the steel from its case slowly, like a man after loving his woman, until the shaft was free. He turned it in the dusky daylight and watched light slide along the raised center ridge.

The sword seemed well made. Nearing four feet in length, it felt like an extension of his arm. He tried a few thrusts and parries. It was good. Very good.

A slow smile spread over his countenance.

"You are mine."

His husky voice rang ominous in the stone enclosure. He swung the blade over his head, spinning on his good leg and dropping to a knee. The weapon reached far in front of him.

"We are one, you and I."

He stood again and whirled the blade, two-handed, swooping in wide figure eights. Captivated by the feel of it, he couldn't stop in time.

With a cry Grier dropped her basket of healing supplies and fell to the floor.

Chapter Nine

"G rier!" Rydar bellowed. The cadence of his heart faltered. He scrambled to her side, stepping fully on his left leg but not marking the blade of pain from the broken limb.

She looked up at him, her eyes wide and her face devoid of color. He crumpled to his knees beside her.

"I'm aright!" she breathed. She reached for the slit in her sleeve, and pulled away blood-smeared fingers. "It's no' deep, thank the saints."

Rydar couldn't understand all her words; he could barely hear past his thundering pulse. The realization that he might have killed her sickened him; the spectre of loss as real as if he had known her all his life.

He helped her sit up and tugged at her gown, anxious to see the wound. She shrugged her shoulders and pushed the neckline of her kirtle below the cut. Blood ran down her arm, soaking into her dress, but the gash didn't penetrate into muscle.

The tower walls seemed to be moving and his field of vision was narrowing. He pulled the hem of his shirt sleeve over his hand and pressed it hard against the wound.

"I no ken you come! I'm sorry!" He slumped against the stone wall, boneless as a worm.

Grier nodded and rested against him. After several minutes, the bleeding stopped. Rydar watched, fascinated, as she fished around one-handed in her basket. She pressed some of the cobweb, along with an aromatic salve he didn't know, into the cut. He helped her bind her arm with a strip of linen from her basket.

"I'm sorry, Grier," he said again.

She laid her hand on his cheek and met his distraught gaze. "I ken. You did no' mean me harm."

Rydar searched her eyes; streaked in deep blues, pupils dilated, framed by long russet lashes. Her lips parted and she touched them with her tongue. She breathed through her mouth. She hesitated.

She turned away.

His breath left him in a rush. He missed his chance. A chance he wasn't looking for. Mustn't look for. Badly wanted, nonetheless.

Skitt.

The two invalids struggled to their feet. Rydar sheathed the sword, but didn't set it down. Instead, he strapped it at his waist.

"It was my Da's." Grier ran one finger over the leather, tracing the design.

"Your pappa, aye," Rydar confirmed. Then, "My *sverd nå.*"

"Aye." Grier looked up at him. "It's your sword now." She collected her basket and left the armory. Rydar watched her disappearing back in awe.

She always understands me.

He crutched after her, thanking God repeatedly for staying the blade.

May 23, 1354

"Once again I apologize for our accommodations," Grier murmured. She set cups of wine in front of Lady Margoh and Rydar and waved toward Rydar's splinted leg. "The hall is otherwise occupied."

Rydar shifted in his chair, his face warming, and wondered if Grier considered him an imposition. She hadn't treated him as such. Still, it was all the more reason to heal quickly and continue on his way.

"Yes, of course." Lady Margoh sipped the wine and glared at Grier over the rim. Rydar had no idea why she wasn't pleased; the wine was quite delicious.

"What are you working on today?" Grier asked.

"Names of things," Margoh answered curtly.

"That sounds bonny!" Grier grinned and turned to Rydar. Her

bruised eye was healing well. "You say your 'speak', too, aye?"

"Aye." Rydar's bemused glance bounced between the women. "We *begynn?*"

Margoh sighed and patted her hand on the polished surface. "Begin. Table."

"Table," Rydar responded. "*Tabellfør.*"

"*Tabellfør,*" Grier repeated.

Margoh only looked at Rydar. "Chair."

"Aye. Chair. *Stol.*"

"Floor." Margoh tapped her fabric-clad foot.

Rydar countered with his boot. "Floor. *Gulv.*"

"Wall."

"Wall. *Vegg.*"

"This one's easy," Margoh purred. "Door."

Rydar laughed. "*Dør!*"

Ceiling. Fireplace. Hearth. Hallway. Stairs. Rydar repeated what Margoh said, and Grier repeated after Rydar. The trio worked their way through the keep, naming everything in sight. When they got to the tapestry in the Great Hall, Margoh faltered.

She glanced at Grier. "Sailors."

"Vikings," Grier stated.

"*Vikinger?*" Rydar pointed, confused. Why did she call the men in the boats 'pirating'?

"Heroes," Margoh added, still facing Grier, her tone a gauntlet tossed.

"Heroes? Or barbarians?" Grier countered angrily.

"Noble warriors!" Margoh barked.

Rydar hobbled between the women before they descended into their own war. "No. Stop."

Grier leaned around him. "Bloody murderers!"

"Victors!" Margoh retorted.

"Rapists! Pillagers! Thieves!" Grier shouted.

Rydar held his crutch with one hand and grabbed Grier's shoulder with the other. He pulled it around so she was forced to face him.

"Stop!" he bellowed.

Grier gaped at him, her face suffused with red. It matched her hair and made her eyes look even bluer. They rounded, as did her mouth. "Oh, my Lord! You're a Viking!"

"I?" he blurted, incredulous. "No!"

"Ye're Norse! You came on a boat!" Grier backed away.

Rydar looked at Margoh, eyes wide in question.

"*Du kom på en båt,*" she translated, watching the exchange with an expression he couldn't name.

He turned back to Grier. "I'm no' *vikinger!*" he protested.

"But you're born of them, are ye no'?"

"Of course he is. Be quite certain," Margoh stated with great authority.

Rydar frowned at her. "What you speak?"

Margoh waved her hand dismissively. "Come back to the table, Rydar."

She whirled and walked toward the dining room. Her backside swayed in exaggerated punctuation and his eyes were drawn there.

"Ach! No' a Viking, ye say?" Grier sneered. She disappeared out the door.

Rydar hobbled into the hallway and slammed his hand against its stone wall, stinging his palm on the cold surface. He never was a patient man and his inability to communicate well infuriated him. He spoke three—three!—*fukking* languages, but he was reduced to childish babble in this country.

And to compound the situation, he couldn't walk any better than an infant! Rydar angrily tried to put weight on his left leg, but the pain was intolerable.

"*Skitt!*" he thundered.

He felt he would explode with frustration at his continual failures. He failed to comprehend his father's dying words. He failed to build an adequate boat. He failed to reach Norway. He failed to save Arne.

And he failed to understand Grier. That was particularly enraging, since she always understood him.

"*Gud forbanner det all til helvete!*" he bellowed, and threw the crutch as hard as he could. It bounced off the wall and tumbled down the hallway. The clatter of wood against stone echoed through the keep.

Margoh's face appeared at the door of the formal dining room, blanched with shock at his strident profanity. He stared at her through the haze of his fury.

"Rydar?" she ventured.

He clenched his fists and ground out his apology. "*Jeg er trist.*"

Hopping on one leg to the staircase, he sank to a step. He rested his forehead on the heels of his hands. His words came out hard.

"No! No Norse. I am sorry."

Margoh appeared in front of him. He raised his head and squinted into her blue-gray eyes. "Go home," he said, not in Norse. "No more learn now."

She tucked his hair behind his ear and ran her finger along his jaw. He smelled her expensive perfume and wondered briefly why she wore it to the lessons.

She whispered, "I'll come back tomorrow. In the morning."

Rydar nodded. "Come back. In the morning. Aye."

He didn't move until she was gone from the keep and he was alone. Then he hopped one-legged down the hallway after his crutch.

May 26, 1354

The summons came in the early afternoon. Fergus MacDonald fell from the roof he was repairing and his arm was injured. Grier walked the half mile to his farm in less than fifteen minutes, even with the stops.

She kent it was foolishness, but she felt as though she was being followed. The back of her neck tingled and she startled at forest sounds that she never normally noticed. Now and again she paused to pick a plant and put it in her basket, to pull off her short boot and tip out a non-existent stone, or set her basket down and stretch her back. She glanced around then, trying to discern if she truly did hear suspicious movement in the woods. But she saw nothing.

But then, if a skilled hunter was tracking her, she wouldn't see anything, would she?

"Ach, ye're going daft!" she chided herself, pushing away memories of Grif's attack. "It's the middle of a bonny day and you're summoning shades!"

Fergus lay where he fell, his legs working in silent agony. His wife fluttered over him in a flurry of useless movement. The man's dark eyes met Grier's and his colorless lips parted in his pale face.

"What have ye done here, Fergus? Will you do anything for my attention?" Grier teased as she knelt beside him. Her fingers skimmed over his shoulder and arm.

The diversion worked, and his cheeks lifted in a stiff grin. "I've a fondness for red hair," he rasped.

"You've knocked your arm from its joint."

"C-can ye fix it?" he stammered.

"Aye. But I'll need some help. Is your boy near?"

Grier sat the adolescent behind his father and had him wrap his arms around his father's chest, putting his head between Fergus's head and the misplaced joint.

"Hold tight now. This will hurt a bit, but no' for long." Grier grasped Fergus's arm, braced herself, and pulled.

Fergus let out a cry that would shame a banshee. His wife screamed as well. A few choice curse words followed before the man realized that his shoulder was fixed. He gaped at Grier.

"Is that it?" he croaked.

"Aye. But you'll be sore for a week or so. And you mustn't move it too much for ten days. You don't want it to come out again," Grier cautioned.

His mouth relaxed into a relieved smile. "My thanks, Lady Grier. You're a good woman. Just like your Mam, God sain her soul." The three adults crossed themselves.

"The next time you wish my attention will ye just come up to the castle, then?" Grier lifted her basket. She winked at the man. "And bring your wife."

On the way back to the keep, Grier watched and listened. But all she heard were birds. All she saw was a brace of rabbits skittering across her path. All she felt was the spring breeze pushing her gown against her body, then pulling it away again.

Shaking her head at her earlier imaginings, she strode purposefully toward home and planned the evening meal along the way. She would check the garden when she got back. For sure there would be new onions.

ᚱᚾ

The mare Salle was in love with Rydar.

Whenever his uneven gait approached her stall every part of her strained in his direction. She pressed her long nose against his chest.

She sidled against him so he could mount her in his awkward manner. She sighed when he climbed on her back. And she did anything he asked of her.

Rydar tried to explain it to Grier when she found him in the stable with his shoulder tucked under the mare's neck, scratching the animal's nose. She carried a basket of onions and spring greens.

"Are ye coming in for supper?"

"Aye," he answered. He closed the gate behind the horse and hobbled quickly from the stable. Salle's plaintive whinny called after them.

"Salle like me," Rydar said.

Grier matched his stride and peered up at him. "How do ye ken?"

Rydar smiled at that. He knew his explanation, limited as it must be by language, would sound silly. "She happy when I come. She moves."

Grier's brow puckered. "Moves?"

Rydar stopped his progress and tucked the crutch under his arm. With his hands he imitated ears flicking, tail swishing and hooves prancing. "Moves!"

Grier laughed loudly.

Rydar laughed as well, realizing he must look quite funny. He wagged his finger in Grier's face. "She love me!"

Grier's expression shifted at those words, but he couldn't read it before she turned away. He felt he missed something important, but couldn't puzzle out what it might be.

Inside the keep, Rydar followed Grier to the kitchen. The coalescing aromas of roasting meat and baking bread made his stomach grumble thunderously.

"By crivens, man, are ye *never* full?" Grier tossed over her shoulder.

Rydar sat at the table and watched Grier finish preparing their meal. His thoughts drifted to his daily ride. The tenants who lived within the castle walls had regarded him with curious suspicion at first. He understood why; an incoherent stranger riding bareback with multi-colored threads in his cheek and wooden spoons strapped to one leg would naturally draw suspicion.

By now, the end of his second week here, he had visited them all: the butcher, the chandler, the brewer, the grooms, the miller, the weaver, the glazier, the carpenter. He communicated as best he could. He found it odd that none of them appeared to have enough to do, yet they complained about a lack of goods. True, according to Grier the population had declined by more than half in the plague's wake, and Grier and Logan's needs seemed few. But it was an unsettling waste of skills.

He needed to think more on that.

"Might be because you do no' use a saddle."

Startled back into the kitchen, Rydar looked up. Grier's piercing blue eyes met his. He puzzled out every word but saddle.

"The wood and leather seat a man rides on," she explained.

"Aye, saddle." Rydar nodded, learning the new word. He said slowly, "No. I do no' use a saddle." He looked at her. "Why is 'might be' that?"

Grier pointed her meat-carving knife at him. "Because she feels you, ye ken?"

Rydar blinked. "No."

"Your legs, your muscles, your warmth?" Grier patted her own thighs with the un-knifed hand. "There is nothing between you and her."

Rydar understood in a gut-warming glimmer.

"She feels me," he repeated. "My legs, my warmth." A mischievous smile split his cheeks. "Like woman? I move her with my warmth legs?"

Grier straightened. Her face turned scarlet. Her mouth worked, her brow worked, her shoulders worked, but no words escaped the plethora of motion. She whirled back to the meat.

"Aye" she croaked.

Rydar laughed to cover his unanticipated and undeniable arousal.

Skitt.

Chapter Ten

May 27, 1354

You *skrive?*"

Morning light pushed through the uneven windowpanes and slanted across the kitchen table. Grier looked up from her book, quill poised over the sheep-skin parchment. Rydar's astonishment irritated her and she frowned at him.

"What?"

"*Skrive.*" Rydar mimicked writing.

"I ken. Aye, I can scribe. And I can read, too!" she retorted with not a wee bit of sarcasm.

"Read," Rydar repeated, thoughtfully. "Aye."

"Can you?" Grier challenged.

One corner of Rydar's mouth twitched. "I read Norse. Latin. German. And I learn…" He pointed at Grier's parchment and grinned at her.

Grier's jaw dropped. "All that?"

She regarded her surprising guest with new appreciation. Even a Viking warrior might become civilized, she supposed. She patted the bench beside her.

"Come here. Let me see your cheek."

Rydar crutched forward and lowered himself beside her. "What you—scribe?" he asked.

"I keep an account of the people I treat; what their ailment was, what I did for them, and how they did after." Grier turned the book to face Rydar. "See? Here you are."

Rydar took the pen and, with an engaging grin, changed the spelling of his name from 'Rider.' Then he added 'Hansen.' And 'Norway.'

Grier read his entries without comment. She was glad to know how to spell his name. But when she saw it written correctly, and in his strong, clear hand, she felt like something inside her slipped into place. She had no idea what it was, much less what she should do about it. For a moment, she was disoriented. The black letters seemed to dance on the page.

Then Grier pushed the book aside. Determined to maintain her equilibrium, she gripped Rydar's jaw and pulled him close to examine the stitches.

"They need to come out."

"Need come out? Aye." His gaze questioned, but she looked away.

Grier retrieved her sewing basket from its home by the hearth. Inside was a tiny razor, very sharp for cutting cloth. She held it up and faced Rydar. "Ye can no' move, now. Be still, aye?"

Rydar started to nod, then froze. "Aye."

Grier carefully cut the thread below each knot, now buried in two weeks of new beard. She thought about how his face had filled out in those two weeks, how his pale skin had gained color, how his cropped hair framed his smile, and those thoughts sent a tickle through her belly. She reached for a small pair of pinchers and gripped the end of one thread.

"It may hurt a bit," she warned.

Rydar waved one hand, and otherwise did not move. He didn't even flinch when she tugged the stitches from his skin. He held out his palm and she dropped the threads there.

"Done. Now don't go tearing it open," she scolded.

Rydar nodded and tossed the tiny knotted bits of cotton yarn into the fire. He skimmed his fingers over the wound, exploring.

"It's most likely time to change the dressing on your leg, as well." Grier wiggled her fingers toward Rydar's bandaged shin. Understanding, he removed the left leg of his hose, then rested that limb on the bench.

Images of him nearly naked after the rescue pushed their way into Grier's awareness. Well formed in spite of his lack of flesh, he would certainly look better now that he ate regularly. She clamped her teeth together and bent over Rydar's leg, not meeting his gaze lest he somehow guess the improper path of her thoughts. She unwound the dirty linen strips that held the wooden spoons-cum-splints in place. When she lifted away the wool padding she was pleased with what she saw.

"Is good?" Rydar asked, reading her expression.

"Aye. It's no' swollen and the bruises are faded." Grier washed the skin gently with vinegar, then rewrapped it with fresh wool and clean linen strips.

"When I can walk?"

Grier pointed an imperious finger in his direction. "Four more weeks! And not a day sooner!"

Rydar rolled his eyes in exaggerated compliance. He pulled his hose on and tied it in place.

Grier stood and put her implements away. She started to speak with her back to him, but realized he wouldn't understand without watching her mouth and seeing her expression. She turned to face him across the kitchen. "I'm sorry."

Rydar's brow lifted. "Sorry? Why sorry?"

"When Margoh was here. I lost my temper." Grier knotted her fingers behind her back. "It was no' proper. I'm sorry."

"*Temperament*. Aye, I ken. Proper?" Rydar queried.

"Right. Acceptable. Ladylike."

"*Akseptabel*; I ken." Rydar patted the bench. "Come here. Let me see your cheek."

Grier could not help but smile at his mimicry and she did as he asked. He faced her and took her chin in his long fingers. Clear green eyes, which she noticed in the morning sunlight held tiny flecks of gold, met hers.

"Vikingers old, not here now. I no' Viking. I no' hurt you. You save me. No Grier? I dead. You ken?" he spoke earnestly. She knew he meant so much more than he was able to say.

Grier shifted, embarrassed. "It was no' you that made me wroth. It was that hen that provoked me." At Rydar's bemused expression, she clarified. "Margoh."

"Ach!" Rydar began to chuckle. "Margoh the Hen!" And he laughed.

Grier winced. "Is it funny?"

Rydar pushed up onto his good leg and bent his arms like

wings. He began to hop around the room, naming off items.

"Chair! Table! Door!" Then he clucked and gestured with one elbow-wing. "Come here! Come here!"

Grier burst into appreciative giggles. She jumped up to join him and snuggled under his left arm for support. They moved around the kitchen practicing words, and then went into the hallway. Grier had one arm around Rydar's waist and one of his 'wings' relaxed so his large palm cupped her shoulder.

"Steps! Wall! Ceiling!" Grier called out.

Rydar said the words as if he were a squawking chicken. Grier laughed so hard, she was afraid she might piss herself. She could no longer speak. Rydar threw his head back and crowed loud as an arrogant rooster. Grier dropped to the floor in hysterics, abandoning her supporting role. Rydar wobbled precariously and grabbed the edge of the staircase for support, wheezing with laughter.

Logan tromped down the stairs. "This is a pretty scene. And you're loud enough to wake the dead! Is breakfast made?"

Grier wiped her eyes. "Breakfast? No, no' yet. I'm in need of eggs."

"Eggs?" Rydar repeated, his eyes twinkling. "Need eggs?"

Rydar screwed up his face and pretended to try and lay an egg. Logan looked at him as though he were daft.

Grier pushed to her feet and grasped his shoulders. "You get eggs from a hen, no' from a rooster, ye foolish Viking!"

For a moment, bafflement dominated Rydar's features. Then he gripped her meaning and crumpled to the floor, bellowing in unrestrained howls.

May 31, 1354

Rydar's grasp of his new language amazed Grier. True, many words sounded the same as Norse and he often mixed up the pronunciations, offering to 'hjelp du' and saying he 'vil komm.' But there were plenty of words that didn't match. Rydar pushed himself hard, unafraid to make mistakes. With Grier's constant help, and Margoh's annoyingly long and frequent visits, he was learning hers so much faster than she could learn his.

But then, he had more at stake, did he not? After all, she was not living in his land; he was living in hers. And he might be here for some time to come, she hoped.

It was this very trail that her thoughts meandered along when she was supposed to be attentive to the language lesson, so she startled when she realized both Rydar and Margoh were staring at her apparently waiting for some sort of response.

"What?"

"Have you a calendar?" Margoh repeated.

"Oh! Aye. I'll get it." Grier left the dining room and ran up the stairs to her sleep chamber. She returned with a large sheet of parchment neatly lined and squared, with numbers in each box and elaborate figures decorating the borders.

"You make this?" Rydar lifted the calendar and examined it closely. "Beautiful."

"Winter nights in Balnakeil Bay are long and dark," she demurred. "It passes the time."

"As I was saying, this is today, the last day of May," Margoh interjected. "Now, birthdays. Mine is in October on the fifteenth." She pointed at the corresponding square. "When is yours?"

Grier reached for the document. "I was born in—"

"I addressed Rydar," Margoh snapped.

Rydar slid his gaze away from Margoh to Grier. "Born in?" he asked her pointedly.

"March. On the tenth," Grier murmured. She refused to look at the rude and irritating Margoh the Hen.

He nodded. "My birth day…" He looked for the name of the month. "June. June twenty. The *Sommer Solverv*."

"The Summer Solstice?" Margoh cooed. "How very special you are!"

"What year?" Grier asked. Margoh pulled back, drawing Grier's glance. The older woman's expression altered and she seemed alarmed. That was interesting.

Rydar wrote '1324' on a slip of parchment and looked up.

"What year is now?" he asked Grier.

Grier pulled the paper close to her and wrote '1354.'

"No… No!" Rydar slumped back in his chair and turned stricken eyes to Grier. "Is not… I am… *tretti?*" Confusion sculpted his features. "How I am *tretti?*"

"Thirty," she whispered.

Rydar ran both hands through his hair. Twice. "Thirty," he

mumbled, incredulity washing over his countenance.

"Did you no' know?" Grier asked.

Rydar's face grew ashen and he stared at nothing. He shook his head slowly.

"Thirty. Is no' right." His eyes lifted to Grier's. Huge pupils obliterated the green, leaving only golden rings around black holes. "Are you much right of year?"

Grier nodded. Rydar covered his face with his broad hands.

"Å min Gud! So much time gone," he moaned. His palms rounded the tones giving his lament an eerie sound. "Å min Gud…"

Margoh reached for the calendar. Her words were clipped. "Let's move on."

Rydar's hands fell loosely to the table and he faced Grier. "What year you are born?"

In spite of the dread that speared through her, Grier wrote '1328.' She lifted her chin. "I'm twenty-six."

He nodded. "Tjue seks. Twenty six."

Grier held her breath and watched for any sign that Rydar thought her too old. Mercifully, there was none. But then, he was older than her and obviously concerned at the moment about his own age.

Margoh stood and set the calendar on the cabinet that held the fine dishes. Grier turned her head and considered the woman's back.

"And in what year were you born, Margoh?" she asked. The question was truly a bit wickit. But Grier wanted Rydar to know that the jillet was older than he, if he didn't know that already.

"I doubt that's of any interest to anyone," Margoh stated, her back still to the room.

"What year you are born?" Rydar restated the question.

Margoh didn't answer at first and seemed to be weighing the consequences of refusing. She whirled and scribbled '1317,' then hissed, and turned the seven into a nine.

She straightened and said, "Now let's move on to—"

"You'll turn thirty-seven this October?" Grier smiled her nicest smile, knowing Rydar could figure out Margoh's years for himself. "I never would have weened it, Margoh. You're so beautiful for a woman of your years."

Margoh flushed and her mouth gaped. She snapped it shut.

Triumphant, Grier rose from her seat. "I must see to supper. Please excuse me."

ᚱᚺ

Tumultuous red hair spread in flames across his bed; auburn, russet, orange, gold, ginger. Skin smooth as fresh cream. Eyes deep as a clear winter sky. Rose-tipped mounds filled his hands, his mouth. Her copper-forested cleft opened.

Rydar awoke with a gasp.

Gud forbanner det all til helvete!

He rolled from his cot and reached for the mantle, two hops away. It only required a few quick strokes before his seed hissed and dissipated in a musky cloud over the banked coals.

He stared at the fire.

She's a virgin. Leave her alone.

"But it's not only swiving," he whispered, arguing with himself. "There's something special about her." She was intelligent. Headstrong. Fearless. Independent. But those qualities did not make compliant wives.

Who was seeking a compliant wife?

"I'm not in any position to marry!" he muttered. Scowling, he turned his back on the hearth's subdued inferno. "I'm already thirty. I haven't a penny to my name. The clothes on my back are borrowed. I eat and sleep under a roof provided by Christian charity. I cannot even do for myself!"

Sitting on the edge of his cot, he stared at the coals and considered the matching inferno that simmered inside of him. Years had passed since he last laid with a woman. The women in Grønnland were worn down, joyless, and they married young to the least objectionable prospects.

Rydar knew he was far from objectionable, and rampant opportunities were thrust upon him. Though he deflected marriage, he did sample the choices as often as he could. However none tempted him enough to stay.

He smiled.

Grier was decidedly not 'objectionable' either. She was beautiful. Rounded and firm and vibrant. Rydar closed his eyes and retrieved the dream image of his feisty feminine savior. He held it, examined it, pondered it, enjoyed it. His yard, long deprived, stiffened again.

He opened his eyes and stretched out on the narrow bed, staring toward the ceiling. He steered his consideration to Margoh; tall, blond, and beautiful in a worldly way. During their lessons she all but swived him on the table.

But the widow paled alongside Grier.

As engaging as Grier was, she mustn't be allowed to hold him here. He must return to Arendal and determine if he had an inheritance. Property was the key. Without it, he would merely be a laborer, a tradesman. Not much to offer any woman, especially at this age.

Rydar rubbed his face with his palms and combed his fingers through his new beard. He felt the healed cut on his cheek and sighed. Blue eyes and red hair floated pleasingly through his mind.

Grier.

Chapter Eleven

June 3, 1354

Rydar rode Salle alongside Logan into Durness. The mile-long road crested over a narrow spit of rocky Scottish stubbornness that protruded straight north into the Sea and sheltered Balnakeil Bay. Behind him, overlooking the Bay, were the castle and its two-and-a-half story keep and three-story round tower. In front of him, a cluster of stone and timber buildings lined up along a narrow street like silent soldiers. A few low residences flowed outward, forming the skirts of their tunics.

Logan was taking him to Malise McKay's house where Margoh Henriksen and her sister, Hanne Larson, currently abided. Once Rydar knew the way, he might come alone for his lessons and not be a burden on Logan's time.

The main thoroughfare of Durness was cobbled with native stones, rounded by the surf. Most of the buildings had stone-and-mortar first stories. If there was an upper floor, that was made of timber and white-washed plaster. Roofs were moss-coated slate.

Rydar frowned, puzzled.

At least half the buildings were vacant. Some doors stood open. Shutters were broken. He asked Logan about it.

"It's the Death, ye ken? Too many died. Others moved away, though I doubt they escaped."

Rydar considered his words. "Men here. They are work, aye?"

"Aye. Though the merchant guild has not met in far more than a year."

"Merk-ant guild?"

"The group of men who control commerce in the town."

"Oh." Rydar determined he needed to ask Margoh to explain that.

He did.

"Every town has a guild. They have standard measures for products, set standard prices, things such as that," she explained in Norse, handing him a cup of spiced wine. He sat in the McKay's kitchen with her, their house being much smaller than the castle keep. "Why do you ask?"

"It seems that there are men at the castle who have skills, but they lack work. And they complain about the dearth of goods. Is it the same for the town people?"

"I suppose. But what concern is it of yours?" Margoh ran her middle finger along the inside of the deeply scooped neckline on her red wool gown. The color went quite well with her blond hair and brought color to her pale cheeks. "What are you considering?"

Rydar raised his gaze and his palms. "I have nothing at all to call my own. All that I had was left behind in Grønnland or lost at sea. But I do intend to continue my journey."

"How?"

"I don't yet know."

She leaned closer. "When?"

Rydar shrugged and sipped his wine.

Margoh's overt trifling made him think of swiving. And swiving made him think of Grier. And bedding Grier wasn't a possibility, so the entire thread of thought—and the widow's actions—irritated him.

Margoh contemplated him in silence for a pace. Then, "Will you journey alone?"

He had not expected that. "I planned to."

"But you might consider a passenger?"

Rydar tilted his head and tried to dissuade her. "It's a very dangerous and unsure passage. The risk would be yours. Entirely yours. Do you understand that?"

She watched him pensively and didn't respond. In the face of her silence, his position must be made clear.

"I will make you no promises. Of any kind," he stated.

Margoh leaned back in her chair, apparently deciding. "I've had promises. I'll take the risk."

She lifted her cup of wine and drained it.

ᚱᚺ

When Rydar returned to the castle, he went looking for Grier. In spite of the plague-devastated population, the lack of industry in the small town puzzled him. He had questions about her tenants and their trade with the inhabitants of Durness. She wasn't to be found in the lower rooms, so he called up the stairs.

Moira's head poked out one of the doors. "She's no' up here."

"You ken where?" Rydar asked.

Moira shrugged. "She was called to a tenant who was hurtit. I dinna ken and she's back." She retreated, offering no additional information.

Rydar sighed, blowing a long breath through loose lips. *She went alone? Again?*

Irritated, he crutched his way into the kitchen for a mug of ale. He stood in the room, quenching his thirst with the pale brew, and caught sight of Grier through the diamond-paned window. She stood beyond the castle wall on the windy bluff facing the sea.

Rydar left his empty mug on the table and hobbled outside to talk to her. But once he crossed the moat bridge, something in her stance slowed him.

She stood with her head lowered, her arms folded in front of her. As Rydar drew nearer he could see her profile. Her expression was somber, and she gripped her crucifix in one hand. The apron she wore was stained with an alarming amount of blood.

The crash of endlessly tumbling waves, agitated by a North Sea wind blowing into Balnakeil Bay, covered the sound of his approach. Unwilling to disturb her thoughts, he stopped and waited. For what, he had no idea.

Grier let go of her necklace and reached for her hair. She unplaited it slowly, loosing abundant red waves to the wind. She shook her head. Her curls streamed out behind her, an undulating copper standard. The hem of her gown snapped and fluttered beneath it. Grier closed her eyes. Unfurling her arms, she straightened her back and lifted her chin to the afternoon sun.

The wind molded her gown against her thighs, her belly, the

curve of her breasts. She looked as though she might take flight. She was a wild creature, at one with the wind and the sky. Beautiful. Gloriously strong. Unfettered. No man could tame her.

No man should ever try, Rydar realized. To do so would quench the very qualities that made her so worthy a companion at the start.

He lost track of time watching her. Grier's arms lowered finally, and her eyes opened. He stepped closer then and she turned toward him. The serene expression on her face seemed to say that she knew he was there all along.

In spite of his broken leg, he quickly closed the distance between them, his eyes never shifting from hers. He was compelled to kiss her and didn't think to resist. He tilted her chin upward with a knuckle and took her mouth with his before he thought better of it.

It was a solid kiss. Firm moist lips met his, pressing, probing, accepting. Sweet breath. Humming sigh. No resistance.

He held her lips possibly longer than he should have, but the contours of her mouth fit against his so perfectly that he didn't wish to let them go.

Though compliant at first, Grier jerked back with a small cry and gasp. Blue eyes widened over the fist that now sealed her mouth. Her brow twitched, displaying surprise, shock. She blinked rapidly.

Rydar knew his amorous ambush had frightened her, and he raised both hands in a gesture of surrender. "I sorry."

"Don't," she sputtered.

He shook his head and his hands fell to his side. "I do no'," he said.

"No! That's no' what I'm saying!" Grier cried. She bit her lower lip. She turned away, as if to leave, but didn't. She rubbed her palms hard against the sides of her skirt and drew a deep breath. With a small gasp of a sob, she faced him again.

Grier reached up and tangled her fingers in his wind-blown hair. Balancing on her toes, she pulled his face down to hers. She kissed him, open-eyed at first, and then he closed his.

Soft full lips. Warm breath against his cheek. Her tongue pushed past his teeth and tangled with his, sending fierce waves pulsating down to his boots. He reached for her shoulders and steadied her so she wouldn't stop.

The taste of her, the feel of her, the little moans that escaped her, turned him to iron. He held himself away from her so she wouldn't notice. Thank the Lord this tunic was long enough to cover the urgent bulge tucked inside his braies.

The kiss suspended the wind and even the raucous sound of the waves disappeared.

Then Grier pulled away from him and he forced his eyes open. He still held her shoulders. Her lips were smudged and reddened, her cheeks flushed, and her eyes out-blued the sky.

"Oh, no!" she wailed.

"What?" Rydar croaked.

She twisted from his grasp, turned and stumbled on the hem of her dress. Grabbing bunches of fabric in both hands, Grier hiked her skirt and bloodied apron above her ankles and ran toward the keep. Rydar felt his soul rip from his body and trail along the ground behind her.

Strength abandoned him and he sank to the ground. He laid back, limbs splayed wide in the course sea grass. Wind rushed over his face, and lifted the edge of his tunic to cool his thighs and parts between. His arousal calmed slowly. His thudding heart took longer.

Why on earth did he do that? Why did he need to kiss her? Was it because she looked so beautiful with her hair streaming in the wind and her gown outlining every curve of her body?

If his recurring dreams were any indication, it was because he desired to make energetic love to her. Repeatedly. To hold her close along his body, feel her supple warmth wrap around him, taste every inch of her skin. Tangle himself in all parts of her glorious red hair. Fall asleep wrapped in her arms.

He saw the image again in his mind: glorious Grier standing on the windy bluff. But this time she was waving goodbye. He was sailing away from her. Forever. And that's when the realization punched him in the gut.

He didn't want to leave her.

"NO!" he bellowed and slammed his fists against the ground, smashing the dry, rasping grass. No. No, no, no! He could not fall in love with her. He must not fall in love with her. He would never stay here. Never.

"Tomorrow I will find a way to leave," he resolved, denying the lure of his desirable healer. "Tomorrow I will make a plan and begin it. This I will absolutely do."

Rydar reached for his crutch and clambered to his feet. He began a slow path back to the keep. His resolution was steel. Inflexible. Cold. Severing.

ᚱᚼ

Grier stomped around her chamber. She could not recall being angrier with herself. How could she have behaved so wantonly? She wasn't a jillet! What on God's good earth had come over her?

She didn't know Rydar was near her on the bluff, but neither was she surprised to see him there. When he came toward her, she kent his intention; every inch of his tall body pulsated with it. She reacted without thinking, kissing him back. Shocked at herself, she pulled away. That should have been the end of it.

But then she returned to him. She kissed him deeply, passionately. She kissed him! What in God's good name did she think she was about?

Grier touched her mouth. She still felt Rydar's lips against hers; felt the scratch of his beard on her chin; felt the grip of his hands on her shoulders. Felt his strength. Felt his desire.

Felt her desire.

Grier crumpled to the floor.

I do desire him. Was it merely loneliness? Was it because he was her only visible prospect?

Or was it because the Viking was so quick to learn, eager to communicate with her? Or his willingness to be of help. Or his sense of humor and the way his eyes glowed when he laughed. Perchance it was because he was becoming the most beautiful man she had ever known.

He was so exotic to her with his startling height and his angelic Norse coloring. His unfamiliar language flowed through her, warming her like fine wine. His hands spoke to her of both rough skills and tender care.

There was a bond between the two of them that she couldn't explain—Grier felt it the first time their eyes met. Did he feel it, too?

"I could love him, I think," she whispered to the empty room. "I wonder—could he ever love me?"

ᚱᚾ

The kisses were not mentioned as Rydar cleaned fish for the supper's stew and Grier baked bread. She nervously filled the air with words, telling him about the gashed thigh she stitched, staunching the loss of blood, and hopefully saving the man's life.

"I'll know in three day's time," she added. "If the wound doesn't fester he should yet live."

"Hm," Rydar grunted. He didn't look at her.

"What were you about today?" she asked. She selected a large onion and fetched her steel cooking knife.

"I ride Salle to Durness with Logan."

Grier spun to face him. Firelight glinted off the sharp blade. "What?"

He looked up at her, his green eyes hooded and his gaze cool. "I ride Salle to Durness with Logan."

"Why?"

Rydar rolled his eyes. "I go to Margoh. Talk lessons. Logan say is good idea I ken the way."

"Oh." Grier hefted the knife in one hand and the onion in the other. She should have kilt Logan when she had the chance. She tried to sound unconcerned though she wondered how much longer her heart would beat. "Will you have your lessons there now?"

"I think yes." He returned his attention to the fish. "You say I ride Salle any time, aye?"

Grier set the onion on the table and hacked repeatedly into the pungent bulb. Fumes rose and stung her eyes. "Aye."

"Now I ride to Margoh."

Now I ride to Margoh. The words cut into her as mortally as she cut into the onion. After their kisses this afternoon, how could he sound so cold? Perhaps he didn't care anything about her at all and was simply in the mood to rut. A typical man. She sniffed as tears ran down her cheeks.

"Grier?"

She swiped at her cheeks with the back of her hand. "Aye?"

"What is wrong?" he asked, his voice softened.

She held up the onion and forced a smirk that she prayed was convincing. "Tis only the fumes. This one is strong."

"Hm," Rydar grunted again and considered her, unsmiling.

She turned her back on those beautiful pastel eyes that saw into her soul and dropped the ragged onion pieces into a pot. Her heart was ragged as well, shredded by his indifference to her.

She struggled to speak casually. "Have you done with the fish yet?"

Chapter Twelve

The call to deliver a babe came as Rydar, Logan and Grier sat down to their supper of fish stew, bread, cheese and cider. Moira tapped her foot and waited for Grier's response. With a hungry sigh, Grier stuffed a slice of bread into her mouth and dropped a wedge of cheese into her clean apron's pocket.

She spoke to the men with her mouth full. "It's her fifth bairn and will likely come fast. I'll go now."

Rydar's eyes narrowed briefly then his gaze fell back to his food. Grier thought she saw his jaw clench.

The wind had slowed with the lowering of the sun. As Grier crossed the castle yard toward the stable, she made a quick calculation: she could walk the half mile to the cottage in the time it would take a groom to saddle and bridle Salle. And besides that, the evening was warm. The turquoise sky glowed with orange-edged lavender clouds.

Grier coveted the few extra moments alone to ponder Rydar's kisses and the way they touched the emptiness inside her. And the puzzling coolness in his attitude afterward. And what it meant to her that he would begin riding into Durness for his language lessons.

She was no wiser, however, at the end of her walk, though her prediction proved true. The babe clambered into the world soon after she arrived, early but strong, and wailing to wake the dying.

Grier sat another hour with the woman to be certain the bairn suckled well and her bleeding stopped, so the summer night's sun was hiding below the horizon when she started home.

In the grayed light she saw her way easily without a torch. Half-a-moon peered askance at her, as if to scold her for being so unwary. The twilit sky lent an otherworldly patina to the landscape and she imagined sounds and movements that were most unlikely.

"Summoning shades is best left for bonny days," she murmured. "Not for nights such as this."

"Hello, missy."

Grier gasped and jumped back. Her basket banged her knee. Hard.

A skinny man with tangled black hair and beard materialized on the path. Threadbare clothes hung loose on his bony frame. Gray skin sunk into his cheeks and bagged under his pale eyes.

"Good evening, sir. Good journey to you." Grier tried to skirt around him, but he stepped in her way.

"No' so fast. What have you there?" He jerked his chin at her basket.

Grier shrugged and forced diffidence into her tone. "Only women's things. Herbs, flowers. Naught of value."

"I'll judge that meself!" He grabbed for the handle but Grier tossed the basket aside.

"Now what did ye do tha' for?" he asked. In the dim light, Grier saw his eyes pass over her. She didn't care for the way his mouth twisted. "As it stands, I'm thinking it's ye wha' might be the value after all."

Grier tossed her head. "I assure ye, sir. You do no' want me."

"Oh? And why no'?"

"I'm poxed."

"I dinna believe you." The man lifted his tunic and rubbed the front of his braies.

Grier stepped backward. The fellow jumped forward and grabbed her jaw with skeletal fingers, twisting it toward the moon. Grier could smell his body odor and sour, ale-tainted breath.

"I said, I do no' believe you," he sneered.

Grier stared at him, determined not to show the fear that twined around her bones like English ivy. "Then risk your own life. It's no concern of mine. I'll die either way."

"Ye're lyin'."

Grier shrugged. "Who lies about death?"

"Awbody lies about awthing," he countered. His numbing grip was bruising her jaw. And the other bruise had only just healed.

"Do you think I care to face God with li-lies on my li-lips?" Grier ground past the pain.

He narrowed his eyes, considering. Then he sniffed her.

"Ye're too clean to be poxed." He shoved her hard and she fell backward. Twigs snapped and damp leaves stuck to her flailing limbs.

Before she could scoot away, he knelt on her belly. Air rushed from her in a rough whoosh and she couldn't breathe in. The man pushed his braies down, rubbing to keep himself hard. Grier's world condensed to tiny black gnats and white fireflies, swirling in front of her eyes and blotting out her accoster.

She struggled, clawing where his face must be and wrestling against the carpet of moldering leaves until her body went limp. Somehow, he avoided her attempts to dislodge him from her body. Then he pinned her wrists against the ground with his free hand.

When the man shifted his position, breath returned to her lungs in a throat-searing gasp and left in the loudest scream Grier could manage. The man slapped her, but she screamed again. He slapped her again and she tasted blood.

"Hush it or I'll use me fist!" he threatened.

Grier screamed anyway. The punch made her ears ring and blurred her vision. She blinked and gasped and tried to make sense of her surroundings. He clamped his lips over her mouth to silence her. Grier's gorge rose at the stench of his breath.

He collapsed on top of her with a guttural gurgle. Grier felt something warm run over her neck and she was certain he had vomited on her. She took advantage of the moment. She shoved him aside and rolled away.

From the corner of her eye she saw steel reflecting moonlight. Grier scrambled to her feet and bolted into the safety of the forest, not seeing or caring where she ran.

"Grier!"

He kent her name? How? She grabbed a tree trunk and used it for protection as she swung around behind it, panting and shaking beyond control. She gagged violently, realizing there was no vomit on her, only blood. Its filth and stink enveloped her. Swallowing the sobs that wrenched her chest she tried desperately to be silent.

"Grier!"

She froze—the voice was familiar. Could it be that Rydar was here?

She peered around the trunk. In the dim light she saw the silhouette of her tall rescuer standing on one leg and leaning on his massive sword. Salle snorted and stomped nearby. Grier stumbled from behind the tree. Rydar hopped toward her on one foot. She staggered in his direction and fell into his arms nearly knocking him over.

"Where—did you—come from?" she gasped.

"I follow you."

She sniffed wetly and dragged the back of her hand under her dripping nose. "Why?"

"Ruffians." His tone was stern and his expression angry. His eyes showed dark and dilated in the dim light. "You no' go alone! Is no' good!"

"What?"

Rydar huffed and repeated his reasoning.

Grier blinked up at him, a realization congealing in her chest. "Is this the first time?"

Rydar paused then shook his head, no.

"You have been following me?" she demanded, her voice rising in pitch.

He lifted his chin, daring her to challenge him. "Aye."

She pulled away from him and glared up at his shadowed features. She was livid. Beyond livid. How dare he? Who did he imagine himself to be?

She yanked at her apron with spastic hands and scrubbed her assailant's blood from her face and neck with forceful swipes.

"Why did you no' tell me?" she shouted.

Rydar gave her a knowing look. "You say no, and I tell you, aye?"

"Aye!" Grier stomped her foot. She gestured toward him with the hem of the bloodied apron crumpled in her fist. "I don't need you! Ye ken?"

Rydar frowned at her and his jaw gaped in disbelief. He waggled his bloodied sword at the path and its gruesome occupant, now headless.

Grier glowered her defiance.

"I can take care of myself!" she shrieked. She whirled around and stumbled towards her basket, her legs tingling and unsteady, and her boots' wooden soles slipping on damp leaves and pebbles.

"Grier!" Rydar barked. "Stop!"

She yelled over her shoulder, "How could you follow me? Who asked you to? Of all the—shite!" She tripped and felt to her hands and knees. Rydar hopped after her and reached down to help her stand. She slapped his hand away.

"Don't touch me," she growled.

"Grier, do no' be wroth!"

"Do no' be wroth? Do no' be wroth!" Grier grabbed for her basket and used its handle to leverage herself up. "What do you ken about it anyway?"

"I save your life!" Ryder shouted.

Grier stomped away from him, turned back to face him, pointed her finger at him, waved it in front of his nose, then dropped a clenched fist by her side.

"You do no' understand!" she cried. She kicked rotted leaves at him. Twice.

"No! I do no'!" Rydar hop-stepped closer. He towered over her, arms flexed. "I do no' understand!" he bellowed. *"Forbannet sta kvinne! Gud forbanner det all til helvete!"*

Grier flinched. She was enraged and she was terrified and she shuddered under the weight of both. Her emotions in turmoil, she searched through their frenetic disruption for words he would understand; words to express the reality of her truly precarious situation.

Rydar glared down at her, the moon's light glimmered in his pale eyes. His jaw jutted forward. He looked absolutely furious.

She could no' blame him.

But she mustn't cry in front of him. After their tumultuous kisses this afternoon, she was determined to grasp any dignity still within her reach. She tightened her grip on the basket handle and swallowed the lump that strangled her words. She spoke, her voice low, her words slow and very deliberate.

"You are a man."

Rydar scoffed. "Aye. Good you see that!" Sarcasm, apparently, transcended language limitations.

She pressed on. "But I am a woman."

Rydar threw his arms wide, his expression disbelieving. "What is your meaning!" he roared.

Grier poked her stiff forefinger hard into Rydar's chest, jabbing him with every word. "My world is no' your world, Viking!"

Rydar's arms fell limp at his side and his shoulders slumped. Glowering, he shook his head. "I do no' understand!" he barked.

Grier sucked in a breath, angry that it came unevenly. "I'm alone."

Rydar stared hard at her, his expression unchanged. "Alone is why—" he began.

"Aye!" Grier interrupted. "Alone *is* why!"

Rydar stepped back. His jaw hung slack and his brow puckered. His eyes never left hers.

Grier kent he was confused. She kent he was working through the English words. She kent she hadn't been clear. But she was about to admit her deepest fear to this unexpected man, and she feared what might happen when she did.

Cursed tears came—yet again—and she was helpless to stop them. But she would not acknowledge them. She would not wipe them away. She wouldn't even sniff back the slime that dripped from her nose and ran along her lips.

Rydar reached out to dry her cheek and she smacked his hand away. She couldn't accept his kindness. Not now. Not at this particular crossroad.

"Say me," Rydar whispered.

Grier lifted her chin. The half moon shone in her eyes and she knew Rydar could see her clearly.

"I. Am. Alone," she said deliberately. She thumbed her chest. "I have to take care of myself. I have to rely on myself. I have only me. Do ye ken?"

Rydar folded his arms. He looked at the ground. He rubbed his beard. "Aye?"

"Rydar!"

He met her gaze again, staring from under a darkly twisted brow.

"If I can no' take care of myself..." Grier paused, and then named her demon. "I will die."

There it was. Out in the world. Acknowledged.

Grier hoped her defiant expression masked her soul-deep terror.

These two attacks in as many weeks—the man with the poppy medicine and tonight—shook her confidence more than she wished to admit. If she could no longer go safely to practice her healing skills, what would she do? Where was her purpose then? To merely play servant to Logan's young bride?

She didn't want to consider that. That was merely a lingering death.

Rydar unfolded his arms. He leaned over and pulled the basket from Grier's grip. He opened the lid and fished out a rag. Without a word, he wiped Grier's cheeks and nose. He was so tender that Grier thought she might scream.

He sighed heavily, and narrowed his eyes. Then he pointed his forefinger and poked her with each word, gently, in the same manner that she poked him earlier.

"You," he said in a voice as deep and powerful as the North Sea, "are strongest woman I ever ken."

Grier was stunned. She opened her mouth, but no words came.

Rydar's finger moved upward and tucked her mussed and blood-wetted curls behind her ear. "I never ken woman so strong like you."

"Strong? Like a man?" she ventured.

Rydar's lopsided grin made a vigorous appearance. "No! No' like man. Different strong. Strong in here." He tapped her chest again.

Tears continued to wash Grier's cheeks but she didn't heed them. Rydar had just given her the greatest compliment of her life. Did he know it? Did this Viking sailor that crashed so unexpectedly into her life truly understand her after all? She sniffed; loud, sloppy and very un-ladylike.

"Thank you, Rydar," she conceded.

Rydar handed her the basket. "We go now."

Grier nodded and gripped the handle. Rydar whistled and Salle trotted to them. Her ears pricked and tail swished as she sidled against Rydar.

The mare does 'move' when she's close to him, Grier realized. Rydar placed his hands on Salle's back and vaulted into position. Then he pulled Grier up behind him. She held the basket with one arm and his waist with the other.

She realized suddenly that he had gained weight. Memories of his gaunt frame faded as she felt his solid presence in front of her. He was stronger; growing even more handsome as he healed. Tonight he had demonstrated considerable strength and he wasn't fully recovered yet.

Grier pressed down the ache, confusion and pain that this day's diverse events kindled in her chest.

He does no' care for me, she reminded herself cruelly. He's riding to Margoh.

Rydar steered the mare away from the decapitated torso of the miscreant and urged Salle toward the castle. Grier shuddered and turned aside. The reality of the night's threat rose in front of her, a spectre of her uncertain future. She squeezed her eyes shut.

It was too much to ponder now, and she was too fragile. She would wait and think about it tomorrow, in the rational light of day. For tonight, she would bathe, and then burn her blood-ruined gown. A sizeable cup of warm mead would help her sleep.

"I have question," Rydar said over his shoulder, tugging her from her morbid thoughts.

"What is it?"

"Now you ken; I come all time, aye?"

Pride gave Grier every intention to object, but the strength that the big, male body in front of her gave her pause. With Rydar, she felt safe and protected for the first time in six years. Besides, a competent guard would bring peace of mind in this increasingly dangerous land. A bit of the hardness she feigned fell away, chipped again by the Norseman's respectful kindness.

"I suppose," she consented, her tone chiding. "If you do no' get in my way."

She felt him chuckle and his understanding endeared him to her.

"I stink. I need a bath," Grier mumbled. "And this gown is ruined." Rydar rested a hand on her leg and rubbed it soothingly.

She was not soothed.

Awareness of his muscled back and powerful arse between her thighs was akin to considering a rich banquet after vomiting violently. She had been accosted, very nearly raped, and a man was killed.

Could Rydar feel her heart hammering? It was trying to break out of her chest.

"You safe now, Grier," he said over his shoulder. "Do no' be afraid."

"Aye. Thank you." Better he thought her afraid, than realize she was responding as a lonely, warm-blooded woman to his very compelling masculinity.

Chapter Thirteen

June 4, 1354

Lightning blinked repeatedly. The day grumbled in response, pulling its gray blanket of clouds lower. It was a good day to work in the kitchen by the fire, lulled by the soft patter of rain.

Grier served Rydar a substantial mug of cider while he finished off yet another loaf of bread, this one with a honey comb. She had a pile of mending to do and this seemed a bonny time to do it. Because of the storm, there would be no traveling to Durness for lessons today. Grier settled on a stool where she could see Rydar easily.

"I have no' eat this," he held up the comb, "after I was boy."

"Were there no bees in Greenland?"

"Bees?"

Grier made a buzzing sound and wiggled her hand in front of her.

"Oh, aye. No. No bees."

"Ye were no' born in Greenland." Grier pulled her threaded needle through the stockings, then gazed expectantly at Rydar.

"No. Norway." He wasn't looking at her.

"How did you come to be in Greenland?"

Rydar considered his sudden fists, resting before him on the table. His brow twitched. "My *pappa* hopes for better there."

"Better than what?" Grier asked, dropping her eyes back to her task. She sensed his unease and thought he might talk more easily if she didn't look at him. She hoped he would, at any rate. He was still such a mystery and she longed to know more of him.

Rydar was quiet a moment then heaved a sigh. "First son gets all, aye?" His tone held no discernable emotion.

She nodded and stuck her needle into the knit garment.

"The—two—son?" his voice lifted in question.

"Second. Second son." Grier kept her eyes lowered, concentrating on her stitches.

"Aye. Second son go to God. And the," he paused.

"Third son."

"Third son is—*solidus*—for king," he reverted to Latin.

"Soldier." Grier did look at him then. "And your father?"

Rydar held up four fingers. "He helps first brother with land and money."

"He was his brother's chamberlain?"

Rydar shrugged. He didn't understand.

Grier waved her hand, ignored the difficult word and pressed on. "So how did you come to be in Greenland, then?"

"He had"—Rydar pounded his fists against each other—"with first brother when I had ten years."

"Do ye ken what it was about?"

"No. He no' say. Nor my *mamma*." Rydar's countenance shifted, the strain and sorrow of the past etched in deepening lines around his mouth. "There is heap o' crying, and we sail."

She lowered her darning to her lap. "Logan's da was chamberlain to my Da."

"Your Da is first?"

"Aye. He was laird. King Robert Bruce gave my grandda, Innes MacGowen, this land about fifty years ago as a reward for battles won against the English."

"Is English close here?"

"No! We're sae far from the English here!" Grier chuckled and shook her head. "MacGowen was raised on the border and he asked for lands as far from England as could be had."

Rydar shrugged. Grier put down her mending.

"England and Scotland have"—she pounded her fists against each other in imitation of him—"for many years. But he grew up on the border, that's why we speak mainly Scots English instead of Gaelic. It's how we were raised."

Rydar squinted at her and Grier recognized his lack of

understanding again. She continued her account slowly, hoping he would catch the important parts. She really wanted him to know more of her. For reasons she didn't understand, it seemed important.

"My Da, Rory MacInnes, drew papers leaving the castle and these lands to his brother, Davy, if something happened to him afore he fathered a son. He believed I would be married and have my husband's lands, ye see. But a son never came and the Death did. When he died so suddenly, everything went to Davy."

Grier paused and bit off her yarn above a knot, using the diversion to once again swallow the bitter resentment over what this chain of events had cost her. If only they had known the devastation their future held, the papers could have been rewritten and she would be laird now. She would have her own lands and her own home.

"And now Logan is laird," she finished quietly. She met Rydar's gaze and saw surprising understanding and empathy. It might be that he somehow understood her situation.

Rydar waved his hand, indicating the castle. "MacDavid? He make this?" he asked, changing the direction of the conversation.

Grier smiled a little and shook her head. "No, it was here for hundreds of years. He just made it better."

"Better?"

Grier gestured while she explained. "He built walls to make separate rooms from the great hall. He moved the kitchen inside. He put glass in the windows. And he divided the chamber upstairs into private sleeping rooms."

"I ken." Rydar nodded.

They sat in comfortable silence a while. The kitchen door was slightly ajar and the patter of rain and the scent of wet dirt filled the space between them. Grier finished the stocking, picked up another, and steeled herself for whatever Rydar's reaction might be to her next words.

"Will you tell me of Greenland?" she asked softly. He never spoke of it and she wondered why. What had transpired there that prompted his very risky departure in that very fragile craft?

A subtle change came over his face, as though an open door was purposely pushed closed, latched, and a bar lowered. Not quickly as in anger, but with deliberate intent. As if what was behind the door needed to remain behind the door.

"I do no' have your words," Rydar demurred, pale eyes hooded. She saw the pink scar on his cheek ripple through his beard as his jaw tightened.

Grier tamped down her disappointment, surprised at the resultant emptiness she felt. "Aye. Another time then."

Rydar pulled himself up by his crutch. He hobbled across the kitchen, stopping at the door to grab a basket. "I get onions," he mumbled over his shoulder. And he stepped into the storm.

ᚱᚺ

He stood in the pounding rain, closed his eyes, and lifted his face to its caress. He inhaled the erotic scents of fertile earth, pungent heather, wet rock, salt spray. For a pace, he simply existed in its cooling and comforting embrace.

Why did Grier have to ask about Grønnland? He was getting better at pushing those memories from his mind. These days he looked forward, not back. Back was death. Life was in front of him; and if not life, at the least a meaningful death in its pursuit. Not a futile death in a dying settlement.

Rydar bent down to pull onions.

He liked onions a lot. He liked them sliced between pieces of warm bread. Or boiled in any stew. He particularly loved them fried with turnips and herbs. Perhaps he'd ask Grier to fry onions with the 'neeps' for supper tonight.

Limping back into the keep, he left both the brimming basket and a spreading puddle in the deserted kitchen. Then he went to his room to change into dry clothes. He took his time, stripping to his braies and drying his skin with his linen shirt. He pulled on a clean pair of hose, a clean shirt and tunic, and looked for somewhere to hang his sopping apparel. He opened a cabinet and draped the items over its door. Curious, he opened the rest of the cabinet's doors.

The tied rolls of parchment inside were far too tempting to ignore. Rydar selected one and unrolled it. It was a map. He tipped it toward the window's rainy light. The castle was outlined and labeled, as was the road to Durness. Looking closely, he saw the layout of the nearby town.

That was interesting enough.

He unrolled another parchment, a map of Scotland. He set that one aside to examine later. The third one made his heart pound with happy disbelief. It was a map of the North Sea and it showed Grønnland, Iceland, Skottland, the Orkneys, the Shetlands and Norway.

Norway!

He was shocked by how close it was. If the map was to be believed, he was already three-quarters of the way home! Rydar measured distances with his fingers and figured he had less than three hundred miles yet to go.

He sat down hard, his heart somersaulting, the knee of his good leg gone weak. He had no idea he was so close. His multiple failures faded in the proximity of the nation so near to the east.

A week.

With a good boat he could be home in a week. Yesterday's resolution to form a plan was suddenly half accomplished.

A hesitant knock on his door diverted his attention. It took him a moment to bring his mind back into Skottland, Durness, the keep, the room. He stood and hopped on one leg to the portal.

"So ye are in here. I saw the onions. Thank you," Grier said. She noticed the map in his hand. "And ye found the maps!"

Rydar looked down at the parchment he held, surprised it was still in his hand. "Maps. Aye."

"I love maps! Do you no'?" she asked, her enthusiasm sincere if her expression was true.

Rydar corralled his thoughts with great effort and answered, "Aye."

Grier leaned forward. "Which have you got there?"

"Um, *Nord* Sea." Rydar hopped back into the room and sat on his cot. He patted it in invitation. Grier followed and sat beside him. He unrolled the parchment and she held one edge. "Here Grønnland," he began. "And here Norway."

"Yes. And here's Balnakeil Bay," Grier offered, pointing.

"Is seven days on boat."

"What is?"

Rydar pinned her with his gaze. "Here to Norway."

She blinked. "Norway?"

"My home." He pointed at the map again, dragging his finger from Grønnland to Balnakeil Bay. "I sail here... to here now. Norway is no' far!"

She looked confused.

"I very near home, Grier," he said softly.

She gave a jerky nod and looked around the room. She retrieved the first map he found.

"Here is Durness," she said, sitting next to him again. "When the rain lets up, we should go, aye?" Grier smiled at him with her lips. Her eyes were strangely dim. "I have no' been there in a good bit."

"Aye?" Rydar answered. Her shifted attitude confounded him.

She stood and moved toward the door. "I've mending to finish and cooking to do."

"Grier?"

She spun to face him, expectant. Her hair, tied back from her face, whorled in shining copper coils around her shoulders. Her clear blue eyes opened wide. They claimed his and commanded his full attention.

Suddenly his question seemed so very wrong. He asked it anyway, not knowing what the right question to ask her was.

"You fry onions with neeps for supper?"

Grier sucked in a breath as if she had something of import to say. It left her body in a long, slow sigh. Her demeanor sagged. The word was so muted, he barely heard it.

"Yes."

June 6, 1354

Rydar stood on the bluff behind the keep and stared beyond Balnakeil Bay at the North Sea. The turquoise sky, thickly woven with fat white ribbons, reached as far as he could see over the constant rolling of the distant navy water. Home was just over there, to his right.

Two days ago he felt triumphant when he found the map. Now he felt hollow, frustrated once again by his constant limitations. How might he procure a boat? He had no supplies. He had no money. He had no help. And June was aging already; the solstice—and his thirtieth birthday—were but a fortnight ahead. Soon he would have no time.

He turned and skirted the keep, not wanting to see Grier while mired in this uncharitable mood. He wandered around the castle yard, talking to the tenants, testing the strength of his leg little by little. He was determined to remove the splint by his birthday, even if Grier objected.

His first chat was with the baker. She kneaded dough on a flat stone, her ruddy arms revealing the strength her job required. It was her responsibility to bake bread for all those who worked at the castle, a job that required far fewer loaves now than before the Death

"You sell bread in Durness?" Rydar asked.

"I could. That man died two years back," she said, breathless. "But I've no' enough yeast."

Rydar watched her, entranced by the rhythm of her pounding, folding, pounding, folding, pounding.

"It would be a help if I could," she continued. "The Death took my husband and I've two sons to raise up." Pound. Fold. Pound. Fold.

"You need yeast?" Rydar asked.

"Aye." Pound. "With the money, I could buy more flour." Fold. "It would be a help."

"Where you can get yeast?"

She paused and pointed with her chin. "The brewer. He uses it to make ale. But it's no' free, aye?"

Rydar thanked the woman and walked to the brewer's barn, using his crutch as a cane. His leg hurt to walk on, but he ignored the pain.

The smell of yeast overpowered all else in the stone building. Oak barrels, set on their sides, rose four high along the outer walls. The brewer was standing on a stool, stirring the contents of a huge copper pot with a wood paddle. Below it, a young apprentice stoked the fire.

Rydar watched for a while, propping up his leg to relieve the persistent ache. Finally, the brewer nodded and climbed down from the stool. He approached Rydar with a wary expression.

"Might I help you?"

"My name is Rydar Hansen." He offered his hand. The brewer took it. "I'm guest in keep."

"Oh, right! You're the one Lady Grier fished out of the sea!" The man wiped his sweating brow on a rag. "How are ye gettin' on?"

"Lady is healer. I heal."

The man was balding and plump, but Rydar thought he was younger than he looked. "You are brewer for long?"

"Only this past year. My father—God sain his soul—taught me everything, and I was his apprentice for six and a half years." The man shrugged. "Not enough for a guild member, but enough to know my business."

"You have helper?" Rydar indicated the adolescent.

"My boy, William." He turned and considered the gangly boy. "And he'll do."

Rydar broached the subject that was tickling his mind. "I talk to Baker. She say she sell bread in Durness, but needs more yeast."

"It's a fine idea. I could supply the tavern there as well, if I had more barrels."

"And yeast?"

The brewer narrowed his eyes, and leaned toward Rydar. "I can't sell it. Unless I have money to buy more."

"With more barrels, you make more money?"

He nodded slowly. "Aye."

Rydar nodded back. "Aye. Thank you." He stood and crutched his way out of the barn and headed for the cooper. That man had a similar situation; he could not make more barrels unless he had more iron bands.

"No man here makes bands? " Rydar asked.

"No' these days." The man crossed himself. "No' since... Ye ken?"

Rydar nodded. "Aye."

So the smithy was in Durness.

And a trip into Durness suited Rydar's restless mood quite well.

Chapter Fourteen

Rydar was like a fox on a rabbit hunt. He ate a quick lunch without Grier. She was gone from the keep without explanation, but his quest called too strongly for him to be irritated by that.

He rode Salle bareback to the McKay's home in Durness. Margoh was surprised by his unexpected appearance, and he apologized to her for coming unannounced.

"No, it's fine! Only allow me to, um…" She rushed from the room, leaving Rydar alone with her sister Hanne.

"Please, do sit down, sir. Give comfort to your leg." She spoke in Norse and gestured toward a chair.

"Thank you, Madam Larsen," Rydar answered in kind. "And are you well?"

"As well as I might be without husband or children. Or a home of my own."

"Perhaps there is yet hope?"

Hanne gave him a contemptuous look. "At my age? You are either cruel, or a jester. And I doubt there is a difference."

Margoh reappeared, her gown changed and her hair covered by a jeweled headdress. "To what do I owe this pleasure, Rydar?"

"I was hoping you could take me to the smithy."

Confusion played over her face and she struggled to maintain a happy countenance. "The smithy?"

"I'll explain on the way." Rydar stood and offered his hand. Margoh's soft fingers were dwarfed by his larger, rougher ones.

"Shall we go then?"

Smudges of red bloomed on her cheeks. "Yes."

Margoh slid her arm through Rydar's right arm and she hugged it close as they left the McKay's. Her hip slid against his with every step. Her offer was uncomfortably clear.

She led him to the smithy at the far end of the town, closest to the sea. "So, the baker needs yeast from the brewer, who needs barrels from the cooper, who needs bands from the smithy?"

"That's it." Rydar glanced down at her. "And I've come to see what the smithy needs."

"How do you know he needs anything?"

He chuckled. "Everybody needs something!"

And he was right.

"My leather apron and gloves are worn through." The smith, also a McKay, held them up for Rydar to see. "So, I can't do big work until I can get new ones."

"What stops you?" Rydar inquired.

"Roy MacTanner is asking too high a price. If I could sell bands to young Gavin MacDonald, I could pay Roy. But he'll no' take credit, and I don't fault him."

"Why Roy wants high price?"

Smithy shrugged. "Ask him."

Margoh sighed. "Are we off to Roy's then?"

"If you don't mind," Rydar answered.

"And if I do?" she muttered, turning in the new direction.

The pair made their way back through town. When they reached Roy's, his wife went to find him, leaving Rydar and Margoh alone outside the tanning. Margoh's hands circled his waist and she leaned against him.

"I've missed you, Rydar," she murmured. "You haven't come for lessons in days." Her head tilted back and her lips parted in offering.

Tucking his crutch under his left arm, he circled her wrists and pulled her hands from under his doublet. "Stop it, Margoh."

"Ahem."

Rydar loosed Margoh's wrists and looked over his shoulder. "Roy?"

"And who might ye be?" the tanner demanded.

Rydar turned to face him. "My name is Rydar Hansen."

Roy's gaze shifted to Margoh. "Aren't you Ellen McKay's sister?"

"This is Lady Margoh Henriksen," Rydar said. He pulled Margoh out from behind him.

"Uh, huh. What are ye needin'?"

"We talked to smith. He needs new apron and gloves."

"And?"

Rydar made a dismissive gesture. "He say your price is high. I ask what you need."

Roy squinted up at the taller man. "What I need?"

"Every man need. Roy need apron and gloves. You need...?"

Roy stared at him for a long silent minute, and then relented. "Hides."

"Hides?" Rydar repeated, hoping for an explanation without having to ask for one.

"Aye. Since the Black—since there are less people here, the butcher cuts less meat."

"Oh!" Rydar grinned at Margoh, who flushed with anger. "Less meat, less hides."

"And higher prices for the ones I can get, aye?"

"Aye. Thank you, Roy." Rydar took Margoh's elbow and turned to leave.

Roy called after him, "Is that all ye wanted?"

Rydar nodded and waved.

The butcher to see was at the castle, so this day's business in Durness was complete. Margoh's face was splotched and her jaw clenched as Rydar limped in silence back toward her sister's home. He wasn't assured what angered her, but he was too distracted pondering his string of conversations to bother asking.

Along the main street, they passed several deserted houses and Rydar stopped. "Who owns these houses?"

"I've no idea." Margoh looked up at him, her suspicion clear. "Why?"

Rydar pushed a door open.

"Don't go in there!" Margoh snapped.

He stepped inside and considered the dilapidated condition of the building. The shutters were broken, sand and dead leaves covered the floor. Walls that may have been whitewashed at one point were splattered with black mold. The air stank of a stale hearth and the droppings of multiple rodents.

Rydar looked at Margoh. "Why not?"

"Because! There was plague in there!"

Rydar shook his head. "The plague is gone."

"How do you know?"

"Grier told me."

"Grier!" Margoh huffed.

Rydar pressed down his irritation. "No one has died in Durness for a year and a half."

Margoh stepped gingerly through the doorway and came so close that he recoiled. With a knowing smile she ran her fingernails up his thigh sending waves of lust cresting over his body. Then she spun slowly and sashayed out of the house.

Gud forbanner det all til helevte! he snarled under his breath.

He followed her out of the house and gripped her elbow. Hard. She smiled up at him, but her smile stiffened when their eyes met. He leaned down and spoke quietly.

"Don't you ever touch me like that again, or I'll cease to behave the gentleman," he warned.

"Why, Rydar. That's what I'm hoping for," she dared to say.

He gave her a look that made men cower. "That's not what I meant and you know it."

Margoh patted the hand that held her arm. "You'll get nothing from that annoying virgin, you understand. And a man like you has needs, does he not?"

The dream image of Grier jumped to the front of his thoughts. He had needs, true. But those needs—denied for so long—had affixed themselves to his red-haired hostess. He shrugged the vision away.

"I have more pressing matters to concern myself with," he said. Giving her arm a tug he started crutching his way back to the McKay's house and Salle.

ᚱᚼ

Grier fingered a bolt of bleached linen, deciding how much to buy. She needed a new chemise and was thinking of making one with long sleeves for winter.

"I needn't wait. I could make both now, if I like!" she muttered.

Shops in Durness were slowly recovering from the Death and her
choices had expanded. So shopping took longer.

But it was also much more fun. Besides the linen, Grier had
already selected a bolt of wool that was woven in an unusual square
pattern of muted greens and browns shot through with orange. She
might make a long tunic for Logan from it. And perhaps one for
Rydar as well.

Grier smiled when she thought of the big Norse sailor. Her
patient. Her savior. Her friend. Yes, they had become friends, she
realized. He was intelligent and he learned her language so quickly.
He possessed a lively sense of humor. He had slipped into her life
quite effortlessly.

Might he yet choose to stay?

Grier made her choice and the shopkeeper bundled her
purchases. She stepped into the street and paused, enjoying a bit of
sun that pushed around a herd of gray-bottomed clouds. She shaded
her eyes and looked down the row of buildings. Was there aught
else she needed? A twirling movement pulled her attention.

Margoh stood several buildings away, outside the doorway of
an abandoned house.

How odd, Grier thought. I wonder what she's—

Rydar appeared in the same house's doorway. Margoh turned to
him and Grier could see her wide smile. Rydar's free hand slid
down Margoh's arm to grasp her elbow. He leaned over to speak in
her ear. She patted his hand. They turned and they moved together
toward the McKay house.

Grier's world faded flat and colorless. She spun around and
began to stumble in the opposite direction, not seeing her path nor
determining a destination. She gripped the bundle of fabric against
her chest and pressed it hard against her struggling heart.

I ride to Margoh.

'Ride Margoh' was more like it! Was he tail-toddling with the
whore? And in that filthy, stinking, abandoned house? Would
Margoh stoop to any disgusting level to claim the Norseman? Even
worse, could Rydar be so easily tempted by a shamefully displayed
bosom and flaunted arse? She would not have thought so.

Grier was furious, devastated, resigned and furious again. She
turned west and stomped her way through the woods toward the
castle, daring danger to meet her.

"God help any 'ruffian' that crosses my path today!" she declaimed. "I'll rip his stones from his sack and stuff them down his damned throat!"

She considered doing that very thing to Rydar.

What about me? And what about our kisses?

Rydar's betrayal of their intimate moment hurt most of all. She had kissed him without reservation, and his response was to claim a heap more'n a kiss from the willing widow. Most likely it was not the first time!

"Shite!" she spat. "I've been a whappin fool."

When she reached the keep Grier climbed to her chamber without greeting Moira. She shut and latched her door, threw the bolt of woven wool onto her bed, and glared at it as if her eyes might set it aflame.

She thought to make Rydar a tunic from it. That woeful, ungrate Viking! After the flighty way he behaved, he didn't deserve such a gift. What would she do now? Grier jammed her fists onto her hips. Her grunt of pique became a quiet groan.

What *would* she do now?

Grier slumped onto the edge of the bed and ran her hand over the wool, staring at the interplay of browns and greens. Those colors would look quite bonny with his eyes. His beautiful green eyes, so pale, so clear. She didn't care to consider the idea of those eyes disappearing from her world forever.

Grier laid down along the thick roll of fabric and pillowed her head on her bent arm. Her hand stroked the wool as if it was the man.

"Please, Rydar. Do no' leave me," she whispered.

She lay still for several long minutes, staring unseeing at the wool, lost in her melancholy mood. Then a rivulet of an idea began to trickle through her mind, the realization of who she was: the strongest woman Rydar ever kent. He said so, himself. And he meant it a compliment.

She didn't feel strong at the moment. When all those she loved fell, and the Death stole both her inheritance and her husbands, she wanted to die. Yet, she fought for life every day as a healer. She met each sunrise with hope. She still found joy in the sprouting of a flower, the colors of the sea, or a winter's eve by the fire.

In light of such, she must be judged a strong woman.

And what might a strong woman do next?

"Fight." Grier's fist tightened on the wool. "Fight for him, and I wish to have him."

She sat up on the bed, frowning. That path posed a substantial risk. She might pour her efforts into winning Rydar only to lose, either to Margoh, or to his determination to sail for Norway. Or the both.

That would be humiliating. Beyond that, Grier wasn't sure she could withstand yet another loss and still find the will to rise in the morning.

But what other choices did she have? Logan would marry Malise McKay and Grier would be their spinster cousin, her livelihood dependent on their charity. No other suitors were within sight. No other land was hers. She wasn't trained for any other vocation. And she was already twenty-six.

"Trying to win him will no' be easy," she murmured. "Margoh's no maid. She'll spread her thighs for him and lose nothing. What have I to offer him?"

Would she take him to her bed?

A small itch tickled her groin. A little ball of pressure developed low in her belly. Grier knew enough to understand her body—and it desired his without question. Bedding Rydar may be her last chance to experience physical union with a man. And what a splendid man he had indeed become.

But to give up her maidenhood? That was a considerable risk. What if a knight in glorious colors should ride into Durness one day and offer her marriage? Would he still take her, knowing that she had willingly wiggled beneath another man? That she was sullied by his bedsport?

Grier chuckled. A knight's appearance at her remote little castle was unlikely in the extreme. But then, so was his taking any other than a maid to wife.

And what if she consented, but didn't enjoy the union? What if the experience of bedding the Norseman left her disappointed?

The little ball of pressure in Grier's belly warmed, sending tendrils of heat twisting through her body. Rydar was a strong, virile man on the outside. He would most certainly be strong and virile between the sheets as well. Of that, she had no doubts. And the consequences—and her imaginary knight—could go straight to hecklebirnie for all she cared!

But I'm already his healer. His savior. His friend. Intelligent enough with a lively sense of humor.

I've slipped into his life without effort.

He might yet choose to stay.

June 7, 1354

Rydar limped in to breakfast, considering how best to explain his request. He spoke to the butcher yester eve after he turned Salle over to the groom, and found that the lack of meat was not because demand was down, but because hunters were scarce.

"Hunting takes time, aye?" the butcher said. "And there are so few able men left and each one's got more'n a darg of work each sunrise."

"So if man hunts and brings meat, you sell hides for less?"

The man shrugged. "I've no use for them. But I have to see to my family, and hides are scarce. So I do what I must."

And that was the answer.

Rydar had the time and he was a skilled hunter. Bows and arrows lined the walls of the tower, idle and waiting. He would sell his prey to the butcher, who would lower the price of hides so the tanner could make aprons and gloves for the smithy, who would sell bands to the cooper to make barrels for the brewer. Then the brewer would sell yeast to the baker who would sell bread in Durness.

And Rydar would have an income to pay for his boat. He only needed the laird's permission to hunt on his land. Logan was bound to say yes. Or so he dearly hoped.

That conversation would have to wait, however. Grier rushed in from the hallway, plaiting her hair. "I've been called to an accident," she said. She pointed with her chin. "Might you fetch my basket?"

"In the castle?" he asked, hopeful he would not need to accompany her and could wait for Logan. He handed the basket to Grier.

Plait done, Grier shook her head and rummaged through its contents. "No, it's a herdsman. Cut his leg open in a fall from a rock. Might be broke."

"Is far?"

Her head popped up at that. Distracted blue eyes focused on his. "About a mile."

She crossed the kitchen and grabbed her remaining wooden spoon. She held it up to him with a sly grin, saying, "You do no' need to come this time, if ye wish to stay here."

But he promised to keep her safe and he was a man of his word. He wagged a finger in her face. "Ruffians," he taunted. "You ken!"

When she smiled at his chiding the summer sky of her eyes deepened, entrancing him. Her voice was smooth and warm. "At the least you're no' waumish about the blood."

She hefted her basket and left the room. Rydar's eyes followed the saucy sway of her hips out the door.

"He'll want me to come quickly!" her voice lilted back to him, rich with amusement.

Rydar was startled into movement. "Aye!"

His mood lifted and he smiled broadly. This was a good turn. Perhaps he could tell her his ideas about commerce along the way. Explaining them to her would help him learn the words he needed to explain those same ideas to Logan. She might even be able to predict Logan's answer to his unorthodox appeal.

He followed Grier's path, quite pleased at the prospect of spending time with her after all.

Chapter Fifteen

June 9, 1354

Rydar's request was made to wait; Logan was gone the rest of that day and most of the next, returning late to sleep and leaving the keep at dawn. Rydar considered going out to hunt without asking, but because he intended to sell his catch, not turn it over to the castle's larder, he needed Logan's permission. He couldn't be so rude to his generous hosts as to act otherwise.

Frustrated by the delay, Rydar rose before the sun on the third day and waited in the kitchen for Logan. He even made the parritch for breakfast.

Logan stepped into the kitchen and puzzled over the victuals. "Who made the parritch?"

"I make." Rydar poured a little milk over his and handed the pitcher to Logan. "And I get milk." He pointed at Logan's chair. "Sit, please. I must ask about hunting."

Logan sat and stared at the bowl in front of him. "How did ye ken how to make it?"

"I always cook in Grønnland," Rydar answered a bit sharply. Days of waiting had sanded away his patience. "Now you eat and I talk, aye?"

Logan nodded and poured milk on his parritch. "Hunting?" he repeated and spooned a dollop of honey over his oats.

Rydar explained the impromptu trail he followed that began

with the baker and ended with the butcher. Logan listened with increasing interest until, by the end, his breakfast was cooling and ignored.

"So you want to hunt and give the game to the butcher?" Logan deduced.

Rydar shifted in his seat. He cleared his throat. "I want to sell to butcher."

"Sell?' Logan frowned and leaned back. "Sell *my* game to *my* butcher?"

Rydar assumed Logan would respond that way—he certainly would have if presented with the same request. Now he would present a second conceit. "Or…"

Logan waved one hand. "I'm listening."

"I keep part for wages."

Logan narrowed his eyes. "Why?"

"Because no man hunts now. I have time. I have skill. You need me."

Logan's mouth twitched. "And if I say no?"

Rydar spread his hands wide and grinned at the younger man. "Other men will need me."

Logan laughed at that and slapped the table. He wagged a finger at Rydar. "Aye, then. And I'll give you one tenth of what you bring."

"Half," Rydar countered boldly.

Logan shrugged, looking unconcerned. "Quarter."

"Third."

Logan paused and stared into Rydar's eyes. Rydar didn't blink.

"Third," Rydar said again. "Or I go to McKay's, aye?"

With a grunt of resignation, Logan offered his hand across the table. "Aye. You may keep one third of what you bring down on my lands."

Rydar gripped Logan's hand. "Good."

"Your idea makes me reflect on something else," Logan began. He stirred his congealing cereal. "Have you ever been to a mercat?"

"What is 'mercat'?"

"A place where merchants and craftsmen bring their wares to sell or trade."

Rydar puzzled through the words. "Merchants? Guild, aye?" he asked.

"Yes!" Logan pointed with his gloppy spoon. Bits of oatmeal fell to the table, unheeded. "A merchants' guild would oversee this sort of thing."

"But guild is gone for more than year," Rydar reminded Logan.

Logan nodded slowly. "And having a mercat fair might bring them back together, then."

Rydar quickly considered that idea and what role he might play to his own advantage. "You tell tenants and town of mercat fair. I talk to men when I sell meat, aye?"

"Aye. Good." Logan ate a bite of cold parritch.

Another possibility came to him. Rydar shifted, resettling in his chair. "To be in mercat, they pay little..." he faltered; he didn't know the word.

"Fee. To reserve their staund," Logan finished the thought. "Aye."

"And I help. I gather fees," Rydar offered.

Logan chuckled. "And how much will this cost me?"

Rydar grinned widely again. "Half."

Logan scoffed. "Fine. You'll keep one third of this as well." He shook his head. "You're quite a knackie, Hansen."

"Thank you." He didn't know the word, but he assumed it was a compliment. "When is mercat?"

Logan thought a minute. "In a brace of weeks?" Then his countenance brightened. "The solstice! There was always a celebration before the—well, before. We can hold the mercat in the day and festivities at night!"

"Festivities?" Rydar asked.

"Music, games, food and drink. To celebrate the longest day!"

"A good day," Rydar concurred. *My thirtieth birthday*. He still couldn't grasp that he was that old. His life was half over and he had nothing to prove for it as yet. He was determined to change that and soon. This was the first step. "Very good, Logan."

Logan stood to leave. "Very good yourself, Hansen."

June 10, 1354

Rydar dressed before the sun crested the northeastern horizon, unable to pretend to sleep any longer. Giddy anticipation coursed through his veins. The agreements with Logan were even better than he intended; between the hunting and the staund fees, he would be able to buy supplies to build his boat much sooner than he first thought. Sailing home to Norway before the weather turned loomed possible.

Arne drifted through his thoughts. Rydar missed his friend, especially living in this strange land. They had been closer than most brothers and sailing onward alone was bound to rekindle his grief. But it must also rekindle his determination that Arne's death be purposeful.

He gathered the quiver, arrows and longbow that Logan let him take from the tower. Limping into the kitchen, he filled a leather sack with cheese, dried meat and a few apples. Then he slipped out the keep's door and headed for the stable leaning on his erstwhile crutch—recently cut short, it was now merely a cane.

The slanting sunshine cast long shadows to the southwest and colored the world in pinks and oranges. Dew fog floated over the ground and filled the hollows. The world was silent, cool, peaceful. Salle pranced through the woods, happy to be out with Rydar. He realized he was happy as well. For the first time in decades, his future held hope. Real, true hope; not hope dreamed or imagined. He laughed his relief out loud.

Rydar shot at any living thing that crossed his path at first, learning the bow and the trajectory of these arrows. He managed to hit a few rabbits and grouse, but he missed a wild shot at a boar. Just as well; he was in no shape to run for his life should he only wound the fierce beast.

The day warmed considerably as the sun swirled in its circular path. Rydar paused by a clear stream and lowered himself to the ground to drink his fill. His leg throbbed and his arms shook. He hadn't been this physically active since his boat splintered and tossed him into the North Sea a month ago. Lying on his back beside the stream he rested his complaining muscles and wiped sweat from his brow.

Through sporadic birdsong there came a crackle of movement in the woods. Rydar forced himself to roll to his knees and he retrieved his weapons. He knelt behind a tall bush and waited to see what sort of creature might appear to share his water.

A slow grin spread his cheeks.

The hind was still in velvet, his stubby antlers fuzzy. Unaware of his destiny, he nibbled on new pinecones and the tender tips of evergreen branches that bordered the stream. The sharp scent of sap colored the air. Under it, Rydar smelt the young male's musk. Moving only his eyes, Rydar skimmed the forest for any companions the deer might have. The young buck was alone.

Rydar slowly righted his longbow and took aim. His arm cramped; he was out of practice and the last several hours of hunting tired him more than he anticipated. His thumb lay against his cheek. He paused to steady himself. Held his breath. Let go.

The hind leapt in the air and fell to the forest floor, trying desperately to kick death away. Rydar limped toward the frantic creature and drew his knife. He cut the dying animal's throat, then sat on the leaf and pine-needle carpet while it bled to death. He was at the end of his strength. But he was very pleased with his first day's bounty.

When he felt able, Rydar pushed to his feet. He pulled the arrow from the deer's chest, rinsed it in the creek, and stuck it back in his quiver. Then he gripped the animal by the antlers, and began to make slow, awkward progress on the quarter mile trek to where Salle was tethered.

ᚱᚾ

Grier decided it was time to move Rydar up the stairs to one of the private sleep chambers. True, he shouldn't be putting full weight on his leg as yet, but she was powerless to stop the stubborn Norseman from doing so. And if she narrowed the distance between them, their new proximity might help her capture the Viking's affection.

Moira aired out the unoccupied chamber between Grier's and Logan's. While the maid re-stuffed the mattress with fresh straw— and added lavender at Grier's instruction—Grier brought up a new feather bed. She ordered the long-unused sheets washed and sun-dried, and carried up the pitcher, ewer and piss pot herself.

"I care to make it specially his, then," Grier murmured. What would make Rydar feel at home here?

"Maps!" she said. "He was fair excited about the maps!"

Should she remind him of his thwarted journey? Her hope was to convince him to stay. But if she put all the maps in the room, including the ones of Scotland and Durness, perhaps he'd grow accustomed to her home here.

Besides, it would show that Grier understood him. With that particular decision made, she went down to the Hall to retrieve the maps. Lastly, she added a pitcher of purple thistles and fresh lavender to the table by the bed.

The effect was quite satisfying. As a final reminder of her presence, she put up her calendar—the one she spent all last winter embellishing.

Grier smiled.

There was no way Rydar could bide in this room for a single day without thinking of her.

ᚱᚾ

Every muscle in Rydar's body objected to further demands. Riding Salle through the forest he saw ample game, but couldn't muster the will to draw the longbow again. Just the idea of climbing down from the horse to retrieve an arrow made him groan.

Wresting the young buck onto Salle's back had drained his reserves; afterward he had to sit and rest, chewing the food from his leather bag while he caught his breath. His broken leg ached tenaciously. If pressed, he would admit that Grier was right. He truly shouldn't be walking on it as much as he had been.

He was three and a half miles from the castle, a journey of just over an hour across the rough terrain. When he finally glimpsed the tower through the trees, he moaned with relief.

"We're almost home, Salle," he said patting the mare's neck. Her ears twitched back at his voice, then forward in the direction of her stable. She stepped a little faster under her double load.

Rydar startled. What did he just say? *We're* almost home? He was so tired he wasn't thinking straight. "Not my home, of course," he declared firmly. "Your home."

He reined Salle to a halt in front of the butcher and offered the buck. The butcher pulled the carcass off Salle's back with less effort than Rydar wished to recognize at that moment, and disappeared inside his shop. He returned with six pence—a week's wages for a laborer—and handed Rydar the coins.

"He's a fine one!" the man complimented. "The meat should be tender yet."

"You sell hide to tanner?" Rydar asked from Salle's back.

"Aye." He nodded and pointed at Rydar. "Ye'll hunt again soon?"

"Aye."

Rydar nudged Salle toward her stable. He had six rabbits, three pheasants, quail and grouse strung across her withers. The buck was substantially more than a third of what he brought, but the hide was what was needful. Tomorrow he would hunt again and make up the shortfall.

If he could move.

Limping toward the keep, Rydar leaned hard on the cane he left in Salle's stall. He wanted nothing more than to collapse on his cot and prop up his fiercely aching leg. He knew the wooden-spoon brace kept the bone in place and his leg would knit in spite of the pain. But he also knew Grier would wish to blister his arse if she kent how badly it hurt him at this moment. He had no idea how to conceal his misery from her. She noticed everything, it seemed.

Perhaps she would be out of the keep, gone on a healing or other such errand. Then, if he asked very nicely when he gave her the small game, Moira might be convinced to bring him the midday meal in his bed.

ᚱᚺ

The door to the keep opened. Grier had been listening for Rydar's uneven gait and she hurried from the kitchen, eager to show him his new accommodations. He stood in the doorway to the Hall, frowning. He turned toward her when she drew near.

"Where my bed is?" he asked. His face was smudged with sweaty streaks that settled in deepening lines across his forehead and around his mouth. He leaned on his cane and his left leg was bent at the knee. He rested no weight on it.

"I prepared a chamber for you upstairs."

He glanced up the stairs. "Why?"

She faltered. "You've been healing so well... And it's more comfortable."

Rydar shrugged. He didn't appear pleased.

"Comfortable?" Grier searched for other words. "The bed is sae big. Soft. The room is cozy. Private. Aye?"

"This day you make me move?" he demanded, scowling. "Why this day?"

Grier bristled at his ungrateful attitude. "Why no' this day?"

He waved his right arm in a wild arc. "I hunt today! Is hard work!"

"And was it a good hunt?" she asked, trying to deflect and understand his irritation.

"I bring rabbits, birds. And deer." Rydar grumbled. He shifted his weight, still favoring his left leg.

She spread her hands. "So why are ye wroth?"

His gaze moved up the staircase under a lowered brow. "Why *this* day?" he barked.

Grier straightened and glowered. "So ye'd be mair comfortable!" she barked back.

Rydar limped to the staircase and began to make his way up. Grier recognized his struggle. She rushed to tuck herself by his side and support him.

"Does your leg hurt fierce?" she asked.

He pushed her away. "Go."

Grier fought the anger that surged through her. "You require some help, and that's clear."

"No, I do no'."

"Aye, ye do."

"No."

"Have ye pushed too hard and hurt it again?" she accused.

He managed another step and winced.

She followed him. "Rydar, do no' be a fool! Let me help you!"

"No!" he snapped and glared over his shoulder. "I go up alone!"

Grier folded her arms. "Ye do no' know which chamber is yours, ye stubborn Viking."

That stopped him. Grier saw the muscles of his jaw working under his light brown beard. "Clean one is mine, aye?" he challenged.

Grier cocked one brow. "Oh. Very clever."

He worked himself up another step.

"Will you be needing anything else?" she taunted.

"Food. Now." One more step. Sweat beaded on his brow.

Grier stood her ground. "Right away, Sir Hansen."

Rydar growled, his guttural irritation sinking down to her. Grier leaned against the balustrade and watched him take the stairs one slow step at a time. "Might there be anything else, your Lordship?"

He turned to glower down at her. "Is your quiet too much to ask?"

She stomped up the steps to meet him. "Is your 'polite' too much to ask?" she mimicked. He waved a dismissive hand at her.

Up another step. Grier saw that under the mottled flush of his anger his face was pale. "Rydar, are you unwell?" she asked, alarmed.

"Fine!" he grunted. Up another step.

"Well, ye do no' look fine."

He didn't respond. Up one more step. He leaned against the wall, his breathing labored. A clenched jaw rippled his cheek. Pausing, he wiped his brow, then struggled up another step.

Grier gripped his arm. "Let me help you."

"You help me fine!" he retorted, jerking his arm from her grasp. "You move my bed!"

"I thought ye might prefer a bigger bed and a more private room!" Grier shouted. "I only thought of you!"

"Oh?" he shouted back. "And did ye think my leg is broke?"

Grier scoffed. "And do *you* ever think your leg is broke? It does no' appear to *me* that ye do!"

Rydar ignored her and took another step. Grier's fists clenched and her nails cut into her palms. She wanted to pummel him. Instead, she screwed up her face and stuck her tongue at his back. Stubborn, pompous Viking. She decided to let him starve a while. Maybe he'd learn a little gratitude

Then he wobbled.

Grier caught him before he tumbled down the stone steps, wedging herself under him and bracing his tall body with her shoulders. She shoved with all her strength and he sat down hard, his arse landing three steps from the top of the staircase. For a moment they simply stared at each other in gape-mouthed shock.

"Are ye aright?" Grier breathed.

Rydar's face scarleted. "Aye," he snarled.

He scooted up the remaining stairs on his bottom. Grier waited until he pulled himself to his feet, then she climbed the steps and stood beside him. Repeatedly wiping sweat from his brow had cleared away some of the day's dust, but Grier could still smell animal musk and blood on him.

"Your chamber is this way." She turned and strode past her parents' room and her own. She pushed open the door of the refurbished sleep chamber. "Here ye go. I hope it's to your liking."

Without another look or word, she pushed past the bad-tempered Norseman and ran down the stairs.

Chapter Sixteen

Grier fled through the kitchen to the back door and bolted from the keep. Though tears blurred her vision she kent the path well. Furious at the man, she didn't slow her pace until she reached the chyngell.

That did not go at all well.

Grier only wished to please the idiotic Viking. She spent the whole morning doing everything she might to make the chamber clean and comfortable for him. She knew he felt awkward when she greeted guests in the dining room, because *he* was the reason for extending that unorthodox hospitality.

And despite his complaining just now, he certainly had not been favoring his leg. The obstinate sailor walked on it every chance he might. It wasn't her fault he overdid himself on this particular day! So why should she be blamed for his pain?

Grier marched across the wet sand at the edge of the waves, going east along the bay's shore. When the land turned north she stopped and realized she was facing Norway.

One week by boat.

"Shite!" she yelped. She spun and tromped back in the other direction. What might she do now?

Grier climbed to the top of a seaside boulder and watched the bay change colors under skittering clouds. The constant tumble of water soothed her as it always did. A fresh breeze caressed her face. Grier closed her eyes. Sometimes she imagined that what she felt was her mother's angelic fingers stroking her cheeks, calming her and reassuring her. She spent hours here during the Death, basking in the memory of her mother's love. She sighed and felt for the crucifix.

Palpable as her mother's touch, an unexplained serenity seeped through her body. Her heart slowed it's indignant pace. When her anger faded the answer came—at least for this day.

"I need to take care of him," she whispered. "Everyone needs taking care of, and Rydar especially."

Kill him with kindness, then, afore she just plain kilt him.

Grier pulled a deep breath and blew out the last of her irritation. *Aye, Mam.*

ᚱᚺ

Rydar listened to Grier's rapid footfalls echo down the stairs. He heard the heavy kitchen door slam open. It did not slam shut. With a quiet groan, he limped into his new chamber, shut the door, and fell across the foot of the bed on his belly. His relieved muscles tingled their gratitude.

The bed smelt of lavender.

A brisk knock on the door woke him. At first he didn't know where he was. The sun had withdrawn from the window, leaving only dusky blue reflections of the sky. He blinked. The knock repeated, with more intent.

"Aye!" he grunted and turned on his side toward the knocking.

The door was pushed open by the backside of an adolescent male holding one end of the big copper bathing tub. Another boy, with a matching face, carried the other end. They were followed by a third copy carrying two buckets of steaming water, which he emptied into the bathtub. Without a word, they left the room.

Moira strode in with a small stool which she placed beside the tub. Then she set about building a fire.

"The boys?" Rydar asked, pointing at the door.

"My brothers," she answered without turning from her task.

"They have same face!"

Moira did turn at that, considering the objects of interest as the trio returned and poured more water into the washtub. "Aye. They're triplets. Morris, Angus and Fergus."

The boys all turned to Rydar, each raising a hand when his

name was called, obviously accustomed to the sensation they caused by being born together and identical. When they left his room Moira followed them out, and then reappeared with a stack of folded towels. The cake of scented soap rested on top. She set the linens on the stool.

The next delivery of water filled the tub. As her brothers filed from the room, Moira turned to Rydar. "When ye've done with your bath, call down the stairs. I'll bring your supper up straight away."

Rydar frowned. "Where is dinner?"

"You slept through that, man."

He startled. "How long I sleep?"

"Long enough," she stated and pulled the door closed behind her.

Rydar rolled off the bed. He was stiff and felt every single one of his thirty years. With a bit of difficulty, he pulled off his clothes and left them in a heap by the foot of the bed. But when he tried to get into the copper tub, he realized he couldn't do so without getting his brace wet.

"No more!" he growled. After all, he'd worn the brace for four weeks already.

Sitting on the little stool, he unwrapped the dirty linen strips and removed the wooden spoon braces. His leg was swollen, mostly around his ankle, and there were raised stripes on his skin where the swelling pressed against the bandages. But a portion of his pain lessened when his leg was freed. He climbed into the water and submerged his whole body in the hot bath.

For the second time since leaving Grønnland he experienced the decadent sensation of wet heat radiating through his body and relieving his pain. His skin puckered like gooseflesh from his calves to his scalp. He closed his eyes and inhaled the steam and the aroma of the flowered soap. This was such a beguiling experience, he might consider repeating it once a month whether he needed it or not.

Rydar soaped and rinsed his body, his hair, his beard. Then he rested again against the tub's tall back and soaked the last bit of warmth from the water. He opened his eyes and considered getting out to answer the demands of his rumbling belly when he noticed the *kalender* on the wall. Grier's *kalender*.

He looked around the room then, at the maps tacked up there.

Then he saw the pitcher of thistles and lavender by the bed. Lavender—the mattress smelled of fresh straw and lavender. The mattress, and featherbed, which were covered with clean sheets.

The hot bath brought up to him. The linen towels and scented soap. The promise of supper served in his room.

Skitt.

When he returned from hunting, beyond exhausted and wracked with pain, all he considered was the overwhelming climb up the stairs. It seemed so insurmountable that he had lashed out at Grier, punishing her for his own weakness.

Until this moment he hadn't noticed her efforts. She created a sanctuary for him here; a comfortable and private sanctuary. And she put up the *kalendar* she made so he might know the days. And, more importantly, she put up the maps so he might find his way home.

Skitt!

How could he be such an ass? He was obviously ill-prepared to mingle with civilized society, the Grønnland settlement's rough culture being his only adult experience. If he planned to walk into the castle at Arendal and claim his rightful place, he had better learn some manners quickly, that much was quite clear.

He would begin with an apology.

Climbing from the tub, Rydar scrubbed himself dry. He hopped across the room on one leg and opened a chest. As he expected, his borrowed clothes waited there. But folded on top was a new garment, one made of tightly woven wool in a square pattern of green and brown. Orange threads the same color as Grier's hair ran through it. He had never seen such fabric. He lifted it out, curious, and held it against his chest.

The tunic was longer and broader across the shoulders than the other clothes Grier lent him. The sleeves reached his wrists. The material was a little stiff. And it was spotlessly clean.

"Å *min Gud*," he murmured. "She made this for me."

Now he truly felt like an ass. Perhaps a herd of asses.

He spied a new linen shirt in the pile of clothing. Aye, most definitely a herd of asses. Big stubborn, stinking, Norse ones.

Rydar donned the new garments and noticed the fine needlework in a fresh wave of heated humiliation. With a resigned sigh, he limped to the door of his chamber and stepped into the open hallway above the stairs.

"Moira?" he called down, hoping to delay facing Grier a bit longer.

But it was Grier's face that appeared below him. She looked up at him, her sapphire eyes filled with such kindness that he forgot what he meant to say. Her hesitant smile spiraled through his gut and his guilt cut deeper.

"Are ye ready for supper, then?" she asked after a moment.

He nodded. "Aye."

"I'll bring it right up." Then she disappeared from his view.

ᚱᚺ

Grier carried the tray up the stairs, chiding herself to stay calm and not to let her turbulent emotions rule. Rydar wore the doublet she sewed, and from her brief glimpse of him on the second floor it seemed to fit perfectly. If he put the garment on, then he must have forgiven her for displacing him unawares on such an inopportune day.

His chamber door stood open so she entered without pause. Rydar sat in a chair next to the bed table; Grier set the tray of food beside him. She noticed with warming satisfaction that the colors of the fabric did match his hair and eyes. The tunic fit handsomely on his long, lean form. She tried not to stare.

"What is supper?" he asked, pushing her consideration from him to the tray.

"Pheasant. After your efforts today, I do hope ye like the way it's cooked."

Rydar took a bite of the roasted meat. His expression shifted from curiosity to surprise to broad enjoyment. "Is sae good, Grier."

"And I fried the neeps with onions, as ye prefer," she offered.

Rydar swallowed the bite of pheasant. His brow lowered and he seemed to be thinking hard on something. Unsure of what to do next, Grier looked around the room and saw his dirty clothes in one pile, and the dirty linen strips and wood spoons in another. She went first to the discarded brace.

"You should no' have taken it off just yet," she said over her shoulder as she collected the bits.

"I can no' get in water, and is on."

"Oh!" Grier stood and turned to face him. "Shall I get fresh linen and tie it up again?"

Rydar's face wound into a blend of irritation and supplication. "And if you do no'?"

Her lips pursed and her eyes narrowed. The Norseman was even more stubborn than she, Grier conceded. He would most likely do as he pleased no matter what she said. She tried to think logically past her objections to what the real consequences might be.

"Well, you've already walked on it. I suppose if you do no' bang into it, it will still heal." She jabbed the spoons at him. "But you'll need to go easy! Ye pushed too hard this day, and you ken."

He acknowledged her words with a crooked half-smile. "I'm sorry, Grier."

"There's no need to apologize to me! If you re-break it, you've no one else to blame and you're crippled, ye stubborn Viking!" She began to gather the soiled clothing.

"No' the leg," Rydar began. "I'm sorry for me. I'm no' kind this day."

Grier straightened and turned to face him. "What?" She heard him fine; she just wanted to hear the unexpected words again.

Rydar stood and closed the gap between them. Grier looked up into his eyes, waiting, wondering. He pushed her perpetually disorderly curls back over her shoulders. His fingers brushed her cheeks. She didn't move and barely breathed.

"You make me a new room. You make it good for me." Rydar pointed first at the items pinned to the walls, then the bed. "Is clean and smells good. You pushed hard this day, aye?" he parroted.

"Aye," Grier murmured.

"Thank you." His pale green eyes searched hers. She didn't know what he hoped to find. She licked her lips self-consciously. Her pulse thrummed.

"Forgiven," she whispered.

He bent lower and his lips brushed her forehead. Then her temple. Her cheek. Their touch stopped her breath and sent shivers of delight rippling down her neck. She turned toward his mouth, closed her eyes, and met it with her own.

His kiss filled her mind with sweet possibilities. The filthy clothes spilled from her hands and she reached for him. His body was warm and firm under her hands.

This kiss was different from their first ones. Softly testing, exploring. At first, only their lips. Then his tongue teased hers and she answered. She may be a virgin, true, but after her three betrothals she kent how to kiss a man. He moaned a little and she leaned against him. Hard thighs pressed against hers, strong arms encircled her. Hot breath caressed her face. The coarse hairs of his beard tickled around her mouth.

Grier relished every sensation. Her breath came faster and her belly tingled. She wanted so much more of him than was seemly, so much more than was safe in her situation. She eased away from the kiss, glad to note he was breathing harder as well. She wasn't the only one affected by their sampled intimacy.

Rydar stepped back and his face was flushed. His gaze flickered around the room. She rescued him before he said anything that might dampen the moment.

"You must be fair starving by now. Sit down and eat, then."

He looked at the heaping tray of food, then back at her. "You eat afore?"

"No, no' yet." Grier gestured vaguely toward the door. "I'll go down and sup in the kitchen."

Rydar made a face and pointed at the table. "Is more food here than even I eat!"

Grier laughed. "I suppose I was a bit generous with the portions."

"You sit. Eat with me." He pointed at the chair. "I sit on bed."

"I was going to have the boys come empty the bath water."

"Sit!" he commanded. "Water will wait!"

Grier sat and served him a plate, then made her meal from the remaining food on the tray. He complimented her cooking so often that Grier began to wonder if he had a particular motive in mind. But he merely lounged on the bed, conversing easily and looking more relaxed than he had since she first found him.

When they finished, Grier called Moira's brothers to empty and remove the copper tub, and then she sent the denuded tray downstairs, along with Rydar's hunting clothes to be laundered on the morrow. When the tasks were complete, and she had no further excuse to dally, Rydar bid her goodnight with a long and confident kiss.

Chapter Seventeen

June 19, 1354

Twenty-nine merchants paid Rydar tippence each to reserve their staunds for the Solstice Mercat and Fair. That made fifty-eight pence; nineteen for him and thirty-nine for Logan.

In addition, he hunted on six of the last nine days. On five of those days, he brought back deer. He now had sixteen pence from hunting, plus the nineteen pence from the Mercat fees.

Thirty-five pence was a very good start, indeed.

Rydar kept the money stored in a pouch he fashioned from a scrap of fabric that Grier gave him. The pouch was pinned inside his shirt.

He felt for the pouch now—which reminded him of Grier—and pondered his small fortune to balance the foul mood he was in. He just spent another irritating afternoon trying to concentrate on language lessons in the crowded McKay household.

Margoh and Hanne had moved into a house that held their sister Ellen and her husband, Malise, her little brother, and a maid. His presence made eight people moving through one parlor, one kitchen, four sleep chambers and a small study, and left no quiet corners. He wondered if Margoh would object to having the lessons back in the keep.

But, he realized, it might be that the lessons would soon become unnecessary. After all, tomorrow at the Mercat, he planned to ask around about building his boat.

ᚱᚺ

Grier stood in the kitchen, hands on her hips and lips pressed in thought. Rydar limped in, scowling. But his expression softened when he looked at her.

"What's amiss?" she asked.

His grin flickered. "You see?"

Grier was amused to note his surprise. "Aye. There's thunder in your brow!"

Rydar shook his head and sighed. "Too much people at McKay house."

"Too many people? For what?"

"For learning speak. Is…" Rydar waved clawed fingers around his head in frantic motion. "Too much noise. Too much—*many*—people."

As frustrated as Rydar was, Grier's heart lightened at his complaint. "I thought you and Margoh would be alone. Are ye no'?"

"No!" Rydar scoffed. "We are no' alone."

All along she pictured Rydar and Margoh snuggled in some secluded corner while the widow murmured in seductive Scots English. The idea of them sitting in the midst of a chaotic household with Rydar struggling to attend the task at hand was a revelation. A pleasant revelation that carried substantial relief.

Rydar poured himself some ale and slumped at the table. Grier bit back her grin and changed the subject.

"Logan is having supper in Durness tonight with Malise and I've no mind of what to cook." She faced her perpetually hungry houseguest. "Is there anything you have a taste for?"

Rydar looked out the window at the mild June evening. "Do no' cook. We eat cheese, bread, butter. Or boiled eggs. Do no' trouble for me."

Her gaze followed his. "Tis a beautiful evening."

Rydar looked askance at her.

So she asked, "Now what's amiss?"

His brows lifted. "Might we eat out of keep?"

A slow smile spread her cheeks. "Aye. We might."

Grier got busy setting atop the table all manner of things they might sup on, while Rydar packed the food in a basket. Grier went upstairs and brought down a blanket for them to sit on. Back in the kitchen, she dug out a bottle of wine from a low cabinet. Rydar's pale green eyes widened in question.

She grinned. "We'll celebrate on our own this night. Your Mercat tomorrow will be quite the event!"

Rydar shook his head but looked pleased. "Is no' my Mercat…"

"How can you say that? You were the one who figured out how to get men working again!"

He pointed at her. "But you tell me I see things right, aye?"

"Aye, and you did. Ye're very cannie."

"And we talk first so I ken all are good ideas, aye?"

"Well… aye."

"And you give me words for I talk to Logan."

Joy bubbled in Grier's chest at his multiple affirmations. "I guess we did it together, Viking."

Rydar smiled his crooked smile. "We are good together." He lifted the basket.

Grier hugged the blanket happily. The pair walked out to the bluff overlooking Balnakeil Bay. She spread the coverlet over the coarse sea grass and they settled to their casual meal. The lowering sun yellowed the sky like melted butter.

"You've been here a month and a half now," Grier began.

"Aye," Rydar said with a mouth full of bread and honey.

"How have ye found it?"

Rydar faced the sea, his expression pensive. "Everything is good. Better than Grønnland."

"You've learnt my 'speak' quite well," Grier said.

He looked at her then, his pale eyes turning golden in the slanting sun. "Aye. But is much more."

"You'll learn. Give it time."

Rydar looked down at the cheese and carefully cut himself a chunk while Grier berated herself silently for being so bold. She mustn't reveal her hope that he'd remain in Durness until he professed feelings for her that went beyond friendship. Whether she would risk opening that door first remained to be determined. For now, she changed the direction of their conversation.

"Do you have any brothers?" Grier poured a cup of the rich red wine and handed it to him.

Rydar's lopsided grin eased over his cheeks. As he accepted the cup, his fingers brushed hers. "No. My *pappa* got girls easy. I am only son."

Grier drew a deep breath, relieved that he was talking. The last time she questioned him about his past, he avoided the conversation by stomping outside into a pounding thunderstorm.

"How many sisters have you?" she asked.

Rydar held up the fingers of his empty hand. "Four. Two more old and two more young."

"And all of you went to Greenland, then?"

"No. My one sister is given to church. She had fourteen years and weak eyes. But a good husband is for my second sister in Norway—before we sail to Grønnland."

"How many years had she?"

"Thirteen."

Grier slumped. "Half my age."

"Your age is good."

"Hmph."

Rydar laughed. Grier always found his lopsided grin so charming, though it made him look the knave. She supposed that was part of the Norseman's appeal.

He continued without her prompting, "I have two young sisters. So I am the one, ye ken? I had my *pappa's* hope."

"So... how does it happen that you were sailing past my home in a storm?"

Rydar's gaze fell to the ground. He pulled up a stalk of sea grass by its roots and twisted it tightly around his fingers. Grier watched them turn red, and when he unwound the grass there were white grooves in his skin. When he spoke, his voice was rough.

"Grønnland dies."

She waited. A breeze lifted an errant strand of her hair and tickled her cheek. Annoyed at the distraction, she tugged it over her ear.

"Boats from Norway stop. We do no' ken Black Death." He peered at her, his intense green eyes narrowed. "We think we are alone to do. No more help."

"I see," she whispered.

"My *mamma* is dead. And my baby sister. The winters are cold, and they are no' very strong. First the rheums, then the fever." Rydar cleared his throat but his voice remained coarse. He looked toward the bay. "We bury Inge in my *mamma's* arms."

Grier watched him surreptitiously while he spoke his pain. His large hands, abraded and calloused from hunting, rested on his thighs. The pink scar on his cheek reddened beneath the beard of his sun-darkened face.

"Was that near past?" she finally asked.

"No. Ten or eleven years, it might be now."

"And your other sister?" Grier ventured.

"Married at fifteen. *Mamma* at sixteen. And six times more, though no' all live after first year."

That was common. Birth was perilous for mothers, life was perilous for bairns. "And she remains in Greenland?"

"Aye."

"And your father?"

Rydar wiped his hands on his hose. "Two summers after my *mamma.*"

"I ken how it feels to lose your parents," Grier murmured.

Rydar took her hand and squeezed his acknowledgement. "Aye, you do."

Grier gripped her crucifix through her gown. Another breeze brushed her cheek and she smiled a little this time. *Mam.*

"In Grønnland, when boats stop, is no' more hope. So Arne and I make our boat." Rydar shook his head. "Is all my fault."

"Your fault?" Grier asked. "How?"

Rydar's shoulders lifted and fell in a guilty shrug. "My idea. Arne is never in Norway. I tell him things so he comes with me."

Grier felt Rydar's failures as if they were her own. She knew what it was to be responsible for another's life. Or death. Her own failures haunted her at the most unexpected times. But dwelling on the disappointments of the past would stand them no good. Another shift in conversation was needful.

"Rydar, are you—comfortable here?" Grier pulled back from saying 'happy.' He had filled out well since she found him, thanks to his insatiable appetite. He was strong and healthy, though of course he still limped.

"Oh, aye. Very," Rydar assured her. "You are good for me."

He offered her the last piece of cheese and ate it when she declined. She repacked the basket.

The sun dipped just below the sea beginning her six-hour path below the northern horizon. High clouds glowed sun-orange on one side and moon-silver on the other. Grier lay back on the blanket. Her gown rippled in the temperate breeze.

Rydar stretched out his long frame beside her. He laced his fingers through hers and she lifted their hands to her lips. She kissed each of his knuckles. When she looked up he was watching her.

"What do you want, Rydar?" she whispered.

He shrugged. "What every man wants."

"That is?"

"I'm thirty on morrow. I want a wife before is late. Bairns. Sons."

Grier drew slow breaths. "You wish to marry?"

"I always want that." Rydar ran his free hand through his hair. Then he hitched up on one elbow and looked down at Grier. His expression was somber but his jade eyes burned into hers. He ran one thumb from her forehead, around behind her ear, and along her jaw.

"I never see hair like yours," he whispered.

Grier reached up reflexively. "Ye mean curly?"

The lopsided grin reappeared. "I mean fire. Looks like fire. Moves like fire." He stroked his fingers through it, tangling a little in its mass. "Beautiful like fire."

Grier licked her lips in invitation and Rydar accepted. Grier turned her body toward him and he pulled her close. She pressed against as much of his length as she could, and ran her hands over the rest of him.

That kiss was followed by another. And then another. The earth seemed to shift beneath her and she held him tighter. The taste and feel of him exploded in her senses, until nothing else existed. Not the bluff, not the castle, not the sea. She floated in a cloud of his earthy scent.

Rydar leaned over her and draped one leg across hers; his knee rested between hers. She felt him harden against her thigh and she warmed in response. Little hums of pleasure escaped her. And him.

When his hand inched upward from her waist and brushed her breast, she gasped at the searing sensation. She tightened her grip on Rydar's doublet. Reason was leaving her, and swiftly.

With a grunt, Rydar broke away from her. The lips buried in his beard were reddened and his breath was tattered. He rolled away from her and flopped on his back, limbs splayed. His jaw rippled and clenched. His throat rolled as he swallowed.

Grier stared at him, her breath uneven and her body trembling. She couldn't stop herself from glancing at the bulge in his braies with guilty regret. Her cheeks flamed.

Rydar's voice was quiet and strained. "I push too hard, aye?"

Though pierced by disappointment and embarrassed at her body's wanton eagerness, what could she say? He was being a gentleman and ignoring his own need. Not claiming more than a kiss. Not taking his own pleasure because she was a virgin. Even if she wanted to lay with him, which she began to believe she did.

She shook her head. "I pushed you as well. I'm sorry."

"No sorry, Grier. I am man, aye? I care for you."

Grier smiled a little and touched his face. "Aye."

Rydar sucked a lungful of air and hissed it out slowly. After several minutes of silence, he took her hand in his again, as if to atone. They both faced the sky as orange disappeared from the clouds, leaving only the moon's silver reflection on their southern faces. Then Grier turned to him and propped on her elbow.

"Why did you no' marry in Greenland?"

One corner of his mouth jerked up. "The women are no' to my liking."

Grier considered that unexpected comment. "What sort of woman is?" she ventured.

"Strong," was his first response. Grier's heart thumped her ribs hopefully. "No' sickly. Strong body and mind. Able to do and think."

"The women there, they fell ill?"

"Aye. Or die birthing."

"That happens everywhere."

Rydar faced her. "I ken. But they can no' read or scribe. They do no' care. Life is too hard."

"It felt like that here, these past years," Grier admitted.

"But you did no' fall." Rydar's smile caught her heart and held on to it. "You sae strong, Grier. I say that afore, aye?"

She turned toward the bay, hoping her heated flush was disguised by the dimly purple light from the sky. Whether she felt strong or not, Rydar thought she was. Perhaps he was right. Perhaps she had more strength than she realized. She would think more about that when her emotions were less scattered.

"I need wife who gives sons. Whole house of sons!" he added after a pace.

"Do you no' care what she looks like?" she could not stop herself from asking, though her gut warned her she would regret it.

He rubbed his eyes. "Well… Aye, I do. A comely lass."

Grier received the blow she anticipated and winced with the hit. She had never considered herself 'comely.' At best she thought she was 'passable.' Spending time styling her hair or sewing the latest fashions from London, or even Edinburgh, seemed a waste of time. Life here in Balnakeil Bay was simple. So was she.

But the elegant Margoh was always finely dressed and never had a lock of her beautiful blond hair out of place. Grier's mood plummeted at the thought of the very attractive, very aggressive, very available widow.

"What do you find comely?" she asked suddenly. "Tall? Blond?" She may as well have rubbed salt in a blister as to ask such a question.

Rydar considered her then, his expression bemused. "Why you ask?"

"I was only making conversation." Grier turned back to the sea, her face tight.

"I can no' marry now. First, I get my land," he stated. His tone allowed no space for argument.

Unlike their companionable silence earlier, this silence was cold and sliced in moon-silvered shards. Grier shivered.

"There's land here," she tossed at him. "Quite a lot of it."

Rydar hesitated, staring toward the constant motion of the restless waves. Moonlight flickered on the water like a legion of silver candles.

"Aye," he said finally. "That there is."

Chapter Eighteen

Rydar grunted, strained, spurted and woke.

With a hissed curse he rolled to his back realizing that, once again, he dreamt that the soft, fragrant mattress beneath him was Grier. And once again, he deflowered his sheets.

Skitt!

The woman haunted his mind and his body. With her fire hair, ocean eyes, earthy figure and determination as forceful as the wind, she personified all the natural elements. He was drawn to her in every way a man could be drawn to a woman and he couldn't deny it. Truthfully, he had no care to deny it. Truthfully he wanted to slip silently into her chamber, climb naked under her bedclothes and follow the lusty path of his dreams.

She would accept him, if her recent behavior was an indication. Something between them had changed. Grier treated him as if she would welcome his courting, should he choose to pursue her. He knew that if he were in her bed right now, she would take him in without hesitation and give him her maidenhood freely. Rydar had no idea how he could be so certain of this.

But he was.

Sheets aside, he had never deflowered anyone and he wasn't about to start now, no matter how attracted he was to his lively rescuer. He expended more effort than he believed himself capable of to halt his seduction of her on the bluff this evening.

But he was puzzled by her reaction; was her question about 'comeliness' intended to prompt a compliment? He didn't think so.

She wasn't the sort of woman to lead a man that way. So why did she mention Margoh's attributes specifically? Might Grier be envious of the older woman?

Was it possible that Grier didn't know how beautiful *she* was?

Rydar grew up surrounded by tall blond women; that sort no longer attracted his attention. But copper curls, womanly curves and sapphire eyes did. And it was helpful that this striking package contained a clever, kind and feisty female. Rydar knew men who grew bored with their wives; Grier would keep a man interested for a lifetime and beyond.

If, he clarified, a man was interested in marriage to begin with.

Interested or not, his thoughts persistently wended a path back to Grier.

Back to her kisses. Back to the feel of her body against his. Her warm, firm and eager body. She made him feel so solid, so strong and so capable. After the crush of his multiple failures, those were heady sensations, indeed.

What about love? Love could keep him in Scotland. Though that idea was once unthinkable, should he perhaps consider it?

"Not tonight," he mumbled. "Perhaps after tomorrow's Mercat is past."

On the eve of the solstice, the night sky through the window was pale purple and glowed pink along the northern horizon. He kicked off his covers and limped to the hearth by its dim light. Before he could sleep he needed again to put out the demanding fire that Grier always set ablaze inside him.

June 20, 1354

Logan drove his cart into town early the next morning after firmly stating that he, Grier and Rydar would be too tired by the time the festivities ended to walk the mile back to the castle.

"And possibly a bit plaistert, truth be told!" He gave Rydar's elbow a conspiratorial nudge.

Rydar grinned; he was in the mood for cutting loose. Getting a little drunk sounded appealing and it might numb the memory of Grier's intoxicating kisses and the scorching caress of her skin.

Fertile clouds obscured the sky and spat annoyingly at the Solstice Mercat crowd as merchants settled their trestles and tents along the cobbled artery of Durness. Rydar wandered amongst them, awed by the variety of merchants and their exotic wares.

Well, they were exotic to him at any rate. Grønnland never offered such an array of choices! Brass workers unwrapped elaborate candlesticks. Silversmiths polished plates and chalices. Bags of pungent, oily fleece filled several wagons. White crocheted lace lay draped over tables. Casks of ale were tapped, releasing their yeasty enticements. Spices he couldn't identify colored the air. Fires tied aromatic ribbons of smoke around hissing shanks of lamb and whole stuffed pheasants.

Three unexpected merchants arrived to join the Mercat. One unloaded crates of protesting chickens—and one cocky and colorful rooster. Another drove a cart stacked with multihued bolts of woven wool that still reeked of bitter dyes. The third presented alluring trays of gold- and silver-set jewels. Rydar fingered a few delicate items that evoked faint recollections of his mother. He wondered if there were still any Hansen jewels remaining in Norway.

Each merchant paid Rydar their tippence and he helped them find an empty bit of street on which to set up their staunds. He gave Logan four pence and put the other two in his pouch. Then, ignoring the ever-present pain in his left shin, he ambled through the growing crowd, stopping at each staund, and chatting as best he was able with the business men—or women—who displayed their wares for sale.

Someone grabbed his arm and he looked down to see the rounded swells of Margoh's bosom pressed against him. Her finger lifted and traced a languorous circle on his chest.

"Where did you get such a unique doublet? I've never seen fabric like this before."

Rydar pushed her hand away. "Grier made it for me. Nothing in the keep fit me well."

Margoh wrinkled her nose, annoyed. "Well, she has an interesting sense of style, doesn't she? Will you walk with me?"

He shook his head. "No. I must make certain the merchants are all satisfied."

She pulled a face, spun and sauntered away, hips swaying, obviously assuming he was watching. Which, of course, he was.

Until she walked past Grier and his gaze rose to meet hers. Grier's eyes softened and her mouth curved in a smile that heated him far more than Margoh's touch ever could. He saw his own desires mirrored in her eyes.

Grier turned and walked away from him. Her arse swung naturally, as it always did. Her curls caressed her straight back. Rydar's couldn't command his gaze to release her. If only he might somehow bed the virgin, and not only in his dreams.

He pulled a penny from his pouch. Resigned, he made his way toward the brewer's tent.

ᚱᚺ

Grier walked among the stalls with Logan and Malise, one arm looped through the girl's. Distracted from the displays, she replayed in her mind the vision of Rydar standing against Margoh. The jillet fondled his chest, fingered his clothes and batted her lashes at the Viking. Her behavior robbed strength from Grier's hopes.

She saw him now, limping through the crowd. So tall—a head above most—and robust. Striking in his Nordic-god looks. When his gaze zigged over the Mercat crowd, Grier ducked behind a canvas; somehow she knew he was searching for her. She couldn't risk him seeing her desperate devotion before she hid it away.

"Here, Malise." She picked up a piece of lace. "This looks like the piece you showed me, does it no'?"

Malise's expression brightened. "Aye! It does that!" She pulled Logan further into the tent. Helping Malise look for lace provided an opportunity to deepen her friendship with the next lady of Durness Castle, undoubtedly a wise path. Malise was less likely to banish a useful companion.

Companion.

"Aye. There's my prospect in a word," Grier muttered.

She gazed down the line of tents and trestles. The street was full of people strolling, chatting, eating, buying, selling. An easy rumble of conversation stippled with laughter rolled toward her. She stayed in the lace tent, peeking out between its canvas flaps. Rydar limped up the street toward the brewer's tent, alone. Whatever Margoh expected had obviously not reached fruition.

Grier sighed her relief.

There was still hope.

ᚱᚺ

Might I stay in Scotland?

The possibility rolled through Rydar's mind endlessly that day. He sought solace in the brewer's tent to rest his leg and ponder that question. Grier was a powerful incentive to stay. He knew the feisty redhead would be a fit companion for the rest of his days, one he would enjoy and never tire of.

Beside that, the obstacles between him and his journey lived and breathed and taunted him with the futility of his quest. He was torn between what stood before him here—a woman warm and desirable—and what might no longer await him in Norway.

When the sun came out after midday, he wandered the street again, the question still unanswered. The Fair's crowd, loosened by successful trade, copious ale and random sunshine, gathered around a brightly-dressed bard. The dwarf stood on a wooden box and sang, recited poetry, and entertained with tales of William Wallace, Robert the Bruce, and their current king, David II. Rydar laughed at what he understood and joined in the play, challenging the bard to a mock battle.

A roar erupted when the diminutive man hopped off his perch and swaggered toward his giant opponent. With a few wild actions, Rydar threatened and then 'spared' the stranger's life. The enthusiastic crowd, he was quite pleased to note, included a clapping and laughing Grier. Rydar bowed to her, acting her champion. She rewarded him with a chaste kiss on his cheek.

As the day aged, Rydar purchased three roasted pheasant legs, grilled neeps and pot of cider, and searched out a quiet spot at the far end of the main street to sit and eat and think. He found a soft patch of sandy ground, and rested his sore leg.

Today was a very good day. Durness was a very good place. Grier was a remarkable woman. Perhaps it was no accident at all that he washed ashore here.

Should I stay in Scotland?

It was fairly obvious that plague was the reason the ships stopped coming to Grønnland; the years lined up aright. Might he make his way back to Arendal only to find that his family was gone and someone else now held Hansen Hall? Might he find he was displaced from his ancestral home just as Grier would be from hers?

In truth, it was very likely.

Rydar drew a deep breath and blew it out slowly. *But what if some of my family survived? If so, he had a place there. A position and a future. And he needed to fulfill his promise to Arne. If he remained here, then Arne died for nothing. He couldn't betray his best friend in that manner.*

But how could he leave Grier?

ᚱᚾ

By the time the sun had circled half the sky and rested lower, Grier found Rydar sitting under a tree, holding a denuded bone and an empty cider pot. She thought of how he looked when he singled her out in the bard's crowd; when he bowed to her, then lifted his chin and met her gaze, his laughing green eyes framed by gold-streaked hair curving around his bearded jaw. He looked so incredibly handsome in the tunic she made for him, and playing the knight of her dreams, that she couldn't help but kiss him. She wanted to shout, *how I love you, you silly Viking!*

Love?

Aye, there it was. With a painful wallop of her heart, Grier realized she loved the stubborn Norseman. And she loved him with all of her being.

How long?

Since she first saw him and pulled him from the North Sea. Once she acknowledged it, it became an irrevocable part of her, an inevitable shift of direction. Her life transformed in both form and purpose. Her chest warmed with relief and clotted with fear.

Should she tell him? Might it make him stay? Judging his mood Grier approached Rydar slowly, a package gripped behind her. He turned at the sound of her steps.

"Grier," he whispered.

"Happy birthday, Rydar." She offered him the package. It was the biggest risk to any future she might yet have with him and she wondered if she was in truth a fool.

He accepted the small bundle. "What this is?"

Grier knelt close beside him on the ground. Her knees rested against his thigh. "Open it."

Rydar untied the twine and the cloth wrapping fell away. He

lifted the circular instrument with a slow reverence usually reserved for the communion cup.

"Is a *kompass*." He looked at her with disbelief. "You give me a *kompass?*"

"Aye." Grier smiled past her burgeoning fear.

Rydar's brow twitched. He ran his hand through his hair. "I do no' have words."

Grier lowered her lashes. "Do you require words?" she whispered. Then she raised her gaze to his again.

Rydar set the compass on the ground with exceeding care, and then pulled Grier to him. Her arms circled his waist and she lifted her mouth to his. He tasted of ale and meat, and his beard tickled her chin. His tongue tousled with hers. His fingers twisted in her hair.

Rydar kissed her with such tender longing that she wondered if he might discern her heart. When their kisses ended she leaned into him. His heart thudded in her ear and his chest swelled and shrank with slow, easy breaths. She rested, content in his arms and his gratitude, glad for this moment that he was hers alone.

Should she tell him that she loved him?

No. No' yet.

ᚱᚺ

Merchants packed their unsold wares and took down their tents in deflating billows of color. An enormous fire was built at the north end of town closest to the sloping, sandy chyngell. Sinews of discordant tones echoed off the houses as musicians tuned their instruments.

The sun burnished the remaining clouds in colors that echoed the celebratory flames, then dipped below the northwest horizon to begin her several-hour swim to the northeast side. Grier and Rydar walked together through the rowdy crowd. He took her hand and held it tight, keeping her close as he ambled with her through the deconstructed Mercat.

"Is good day, Grier," he said. "Very good day."

"Are you happy?" she asked.

Rydar paused. "Aye."

"Me, too." She rested her head against his upper arm. Leaving the celebration behind, they continued to walk north toward the sea until they reached the sand. Grier stopped and turned to Rydar.

He took her face in his hands. His lips lowered to hers. Soft at first, they soon asked more of her and she answered without hesitation. A small moan escaped her and she gave herself over to his mouth, his tongue, the forceful caress of his breath on her cheek. He rocked in a circle while he kissed her, spinning slowly, and she lost any sense of where she was. She held him close, her body pressed against his, savoring heady sensations that nothing else, and no one else, had ever caused her to feel before.

When the kiss ended, she knew it was time to tell him of her love. She pulled a deep breath to bolster her courage. "Rydar?"

"Aye?" His gaze wandered over her features.

"I—" She paused and tried to think past the roar of her pulse. "I—"

"What, Grier?" Rydar brushed his knuckles along her jaw. Then he looked beyond her. Confusion furrowed his brow. "What *that* is?"

His eyes widened. He gripped Grier's shoulders so hard that she winced. His stare touched hers, and then soared above her again.

"Wh-what?" She looked over her shoulder. "The boat?"

Rydar pushed past her and loped unevenly toward the dark structure. Hidden from the main thoroughfare behind a withering and abandoned house, the vessel sat poised just beyond the water's reach.

He called back to Grier as she stumbled after him. "Who is boat?"

"It belonged to Rabbie Campbell," she said when she reached him. "He's been dead these three years."

"Who is boat, now?" Rydar demanded. He wasn't looking at her; he was pacing off the size of the boat and running his hand over her planks as he did so.

"No one's, I ween. He had no sons. No one's touched it since he fell." Grier's growing unease had nothing to do with the prompted plague memories. Strangling fear began in her breast and twined up to her throat. Her knees went weak.

"I build it, I finish it," Rydar stated. His eyes glowed in the pale light. "Is my boat!"

"Will you be a fisherman, like Rabbie?" Grier asked. *Please*

God, let that be his new plan.

He did not seem to hear her. "Twelve walks long and six wide," he said. "That will do." He leaned back and looked up at the mast. "Good."

He was climbing up the side, now. He straddled the edge and called down what he discovered. "Braces for top *dekk*, low *dekk*, and *lagring* in bottom. Only needs boards for *dekks*."

"Rydar?"

He disappeared into the craft without answering. Grier heard the creak of straining rope and the rudder began to wag back and forth like the slow tail of an old hound. His cry of, "Works!" floated to the edge and spilled down on her.

"Rydar!" Grier cried, frantic to reclaim his attention.

His head reappeared and he grinned down at her. "My boat!"

"Come down!" she urged.

He threw his legs over the rim and lowered himself to arms' length, then let go and dropped to the sand. He tumbled back and fell hard on his arse.

"Ow!" he yelped.

"Watch your leg and ye do no' break it again!" Grier barked.

He stood awkwardly and brushed sand from the back of his clothes.

"Do ye plan to fish?" she asked again, trying to keep the panic from her tone.

"What? No." He stopped brushing off his clothes and his brow crinkled when he considered her. "Why you ask?"

"The boat, Rydar! Why do you want the boat?" she demanded. Her tone sounded shrill, even to her own ears.

He looked back over his shoulder at the half-finished structure, the ominous embodiment of her fear, and then faced her again. His levity evaporated. In the evening's lavender light his eyes were colorless, their pupils dilated. His gaze fell to the sand at her feet. After a pace, it wandered up her form until his eyes met hers.

Grier's heart began to leap in protest, banging frantically against her chest. She couldn't feel her legs. He looked at her so intently that she couldn't breathe.

She kent the answer before he said it and she felt her soul cleave apart.

"I sail home, Grier. To Norway."

Chapter Nineteen

There you are, Grier! And Rydar!" Logan's voice called to them over the sound of crashing waves. Or maybe 'twas the sound of her crashing hopes. "We wondered where you two got off to!"

Grier forced herself to turn toward her cousin. Her head felt oddly heavy and she thought she might faint because her heart refused to keep a steady rhythm. Logan pulled a skipping Malise by one hand. The girl's wide smile was echoed in Logan's joyous expression.

"We have news, Grier!" Logan said. The couple halted in front of her. "Do ye care to guess?"

Grier wagged her head unevenly. Her mouth was dry as dead leaves and she wasn't able to talk. Just as well. She couldn't form a coherent sentence at that moment if her very life was dependent upon it. She sensed Rydar beside her but she couldn't acknowledge him.

"We are betrothed, of course!" Malise chirped. "We are to be wed!"

"Can you believe it, Grier?" Logan laughed. "It happened so swift!"

Grier knew she should speak now. It was expected. She levered her mouth open and hoped the appropriate words might tumble out on their own. They did not.

Rydar stepped forward and held out his hand. "Good! Is very good, Logan!" Rydar said. The deep blade of his voice pricked Grier to speak.

"Aye. God's grace to you both," she squeaked. It was hard to talk when she struggled just to keep breathing.

"Thank you, Lady Grier. Sir Hansen." Malise beamed at her intended. Logan looked inches taller and broader in his joy.

"When?"

The abruptness of Grier's tone drew three puzzled pairs of eyes. She didn't care. She needed to know how much time she had and she needed to know now.

Logan cleared his throat. "In a month. We thought July twentieth."

"Aye. One month." Grier didn't recognize her own voice.

"What are you doing over here by Rabbie's boat, anyway?" Logan asked, as if he was suddenly aware that a world existed outside of his beloved's smile.

"I finish boat!" Rydar exclaimed.

Logan nodded, and then frowned. "Why?"

"I sail home. To Norway."

"Oh! Braw idea, Hansen! No one has touched the craft since Rabbie died. Most likely afeared of the plague, though it's gone." Logan gripped Malise's elbow. "But come with us now, aye? Malise's Da has brought out his best wines and the musicians are playing!"

Logan and Malise turned and hurried toward the sounds of revelry, arms linked and heads together.

"Grier?"

Rydar's voice sliced through any reserve Grier might have had. She jerked her chin up and met his worried gaze.

"We go?" he asked.

She bounced a nod. "Aye," she growled. She stomped forward and didn't care a wee bit if he followed or not.

June 21, 1354

Grier's tongue was glued to the roof of her mouth. She blinked and squinted toward twin blades of sunlight that sliced in through her eyes, and out through her temples. Her bladder demanded to be emptied. Her stomach quivered dangerously.

She rolled from her bed. The room tilted, the walls moved in and out, and the floor wobbled. Grier held one wall in place and squatted over the piss pot, all the while commanding her stomach to be still. It refused and she vomited sour wine onto the wood floor.

"Shite," she mumbled. She hadn't the strength to clean it up. She crawled back to her bed and pulled a pillow over her face. Her forehead throbbed with her pulse.

The last thing she remembered was convincing Logan to refill her wine goblet. She was still able to stand, she recalled, as long as she kept one hand on the table. She wasn't drunk enough yet. She could still think. She could still feel. Her soul could still bleed.

Oblivion finally arrived.

Another memory swam through her befuddled mind: Rydar, carrying her up the stairs. How did he manage that with his leg?

Must be better. Six—seven?—weeks. Aye.

Then Grier remembered why. With a gasping sob, she sought the mindless solace of sleep once again.

ᚱᚾ

During last night's celebration for Malise and Logan, Rydar met a young man speaking Norse. As he and the boy talked, possibilities bloomed.

He was eighteen and had come to the Mercat with his sixteen-year-old brother and nineteen-year-old cousin. The three were fishermen from the Shetland Islands and they had come to Scotland to try and make their way. Rydar asked the young man to meet him at Rabbie's boat this morning to discuss an arrangement that might suit all of them quite well.

While he rode into Durness he thought of Grier. Logan's announcement of his impending wedding had affected her much harder than Rydar would have expected. She was stunned to the point of speechlessness. True, Malise would soon be the lady of the castle; but Grier knew it was bound to happen. She told him as much.

Then she purposefully tried to drink herself senseless, something he never expected of a woman like her. Even though Logan watered her wine, she was obviously not accustomed to drinking such a large amount. She managed to accomplish her goal in spite of her cousin's efforts. When she could no longer stand, Rydar carried her to the cart and cradled her on the bumpy ride back to the keep. Then he bore her up the stairs and laid her in her bed.

He stood over her, twisted her thick, disobedient hair out of the way, and stroked her cheek. Curled on her mattress she looked so small, so vulnerable. All her courage and determination seemed to have evaporated leaving behind a frightened woman, hurt and alone. Rydar longed to ease her pain and her fear, the way she helped to ease his. But how could he change her situation? With the serendipitous discovery of the boat, he was most definitely leaving Scotland.

And leaving her.

Rydar reined Salle to a stop. He didn't move and barely breathed as the notion sprouted, grew and solidified.

Take her with you.

"I can't ask Grier to leave everything she has ever known!" he blurted. Salle startled and sidestepped at his sudden and loud protestation. He patted her neck to reassure her.

He had nothing to promise Grier. He didn't know if he even had a home. A family. A position. An income.

How could he, in good conscience, ask Grier to leave the only home she had ever known and follow him into definite uncertainty, probable danger and possible ruin? Ridiculous! Why would she even consider it?

"No sane woman would do such a thing!" he declared. "Even for love!"

Love?

Again that possibility prodded him. Did he love Grier?

"What is love anyway, Salle?" he grumbled to the mare, avoiding his own question. Her ears flicked back to him and her head bobbed. He knew he needed to answer that question first. Because if he didn't love Grier, then he would simply thank her for all she did for him and sail away.

But if he did love her, he must decide whether it was better to leave her behind, safe in her life's home, or take her on his perilous journey to the country of his birth. And if he asked her to come with him, shouldn't he offer marriage first? Wasn't that necessary to preserve her reputation and assure her of his sincere motives?

"I better settle my own course first, Salle." Rydar nudged the mare forward. "But if today turns out as I hope, I'll be in a promising position. Then, if Grier ever declares her love for me, I will surely ask her to consider joining me!"

Grier must speak her love first, Rydar decided as he entered Durness. Only then would he be sufficiently certain of her feelings to present the possibility of her accompanying him; both into marriage, and into the precarious Norse unknown.

ᚱᚺ

Kristofer, a lanky, blond eighteen-year-old with a thick reddish beard, was waiting beside the boat, sitting in its shade. He scrambled to his feet as Rydar approached, looking inordinately relieved. He waved. Rydar halted Salle and dismounted.

"Where are the other two?" Rydar asked. He tethered Salle to a sea-smoothed stump poking crookedly from the sand.

Kristofer pounded his fist against the side of the boat. The banging of boot soles on wood preceded two bodies clambering over the edge of the craft. They dropped to the sand beside Kristofer and straightened, flanking him.

"This is my brother, Lars," Kristofer began. "He is sixteen and very strong."

Rydar nodded and extended his hand. "Rydar Hansen."

A stockier copy of his older brother, Lars gripped Rydar's fist with the obvious intent of displaying his strength. "Sir."

Rydar suppressed both his grin and his grimace. The boy was strong indeed.

"And this is our cousin, Gavin," Kristofer continued. Gavin was darker than his cousins and a little taller. Rydar shook his hand as well, relieved not to be subjected to a second display of youthful manliness.

"Has Kristofer explained to you what we discussed yester eve?" Rydar asked.

The trio nodded in unison.

"And are the terms amenable?"

Gavin stepped forward. "I beg your pardon, sir, but am I to understand that all you require of us is to help you finish constructing this vessel and make her seaworthy?"

"Yes. And then you sail with me to Norway as my crew when she's completed."

Gavin glanced at Lars, then met Rydar's eyes. "And once we

have reached Norway, you will stay there and—"

"And the boat belongs to you three. Yes." Rydar smiled. "I'll have no further use for her. She will be yours in exchange for your labors."

Relieved grins spilt the youthful faces.

"I'll arrange to purchase lumber from the carpenter today. We'll begin to work tomorrow. And every third day, I'll need to hunt in order to pay for supplies. You boys will work without me those days," Rydar explained. "I plan to sail in a month or less. Is that satisfactory?"

"Yes, sir!" Lars exclaimed.

"One more thing, sir?" Kristofer shifted uneasily and glanced at the other two.

"Yes?"

"Sir, might we sleep in the boat?"

Realization washed through Rydar. "You have no home here, have you?"

Kristofer shook his head. "No, sir."

"But we can fish!" Gavin insisted. "And cook over a fire. All we need is a place to lay our heads."

Rydar nodded. "It might be quite prudent to have you sleeping here. Keep any mischievous ruffians away, eh? Yes. That's a very wise plan."

Three sets of shoulder relaxed.

"Do you have any more questions?" Rydar asked.

Three heads wagged.

"I'll see you tomorrow then. Get yourselves settled today." Rydar untied Salle's reins. He mounted the mare and turned her toward the main street of Durness. As he rode away, he heard the sounds of boyish jubilation erupt behind him.

He grinned.

When he saw the McKay's house, Rydar realized that the entire exchange with Kristofer, Lars and Gavin had been in Norse. And now that he had the means to leave Scotland, he no longer needed to pursue their language.

Ryder reined Salle away from the main street and toward the road back to Durness Castle.

ᚱᚾ

Logan sat across from Grier at the kitchen table. Excitement shot out of him like lightning; the air fairly crackled around him. Grier sat very still and nursed a steaming mug of gingerroot and mint for her rebellious stomach with willowbark added for her aching head.

Never again will I act so foolishly, she resolved. *It is no' worth the price.*

"So I'll fetch Malise every morn after breakfast and return her home after the midday meal!" Logan leaned back looking very pleased with his plan.

Grier hadn't been listening to him. She tried without success to recall what he said.

Logan tilted his head. "Will that suit you, Grier?"

"Ev—every morn?" she stammered.

"Well no' on Sundays, of course!" Logan demurred. "But there's a heap to learn about running the castle. I see no reason to put it off, do you?"

Oh. Teach Malise to run the castle. Every morning. Grier drew a bracing breath. "No, Logan. I think you're wise to start right off. There truly is a heap to learn."

"I kent ye'd agree with me, Grier!" Logan pushed to stand. "I'll go to her now and tell her. We'll begin on the morrow!"

Grier squinted one eye at him. "The morrow?"

"The wedding is in four weeks, Grier. That's no' much time, aye?"

Grier's stomach clenched and threatened to pitch what little it held at Logan. She managed to clamp down the urge, and forced a tremulous smile.

"No' much time at all. You go and tell her, then."

Logan stepped close to Grier and surprised her with a brief hug.

"Thank you, Grier. For everything." He swallowed and his face reddened. "You are the only family I have left, ye ken. I owe my life to you. Ye'll always have a home here."

Before Grier could speak, Logan spun and strode from the room. The door to the keep creaked open and clanked shut.

Grier's head dropped to her folded arms. Despair crushed her and she wept under its weight.

ᚱᚿ

By supper time, Grier was able to look at food again without growing nauseated. Two loaves of bread were finishing in the ovens, and she stirred a thick rabbit stew over the fire, made from the bounty of Rydar's hunting expeditions.

Rydar. What was she going to do about him?

"I love him, I do," she murmured. "And he'll sail away in a few weeks and I'll no' ever see him again." She pulled a breath, pushing against the heaviness of loss that squeezed her chest.

Grier removed the bread from the ovens and set the pot of stew on the table. Grabbing the water bucket, she went outside to the well. She started to pull the bucket of fresh water up from the dark depths but stopped. Letting the bucket tumble down to a distant splash, she dropped on the grass to logically ponder the paths before her.

Grier held up a single finger. "I can stay here, teach Malise, and go on with my life without changing a thing," she said. While expected of her, it was not a particularly inviting path. It was the path of surrender and it left her with nothing of her own.

She held up a second finger. "I might move away from Durness. I might even go to Edinburgh. Try to make my own way." It may be she could practice healing, or open an apothecary shop. Even if she hadn't ever known a woman who'd done such a thing, surely someone had.

Then she held up a third finger and stared at it in silence for several minutes. This was the hardest one. The one she ached for. The one she could not choose on her own; it was dependent on *him*. But once she said it aloud, she kent it was the one she would pursue.

"I could go to Norway with him," she whispered.

Grier waited. The earth didn't crack open; lightning didn't fall from the sky. The sea didn't crest over the castle wall and claim her. Only a soft evening breeze and the warming colors of sunset surrounded her.

"That's it, then," she resolved. She felt as if one huge stone was removed from her breast, only to be replaced by another just as heavy.

"I can no' just tell him I'll go! What if he does no' wish me to?"

She stood and began to tug at the rope, lifting the laden bucket from the well and spending her frustration on the straining effort.

The answer was obvious and infuriating. Infuriating because she couldn't compel it to happen.

"I can only go and he asks me to," she muttered. "And that's the way of it."

Grier grabbed the handle of the bucket and unhooked it from the rope. She paused. A black vine of familiar despair trailed through her gut. She tried to draw a breath deep enough to strangle it.

"How did I come to this?" she wondered aloud. "Less than two months ago I pulled a stranger from the sea. Now, my own future and my own happiness rest on the whim of that stubborn Viking!"

Chapter Twenty

R ydar stood in the kitchen and snuck a taste of the rabbit stew. Grier must be recovered from the previous night's overindulgence if she could cook such a rich meal. Light from the kitchen's doorway dimmed and drew his attention.

Grier paused there and her cheeks scarleted, making her eyes look like liquid cobalt. She straightened her shoulders, then one brow lifted and her lips curved.

"It seems a changeling took my place yester eve," she said as she moved into the room. "Did you perhaps see her?"

Rydar was charmed by her unexpected words. "Aye. I did."

Grier hung the bucket of water on the fire hook to heat. She considered Rydar over her shoulder. "I understand she behaved rather foolishly. Has she ruined my good name?"

"No, Lady Grier." He bowed from the waist. "All there kent she is no' you."

She turned to face him. Her smile tugged at his heart; her unassuming beauty tugged at parts lower.

"I'm quite relieved," she said in a soft voice. "I would hate for you to think less of me."

"No. No' less." Rydar reached for her hand and struggled to express his thoughts in the still-unfamiliar tongue. "Many things change at one time, aye? Is very hard to change you at same time." He shrugged, hoping Grier understood him. For a moment he reconsidered the language lessons.

"Thank you, Rydar." Grier lifted his hand and pressed it to her cheek, so warm and smooth against his rough skin. Her eyes fluttered up to his. "Ye're a very fine friend to me."

His eyes fell to her parted lips and he leaned toward her, drawn by their invitation.

"Rydar!"

He pulled back as Logan's voiced bounced down the hall, frustration and disappointment coloring his response to the laird.

"Aye." he growled.

The younger man rounded into the kitchen.

"I have no' seen you today, but Malise said ye were in Durness. Were ye about the boat?" Logan sniffed the stew and grabbed a bowl. "It smells sae good, Grier! And I'm famished! Here—" He handed Rydar a bowl. "Tell me about it, then."

Rydar chuckled at Logan's exuberance, his own irritation eased by Logan's boundless enthusiasm. He sat at the table, filled his bowl and broke off a chunk of warm bread to dip in the steaming stew.

Logan took his place and Rydar waited for Grier to join them before he explained about the three young Norse fishermen from the Shetland Islands, and the deal he struck to exchange their labor.

"I talk to car-pen-ter today and have wood on morrow." Rydar looked hard at Logan. "I use tools, aye?"

Logan nodded and swallowed a bite of stew. "If my men are no' using them."

"I no' keep tools, only use tools," Rydar clarified.

"I understand."

"And I hunt. On third days."

Logan smiled knowingly at him. "Ye must pay for the wood, aye?"

Rydar grinned. "Aye… I no' a rich laird like you!"

Throughout their conversation Grier had been pale and silent, but she chuckled at that. Logan poked him in the ribs.

I shall miss Logan, Rydar thought suddenly. The young man had been a steady and helpful presence for him here in this unfamiliar land.

Rydar turned to Grier and caught her watching him. He winked at her and she blushed, looking adorably embarrassed, and yet undoubtedly pleased.

Perhaps she could grow to love me yet.

June 24, 1354

Little about Grier's life was the same as it was before the twin debacles at the Mercat Fair. The most immediate change was the appearance of her new apprentice, Malise McKay. Logan rode into Durness after breakfast each morning to fetch his intended and deposit her into Grier's tutelage.

Grier began to lead the young woman through the tasks required to assure the keep and castle were well run. Malise was obviously overwhelmed by the prospect. She repeatedly asked Grier, "But ye'll be here, aye? To help me?"

"Aye," Grier answered to calm the girl, though truthfully she was not at all certain of what she might yet choose to do.

After the midday meal on the first day, when Logan returned Malise to her home, Grier climbed the stairs and stood before the closed door of her parents' bedchamber. She rested her hand on the latch, but could not force herself to push it open. In the face of her lost future, it was as if the door was solid stone, and her strength that of a gnat.

"Oh Da, Mam. I always thought I would bed my husband here," she whispered. "No' my cousin Logan and his child bride…"

Unable to move beyond her grief, Grier put off for a day the mournful task of removing her parents' remaining presence there. Her father's clothing, her mother's jewelry, the coverlet and curtains that had always adorned their bed; somehow having those things in place made it seem as though her parents were only away. Not forever gone.

She was no more successful on the second day.

Grier stood in the hall and leaned her forehead against the wooden portal. She couldn't resign herself to the rapidly approaching end to her life as she knew it. The prospect of living out her days as a servant to Malise seemed a dark cave that swallowed any light of hope.

"It might be I save this task for last," she reasoned. "I'll wait until Malise is able to do for herself a bit, and then I'll take the time to prepare their bridal bed."

Grier turned her back on the chamber door and went down the stairs to find another task—any other task—to occupy the rest of her day.

The more subtle change in her life encompassed the dooming shift in purpose for Rydar's absences from the castle. On the first two days, he returned from his boat very late and very hungry. Though he tried to converse with her, exhaustion stole his English words and he fell silent, all but sleeping at the kitchen table when he finished his meal.

The third day, when he returned from hunting just after midday, Grier waited for him. She accepted the game he brought, then sat him down and fed him.

"Are ye no' eating then, ye foolish Viking?" she asked as she ladled him a second bowl of fish stew. "You do no' have weight to spare, ye ken! It's my cross to bear to try and fatten you up!"

Rydar grinned with his mouth full. "I no' take your food. I eat after, aye?" he mumbled.

"Is that so?" Grier squinted at him. "And what about the boys?"

Rydar looked confused. "The boys?"

"Do they eat?"

"Oh!" Rydar paused, frowning. "I no' see they eat."

Grier pointed her ladle at him in accusation. "So you're starving them as well, are ye?"

Rydar looked at her, his face a comical blend of realization and embarrassment. "Boys hungry, aye?"

"I would expect so." Grier shook her head and grabbed the opportunity. "Starting on the morrow I'll bring ye all a solid meal in the midday."

"Is too much work, Grier," Rydar objected. But not too strenuously, she noticed.

"Blethers! Malise is taking over the keep. I've both the time and the inclination. And ye've naught to say about it, Viking!" She jammed the ladle back into the remaining stew then tossed him her most beguiling smile.

Rydar's head pitched back and he guffawed. His booming enjoyment echoed around the kitchen and his pale green eyes glowed with mirth.

"I not say 'no'!" he laughed. "You come. You bring food. Is *your* say, aye?"

Grier happily filled his bowl for the third time, satisfied in her suggestion and very glad of his enthusiastic response.

July 3, 1354

Rydar straightened his back and tugged his shirt off over his head. He used it to mop sweat from his chest and then tossed the damp shirt to the ground. The Scottish sun was strong today and it glittered atop the North Sea's undulating surface. Rydar scooped a cup of cool drinking water. He looked west, but didn't yet see Grier. So he turned back to the boat.

On the first day that he and the young Norse fishermen started work on the vessel, Rydar led them to the water's edge and drew his ideas in wet sand. The boys nodded politely as he talked, but glances bounced between them like juggler's balls.

Rydar paused in his sand-sketching. "What is it?"

Kristofer cleared his throat. "We had some ideas…"

"Go on," Ryder urged.

"It's not that anything is wrong with your plans, sir!" Lars squeaked.

Rydar chuckled. "I understand, Lars. Tell me what you were thinking."

"Well, the boat is to sail to Norway, and then be ours when you've done with it. So we'd like it fit for longer voyages, not only fishing," Kristofer explained.

"We thought we might like to explore the world ourselves," Gavin added.

"While we're still young yet." Kristofer's eyes rounded with horror as soon as the words were out of his mouth. "Not that you're old, sir!"

Rydar gave him a patient smile. "I am not as young as I once was, nor as old as I shall be, God willing."

Kristofer blinked, looking a bit confused.

"May I draw what we thought of, sir?" Gavin held out his hand for the stick. Rydar handed the boy the branch and stepped back.

Gavin spoke as he sketched. "We thought of only two full decks, one on the bottom for storage, and one above it as the main deck… We wanted to build a cabin at the bow that would be for cooking and gathering together out of the weather… At the back we thought a separate sleeping cabin."

Lars nudged his older brother. "Show him where the rudder's handle will go."

"Oh! Here." Gavin stuck the stick in the sand. "See, we'd make the tops of the cabins the third deck, but part would be in front over the kitchen cabin, and part in back over the sleeping cabin."

"Here's the mast," Lars added in his eagerness to be involved.

Rydar was impressed. The design was well thought out and practical. He nodded and slapped Gavin's shoulder. "You've convinced me. It uses no more wood than my plan so it shouldn't cost any more money. But," Rydar considered the teens, "it will take a bit more time."

"We will work hard to see it still done in a month," Kristofer assured him.

"Or less!" Gavin added.

Rydar laughed. "Then I agree! Shall we get started?"

Now the bottom storage deck was finished and they were installing the main deck. Lacking the iron nails of his native homeland, Rydar used a brace and bit borrowed from Logan to create peg holes to fasten down the rough boards he bought from the carpenter. The four men worked together in an easy rhythm. At this rate, the boat might truly be finished sooner than he expected.

"Lady Grier is coming!" Gavin called down.

Rydar turned from the water bucket to see her slowing Raven to a walk. Two deep food baskets hung on either side of the gelding's saddle and Rydar wondered what delicacies she brought this day. Grier smiled and waved. Rydar smiled and waved back. And he experienced the odd lightening in his chest that always accompanied her arrival.

He recognized that his days working on the boat rotated around Grier bringing their midday meal. The hour she spent feeding him and the Norse teens, then examining their progress with sincere interest, seemed to give him the impetus to work through the blisters, burning muscles and aching shin that plagued him daily. She always left him with a soft kiss on the cheek and a squeeze of his arm, and the reminder not to stay so late that his supper was burnt.

She took very good care *of* him. Did she care *for* him?

It seemed that she did. But her enthusiastic regard for his labors confused him, because the sooner he finished, the sooner he would leave her. Did she hope he might change his mind? Or was she resigned to his departure?

"I fried the neeps with onions," Grier said and handed Rydar one of the baskets. "Then I made them into pasties with the grouse."

His mouth watered at the aroma and description. "Will be good, Grier. Always good!"

She blushed and gave him a knowing grin. "You're always so hungert that I could bring hay soaked in ale and ye'd thank me!"

"Aye, is true." Rydar shrugged and laughed. "With much ale!"

The first day Grier came to feed him, Rydar saw the longing in the young fishermen's expressions. When she brought out the victuals, they stared openly. And when she told them the food was for them as well, Rydar thought Lars might cry. Grier was right; the boys were starving. He hadn't considered that, but she had realized it first off. He loved that it was so ingrained in her to be aware of others and do what she could to alleviate their discomfort.

God knew, she had alleviated his.

Kristofer, Lars and Gavin appeared and Grier handed out the generous meat pies. She served them all apple cider and fresh pears. Afterwards, Rydar led her up the ladder into the boat and showed her the day's progress. As she always did, she praised his handiwork and his dedication.

He wished again that he knew what she held in her heart. But he didn't dare ask her; he couldn't risk swaying her choice here, should things go badly for him at home in Arendal. He would never forgive himself for putting her in the midst of that sort of treacherous situation. No, he must be patient. He must wait for her to come around. In the meantime, he would remain as attentive, as helpful and as close to her as he was able.

Rain clouds gathered that afternoon and cooled the men. So when Rydar climbed out of the boat to retrieve another finished plank he was surprised to see Margoh standing with the young men, chatting rapidly in Norse. Her steely gray gaze shifted to him and cut the pleasant greeting from his mouth. She folded her arms and waited in silence for the boys to get on with their work, and for him to approach.

"Welcome, Lady Henriksen."

Margoh's blue-gray eyes flicked to the inquisitive faces of Kristofer and Gavin, then to Lars who popped over the edge of the boat behind them. She looped her arm through Rydar's and tugged him across the sandy chyngell toward the waves' edge.

"Where have you been these past two weeks?" she demanded once they were away from the curious young men. "And what in the name of Thor are you doing?"

"Do you refer to the boat?" Rydar asked coolly.

"I don't know! Do I?" Margoh countered. She stopped walking and turned to face him. "I haven't seen you since the Mercat Fair. You haven't come for lessons. What am I to think?"

Rydar gripped Margoh's shoulders. "You're to think that I'm a lucky man!"

Margoh's brow crinkled. "Why?"

"Because Rabbie Campbell died of the plague!"

Margoh knocked Rydar's hands from her shoulders then swung her tight fist hard into his arm, stinging his skin and most likely leaving a bruise. "If you don't tell me right now, Rydar Hansen, you'll feel my knee next and it won't be in your thigh!"

Rydar lifted one annoyed brow, refusing to rub the twinge from his arm. "Rabbie died before he finished his boat. Now I'm finishing it—with the help of those three fishermen—and by the end of the month I'll sail home."

Margoh's jaw dropped. She spun around to look at the boat, then spun back to face him.

"You mean to Norway?"

"Yes, of course, to Norway. To Arendal specifically."

She stared at him, blinking with increased rapidity. "Take me with you!" she blurted.

Rydar fell back. "What?"

Margoh reached for his wrists and sunk her nails into them. "Take me to Norway with you, Rydar."

He had not believed her when she first mentioned accompanying him, back when he was injured, had no money, and no visible means to accomplish the sea travel. He assumed her words were merely part of her attempted seduction.

"You were serious about this?" Rydar asked.

Margoh's grip tightened. "Why wouldn't I be? There is nothing for me here!"

"What is for you there?" he demanded.

"Family. Cousins of my husband." Her voice was rising in pitch. "They are in Áslo."

Rydar was too stunned to think of a response other than, "How far is that from Arendal?"

Her shoulders jerked up. "I—I don't know."

"Once I reach Arendal I am giving these boys the boat in exchange for their labor," Rydar explained. He pulled his wrists from her grasp and dragged his fingers through his hair. "How might you—"

"I don't know!" Margoh shrieked.

Rydar stared at her, and then looked away. He shook his head in surprise, losing the words of any language

"Rydar, please! Give me a chance to work these things out! I've only just now heard of your plans," she pleaded with considerable force.

Rydar looked at her again. Her desperation was clearly etched in the deepening lines of her face. She looked old, tired. But what was her intent? Was she desperate to leave Durness? Or to get to Norway? Or to be with him?

"Margoh," he began.

She stepped closer and pressed her fingers to his lips. "I know what you're going to say, Rydar. You said no promises. You said the risk was mine. Am I right?" Her fingers drifted away from his mouth.

Rydar's jaw rippled. "Yes."

"All I'm asking for is to sail with you." She looked up at him with wide gray eyes that matched the rain clouds above. "Please, Rydar. I want to start my life over again somewhere else. Before it's too late and my chances have flown."

Rydar tried to think, but his heart was screaming so loud, *what about Grier?* that no reasonable thoughts would form. Something of his reluctance must have shown because Margoh paled and her chin quivered.

"Don't say 'no' yet. Think about it," she whispered. "I beg this of you."

Rydar was in a tight corner. To deny Margoh because he hoped Grier might declare her love and accompany him might very well leave both of the women stranded. At the least he could consider Margoh's request.

"I promise to think about it, Margoh. But the boat is small and the journey will not be comfortable," he warned.

"I understand. Thank you." Margoh slipped her fingers into

Rydar's hair and pulled his head down to hers. She kissed him quickly. He jerked away.

"I'm not part of the bargain," he growled.

"Yet," she claimed before turning in the direction of her home.

Rydar ignored the three pair of impressed male eyes who had witnessed two beautiful women kiss him in as many hours. He squinted at the darkening clouds and called an end to the day. Without the sun it was hard to be sure of the time, and he was bone tired and sore. Before he left, he reminded the boys that on the morrow he would hunt and they would labor without him.

On the ride back to the keep—as truthfully happened every day—Rydar felt enveloping relief as he drew closer to Grier. She was a candle and he was a moth. Or she was a magnet and he was steel. Or she was a beautiful, bright, talented and warm woman.

And he was very much a lonely man.

Chapter
Twenty-One

July 8, 1354

Grier rode toward the keep after another painful afternoon spent watching Rydar work on his boat. She would not have counted it possible, but the man grew more glorious with each completed day. Blessed by hours of sun, his skin grew bronze and his hair gilded with streaks of shining gold. Holding still he looked like a pagan statue.

As he worked, Rydar's bare arms and back glistened with sweat, enhancing each groove and bulge of his straining muscles. Lifting boards, carrying planks, drilling peg holes and pounding in the dowels required considerable effort.

Fitting the pieces into a waterproof vessel without causing leaks was tight work, he explained to her. If a board was short-cut, it must be remade and the work redone. But now they were starting on the cabins and the shorter planks could find a use.

Rydar always seemed so glad to see her. His lopsided smile flashed brilliantly when she approached and he stopped what he was doing to meet her. When she looked into his pale green eyes, she felt as though she was exactly where she belonged.

If only he could feel the same about her.

Grier wondered at times if all of her efforts were wasted. Even though she brought him delicious meals, fussed over his boat, complimented his skills and accomplishments, and kissed him tenderly before leaving, he did not seem to understand how much she cared for him.

"I want to go with you, ye contermacious Viking!" she muttered. "I love ye and I want to make *your* life into *my* life as well!"

An uncomfortable thought occurred to her: might it be that he thought she was glad he was leaving? And that was why she was so enthusiastic about the boat?

She shook her head. "If ye think that, Norseman, then ye're more stupit than even I can fathom!"

Lost in her thoughts, Grier let Raven set his own pace back to the castle. She paid him no mind until he snorted, tossed his head and sidestepped across the wood bridge. She reined him in and looked to see what had upset her mount.

Tethered outside her stable stood a huge gray warhorse. He wore a massive leather and wood saddle glinting with polished metal trim. Beside the fierce-looking stallion was a dark brown gelding of similar size and trappings. Grier dismounted and handed Raven off to her young groom. When she asked who had arrived, he shrugged.

Grier walked toward the keep, wondering why anyone so obviously wealthy and powerful would bother to ride as far north as little Durness Castle. Both of the huge animals swung their heads toward her and watched her passage with interest. They shifted their enormous iron-clad hooves as if eager to be moving on.

In the Great Hall, a man stood with his back to the doorway. Broad-shouldered and tall—though not so tall as Rydar—he was powerfully built and finely dressed. Over a black velvet tunic he wore a purple silk mantle stitched with a raised pattern of gold and red threads. Knee-high leather boots over black hose enhanced the massive muscles of his long legs. He turned at the sound of her footfalls, and tugged black leather gloves from his fingers.

He tilted his head and dipped his chin. "Madam? Is the laird of this castle to be found?"

Grier's mouth flapped stupidly, for the moment silenced by the imperious stranger. The mantle was clasped across his chest with gold-set jewels. The crow-black hair tied at his nape was completely free of gray, and his eyes shifted from green to gold to brown and back again as light played over them. She managed a slight bow.

"I beg your pardon, Your Highness. I am Lady Grier MacInnes, mistress of the castle for my cousin, Laird Logan Roy MacDavid."

The man's mouth tugged up at one corner while his eyes swept over her, openly curious. "I'm no one's 'highness' my lady. Merely a loyal knight and courtier to our King David."

"Oh!" Grier stepped forward. "And is he freed, then?"

The man considered his limp gloves. "Ach, no. He remains in the Tower of London, a prisoner of the English king, Edward III."

"But it's eight years since he attacked England on behalf of France!" Grier exclaimed.

"Aye, 'tis true. I would expect Edward to kill him or free him, but he's done neither."

"What stays his hand, do ye think?"

The knight tilted his head at Grier and seemed to be re-evaluating her. She felt her face heating at her own outspokenness, and self-consciously smoothed the skirt of her plain woolen gown. If only she had dressed better before seeking out her guest.

"There is talk of a generous ransom, my lady," he answered.

"God save King David," Grier murmured and crossed herself.

The courtier slapped his gloves against one palm. "Aye. He will."

Grier lifted her chin and stood straight as befitted her station. "And you are, Sir?"

Boot heels clacked together and he bowed slightly. "Lord Andrew Drummond."

"And how might we be of service to you, my Lord?" Grier asked.

"It has been my duty these past months to travel the northern lands and assess Scotland's strengths—now that the plague is past—on behalf of our King." Lord Andrew's commanding voice rumbled like North Sea waves, powerful and deep.

Grier frowned. "So you have spoken to him?"

"Many times, my lady. The road from Stirling to London grows quite wearisome."

Lord Andrew's expression lost its charm then, and he suddenly looked as tired as he must be. Durness was over two hundred miles from Stirling, and London over four hundred miles further south. And Lord Andrew had obviously not traveled a straight path, as he described his particular mission. Grier felt the weight of his weariness as if it was her own.

"There are two horses?" She waved one hand toward the door.

"My vassal."

"Of course." Grier turned as a younger man appeared in the doorway, dressed much like his knight; without the jewels but with obvious weaponry. He looked very much like a blond Logan.

"Kennan, this is Lady MacInnes, our hostess," Lord Andrew said before Grier could speak.

Another pair of puzzled eyes, these gray, passed over her. He bowed. "My Lady."

Grier nodded her greeting. "If you gentleman will please be comfortable, I'll see to your food and your lodgings."

"My thanks, Lady MacInnes." Andrew's golden eyes sparkled with something surprising that Grier couldn't name.

ᚱᚺ

"Moira!" Grier ran out the keep's kitchen door to the yard. "Moira, come quickly!"

"What's amiss, Lady?" Moira appeared, breathless and red-cheeked.

"We've guests! A courtier from King David!" Grier blurted.

Moira looked like she might swoon. "A true courtier? Whatever's he doing here?"

"Assessing for the King. And he's got a man with him. They'll both be lodging in the keep. We've got a heap to do and quickly!" Grier glanced around. "Can you bring your mither and your brothers straight away, then?"

"Aye!" The maid turned to go but faced Grier again, frowning. "And where will we put them?"

Grier wouldn't allow herself time to think about her answer. "Lord Andrew will stay in the master's bedchamber."

Moira backed away, her eyes wide. "Your Da's chamber?"

Grier stepped forward and grabbed the girl's arm, shaking it as she spoke. "There's no plague nor shades in there, do ye understand?"

"Yes, Lady." She gave a wee nod.

Grier let go of her arm. "Now go! We've a darg to do and little time to do it!"

"Yes, Lady!" Moira ran toward her family's cottage.

Grier hurried back into the kitchen and prepared a light meal of smoked meat, cheese, bread and butter, pears, wine and ale. She carried a tray into the formal dining room, then collected her guests and sat them in there.

"Supper is a few hours away, yet. I thought ye might be famished. If you'll excuse me, Lord Andrew, I'll go see to your chamber."

"Aye. My thanks again, Lady MacInnes." Once more his golden-brown eyes glittered with something beyond Grier's reach, though it was not at all unpleasant. She stared at him longer than was seemly, until his brow wrinkled curiously.

Her face grew warm. Giving him a slight bow, she departed the room with haste.

It required two full hours, and five pair of hands, to dust and mop out the master's chamber. The old sheets were stripped and burned, the mattress re-stuffed, and made up with clean sheets. Everything in the room was washed until it shone. Grier was exhausted even with all the extra help.

Moira's mother was pressed into her previous role as the keep's cook and she went to the kitchen to begin the formal meal. The triplets dragged the copper tub upstairs and filled it so that Lord Andrew might soak away his road-weariness. Grier escaped into her own chamber to wash as best she could and dress herself appropriately for her important guest.

When she lifted a brown velvet gown from the bottom of her chest, she struggled to hold back the tears that clawed at her throat all afternoon. It was hard enough to be forced to remove any trace of her parents' presence that lingered in their chamber, but now to don the dress that was to be her wedding attire approached the limit of what she could withstand. She knelt on the floor of her room, the rich fabric clutched against her cheek, eyes closed, waiting.

Waiting for what?

She hadn't any idea. Her life this day was a mass of confusion.

Logan would marry in less than two weeks. Rydar worked from dawn to dusk either hunting or finishing a boat to sail away on. And now a stranger—a handsome, traveled and wealthy courtier—landed unexpectedly on her doorstep. And he smiled at her like no man ever had.

Her befuddled reverie was disturbed by heavy footsteps outside her door.

Logan!

Grier jumped up and slipped the gown over her head. The long sleeves flared outward, as did the hemline, which lengthened to a small train in back. She dug out a cream-colored silk snood trimmed in silver threads to tame her rebellious hair, and a silver-linked belt to accentuate her waist. She pulled her crucifix from inside her gown and let it hang against her breast as ornamentation.

With a sigh and a shrug, she went after Logan to explain what had occurred.

ᚱᚺ

Rydar opened the door to Rabbie Campbell's house and leaned his head inside. The cottage smelled damp and stale, and a thick layer of undisturbed dust coated every surface. Apparently no one had entered the house after Rabbie made his final exit. Rydar walked through the parlor room and into the kitchen. Dirty bowls and abandoned food, long since turned to colorless rock-like bits, rested on the table. A rusty pot hung in the fireplace. Beside the hearth, a ladder poked through an opening in the low ceiling. Most likely that was where Rabbie slept, warmed by the kitchen fire.

I won't find what I'm looking for up there, I don't expect.

Rydar opened a door at the far side of the kitchen. The tiny room was windowless and appeared to be the larder. A side of bacon hung from the roof, dirty and dry. Not at all the sort of place to store iron fittings for a boat. Rydar closed that door and returned to the parlor.

It might be he should search the outbuilding yet again; perhaps he overlooked them the first time. It was, after all, the logical place to store such things.

"That would be assuming Rabbie lived long enough to have the fittings made," Rydar muttered. He stood in the front room and considered the mess that surrounded him. Nothing but overturned chairs, a table, sideboard, an empty chest, and rolled up carpet covered in a linen sheet.

Rolled up carpet?

"And why would the carpet be rolled against the wall," Rydar wondered aloud. Curious, he pushed the chairs aside and knelt beside the cylinder of fabric. He tugged the edge of the linen away and found—more linen. His heart began to jump against his ribs.

Could it be?

Rydar gripped the edge of the material and stood. He backed away slowly, unrolling the cumbersome log. There was no carpet, only yards and yards of unbleached linen.

"Oh my God in Heaven!" He dropped the fabric and leapt to the front door. "Kristofer! Lars! Gavin!" he bellowed.

"What's amiss?" Gavin's voice floated to him. All three bodies began to move in his direction.

"Come quickly! You won't believe it!" Rydar clapped his hands and wiggled his entire body in an impromptu dance. "Hurry!"

The boys tilted forward in unison and began to run. When the three young men tumbled into the house, their boots thundering in the small space, Rydar turned and waved an upturned palm at the linen lump.

"Do you know what that is?" He tried to appear calm, but his eager voice betrayed him. "Do you?"

Gavin's jaw dropped. "Is it? Thor's thunder! It is!" He began to bounce.

"What?" Lars looked to his older brother for help. Kristofer's laugh started as a chuckle, but soon he and Gavin were jumping up and down together, whooping with joy.

Lars turned to Rydar. Rydar's cheeks ached with the width of his smile. He could order fittings from the smithy, and would do so today, but this was one indispensable piece of his plan that he had not yet puzzled out. And God had it wrapped up like a gift, waiting patiently for him to come find it.

"Sir Hansen?" Lars squeaked. "Is it a sail?"

Three male voices of varying octaves answered in a beautiful chorus, "Yes!"

ᚱᚼ

The smithy knew exactly what Rydar needed for the boat. And after Rydar's help with the new leather gloves and apron, he was willing to do the work at a reduced price.

"Is no' needed," Rydar demurred. "I hunt for money."

"Blethers, Hansen. After what ye did with the Mercat Fair, and how ye got all the craftsmen what they required? Ye're a bit of a hero, ye ken?"

"Did Rabbie no' have boat parts made?" he asked. "He has a sail."

"Aye, he gave me orders. And I had much of it finished when he died." The man paused and crossed himself. "But I melted the iron for other things, a long time past. He weren't going to use them, aye?"

"Aye." Rydar nodded.

"But ye found the sail?"

Rydar smiled. "Aye."

"That's good, then." The man offered a hand that dwarfed Rydar's. "See me in three day's time. I'll have what ye'll be needing."

"Thank you." He pumped the man's arm. "Thank you."

Rydar was beyond jubilant! Riding back to the castle in the polished-copper light of evening, all of creation seemed to congratulate him. Birds sang only for him. Squirrels danced through the trees because of him. Clouds nuzzled the sun to reflect her glory for his eyes alone. He laughed aloud and slapped his thighs. This day's events could not have gone any better!

He considered the sail to be a God-given blessing for his voyage. If ever he doubted his path before, on this day he knew for certain that he was following the destiny intended for him. Finding the boat was one thing; finding the Norse boys was another. And if all good things came in threes—like the Father, Son and Holy Ghost—then the discovery of the linen sail completed the trilogy.

He could not wait to tell Grier about the sail. He knew in his heart that she would understand about the trinity of events and believe the same way he did: that his journey home was God's plan. She would share his excitement, he was certain of it, because she truly understood him and his need to return to Norway. He imagined her smile and the twinkle of her eyes. He would kiss her well in celebration.

And she would kiss him well in return.

Rydar kicked Salle to a brisk canter, so eager to speak with Grier that he couldn't allow the mare to set her own pace on the road back to the keep. He had not been this optimistic in decades.

Rydar slowed Salle to a trot to cross the wood bridge. Unusual activity around the stable drew his immediate attention and he reined the horse to a walk. Salle began to prance, straining against her bridle. Rydar dismounted and led the skittish animal toward her home, wondering what was happening. Salle whinnied.

The answering call from the stable was loud and urgent, sounding unlike any of the animals that resided there. When Rydar reached the open door, he saw the two huge war horses tied in the stalls. Metal-edged saddles rested on trestles and a man Rydar had never seen before was cleaning them. The gray beast, a stallion, turned toward Salle and called to her again. Salle side-stepped and seemed to hide behind Rydar. She stamped her feet and bumped his back with her long bony nose.

"Who you?" Rydar asked the stranger.

The stocky blond met Rydar's gaze, obviously puzzled at his truncated speech. So Rydar spoke again, with deliberate authority.

"*Mitt navn er Rydar Hansen og jeg er fra Norge! Hvem er deg?*"

The man's mouth worked, but no words of response exited his surprised countenance. Satisfied that he no longer appeared to be an imbecile, Rydar addressed the man in the best Scots English he could muster.

"My name is Rydar Hansen. I from Norway. Who you?"

The man dipped his chin. "Kennan Fraser. Vassal to Lord Andrew Drummond, knight and courtier to King David."

Rydar's brow lifted. "King David of Scotland?"

"Aye. Did ye think 'twas King David of the Bible?" he snorted.

Rydar straightened his six-and-a-half feet of sunburnt muscle and glared down at the servant. He didn't understand all the man's words, but his tone was clearly rude. Rydar thrust Salle's reins toward him.

"Take care my horse."

Startled into compliance, the man accepted Salle's reins, though it was not his job to do so. Rydar spun and stomped toward the keep, vastly irritated and pondering this unwelcome interruption of his plans.

Who was this Lord Andrew? Obviously a wealthy man to judge by his horses and tack. He must be powerful if he was both a knight and a courtier to the King of Scotland. What was he doing visiting a small village like Durness, and a small castle like Grier's? Was Grier in any sort of danger?

Instead of only his hunting dagger, Rydar wished he had his long sword to hand, not resting against the wall of his sleep chamber. He drew a resolute breath and heaved open the door of the keep, having absolutely no idea whether he would face friend or foe once inside.

ᚱᚻ

Grier heard the front door open, but Lord Andrew was in the midst of an impressive tale and she daren't look away. Only when he paused, and his gold-brown gaze lifted over her head, did she turn to see who had entered.

Rydar stood tall in the doorway to the Great Hall. His linen shirt was filthy and one sleeve was ripped. His hose were dusty and stained with pitch. His hair was windblown. His brow burnt red by the sun.

He looked like a rough tradesman, not the intelligent and educated man that he was. Grier needed to assure that Lord Andrew understood Rydar's true nature and position—in defiance of his defiled appearance—before the handsome knight said or did something inappropriate.

"Sir Hansen! I'm sae glad you've returned from your labors!" Grier crossed the room toward him, attempting to reassure him with her tone and her expression.

He did not appear reassured. He frowned at her. "Aye?"

Grier gestured toward her guest, but kept her gaze nailed to Rydar. She spoke clearly so he might understand. "May I present Lord Andrew Drummond, courtier to King David?"

Rydar nodded and glanced at the regally dressed man behind her. "Of Scotland."

Grier gave a puzzled grin. "Well, of course. Where else?"

Rydar's pale green eyes returned to Grier and he looked her over from snood to slippers. He seemed confused. Stunned, even. That might explain his unusual response. And why she felt completely disrobed by his intense perusal.

"Why he here?" he asked, staring hard at her.

"Lord Andrew is assessing the northern lands. After the Death. For the king," Grier stammered. Rydar shrugged. His gaze narrowed and bore into hers.

"Assessing? Well, he is determining our resources..."

Rydar shrugged again. His stare became a glare. Why was he wroth?

Grier searched for simple words to explain. "Resources are our men and our sheep and our cattle... Do ye ken?"

"Aye," he grunted.

Grier turned to Lord Andrew who regarded Rydar with a bemused expression. His consideration shifted to her and one eyebrow quirked in clear question.

"May I present, Sir Rydar Martin Hansen of Green—land. Norway. Of Greenland and Norway." Grier felt her face blaze. She was making a muddle of this. She couldn't even recall all of Rydar's names.

Petter-Edvard.

Shite.

Rydar bowed his chin, but nothing else. He didn't smile. "Pleased to meet you, Lord Andrew."

"The pleasure is mine, Sir Hansen." One corner of Lord Andrew's mouth lifted in obvious amusement. "Of Greenland and Norway."

Grier tensed, horrified at the jibe, but Rydar ignored the slight and addressed her again.

"Bath."

A bath was an excellent idea. "Aye. Of course," she said, relieved. "I'll have Moira order the boys."

"Good." Rydar disappeared from the doorway.

"Shall we wait supper for you?" Grier called after him.

He didn't respond.

Chapter
Twenty-Two

Rydar assured Angus, Fergus and Morris that a cool bath was truly preferable on this warm day. He was already heated from the day's sun, labors and excitement, and he didn't wish to wait for hot water. He intended to return to the Great Hall as quickly as possible.

His first impression of the heavily jeweled Lord Andrew was suspect. Richly dressed and strikingly handsome—so much so that even another man would note it—the knight was smug, obviously accustomed to being the most important man in any given room. Rydar needed to make certain that the man, and his importance to the King of Scotland, were not a danger to Grier.

Grier! He had not recognized her in the Great Hall before she turned around. When he saw her, his breath rushed from his body and he could not command it to return. She was stunning beyond mere words. The brown velvet of her softly clinging gown enhanced the warm tones of her flawless skin. The silver belt rode the top of her hips accentuating her narrow waist. And with her tempestuous ginger-colored hair corralled, her blue eyes, full pink lips and strong cheekbones demanded his complete devotion. She was the most beautiful creature he could imagine. He was completely and utterly hers.

And now he must dress appropriately and dine with Lord Andrew. Rydar took rapid but deliberate care with his appearance, keenly aware that he looked like a common cotter when he was first introduced to the knight. He must alter that impression and quickly, leaving no doubt that he was strong, capable, and willing to protect Grier in any manner required.

But for a moment, Rydar slowed his hasty transformation to consider another side to the shiny gold coin that was Lord Andrew.

Rydar was born into a society of which he was ignorant, but determined somehow to rejoin. He knew little of the etiquette of nobility. The courtier was a powerful man and Rydar might learn quite a lot by observing him. The lessons were needful before he returned to Hansen Hall in Arendal.

Having no mirror in his chamber, Rydar managed the best he could with comb and clothing, and hoped the hurried result was adequate. He rushed down the stone stairs toward the sound of conversation. The rich aromas of supper rumbled his belly.

When he appeared in the doorway of the dining hall cleaned, groomed, and dressed in the blue velvet-and-pearl doublet, dark gray hose and tall leather boots, all conversation halted.

Rydar silently met the widened eyes of everyone gathered there: Logan, Malise, her father, Lord Andrew, and Grier. He straightened his shoulders and strode confidently into the room, refusing to limp in spite of the agonizing pain in his shin.

ᚱᚺ

"I'm sorry I late." Rydar gestured at the bountiful meal spread across the table. "Please, eat."

Logan hopped up from his laird's seat and dragged a heavily carved chair to the table's side. "Sit here, Rydar. Beside Grier."

"Thank you, Logan." Rydar eased into the chair and nodded a reserved greeting across the laden tabletop to Lord Andrew. He felt for Grier's hand under the table and squeezed it; for what reason, he couldn't say. He was simply compelled to do so. When she squeezed back, his world righted and felt rational once again.

"Sir Hansen, the Lady Grier has told me that you've come all the way from Greenland in a very wee boat." Lord Andrew paused in cutting his smoked salmon. His amused consideration of Rydar implied his question.

"Aye." Rydar determined not to say more than necessary until he could thoroughly evaluate the knight.

The courtier waved his knife and changed the direction of his query. "So tell me: how did Greenland fare with the Black Death?"

That shift was interesting. Rydar shook his head. "Is no Black Death in Grønnland."

Lord Andrew sat back, incredulity sculpting his neat, aristocratic features. "And how did Greenland manage to escape a plague that kilt more than half o' Europe, then?"

Rydar took a leisurely bite of his salmon before he answered. "Boats no' come, five or six years. Grønnland is alone, aye?"

"What boats are those?"

"Boats from Norway." Rydar sipped his wine. He lifted his goblet in salute to Logan and changed his own direction, hoping to knock the knight off balance. "Is good, Logan. Very good."

"Thank you," Logan answered, looking pleased.

Rydar faced Grier. "Salmon is best," he complimented.

Lord Andrew grunted, obviously irritated at Rydar's cryptic answers and lack of predictable attention. Grier blushed, smiled, and kicked him under the table. Hard.

"The boats from Norway brought your supplies, did they no'?" Grier's blue eyes darkened in warning.

"Aye," he said. Then to placate her he added, "But with no boats, Grønnland dies."

"And that's why you sailed for Norway." Grier prompted.

"Aye. In a very wee boat." Rydar mocked Andrew's words, risking another kick from Grier. Before she could retaliate, he gestured toward Logan with his fork, shifting the diners' attention. "And near die in Balnakeil Bay."

Lord Andrew's eyes jumped to Logan.

"We—that is Grier and myself—pulled them from the sea in the midst of a wickit storm," Logan explained to the knight. "If it weren't for Grier's considerable skills, Rydar might have faced the same fate as his shipmate—God sain the poor man's soul." He crossed himself, as did Grier.

"Rydar was fair battered and his leg was broke," Grier interjected.

Lord Andrew scrutinized Rydar then, as if searching for remnants of injury. Rydar held the nobleman's gaze while he slowly chewed another bite of smoked salmon. He suddenly felt as though he was in a game of chess with the knight. If Grier was the coveted queen, what piece was he?

And did it matter? Even a pawn might take a queen if it plays well.

The knight's expression softened at the new information concerning their appealing hostess. His golden gaze abandoned Rydar to caress her instead, and he pursued the angle with obvious interest.

"Is that so, my lady? Ye're a healer?" he asked Grier.

"She's a fine healer, she is." Logan grinned at his cousin. "There's none better."

Andrew gave Grier a slow, sultry smile that twisted Rydar's gut.

Truthfully, any man with a pulse would be intrigued by Grier's knowledgeable conversation, warm hospitality, and the way her firm curves moved beneath the soft velvet of her gown. She was enchanting.

But it grated on Rydar to watch Lord Andrew respond like any man. He knew he must hide both his affection for Grier and his distrust of the courtier. So he unclenched his jaw and forced his tightly fisted hands to remain below the table's top.

Grier dipped her chin and her cheeks flushed beautifully at Logan's praise. Then she blinked up at Rydar. Her sapphire eyes begged his cooperation. Gazing into their twin seas helped him relax, though it also encouraged a too-familiar twinge in his groin.

Lord Andrew frowned. "How long past was this rescue?"

Grier paused, and then turned to face Lord Andrew again. "The middle of May. It might be eight weeks now."

"Your leg is well?" he asked Rydar.

"Aye." The last thing Rydar would confess to this man was the residual pain that plagued him daily. "I very strong."

Lord Andrew squinted at him. "And ye speak Scots?"

"I learn."

"So quickly?"

One corner of Rydar's mouth lifted. "I very cannie."

Lord Andrew nodded his narrow-eyed acknowledgement. "What will you do now?"

Rydar hesitated and his smirk disappeared. "I... go."

"Where?"

He couldn't face Grier now; she mustn't see his desperate longing. He kept his gaze fixed on Andrew. "Norway."

"How?"

"I finish boat."

"When?"

Rydar drew a breath to answer, but before he was able Logan injected, "No' until after our wedding, of course!"

Malise smiled at Rydar and spoke for the first time since he entered the room. "You will stay, Sir Hansen, will you no'? Logan wishes you to be there. As do I."

"Aye, Hansen." Logan took Malise's hand before pressing his case. "I hoped ye'd do me the honor of standing as my witness."

Rydar was pinned. He pressed his lips into a semblance of a smile and nodded slowly at the young couple. Though he hadn't thought it through, he truly couldn't leave before seeing Logan, his generous host, rescuer and friend, married. That would be rude. Of that much he was sure.

"Aye," he said. He daren't look at Grier, afraid of revealing how much he desired her company on his journey. "I go after wedding, of course."

"Good!" Malise grinned. "I know Aunt Margoh will want you there as well!"

Rydar wondered if it was his imagination, or if Grier stiffened at the mention of Margoh's name. He bounced a quick glance to see if anyone at the table seemed to notice. No one else was looking at her. It occurred to him, then, that he hadn't answered Margoh's request to sail to Norway with him. Time grew short; he must decide.

"This little castle is interesting." Andrew's words jerked Rydar's attention back into the room. "But other than providing a deterrent to invading sailors from the northern lands," he smiled condescendingly at Rydar, "how else might these lands serve King David?"

Another change of direction. Rydar waited to see who might speak first.

"Three months back and we'd be in a sorry state for sure," Logan began. "But Sir Hansen managed to bring together the remaining merchants of Durness for a Mercat Fair."

"And the surrounding lands, do no' forget!" Grier added.

Rydar startled. Did he hear pride in her tone? Was that over him?

Logan nodded. "Aye, that he did."

The knight didn't look at Rydar. "And this was successful?"

"Very!" Logan enthused. "We had thirty-two staunds. And considering how many are gone now, that's a right fine number."

Rydar felt his cheeks warming with embarrassment and shame. In truth, he had not helped create the fair simply to benefit the town, as Logan made it seem. Besides the unpredictable hunting, the mercat was the only path that he had yet come across to fund his journey. Helping the merchants of Durness was simply an added bounty.

Lord Andrew drained his wine goblet and set it carefully in front of his platter. "But Sir Rydar is taking his boat and going to Norway," he said deliberately.

"And the Mercat Fair will return. I'll see to it, myself. It was a whappin success for everyone!" Logan answered. His forceful declamation relieved Rydar's uneasy conscience a bit.

"That's braw, Logan. King David thanks ye for your loyal support." The courtier considered Grier, then. He looked intently at her. "And what of you, my lady?"

"And what *of* me?" Grier asked; her impudent tone reflected her visible confusion.

Now Rydar's attention was nailed to the man. This would be the knight's pivotal move. His attempt to corner the queen.

"Your laird will marry and bring new life into the castle. Your guest returns to his home, but not before creating a mercat to awaken local commerce after the Death."

"Aye." Grier glanced at Logan and Rydar, then faced Andrew again. "And?"

The knight leaned his elbows on the table and laced his fingers. The way his eyes traveled over Grier made Rydar wish to challenge the man with his long sword before the next course was served. He gripped the arms of his chair to hold himself in his seat.

"And what have you to offer your king, Lady Grier?" Andrew murmured.

Grier shoved her hands into her lap and straightened in her seat. "My loyalty, of course, Lord Andrew."

"Is there no' more?" the courtier pressed.

Grier lifted her chin. "I served him well during the Death and beyond. He has plenty more subjects now, than he'd have without my assistance, and 'tis true!" she exclaimed. "What else should he require of me?"

Lord Andrew stared hard at Grier, his expression unreadable. Grier didn't move. Logan cleared his throat. Rydar allowed a half smile, proud of the lively woman beside him.

"Ye've considerable strength, Lady Grier." Andrew leaned back in his chair. "I think there's much more ye might offer. I shall have to remain here until I discover exactly what that might entail."

He addressed Logan, though he still stared at Grier. "Will that suit you, Laird MacDavid?"

Logan nodded. "Aye, of course, Lord Andrew. As ye wish."

There it was: the knight's move. And the queen was adeptly cornered.

Then Rydar silently cursed his boat—and his destiny—for requiring him to leave the castle every day. He cursed his limited language here. He cursed Grier's beguiling beauty, her strength, and her friendship. He cursed Lord Andrew for his obvious interest in her.

And above all, he cursed his unwillingness to risk her prospects and ask her outright to journey with him.

ᚱᚺ

Grier undressed in her room, amazed that her limbs held the strength to do so. She expected to simply crumple to her sheets once her duties as hostess were, at the last, completed. Lord Andrew was comfortably ensconced in the master chamber. Kennan had Rydar's former pallet in the Great Hall. On the morrow the pair would ride forth and explore the town of Durness. Once they assessed the village, they would ride further afield seeking farms and crofters. No holding was too small, apparently, to escape King David's attention.

And Andrew would stay to press his cause with her, whatever that cause may be.

Grier climbed into her bed and lay back on her pillow. She closed her eyes and thought of how Rydar looked when he appeared in the doorway for supper. His gold-streaked hair was combed and

tucked behind his ears, and hung below his jaw. He wore her
father's best doublet, the light blue velvet that was pleated with
pearls; the color turned his light green eyes nearly turquoise.

Standing so very tall in the dining room entry, he was more
magnificent than she had yet seen him. Strong and healthy, with
good color. His hard-muscled legs were visible through the tight
knit hose and his broad shoulders strained the fabric of the tunic. As
he sat down beside her, she smelt the flowered soap.

When he reached for her hand, she felt whole. Her heart jigged
in her chest and her belly warmed. Rydar was the most compelling
man she had ever met. She loved him completely and wished to tell
him so.

Perhaps she should. Perhaps it was time.

A scratching at her door made her spirit sag. She was far too
exhausted to attend a birth, that being the usual call in mid-night.
But duty determinedly pried her eyes open and obligation shoved
her out of bed.

"Coming," she mumbled, reaching for the door's latch.

Rydar stood outside her door. The doublet gone, his untied
linen shirt billowed atop his braies and hose. His feet were bare. As
his gaze raked over her body, she realized that she wore nothing but
her shift. Whirling toward her bed, she yanked a blanket and
wrapped it around her.

"What do ye need? Are ye ill?" she managed. Her cheeks must
be glowing they were so hot.

"I come in?" he whispered, and shot a meaningful look toward
the master chamber.

"Aye," she whispered in return and backed away from the
portal.

Rydar slipped into the room and silently closed the door. He
moved toward Grier's open window where the pale summer's night
sky glowed a hazy pinkish gray. She followed, curious.

"What is it, Rydar?"

He frowned a little. "Lord Andrew? Might no' be good, aye?"

Grier was surprised at that assessment. "What do you mean?"

"He is sae… uh… *skitt!*" Rydar combed his fingers through his
hair and tried again. "Smiles too much, aye? He thinks he kens too
much."

"Oh! Too sure of himself, is he?" Grier tried not to grin.

"Aye." Rydar's face twisted in frustration. "He is... ruffian."

"Ruffian?" Grier repeated in disbelief. "No, Rydar, Lord Andrew is the hintside of a ruffian, I assure you! He's a courtier of the king."

"No' ruffian in what he does." Rydar waved his hands as he tried to explain himself. "Ruffian in what he brings. To you."

Grier tugged at the blanket, though it sagged lower on her body and covered less of her. "Ruffian in what he brings to me... What do ruffians bring? Danger?" Her eyes widened. "Do you think Lord Andrew is dangerous?"

"No' to all," Rydar clarified. "To you."

"Me?" Grier gazed up into his eyes. In the dim light they were unusually dark and intense. He stood close to her and she could feel the warmth of his sun-burnt skin. She still smelt the flower soap on him. "How is he a danger to me?" she whispered.

Rydar's gaze fell down her body. He slowly lifted a hand and cupped one breast that the blanket had abandoned. His thumb brushed its tip through her gown, setting it on fire.

"You sae beautiful. He takes you," he murmured.

Grier froze at Rydar's touch. Her heart exploded and she couldn't breathe. She let go of the blanket and it tumbled around her ankles.

Rydar's gaze met hers then. He wasn't smiling; he looked angry.

"You think I'm beautiful?" she rasped.

"Aye." The word was choked.

Grier threw her arms around Rydar. The winey taste of his tongue intoxicated her. He lifted her off the ground and she wrapped her legs around his hips without thinking about it. His heat was caught between them, hard and damp against the fabric of her shift. A fluid urgency spread outward from that spot and set her aflame. His deep, soft moan rumbled in her ear and she answered with one of her own. Her body demanded that she take him to her bed.

Now.

"Rydar..." she murmured against his lips.

He suddenly lifted her away from him, almost dropping her on the floor. She tripped on the blanket and staggered back. He grabbed her elbow to keep her from falling.

"*Å min Gud!*" He let go of her and backed away.

"Rydar, wait…" Grier pleaded.

"No!" He splayed his hands in front of his chest. "I no' a ruffian. I no' take you."

"But—"

"No, Grier!" he growled. He truly was angry now. His eyes were black holes and his body vibrated with wrath. He jabbed himself with a thumb. Each word came out louder than the one before it. "I better than that!"

Grier grabbed the window's ledge. She shook with desire and desperate disappointment, and determined not to stare at the stiff appendage tenting Rydar's braies.

He came to warn her of a danger and he refused to become that same danger to her. He was right; he acted the gentleman.

What might he do if she professed her love for him?

"Rydar," she began. Her nerves failed and the words strangled her.

He narrowed his eyes. "Grier."

"I—I have something to tell you…"

Rydar stiffened. "And I you."

Grier blinked. "What?"

Rydar's mouth twitched and he took several breaths as though to speak. His hands moved to his hips and his brows bunched. When he finally spoke, she had to strain to hear him.

"I find Rabbie's sail."

Grier's legs buckled. Defeated, she sank to the floor in a boneless heap of body and blanket. She commanded her lungs to inflate, though her tightening ribs tried to prevent it. She stared, unseeing, at the wavering floorboards of her chamber.

"Oh." She tried to swallow, but there was no moisture in her mouth. "Good."

Rydar knelt in front of her, too far away for her to reach him. "I want to tell you and I come, but Lord Andrew…" his voice faded.

"Aye," she grunted. Everything was wrong, now. Horribly, dreadfully, appallingly wrong.

"You tell me something?" he prodded, his tone so tender that it shredded her soul. She wanted to scratch his eyes out in return.

"I, uh, cannot bring your dinner. Tomorrow," Grier stumbled through the first thing that occurred to her to say. "I must be, um, available. To Lord Andrew."

Rydar leaned away from her. "Aye."

"I'll send it with Moira," she promised. "You'll no' go hungry."

"Thank you." Rydar murmured. He climbed slowly to his feet and held out one hand. "Come, Grier," he whispered.

Grier shook her head. "You go on back to your room," she said, forcing herself to look at him. His beautiful face held a mix of concern and regret. He must be sorry he had touched her.

She felt for her crucifix, and knew part of her was dying. "I've some—praying—to do."

Rydar's hand fell limply to his side. He stared at her as if he wished to say something more, but Grier was frightened of what that something might be.

"Goodnight, Rydar," she said before he could speak again. "Sleep well."

"Goodnight," he answered stiffly, adding, "my lady."

Chapter
Twenty-Three

July 12, 1354

H eavy-bottomed clouds hovered over the eastern horizon, the last remnants of three gray days of soft, steady rain. Grier walked along the bluff behind the castle, enjoying the afternoon's sunshine. She hadn't been to Durness, nor to Rydar's boat, since Lord Andrew arrived. Her hours were filled with preparations for the sort of service that a courtier and knight of his status expected.

Each morning after breaking their fast, Andrew and Kennan rode off on their great destriers dressed in their fine velvets and armed with heavily jeweled weapons. The pair was impressive and intimidating, which Grier assumed was their intent. They returned at the end of the day with word of who was expected to join them in the keep for the formal meal that evening.

Then Lord Andrew would retire to the master chamber to change for supper. Grier made certain he had warm water and fresh towels, that his clothes were laundered, his fire was lit and his bedding aired. She worked with Moira's mother on the daily menu and helped the older woman prepare the food. Grier didn't wish her hospitality to be found lacking in any way.

Lord Andrew invited the most prosperous and influential men from the surrounding lands to dine at the castle. Uncomplimentary of the carefully crafted dishes that were presented, Grier bit back her desire to point out the special herbs used, or the sauces created to enhance the meat or fish. The courtier was obviously accustomed to rich food and didn't mark it.

Instead, he spent the mealtime asking question after question about the economic status of his guests' particular holdings.

"How many acres do you own?" Lord Andrew asked each man who sat at her table. "Are they being worked to their best advantage?"

"Your Lordship is aware of the Death," they would answer. "So much land lies fallow now, there simply aren't enough able bodies to till the soil…" Or shepherd the livestock. Or clear the land. Or accomplish whatever tasks remained incomplete.

Lord Andrew was unmoved. "Surely there are those looking for work, are there not? Displaced individuals—or orphans—who must sustain themselves."

"My Lord," Logan interjected. "The dearth of laborers, if any are to be found at all, has sent wages too high for the common estate holder."

Lord Andrew sipped his wine and set it carefully aside. Each evening, he placed the same charge on the guests: "Those who have serfs must no longer allow them to purchase their freedom. They must remain where they are and labor as they always have."

This declamation was met with uneasy glances. Silence reigned until someone gathered enough courage to say, "They will no' stay. They've gone to where they're paid more than I can give them."

"Or they've claimed land that's been abandoned for themselves," Logan added.

Lord Andrew stood and circled the table. Hands clasped behind his back, brows drawn together and lips pressed in thought, he seemed to be considering what he heard. But by the third night, Grier knew that what came next was a carefully crafted speech, one she had memorized by now.

"Gentlemen—for indeed, we are an assemblage of gently born men, are we not? Perhaps, living so far north in this exceptionally beautiful country, you are not aware of Scotland's overall condition. Our own King David II languishes in the Tower of London where he has been held prisoner these past eight years. Our government, its body decimated by plague and lacking leadership, flounders in its attempt to maintain order."

Pause, take a sip of wine.

"Edinburgh's businesses are disrupted. Debtors have died and their bankrupt creditors find there is simply no one left to collect from. Construction has halted and guilds have lost their craftsmen."

Grip the shoulders of the most vocal man in the room.

"Do I paint a bleak portrait? Aye, I do. I'm afraid 'tis a portrait startling in its reality." Give the shoulders a shake. "So what are we—the powerful men of this land—to do? How might we restore Scotland to her rightful glory?"

Grier couldn't meet the eyes of her guests; to a man, they stared downward, not willing to give the unpalatable answer. She couldn't blame them. Every Scot left alive was struggling to find footing in a demolished society that—obviously—no longer operated under past restraints.

Besides that, rumors abounded of a ransom payment to free their king from England's King Edward. The assembled landowners kent that much of what profit they still made might be claimed for that purpose.

Lord Andrew always ended his speech the same way: "Have no fear, my lords. Our beloved Scotland will survive this trial. Her sons are loyal and generous men, whose willing sacrifices always see her through."

He lifted his chalice. "I give you King David!"

Every man present rose to toast the king. After all, they weren't treasonous. Only cautious, and standing on the edge of ruin. Smiling, Lord Andrew encouraged everyone to sit and continue to enjoy the repast.

No matter how many joined them for dinner, Grier noticed that Lord Andrew always sat himself directly opposite her. He watched her intently throughout the meal. His golden brown eyes and sultry smile made her heart pound. Many times she was so unnerved that she struggled just to swallow her food. The knight was regally handsome, charismatic and intelligent in conversation, and obviously quite interested in her as a woman.

What kept her balanced was the presence of the man who always sat by her side.

Lord Andrew may face her, but Rydar flanked her. His lengthy bulk and quiet dignity restored her calm. So many times when she found herself on the edge of irritation she turned to look at him and his comprehending smile soothed her. She relied on the Norseman to get her through the nightly formal occasions without voicing strident opinions that might challenge or offend the knight—and by extension, her king.

Stretching in the balmy afternoon, Grier smelt the salt of the sea. A trio of noisy gulls circled overhead, sparring and bickering with each other. The bright summer sun warmed Grier's back and thighs while the breeze cooled her. She untied her hair and combed her fingers through it, lifting it off her neck. Sporadic gusts enticed her heavy curls to play around her shoulders and tickle her cheeks.

She smiled. *Mam.*

All of her life Grier loved watching the sea. She loved the constantly churning surf with its shifting blues and foaming whites, and the way the sun spattered it with diamonds. Standing on the bluff under an endless sky, Grier's spirit was renewed.

A movement by the castle wall pulled her attention. A tall, broad-shouldered figure clad in a pleated linen shirt, dark gray hose and high black boots strode along the bluff toward her, moving much like the warhorse he rode. Suddenly self-conscious about her casual appearance, Grier smoothed her wind-tossed curls and retied them with the leather thong.

ᚱᚺ

Rydar had hunted on two of the three days of rain, using the steady showers to mask both his sound and his smell. He was not as successful as he would have been, had he kept his mind on the hunt, and not on the irritating presence of the knight in the keep.

When Salle whinnied, Rydar paused on the middle deck of his boat and wiped sweat from his brow. He pulled a lungful of the damp afternoon air and smelt the salt of the sea. Squinting against the afternoon's sunshine, he faced the mare's direction. Moira dismounted from Raven and approached the boat with the same basket that she had carried their food in for the last three days. Since Lord Andrew arrived in Durness, Grier had not come to them.

The Norse boys saw Moira and clambered loudly over the side of the vessel, each claiming to be hungrier than the others. At least the food was abundant and tasty, even if the courier disappointed. In actuality, the boys weren't disappointed. They scampered around, obviously vying for the giggling maid's favor.

Rydar waved a greeting and forced a smile. After the night Lord Andrew arrived, and Grier kissed him so passionately that Rydar very nearly lost control and took her to her bed, he hadn't found an opportunity to speak to her alone. He worried that he had frightened her.

He knew he frightened himself. He very nearly tossed her on her back, pushed her knees to her shoulders and thrust himself so far into her that they melted into one body.

It required three fitful nights of tossing in his own bed for Rydar to face the truth: he truly was deeply, desperately and devotedly in love with Grier. She embodied everything he hoped for in a woman. She was intelligent and educated. She was capable and fearless. She was confident and strong of character.

And she was beautiful. Her copper curls slid over her shoulders like liquid fire. Her blue eyes drowned him like the North Sea had failed to. Her narrow waist, firm bosom, and rounded arse begged to be touched.

Even now, standing on the deck with the sail puddled at his feet, the spar swinging around the mast, sunburnt, windblown and with bits of wood stuck to his skin, he stiffened thinking of her.

"When might I tell her?" he mumbled, brushing wood chips from his cheeks. He tried to comb his fingers through his hair, but couldn't get through the wind-tied knots. His impatient belly rumbled, so he gave up and moved to the boat's edge to climb down.

Logan MacDavid and Malise McKay would marry in eight days. On the ninth day, he was free to sail home. That didn't leave him much time.

"I'll tell her tonight, though I won't ask her to sail with me. I'll leave the asking to her," he said to himself as he dropped to the sand. "But I will tell her how I feel. Tonight."

ᚱᚺ

As Grier corralled her hair, Andrew loosed his. Black locks pooled on his shoulders like wet ink and dripped down the sides of the beard-shadowed jaw that Kennan shaved clean each morning. The summer's wanton breeze pressed his shirt against him, and Grier could see the bulges and grooves of his chest through the cream-colored fabric. He was a splendid example of raw masculinity choosing to be controlled by convention. She had no doubt he was a powerful and unrestrained implement in battle.

"You've returned early this day, Lord Andrew," Grier said. "Have ye finally examined all parts of our fair village?"

The knight's laugh displayed a perfect row of top teeth and an incomplete row of bottom teeth. Lost a couple of those in a battle, he'd said at breakfast the first morn.

"Not quite all," he answered. "But what's left to examine lies closer to the keep."

Grier frowned a little. "And what is that, Lord Andrew?"

The courtier sank to the sandy, sea-grass covered bluff and stretched out his long legs. He patted the ground beside him. "Will you join me, Lady Grier? 'Tis too beautiful a day to waste standing behind stone walls and wooden doors."

Grier lowered to her knees, curious.

"First of all, it's my wish that ye'd address me less formally."

"Aye? And how should I call you, then?" Grier asked.

"Well, my family called me Drew when I was but a sapling. Those close to me still do."

Grier could not imagine that the massive warrior ever resembled a 'sapling' and the idea that the man had a family and friends startled her for some reason.

"Ye have family?" she blurted.

Andrew lifted one brow in amusement. "Aye, my lady. I did no' spring forth from the ground, fully formed and astride my horse. My existence came about in the usual way."

Grier's face heated but she smiled, relieved that he wasn't offended. He leaned a little closer to her.

"Will you call me Drew as well, then? I'd be honored to count ye among my friends." Lord Andrew's voice rumbled softly, blending with the voice of the sea. The notion that Lord Andrew might use such a request to lull her to his side for some political reason did nudge Grier. But she daren't refuse him. And what was his side, precisely?

"Nay, Lord—Drew. The honor of your friendship is mine," she demurred.

Drew nodded his thanks and turned his gaze toward Balnakeil

Bay and the sea beyond. "Tell me the history of this castle. Has it always been in your family?"

Grier shook her head. "These lands were given to my grandfather by Robert Bruce."

Drew did not appear surprised. "And before that?"

"Oh! Well... before that, it was a bit run down. I'm afraid I have little knowledge of those days."

Golden eyes returned to hers. "Before that, this was Scotland's farthest northwest defense against the Vikings. Many battles were fought here. It's said the sands were soaked red with blood."

Grier shuddered at the idea of her pristine white chyngell being the site of such carnage. "I'm glad those times are past," she murmured.

"Are they?" Drew challenged.

"What do you mean?"

"If I'm no' mistaken, ye're aiding a Norseman of Viking heritage in the keep yourself."

Grier scoffed. "Rydar is no' a Viking! He's merely a man who's trying to get back to his home."

"And he'll reach there with complete knowledge of these fortifications, will he no'?" Drew pressed.

"Are ye thinking he'll return with a fleet and attack us?" Grier could not imagine such a turn of events.

"It's been done, my lady. Many a time."

Grier shook her head. "I've come to know the man well. He's strong and capable and intelligent and determined. But he's no' violent. He only wishes to reclaim what is his. And what is his is in Norway."

"Why are ye no' married?"

"To him?" she gasped, wondering if her desires were evident to everyone. Panic surged through her at the idea. Had Rydar noticed? And then ignored the knowledge?

Drew grinned, obviously amused by her misunderstanding. "Married to anyone," he clarified.

"Ah." Though momentarily relieved, the conversation was now heading in another uncomfortable direction. "Twas the Death, of course."

"How?" Drew asked softly. He was quite close to her now. She could see herself reflected in his changeling gold-green-brown eyes, and framed by his thick black lashes.

Grier swallowed her past sorrow. It was time to look forward. "I was betrothed thrice in six years, but none survived long enough to stand beside me at the altar."

Drew's head tilted and his gaze traversed her features. "How long past was that?"

"It's over two years, now, since Aleck died."

"And no man has won your heart since?" He stroked her cheek with one warm finger and then ran its tip behind her ear. "I find that hard to believe, Lady Grier."

She fell silent, unable to think of an appropriate response. She had never done well at fabricating and was certain Drew would see through any attempt at deception. Yet she couldn't tell him the truth, either, since her heart was set on a man who may not care.

She settled for, "There are precious few available men left in Durness."

"It might well be, my lady," Drew tipped her face to meet his, "that you should look beyond Durness to find your heart's desire."

Shocked, Grier realized he was going to kiss her. Her eyes burst wide open and she refused to look at his mouth. She leaned back ever so slightly, scrambling for an excuse—any excuse—to avoid the encounter. Terrified of what his kiss might mean, she held her breath unaware.

Drew paused. His brows pulled together. "Do you fear me, Grier?"

"N-no…" she stammered.

Chapter
Twenty-Four

W hat about tonight?"

Rydar whirled around. Margoh walked toward him, her hips swinging wide. The low neckline of her lavender gown was cut straight across and a ribbon tied the fabric below her bosom. Blond brows gathered over gray-blue eyes.

"Who were you talking to?"

Rydar shrugged in an offhand manner. "Myself, only."

"And what about tonight?" Margoh prodded as she stopped in front of him.

"I was thinking that Logan and Malise will marry in just eight days. I need to speak with Logan as to what my responsibilities are as his witness. That's all." Rydar was pleased with his impromptu explanation, adding, "I'm unfamiliar with the Scotch customs."

"Oh." Margoh glanced at the three young men crowding around Moira. "Where is Grier?"

"Lord Andrew keeps her occupied," Rydar said as casually as he could manage, though the thought raked painful gouges through his gut. "There is apparently much to do when one houses a guest of such high rank."

Margoh smirked. "He's a very handsome and very powerful houseguest. Wealthy, too."

"So?"

"What woman wouldn't choose to spend as much time with him as she could?" Margoh's smirk tightened. "Are they often in the castle alone?"

Rydar rolled his eyes. "And how would I know that? I'm here all the day!"

Margoh lowered her voice to a suggestive level that slid neatly between his doubts. "How does she look at him? How does he look at her?"

"That's enough."

"Why, Rydar? What business is it of yours if she's bedding the knight?"

"I said that's enough," he grumbled. Though certain she wasn't taking the courtier to her bed, Grier might be considering the man. From the looks he gave her across their meals, the courtier was definitely considering her. Rydar resolved to let nothing stand in his way tonight. He would speak his heart to Grier before it grew too late.

"Is there something you wanted, Margoh?"

Her voice lightened some. "Yes. But have you eaten?"

Rydar shook his head and looked toward the feeding frenzy that surrounded Moira.

"Have you left me any food?" he bellowed. Looking guilty, the three boys backed away and sat on a sea-smoothed log with their victuals.

Moira hurried over with the basket. "I've saved yours specially. It's under the cloth."

"Thank you, Moira." Rydar lifted the cloth and retrieved a warm meat pastry, a chunk of cheese, an onion and partial loaf of bread.

"I've ale for you as well," the maid said. "It's tied to my saddle."

"More thanks, Moira." Rydar smiled. At some time in the past two months, the girl apparently decided he wasn't going to eat her alive after all and now treated him quite cordially.

"Sit down, Rydar," Margoh urged. "I'll bring the ale."

She returned with the ale pot and sat close beside him. When his meal was half swallowed and the ale half gone Margoh spoke again, asking, "Have you decided yet?"

Rydar needn't ask to what she referred. The problem was, he had not decided.

"We must understand each other clearly, Margoh," he began. "What are you asking me for?"

"Only passage." Margoh's voice pulled tight. "I don't wish to stay here in Scotland. I want to go to Norway."

"You *do* have family there?" Rydar pressed.

Margoh nodded. "In Áslo. My husband's family."

"And they will welcome you? Provide for you?"

"I believe—yes." Margoh shifted her seated stance. "Yes."

"I'm only going as far as Arendal," Rydar warned.

"I know."

"I don't know how much farther it is to Áslo."

Margoh considered the three young men sitting nearby. "They will take me."

Rydar startled. "Have you asked them?"

"Not yet." She faced him again, her eyes glittering. "But I have money. And they have need."

That was most likely true, Rydar realized. "What of Hanne?" he asked.

Margoh's lips pressed to a brief line. Disgust radiated from her. "My sister believes she is old and her life is over. If she wishes to play dead, then I'll leave her to do so in peace!" she spat. "I still have much to offer and more of life to experience!"

"She knows of your plan?"

Margoh nodded. Some of her ire faded from view. "She does. She thinks I'm a fool."

"Why is that?"

Margoh faced him straight on. She gathered her knees under her and her eyes widened a little as she stared at him. Rydar was half afraid she was about to hurl herself at him.

"Because I know I can find love again," she claimed. Her voice was low and husky. The neckline of her gown gaped some. Rydar yanked his gaze back up to her face.

"In Áslo," he repeated with deliberate finality.

Margoh blinked slowly. "Somewhere," she whispered. "With someone."

Rydar shoved the last bit of bread and cheese into his mouth and wiped his hands on his hose. He stood and offered his hand to

Margoh.

"I must get back to work," he told her. "We're attaching the sail today."

Margoh took his hand, but didn't stand right away. "You haven't answered me, Rydar." She pulled herself up slowly and leaned forward. "I have offered you payment. Will you collect?"

Rydar felt his face heat with irritation. "No, Margoh."

"Never?" She moved a little, rubbing against him. "Please don't say never, Rydar."

Rydar stepped back. "I must get back to work."

"Am I going with you?"

Silence sailed between them as solid as the boat itself. What if Grier decided to come with him? How would she feel if Margoh was on the boat? Well, there were two sleeping cabins on the middle deck; one for each woman, should it come to that. And each one would know her place in his life before they sailed. He'd make absolutely certain of it.

One would be his passenger, the other his passion.

The decision was made. "I suppose so."

Margoh wrapped her arms around him. "Thank you, Rydar. I am very, *very* grateful." She lifted her face, waiting for a kiss.

The easiest way out of the awkward moment was to plant a quick peck on her brow. "Good. Now go."

ᚱᚾ

After a couple hours' labor, the spar and mast were ready to be connected to the sail. Rydar and the boys debated who should climb the mast to string up the sail but Kristofer solved the argument by simply shimmying up the pole while the others talked. Once the young man was atop, Rydar tossed him the rope. He strung it through the iron pulley at the apex of the mast and dropped the end down. Rydar began to hoist the sail.

The wind had been a capricious guest all day, but now it was absent and the sail hung limp. All the men watched as the huge panel of white linen rose higher and higher. The sun shone through it, making it translucent. It was hard to imagine that something so ethereal in appearance was strong enough to drag the boat hundreds of miles across the open sea.

When the sail reached the top of the mast, a cry of victory erupted from the four. Rydar tied the sail's rope to an iron brace that was fixed securely to the outer wall of the sleeping cabins.

"And there's a sight to be seen, boys!" he shouted, giddy with the knowledge that his journey couldn't be stopped now. The boat was completed but for finishing touches. Kristofer began his monkey-like descent down the mast. Lars stood on the middle deck and Gavin stood on the upper deck. Both boys beamed at Rydar.

The sail began to undulate from the top down. Caught in a small breeze, it lifted slightly, then drooped. Rydar heard a noise he knew he should recognize, but his recognition came too late.

The hiss of wind through stiff sea grass was upon them quickly. The sail snapped open, its creamy smooth belly suddenly bulging. It pushed the untethered spar around the mast with astonishing speed.

The horizontal pole swung across the middle deck propelled by the sail, the wind, and its own tree-trunk weight. Alarm shot arrows through Rydar's chest and sapped the strength from his limbs.

"Look out!" he shouted, though he knew it wouldn't save Lars from being pinned against the rail.

The thick pop of Lars' arm breaking made Rydar's knees wobble. The young man loosed a scream that would banish a banshee.

Rydar felt like he was swimming through the air as he moved across the deck. He tugged at the spar, jerking it away. Gavin jumped to tie it down. When the spar released him, Lars looked at his mangled limb and his face contorted into disbelieving shock. His eyes rolled back and he slumped to the deck in a ragged, bleeding heap.

Rydar shifted instantaneously to captain, taking charge and barking orders.

"Come here! Come here!" He motioned to Kristofer. "Help me lay him out straight!"

The young man did so, but then sat down hard on the wood, staring at the piece of bone that protruded from his younger brother's shattered arm.

"Gavin!" Rydar hollered. This was no time for shock—they must act quickly to save Lars.

"Sir?" White-faced, Gavin appeared beside him.

"Ride to the castle and bring Lady Grier! Quickly! Take Salle and whip her to death if you must, but bring the lady and bring her now!" Rydar demanded. "GO!"

Gavin didn't hesitate. He vaulted over the edge of the boat and was gone.

ᚱ ᚺ

Andrew's lids lowered over his eyes in a sleepy, sensual way. "Certainly you have kissed a man before, have you no'?"

"Well, yes…" Grier admitted.

The tip of his nose brushed hers; his parted lips were only a breath away. "And, so?"

"I—it's only that—I mean…" No good reason came to her mind, which merely conjured the image of Rydar's lean bearded face and pale green eyes, that not in any way helpful in this particular situation. "What do you—"

A desperate shout from the keep interrupted them. Grier turned toward her salvation.

"Lady Grier! Come quick! There's been an accident!" Moira screamed. "At the boat!"

Grier moved before Moira finished calling her. Jumping to her feet, she hiked her skirt way above acceptability and ran toward the keep as fast as she was able. Her heart rammed her ribs and blood roared in her ears, urging her on.

Please, God, do no' let it be Rydar!

Moira disappeared through the castle gate.

Grier ran over the wood bridge, past the gate, into the kitchen, and through the keep to the front door. Gavin sat outside on the steps with his face between his knees and Moira was admonishing him to keep it there. Salle panted in the yard, head down and sweat foaming over her flanks.

Grier dropped to the step below the boy. "Gavin! What happened?" she cried, unable to stay calm.

The young man raised his head, his face a distressing shade of gray. "Twas an accident. The wind caught the sail and spun the spar. None of us could catch it…"

"And?" Grier knew she sounded hysterical. She didn't care.

"And it broke his arm. Bad. The bone came through." Gavin's eyes widened abruptly. He turned aside and vomited on the step.

Grier leapt out of the way.

"Moira! Get my basket!" she shouted. The maid straightened and hurried into the keep. Grier resisted the aggravated desire to shake Gavin until she learnt what she needed to know. Her terrified stomach threatened to mimic his.

"Whose arm was caught?" she demanded, even though the boy was not yet recovered. "Whose!"

Gavin wiped his mouth on his sleeve, swallowed roughly and coughed. "Lars," he squawked.

Hot relief rushed through Grier, with guilt close on its heels. Her arms and legs tingled with the conflicting emotions. She drew a deep breath to steady her nerves and turned to Salle. The mare was too winded to carry her back to Durness quickly enough. For all Grier knew, Lars could be bleeding to death. Moira thrust her basket in her face, reclaiming her attention.

"Is Raven in the stable?" Grier pressed. "I must go quickly. The boy might—" She caught Gavin's horrified gaze and stopped. "I must go as quickly as possible."

A deep voice behind her responded, "I'll take you."

Drew leapt past her and bellowed toward the stable, "My horse! NOW!"

Kennan ran from the stable, leading Drew's gray stallion. In her fear, Grier had forgotten the knight's presence, but at this moment he was her hero. He mounted the prancing warhorse and reached down for Grier's hand. He lifted her without visible effort and set her in front of him.

"Hold your basket, and I'll hold you!" Drew commanded. His arms circled her and he kicked the steed into motion.

Grier leaned against the knight, eyes squeezed shut, momentarily afraid for her life. The animal beneath her shot forward in a ground-devouring gate. Grier risked opening her eyes, but their speed blurred everything they passed. She tried without success to relax in the steely arms that held her, keenly aware of how secure she was in the knight's sturdy grasp.

Chapter Twenty-Five

Blankets!" Rydar barked.

Kristofer raised his eyes to Rydar's. He looked confused, his face a mess of red splotches on slack, pale skin. Rydar tried to recall the things he saw Grier do for the injured she tended. He remembered they often started to shiver and she covered them with blankets.

"Kristofer! Go below and bring me all of your blankets. Quickly!" Rydar urged.

The boy jerked a nod and rolled to his feet. He disappeared through the opening in the deck. A moment later, blankets fountained out of the hole and spilled onto the planks. Rydar grabbed them and covered Lars, then folded one and put it under his head.

Lars' eyes blinked and he started to squirm as his senses returned. "O-o-h-h-h!" he groaned.

Rydar knelt by the young fisherman's head and rested the heels of his hands on Lars' shoulders, immobilizing them.

"Hold still, Lars. Don't move," he said calmly. "Lady Grier is on her way."

"M-y-y-a-a-a-r-m!" he wailed. His lower body twisted in pain and panic.

Rydar waggled his head at Kristofer so the boy would come closer. "Help me," Rydar said. "He must hold his arm still!"

Kristofer, visibly shaking but obedient, approached and dropped to his knees beside his younger brother. He leaned over the squirming boy.

"Lars? Can you hear me?"

Lars' eyes rolled wildly then settled on his sibling. "Kris?"

"Lars, you have to hold your arm still," Kristofer said, his voice cracking. He laid his hand on Lars' left cheek and pushed his face away from the injury. "Don't look at it."

"Will I lose it?" Lars cried. "Will I lose my arm?"

A visibly terrified Kristofer looked at Rydar. The answer hung in the air, a breathing thing waiting to be spoken. Rydar swallowed thickly and decided to tell the boys what they needed to hear.

"No, Lars. Not if you hold still."

Rydar felt the boy's body relax a bit. Kristofer kept his hand on his brother's face, but Lars wasn't trying to turn toward the break.

"L-lady G-grier? She'll know wh-what to d-do?" Lars stammered. He was starting to shake. Kristofer tucked the blankets closer around his brother's prostrate form.

"She fixed my leg when it was broken."

"Your leg was broken?" Kristofer asked, surprised. "When?"

"About two months ago. And see?" Rydar smiled at Lars. "You can't even tell!"

Lars relaxed a little more then.

So did Kristofer. "She's a good healer, is she?" he asked.

"Yes. She is." Rydar mentally crossed himself and said a silent prayer that he hadn't just lied to the boys. "The best I've seen."

The pounding of iron-shod hoofs pulled their attention. Rydar stayed where he was and kept Lars still, but Kristofer stumbled to his feet and ran to the boat's edge.

"It's Lady Grier! She's come on a big gray warhorse with the King's man!"

Skitt.

Rydar was not pleased that Lord Andrew was here. As he watched the edge of the boat Grier's head appeared. Then her body rose up as if being pushed from below. Kristofer helped her climb over the rail and reached for her basket. A moment later, Lord Andrew pulled himself onto the vessel.

Grier's gaze, intense and questioning, met Rydar's. He shrugged a little, then shook his head slightly. He understood her silent query, but he truly didn't know if she could save the boy's arm. She moved close and knelt between Rydar and the injured appendage.

"Lars, my boy. What have we got here?" she cooed. She plucked at the bloody sleeve, pulling it from the protruding bone. Her eyes narrowed.

"It hurts awful bad, Lady." Lars' chin trembled and tears started to leak from his eyes.

"I imagine it does, Lars." Grier opened her basket and retrieved a small pottery jug. She pulled the cork from its mouth.

"Will ye save it, Lady? My arm, I mean?" he whispered.

"Aye," she assured him. "But first I'm going to give ye some medicine to stop the pain. Is that aright?"

Lars nodded.

"It's a bit bauch on the tongue," she warned.

"Aye, Lady." Lars sniffed and gulped determinedly. Then he licked his lips and opened his mouth.

Grier dribbled the dark, bitter liquid into the young man's mouth, waited, and dribbled some more, all the while talking soothingly in his ear. Lars' eyes slowly blinked shut and Rydar felt the boy relax completely. He removed his hands from Lars' shoulders.

Grier looked up at him. "You did a braw job with the blankets, Rydar. And holding him still might have saved him from bleeding to death."

"I watch you and learn," he demurred, though pleasure from her praise warmed him throughout.

"I've a sharp dagger." The hard intrusion of Lord Andrew's voice startled Rydar, who had managed to forget the courtier's presence for a pace.

"For what?" Grier asked, her brow lowering.

"To take the arm off, of course!" he stated. "It will require a dagger sharp as a razor plus a bit o' muscle to cut it through." He moved forward with the lethal implement gleaming in his hand. Kristofer cried out a wordless wail of denial and thumped to his knees on the deck.

"No!" Rydar shouted. Grier grasped his arm in warning.

"Drew, I'm going to try and save his arm," she explained, still using the calming tone.

She calls him 'Drew' now? Rydar's previous pleasure vanished, replaced by a sense of looming disaster.

Andrew shook his head. "I've seen many such wounds in battle. There's no hope for the arm. 'Twill only fester and kill him!"

"I differ with ye, Drew." Grier lifted a larger corked jug from her basket. Then she handed Rydar a small knife. "Will you cut away his shirt?"

Rydar set himself to do her bidding when he felt Andrew's large hand clamp down on his shoulder. He froze. A crimson surge of rage made it impossible for him to see the fabric in front of him.

"Hand off me!" he snarled.

Andrew didn't seem to hear him. "Grier! I must insist! This boy's only chance of survival lies in the removal of his arm and the burning of the stump. Now move aside and let me be of service!"

Rydar straightened quicker than an untied spring. He whirled to face the knight and held the tiny knife close to the man's face. He was taller than Lord Andrew and used that to his favor, staring down his nose into the broad man's startled golden eyes. How he longed to let the knife slip—only a little—and draw blood from this pompous nobleman who dared to challenge healing skills he had not yet witnessed.

"Lady. Grier. Say. No." The Scots English words were hard, separate, and distinct.

"Rydar, stop!" Grier cried.

"Are you threatening me, Viking?" Andrew sneered. The deadly dagger he held moved into the corner of Rydar's vision.

Rydar lowered the small blade. "No' threatening. I warn."

"Warn? Me?" Andrew scoffed and wagged his knife.

"Aye," Rydar grunted, glaring at the knight. Only a little cut. Over his eye. It would bleed a decent amount and leave a scar. His fists tightened.

"Ye're an intruder in this land, Hansen. I could easily remove your hide to Edinburgh's dungeons for such a crime!" Andrew pressed.

"Aye." Rydar didn't move or soften his expression, and he struggled mightily as fury nearly overtook reason. The small knife in his hand begged to be used.

The courtier lifted one brow. "Touch me, Viking. See what I do."

"Drew, let him be!" Grier pushed herself between the two men. She splayed her hands against their chests and straightened her arms. She faced Andrew. "I require Rydar's help, Drew. He's learnt much about healing and he's helped me many times afore!"

Lord Andrew threw a dark look down at the resolute burst of orange and blue flame that stood between them. Rydar drew an angry breath and stepped away. He turned his back on Andrew and set to his assigned task, choosing to pointedly ignore the courtier. That was more of an insult to the man than any tossing of words could be.

And killing him now would only distract Grier from the more important task at hand.

"I must be about my business here and quickly," she stated. "I thank ye for your offer and should I find the task daunting, I'll make use of it. But for now, leave us be, I beg you!"

Andrew stood motionless for a long minute before he deigned to give way. Grier knelt beside Rydar again, holding the jug. He had finished cutting away the sleeve.

"I'll pour the wine over it now," she said in a quavering voice, and did so. A soft moan escaped Lars and the fingers on his broken arm twitched. She pulled a deep sigh and nodded. "Tis a good sign."

Grier took the knife from Rydar. Grimly determined, she sliced into the skin and muscle around the exigent bone and spread the enlarged gash with her fingers.

Rydar looked for Kristofer and saw him still kneeling a few feet away. "Can you bring a narrow piece of wood to brace his arm?" he asked. Kristofer nodded and climbed unsteadily to his feet. He disappeared through the deck to search below.

"What did you say to him?" Grier asked.

"Wood... spoon," Rydar pointed at the arm.

She looked a little puzzled. "Aye? Well... Might ye grip his wrist and straighten his arm?"

Rydar fixed his attention on Grier and tried to adjust the arm exactly when and how she needed him to. She wrested the splintered bone end through the opening she had cut in the muscle. Bent close, she closed her eyes, relying on touch and sound to tell her when the bone was correctly aligned. Rydar was amazed that she could accomplish such a thing, but he had seen her do it before and knew she was capable.

"There," she whispered. She opened her eyes just as Kristofer nudged Rydar with a slim board about two feet in length.

Rydar held Lars' wrist with one hand and passed Grier the board with the other. He grinned a little. "Wood spoon, aye?"

"Oh! Aye." Grier chuckled. "Ye'll be a healer on your own soon."

Rydar missed her words because he was momentarily lost in the blue of her eyes and the lilt of her voice. Grier slipped the board under Lars' arm. She lifted a length of linen and a wad of wool. To Rydar's surprise, she handed them to him.

"Use the wool to pad the linen strips. And do no' tie it too tight, ye ken?" she instructed. "Remember how your leg was?"

"Aye." Rydar began his task, pleased that she trusted him to do it right. Grier threaded her needle and soaked it in watered wine. Then she flushed the gash—made by the broken bone and her knife—with the same liquid before she set about sewing it closed.

Grier and Rydar worked side by side, silent and intent. He sensed when she needed him to move out of her path, or help hold the skin closed while she stitched it. She similarly pulled back when Rydar had to slide the linen under the wood and he shifted to wrap Lars' upper arm. It was a dance in which each partner correctly anticipated the other's moves. It was a dance of reparation. And it was a dance of unpredictable intimacy.

When they finished, Rydar took Grier's hand gently in his. He smiled into her eyes. "You are healer, Grier. Is very good work."

"It's no' finished yet," she breathed. Her gaze fell on his lips. He almost forgot himself and kissed her before Andrew made his presence known once again.

"Lady Grier?"

Her eyes left Rydar's and he ached to reclaim them.

"Yes, Drew?" she answered, facing the knight.

He appeared perplexed. "What else is to be done?"

Grier abandoned Rydar's hand and climbed slowly to her feet. "He mustn't be moved."

"How long?" Rydar asked her, thinking of their imminent journey. And thinking as well that, if he desired her gaze and her touch this strongly, how could he possibly think to leave her behind in Scotland and yet continue to live?

"A week at least. And he must be kept warm and watched for

fever." Grier seemed quite certain of her instructions.

The wedding was eight days away; Rydar hoped to leave in nine. Lars could still sail with his brother and cousin, even if he was injured. That information was acceptable—especially if his healer was on the voyage as well. He needed to make that happen, whatever it took.

"I watch for fever tonight," Rydar offered. Though it would take him away from Grier and forestall his decision to tell her of his feelings, the warm look of gratitude she gave him was well worth the delay. "Kristofer and Gavin next nights, aye?"

"I'll sleep beside him!" Kristofer added. "Every night!"

"He'll be in pain, and that's for sure," Grier said. Her mouth puckered and she tapped her lips with one fingertip. "I'll need to return and give him more poppy medicine."

"I'd be pleased to escort you back following the evening meal," Lord Andrew stated. "And return you safely to the keep afterwards." He glanced a challenge at Rydar.

"I go to keep for meal and blankets. I come back and you come, Grier." Rydar smiled at the knight, throwing a challenge of his own. "And then I ken you are safe."

Chapter
Twenty-Six

July 16, 1354

With Grier's permission, Gavin created a bed for Lars in the boat's front cabin. They carried him in there the second day, but only after Grier tied his splinted arm to his side. It was a bit awkward, but Lars was so relieved to still have his arm intact that he thanked her constantly and didn't complain.

Nor did he complain about the pain. She told him to move his fingers and flex his hand to keep his blood flowing, and he did so every time she was with him. She checked the stitches daily for infection, though she knew that danger had most likely passed— Lars ran a slight fever, but it had lessened in only two days.

He was healing beautifully. There was only one remaining concern.

"I do no' think the stitches should come out for another ten days," she remarked to Drew as they walked together along the main street of Durness. She was looking to purchase enough wine for the wedding dinner. The McKay house was too small to host the celebration, so the dinner was to be held at the keep.

The knight held Grier's arm tightly hooked through his. "Why is that a problem?"

"Because"—Grier beat down the slithering despair that snaked through her gut—"they plan to sail for Norway in five."

Drew waved his hand as if to wipe away her concern. "I'm certain someone at their destination would be capable of removing the threads."

"Aye. I suppose so." Grier could not stop herself from glancing in the direction of the sea. And Rydar's boat. "It might be Rydar can do it…"

Lord Andrew stopped walking. He stared into one of the many abandoned buildings that lined the main thoroughfare of Durness. His demeanor shifted and he looked defeated.

"It's like this everywhere."

Grier was surprised to see the unflappable knight's features so drawn. "Empty houses?" she ventured.

His jaw clenched and loosened. "Aye. And it's worse in England."

"Worse?" Grier asked, skeptical. "I can no' imagine anything worse."

Drew's eyes met hers, dull and lifeless. "I have been through so many villages that had no living souls left, that we rode through the night rather than rest in the omnipresence of death. I have seen shallow graves with so many bodies that the earth could no' contain them, but spilled them out."

She gripped her crucifix and crossed herself, trying to ignore images that the horrific description placed in her mind. "Merciful God in Heaven."

"In all my travels I have no' found a family intact, nor a single estate untouched. It is as if God Himself was clearing the land of humankind."

Grier nodded. Though her own faith remained strong, many around her had abandoned the church for exactly that reason. Some went so far as to curse Pope Clement VI for being unable to persuade God to have mercy. Or worse—for bringing His judgment.

"Was it so bad here?" he asked.

"No," she admitted. "Not quite half of our people died. But then some of their family members moved away, looking for relatives or to save themselves."

"Eight out of ten, Grier. In cities where they were living on top of each other, places like London, Edinburgh, Paris and Sienna, that many died. No' all of plague, but when the adults died, their bairns froze or starved." Andrew gazed down the cobbled street.

"And yet, our King sends ye to raise support?" she asked.

"Aye," he grunted.

"If he's been in the Tower all through the Death, can he truly know what hell descended on us?" And if he did, she realized, Lord Andrew wouldn't be standing in front of her now.

Drew's gaze swung back to hers. Their golden specks glinted in the sun. He shook his head slowly.

"No. I've told him, of course. But he's only seen London's struggles from the safety of his prison. He thinks I exaggerate to explain my limited successes."

"I'm sorry, Drew. Ye're path is no' an easy one," she empathized.

He turned to face her and took both of her hands. "My lady, I have a matter of grave import to discuss with you."

"Here?" Grier blurted. "On the street?"

The knight chuckled a little. "Nay. But I would ask that ye ponder a question until this evening when we might discuss it properly."

The despair of Rydar's impending departure uncoiled in her gut and began to twine through her chest. "What question?"

Drew bent forward and pinned her with intense consideration. His voice rumbled toward her like soft thunder. "Lady Grier, what holds ye here in Durness?"

Pinpoints of black and white swam through Grier's vision and she suddenly felt quite hot. "I need to sit down," she croaked. "'Tis a warmer day than I realized."

Drew slid his arm around her waist and pushed her into a tavern. He ordered the maid to bring her a cooled glass of cider, then watched her oddly as she gulped the liquid and asked for another.

"Are ye ill, Grier?" he asked. "I'm sorry I spoke so plainly about our unpleasant past. It was insensitive of me…"

"No, it's no' that." Grier wasn't sure what was wrong with her. "I believe, it's only that, well with all the wedding preparations, I think I've neglected, I mean I… What do I mean?" Confused, she looked into Drew's concerned eyes.

"I'm no' certain I ken," he answered, his changeable irises shadowed by lowered brows.

"Neither do I," she sighed.

The pair sat in silence for several minutes, and then Grier straightened in her seat and lifted her chin. She had no desire to wait several long hours to hear what Drew had in mind, knowing that such waiting and wondering would only lead her down paths of unbridled imagining and brutal trepidation.

"Drew, would you please tell me what ye're about?"

"Here?" he mimicked. "In a tavern?"

Grier tilted her head. "It will no' help your cause to wait, I assure you."

Drew laughed at that. "Ye're an interesting woman, Grier."

"Aye."

That made Drew laugh again, but Grier was no closer to discovering his mission. She decided to try a different tack. She folded her arms and leaned back in her chair and stared at Drew in cold, stone-like silence.

He sipped his ale and seemed to be pondering how best to begin. He chose, "Ye're quite a skilled woman, Grier."

That piqued her interest. "Skilled?"

"Aye. At healing, amongst other things."

Her expression didn't change. "Thank you."

Drew smiled again. "Ye're making me laugh and it's no' a laughing matter."

"What is no'?" Grier pushed. Her nerves were already strung tight as a bow and she believed she would go daft with his delays.

The smile faded. Drew leaned forward. He crossed his arms and rested his elbows on the table. The beautifully carved planes of his clean-shaven face stilled and his eyes deepened in color as his pupils widened. At that moment, Grier found him handsome beyond description.

"I have never seen anyone attempt to save an arm as mangled as that boy's, much less succeed."

Grier warmed with the unexpected praise. "Thank ye, again."

"Do you know how grateful your King would be if you would come to Stirling and avail yourself to his knights?"

Grier's jaw fell open. "You want me to go to Stirling?"

Drew dipped his chin. His eyes glowed under thick black lashes. "You would be well compensated, I assure you."

"You want me to go to Edinburgh!"

His hands spread wide. "My lady, you would be the most

sought-after healer in Scotland!"

"But Stirling?" Grier squeaked.

"Would ye prefer Edinburgh? You might be allowed to live there, I suppose." Drew's brows pulled together as he considered the option.

Grier pressed her hands to the sides of her head, afraid it might tumble from her shoulders in shock. "Lord Andrew. I'm an unmarried, unendowered woman with no male kin to travel with her and ensure her safety. What might ye be thinking?"

A slow smile spread Drew's cheeks. It was the same sultry smile that made it hard for Grier to swallow her supper. Now it caused her heart to flip.

"I might be thinking that you're a beautiful woman. I might be thinking that ye'd make a desirable wife."

Grier jumped to her feet, knocking her chair to the floor. "You wish to marry me?" she shouted.

Drew glanced uneasily around the tavern crowd which was mercifully sparse at this time of the afternoon. "Please sit down, Grier, and do no' announce our conversation to the world, aye?"

Grier blushed, righted her chair and sat. "Do you wish to marry me?" she whispered.

"What I wish, is to get to know you a bit more. And yes, marrying you is what I'll consider."

She was aghast. "Do ye no' have a care for what I wish?"

The knight chuckled. "Of course I do, Grier. But ye're a cannie woman. When the right opportunity presents itself..." He shrugged as if the answer was obvious.

"Ye seem a mite sure of yourself," she observed. That was Rydar's first observation of the man, she recalled. And it was not a compliment.

"I am," he replied.

Grier sagged in her chair, unable to dispute his confidence. "When do ye expect my answer?"

Lord Andrew reached for her hand. He squeezed it lightly and rubbed his thumb over her skin sending a delightful shiver between her shoulders. "As soon as possible. I must be on my way quickly."

Grier frowned. "I could no' leave afore the wedding!" came out of her mouth before she could stop it. Good God in Heaven! Now he would think she might be willing!

Drew grinned. "If you assure me your answer is 'aye,' then I'll wait for ye."

Grier stared at their entwined hands. His fingers were long and dark, hers slim and white. His nails were neatly trimmed. Hers were a little bit ragged. "I—I'll need time. And I'll need to discuss this with Logan."

"Of course."

"Ye'll understand that I had no forewarning?" She drew a deep breath. "I'm somewhat flummixt at the moment…"

"I do, Grier." He lifted her hand to his lips and kissed each finger. She watched him and could not help but wonder how his lips would feel against hers. When he spoke again, his voice was surprisingly rough. "And you understand that I had none either? That as surprised as ye might be, I am doubly so?"

Grier did not find that statement particularly comforting.

Drew's lids lowered sleepily. "Twas no' my expectation to ever come across such an impressive set of skills wrapped in such an attractive parcel."

Grier could not think of one single thing to say except, "Thank you."

ᚱᚾ

Though it was neither his intent nor his desire, Rydar slept on the boat with Lars for the three nights following the accident. Pain woke Lars in the middle of the night, and Rydar gave him the poppy medicine that Grier entrusted into his care. Sleep returned to the boy, lasting until it was time to rise and begin another boisterous and distracting day.

Sleep eluded Rydar, however.

His ironic desire to keep Grier safe—from both ruffians and self-important courtiers—by taking her with him was a riddle he couldn't solve. The aftermath of the Black Death was clear in every part of Durness. The actions of the lawless he had seen firsthand. Logan's wedding and Grier's subsequent displacement would put her in a precarious position, and only a good marriage could restore her situation.

But if they sailed—safely—to Norway, he had every reason to believe that he would find the same conditions there. And he couldn't promise a good marriage; he was a pauper today, and had no assurance that his circumstances would change once he returned to Arendal. He was likely to spend what remained of his life in a trade.

How would that keep Grier safe? It wouldn't.

But how could he ever leave her? He couldn't. She possessed his soul.

Skitt. He shifted position and waited for the sun to rise.

With one man down, Kristofer, Gavin and Rydar labored longer hours to complete the boat. During the past month, he grew to sincerely care for the young fishermen. They were all hard workers and they had dreams to catch, not only fish.

But the work was so consuming, he was only able to make one trip to the castle keep during that time. And when he did, Grier wasn't there.

"She's gone on an errand wi' Lord Andrew," Moira told him.

Rydar nodded grimly. *I should have cut him when I had the chance.*

By the fourth midday after the accident, the boat was finished. Rydar stood on the rear top deck and stared at the completed vessel, examining every inch in his mind, determining that nothing was forgotten. He called out questions that sent Gavin and Kristopher scrambling for answers, but every task he thought of was complete. He wiped sweat with his fisted shirt, and scuttled woodchips from his hair. His burnt skin tightened across his cheeks and shoulders. He kept his weight off his throbbing shin. Satisfaction suffused his soul.

It was time to launch the boat into the water and test her seaworthiness. Rydar talked to the residents of Durness and assembled a group of men to come the next morning and help pull the vessel across the thin strip of sand and into the sea.

Then he headed for Durness Castle and Grier. This evening he was a man with a mission and he wouldn't allow anything to stop him in its fulfillment.

Rydar asked Moira if he might have a warm bath and he dug out the best of his borrowed clothes. Tonight he would talk to Grier alone, even if that required he stay until dawn. He would tell her that she was his sun, his moon, his reason, his life. And he did not wish to live one single day of it without her.

Then she would ask to go with him. She would willingly face his uncertainty by his side, secure in his unfailing love for her. No matter what he endured, she would be his support and his succor, his healer and his strength.

ᚱᚺ

Grier paced around her room in spastic whirls and waited for Logan. Her door stood open so she would see him when he returned to wash for supper. Drew's proposal today had her stomach clenched so tightly, she was afraid to take even a sip of water. She must think of a way out. A way to say no. A reason that would be both believed and accepted.

Because she loved Rydar so strongly, she would decline a position in King David's court to follow the stubborn Viking on his quest to reclaim his future. And if his quest proved a failure, she would be happy to live as a common villager as long as he slept by her side for the rest of her life. But she couldn't admit this to anyone until Rydar asked her to join him.

The entrance to the keep opened and shut, and the echo of boots resounded up the steps. Grier hurried to her doorway. "Logan? Is that you?"

"Aye." His head appeared above the level of the second story floor. "Do ye need me?"

"I do." Grier waited until he topped the stairs before continuing. "Might we speak in private?"

Logan regarded her curiously. "Aye. Come to my chamber while I wash."

Grier followed her younger cousin into his room and closed the door behind her. Logan pulled off his shirt and soaked a linen towel in a basin of water. As he wiped the day's sweat and dirt from his skin, Grier began to tell him of Lord Andrew's surprising suggestion. Logan stopped his ablutions and stared at Grier.

"He wants to marry you?"

Grier's pride was pricked by his evident surprise. "Is it so unbelievable, then?"

"Aye. Well, no. I mean ye're a fine catch. But it's so fast," Logan sputtered. "So he asked for your hand?"

"Perhaps. He wants to take me to Stirling," she clarified.

"Oh." Logan frowned. "When?"

"When he leaves Durness."

"When is he leaving?"

Grier drew a long breath. "If I agree to go with him, he'll wait until the day after your wedding."

"That soon? And ye'd be gone?" Logan looked stricken. "With him?"

That was odd. "Why no' with him?" Grier probed.

"I thought that ye—well, never mind." Logan shook his head, tossed the soiled towel on the table and pulled a clean shirt from his coffer. He slipped it over his head and shoved his arms into the sleeves. Finally he turned to her and asked, "What do you want, Grier?"

Grier looked away. She couldn't tell him the truth and she didn't want him to see it in her eyes. "I do no' wish to go."

"Why?"

"I'm no' willing to leave Durness." *Unless Rydar asks me to go with him.*

"Ye'll no' have another chance with him if ye turn him down," Logan murmured.

Grier looked at him then. "I ken."

"Are ye sae certain of this?"

"I am."

Logan sighed. "That explains why he asked me this morn if I was your guardian."

"He did?" Grier bristled. "What did ye say?"

A smiled tugged at the corners of Logan's mouth. "I told him ye had a fine mind and a strong will of your own. Whatever ye decided to do was what ye'd do. Nothing I approved or disapproved would have any hold on your decisions!"

Grier laughed, relieved that she didn't have to fight her cousin.

"When will ye tell him?" Logan asked.

"Tonight. After the meal." Grier heard Rydar's door open and close. Was he back? Was the boat finished?

The fearful ache in her chest dissolved, then shifted to an entirely different need.

Chapter Twenty-Seven

When Rydar sat down to supper, Grier thought he was in a good mood. But Lord Andrew proved unusually attentive and solicitous, and by the end of the meal the Norseman's body simmered with suppressed anger. Grier longed to confess her feelings to him, but first she must speak with Drew and decline his offer.

"Might I have a moment with ye, Drew?" Grier asked when the last of the food was consumed and the last of the wine, drunk.

His grin was self-assured. "Of course, my lady."

Logan stood and moved toward the door. "Come on, Rydar. Let's go into the Hall, aye?"

"Aye." Rydar straightened slowly, as though he wished to remain. He paused and considered Grier so intently that she almost hurled herself into his arms. Before she could think of what to say to him, he twisted around and followed Logan from the room, closing the door solidly after him.

Drew rounded the table. He lifted Grier to her feet and his lips met hers in a dominating kiss. She allowed it, but she was strangely distant. She found herself thinking about how Drew kissed, rather than being drawn into him.

She found herself comparing his kisses to Rydar's.

Drew's lips released hers and he leaned back. His changeable eyes were dark and smoky; his expression, tender and confident.

"My lady, do I hope for your favor?"

"Well…" Grier faltered.

A shadow of disbelief flickered over his face. "Grier?"

Grier took a protective step back. "Drew."

"Aye?"

"I am sae flattered by the confidence you've shown in me," she began. "I truly am."

Black brows formed rank. "But?"

She lifted her chin. "But I shall have to decline."

"What!"

"I can no' go with ye to Stirling. I'm sorry, Drew."

Closing the gap between them, he stroked her cheek with the knuckles of two long fingers. "What is it, Grier? Do ye require more time?"

"Time?" she repeatedly blankly.

"I ken it's a very big decision to leave your home sae suddenly." His voice rumbled softly like the constant waves on her chyngell. "Ye were no' prepared."

"That is true, Drew. I was no' prepared for your proposal," she deferred. "But—"

Drew silenced her with another kiss. He tasted of wine. Grier waited patiently until he ended the kiss and said, "Your offer was quite generous—"

"Aye," he whispered against her cheek.

"—yet it's no' the sort of life I desire," she finished the sentence.

"Do ye desire me, Grier?" he breathed. His fingers moved up her back and tangled against her scalp. It gave her gooseflesh. She pulled a slight gasp.

"You're a desirable man, Drew. There's no argument to that."

"Many women at court have vied for my favors." He held her gaze. "It's no' a boast. 'Tis the truth. But ye've captured my imagination, Grier."

She swallowed nervously. This was harder than she expected and in so many ways. "I have?"

"Aye, like no other woman afore ye." Drew nuzzled her neck with a warm kiss that sent tremors skating along her spine. "I desire you, Grier MacInnes."

Grier shrugged away from him. "I—I can no' go with you,

Drew," she repeated, her resolve under siege but still firmly in place. "I am flattered, and I'm sorry as well."

He straightened and glared down at her, tense and intimidating. "If ye turn me down, Grier, the offer will no' be repeated."

She nodded slightly. "As I would expect."

His manner eased. "Have ye any idea what ye're about, my lady?"

In spite of everything, she was beginning to doubt her own wisdom. "I believe... I do."

"Is that your final answer, then?"

For a heart-twisting moment, Grier wondered if she had indeed gone quite daft. Another offer from a handsome knight and wealthy courtier would not come her way again. She was tossing it off in the slim hope that a Norseman—acquainted with her for only two months—loved her and would take her with him to an unknown land and an uncertain future.

Yet she was compelled to take that chance. Rydar owned her heart completely and she must follow it. She straightened as well, refusing to cower.

"Aye, Drew. It is."

ᚱᚺ

When Rydar left the formal dining room, he didn't follow Logan to the Hall. Instead, he stomped through the kitchen and out the back door of the keep. He loped across the yard and through the gate, over the bridge, and along the bluff. He stretched his stride and ran as hard as he could until his chest burned and his legs threatened to drop him to the ground. He slowed to a limping walk and threw an angry look over the bay.

"What the hell do I do now?" he shouted.

The waves scolded in unrelenting rhythm: go back. Go back. Go back!

Rydar spun and marched angrily in the direction from which he'd come. I suppose I shall have to go this way at some point anyway, he reasoned.

What was going on between Grier and the knight? The man was obviously courting her. Perhaps he had already made her an offer. Perhaps he had already spoken with Logan. Perhaps she was considering accepting him. After all, she had no other offers, had she?

Was he too late to proclaim his love?

Rydar panted his way back through the kitchen door, drawing puzzled looks from Moira and her mother. They paused in the washing of the evening's dishes and stared at him.

"Are ye well, Sir Hansen?" Moira ventured.

"Aye. Grier?"

"She's in the dining room with Lord Andrew."

Skitt. "Logan?"

Moira glanced at her mother, eyes wide. "I dinna ken."

Rydar snorted his frustration and went in search. He found Logan still in the Great Hall, staring into the fireplace. He held a goblet and swallowed a long drink.

"Logan?" Rydar approached the younger man.

"There ye are. Were ye at the privy?" Logan gestured with the goblet. "Wine?"

Rydar shook his head. The door to the dining room slammed open and the deep clack of boot heels approached. Lord Andrew paused in the doorway and shot Logan with an angry glare.

"I'll leave on the morrow!" he grumbled. Then he threw open the front door to the keep and exited without closing it.

Rydar stared after the man, exceedingly relieved at the sudden declamation, but puzzled as to what precipitated it. Logan walked past him to close the keep's door. The look on his face was odd.

"What is amiss?" Rydar asked. Before Logan could answer, Grier ran to the staircase. Rydar leapt after her.

"Grier! Wait!" he shouted.

She was halfway up the stairs. She stopped and looked over her shoulder. "No' now, Rydar. I can no' talk to you just now. I'm sorry..."

Her voice tripped over a loud sob. She slapped a hand over her mouth and her blue eyes spilled, wetting her flushed cheeks. She spun and rushed up the steps. The door to her chamber slammed shut.

Rydar turned to Logan, immediately deciding that if the younger man didn't tell him what had transpired, he would beat him until he did. "Logan! What is amiss!"

Logan's shoulders sagged. "Come have a glass of wine. I'll tell you all I ken." He walked back into the Hall.

Rydar followed, his heart bashing with dread. Over two gulped glasses of wine, that dread took ominous shape as Logan explained that Lord Andrew offered Grier a position at King David's court. A marriage between the two of them was to follow shortly. Rydar fought to appear calm knowing that either his worst nightmare or his greatest hope would be revealed with Logan's response to his next query.

"What she say?"

Logan pulled a deep breath and let it out slowly. "Grier declined the offer."

"Declined?" Rydar demanded. "What means 'declined'?"

Logan paused, surprised. "It means she turned him down." When Rydar frowned and shook his head, he added, "She said no."

Rydar's knees gave way and he sank onto the closest chair. "No? She say 'no' to Lord Andrew?"

"Aye." One corner of Logan's mouth quirked. "It appears he was none too pleased!"

"Why?" Rydar barked. "She say you why?"

"Aye." Then Logan's expression clouded over like the sky above the North Sea.

"Why?"

Logan refilled his goblet and held the jug toward Rydar. He wagged his head and waited. One obstacle was removed: Grier had refused Lord Andrew. But he had to know why. Dare he hope her reason had anything to do with him? *Please let it be so.*

"Logan! Why?" Rydar pressed, hard.

Logan's voice was soft and the words he delivered were a quiet irrevocable death. "She said she was no' willing to leave Durness."

The room flattened, gone colorless like a woodcut print. Rydar knew his heart still beat. He knew his lungs filled with air and expelled it only to repeat the process. His eyes still saw and his ears still heard. But he couldn't feel anything.

Because Grier was not willing to leave Durness. Not even for marriage to a handsome, wealthy and powerful knight. Not even to be a member in King-David-of-Scotland's royal court. Not even for the chance to live in a true castle with other lords and ladies with titles and wealth and position.

So what chance did he have?

Because Grier was not willing to leave Durness. Especially to sail the North Sea in a small fishing boat. With three young men and one penniless thirty-year-old who—probably disinherited—had nothing of substance to offer her. To leave the safety of the only home she had ever known, and the only family she had remaining, for an uncertain future in a strange land with an unfamiliar language.

All Rydar could offer her were possible poverty, no assured position and a guaranteed struggle. What capable woman with a fine, quick mind would even consider such a bargain? Not one who turned her back on a desirable and powerful knight, that much was certain.

Grier was not willing to leave Durness.

Rydar set his wine goblet on the closest flat surface, stood on numbed legs, and stumbled from the keep without uttering another word.

July 17, 1354

"One. Two. Three!"

The sixteen men roped to Rydar's boat strained forward, dragging the heavy craft across the sand. They paused to rest, then readied again.

"One. Two. Three!"

Rydar's deep voice was loud enough to reach Grier, who watched from a distance. Faces reddened and muscled bulged. Feet sunk into sand.

"One. Two. Three!"

They reached the waves' closest edge.

"One. Two. Three!"

The bow was in the surf. Men dropped their towropes, then splashed and stumbled to either side of the rudder to push.

"One. Two. Three!"

Surging breakers grabbed the hull and lured it into their grasp.

"One. Two. Three!"

The boat began to dance. Rydar, Gavin and Kristofer scrambled up the ropes and heaved themselves onto the deck. They twirled the sail to catch the wind and the craft slammed deeper into the waves, diving through foamy peaks and reaching for the open sea. A guttural shout of joy burst from the men on board. They waved frantically at the crowd on the chyngell, who waved back, grinning.

Rydar took the rudder and Gavin the sail. Kristofer ducked into one of the tiny cabins before reappearing and dropping below the deck.

That must be where Lars is, Grier thought. She rubbed her eyes, scratchy and dry from a night spent sleepless and crying. She didn't think Rydar had noticed she was there. That was just as well. Her red, swollen eyes were underscored with dark smudges. She looked a mess.

Grier hoped to ask him what it was he wanted to talk to her about last night on the stairs, but she found him far too busy for her to interrupt. And now that the boat was launched for testing, he would be gone for hours. No need for the basket of food now.

She turned Raven back toward the castle.

Lord Andrew was much more distraught by yester eve's refusal than she would have expected. Recalling it now prompted another round of stinging tears. She wiped them on her sleeve.

Drew had wiped a tear, too, though she pretended not to notice. Grier wasn't sure whether it was his heart or his pride that was more wounded, but truly wounded he was. When she tried to leave the dining room, he nearly begged her to reconsider, offering to remain in Durness to give her the chance. When she declined him yet again, he shot her a look of such desperation that she nearly relented just to give him ease. She had never in her life hurt anyone in such a manner.

Then he pushed past her, chucked the dining room door open and strode away from her, irrevocably severing her opportunity. She heard the pain in his voice when he told Logan he would leave in the morning. She imagined how he might spend his last night here, trying to forget the impudent elderly maid who dared to refuse him, a powerful courtier knight of their King.

When Grier left the dining room to seek refuge in her chamber, she didn't expect Rydar to be waiting for her. She couldn't speak to him. Her composure was unraveling like yarn and tangling her emotions. It was all she could manage to see beyond her tears and not trip on the stairs.

All through the pale night hours, logic tortured Grier. The offer from Drew was truly astonishing. She never heard of anyone who was handed such an enviable prospect. And the man himself was handsome and his behavior above reproach. Marriage to him would most certainly be an adventure. She might even grow to love him, in time. The knight was everything a maid dreamt of and pretended over through her adolescence.

Had she been a fool?

When she heard Drew return to his room, many hours into the night, Grier silently opened her door and approached the master chamber. Her trembling hand reached out to knock, but retreated. She stood outside his door on the wood floor, her bare toes curled, her arms wrapped around the waist of the cloak she threw over her shift. The knight was indeed, everything.

Everything but Rydar.

Grier tiptoed quickly to Rydar's chamber, suddenly afraid Drew might open the portal and discover her standing there. Rydar's door gaped. He had apparently returned to sleep on his boat yet again. Dim light from the summer sky snuck through the open window. It was more than enough to see by.

The room was neat. Though he had scant few items to call his own, what he had was folded and orderly arranged. She saw the copper tub and realized he had smelled of soap at supper. She was so distracted by her pending conversation with Drew, she hadn't noticed. Why had he bathed tonight? Did it have anything to do with what he wanted to tell her? Or perhaps ask her?

Grier melted onto Rydar's bed. A certainty descended over her, draping her in serenity. She had been right to decline Lord Andrew's proposal. The way she felt about Rydar precluded her feelings for any other man.

She rolled onto her side and let her gaze inhale the details that reflected the man. In them she saw quiet, unfailing and undeniable courage. Rydar faced even more adversity than she had, and yet he remained unbowed. Throughout the challenges of loss, language, and living on charity he acted with unwavering dignity. He rose triumphant. His goal was within his reach.

And that was more impressive to her than all the jeweled weaponry and velvet trappings of the royal knight.

Climbing from Rydar's bed, Grier straightened his covers. She padded back into her own chamber and latched her door. The sky was changing from pale lavender to pink. When the sky was golden orange, Lord Andrew's door latch opened. His footfalls clunked down the stairs. Grier listened until he was gone. She had not slept at all.

Now she was so exhausted, she was in danger of falling as Raven plodded home through the hazy, humid summer day. Without their royal guest, her daily life would return to its previous simplicity. For three days.

"Then Malise will be the lady," she muttered. Her head pounded with her pulse and all she could think of was her bed. She couldn't think of what would happen on the fourth day when Rydar set sail for Norway. Another unwelcome wash of tears flowed down her cheeks.

Grier told Moira she wasn't feeling at all well and instructed the maid not to wake her, not for any reason. She stripped and climbed under her cool sheets. Lying on her back, she covered her eyes with her pillow to block the watery afternoon sun outside her window. Grier felt for her crucifix.

Please, God, let him ask me to go with him.

Chapter
Twenty-Eight

Rydar returned to the keep in a foul mood. First off, Grier came to the chyngell today for the first time in nine days and Rydar had managed not to think about her at all for almost a full hour before he saw her there. Her ginger hair blew around her shoulders like russet angel's wings as she sat astride Raven. The vision made his ravaged heart beat hopefully again.

She didn't approach him, but he couldn't blame her. He was in the midst of sixteen men who were tugging his boat into the sea. He was shouting directions and orders, and once the vessel began to slide forward he daren't stop them so he could quickly declare his love to the maid, and then run back to the boat.

And then the water took his boat and tickled her, and Rydar had to tame her. He leapt to the rudder and Gavin to the sail, and their maiden voyage around the bay commenced. The craft responded well as Rydar learned the feel of her. He was very pleased. Until Kristofer shouted to him from the compartment below.

She was leaking.

Not badly; she wouldn't sink overnight. But three years of sitting dry had allowed a batch of tiny fissures in the hull. And that flaw was enough to multiply Rydar's frustrations by tenfold. Now the boat waited, leashed like a disobedient mutt to the small pier that tethered Durness' fishing boats, until Rydar could begin to repair the cracks.

Tonight, however, he was determined to talk to Grier, no matter what—or who—was tossed in his path. He washed himself and put on a clean shirt, then went looking for her. He only found Moira.

"Where Lady Grier is?" he asked politely.

"Sleeping." That answer wasn't satisfactory, so Rydar followed the maid into the kitchen.

"Sleeping early or sleeping late?" he tried.

Moira's sweet face twisted in confusion. She opened the food basket that rested on the table, and pulled out the victuals. Rydar tried again. He pointed at the midday meal covering the kitchen table.

"She sleeps first, then eats supper? Or she sleeps early for all night?"

"Oh!" Understanding loosened Moira's countenance. "I dinna ken for certain. She went abed this afternoon. She said her head pained her awesome."

"You will wake her?" Rydar suggested.

"No, sir. She said I'm no' to wake her for any reason at all." Moira's eyes widened. "She was sae determined about that."

"She sleeps all night, then?" Rydar prodded, frustrated yet again.

Moira shrugged.

Rydar combed his fingers through his hair. "Logan?"

She gave him a sympathetic pout. "He's dining with Lady Malise and her family."

Skitt.

Skitt skitt skitt skitt skitt! Rydar dropped into the nearest chair. He was hungry, having missed the midday meal on the boat. But his irritation at the events of this day took away his appetite. Still, he knew he needed to eat whether he felt like it or not; meals would likely be lean on the coming sea journey.

With a disgusted sigh, he helped himself to the food that was probably meant to be his hours ago.

July 18, 1354

Grier drew a deep breath and stretched, reaching her arms out from under her sheets and pointing her toes to the bottom of her bed. Her headache was mercifully gone, though her eyes still felt puffy and dry. She stretched again to get her circulation going and wondered what she might make for supper.

Oh, aye. The basket of food. That suited her mood. After a week-and-a-half of rich meals, she looked forward to a simple repast of bread, cheese and apples.

The light outside her window was weak and she smelt rain. That was no surprise; weather in Scotland was always unpredictable, and on the coast even more so. Though the morning was hazy and humid, the late afternoon rain was a relief.

Grier tossed back her covers. She pulled on the gown that she wore earlier in the day and still lay draped across the foot of her bed. She brushed her hair and tied it back. Then she opened her door and went downstairs to the kitchen.

Moira was there, alone. Something about the look on her face was odd. "Well, good morn to you, Lady Grier!" she chirped. "I trust ye slept well!"

"Aye, thank you." Grier quirked her brow at the maid. "Where is the basket I prepared for Sir Hansen?"

"He finished it last night. For his supper."

"Last night?" Grier looked out the window at the drizzle. It was impossible to determine the position of the sun. "What do ye mean last night?"

Moira touched her arm. "Are ye well, Lady Grier? Ye slept so sound and I did no' wake ye, as ye instructed."

Realization knocked Grier. "I slept all afternoon? And all night?"

"Aye. Ye were sae peaked, Lady." Moira smiled softly. "Ye look more like yourself today. I ken it did ye good."

Another day gone. And another night. And another chance to ask Rydar what he wanted to tell her. "What time is it?" Grier demanded.

Moira blinked. "It's about ten. Midmorning."

"Rydar will already be sailing his boat," Grier moaned. She slumped into a chair.

"Oh, no, Lady. It had a leak."

Grier straightened. "A leak? His boat leaks? How do ye ken?"

Moira set a bowl of oat parritch in front of her. "He told me last night, while he ate."

"Did it sink?" Her stomach did.

"No! It was no' that bad. But he'll be fixing it this morn, and no' sailing it again until the morrow."

Relieved in so many ways, Grier jumped up and hugged the startled girl. "Pack the basket again, Moira! I'll take it to him straight away!"

"Ye have no' taken nourishment since yester morn, Lady Grier! And ye'll go nowhere until ye eat your parritch!" Moira jammed her fists onto her hips in imitation of Grier's frequent stance. "And ye'll hurry back after because you've more'n a darg yet to do before the wedding! 'Tis only two days away!"

Grier stared at her maid in gape-mouthed shock. Then she plopped back in her seat and scooped a large bite of parritch into her mouth.

"Yes, miss!" she mumbled with her mouth full, too happy to argue.

ᚱᚺ

Rydar shaved another narrow piece of wood. He dipped it in melted pitch and wedged it into the tiny crack. Water finally stopped seeping through.

"That's got it!" he said. He looked at Gavin who was bent in half beside him, watching intently. "At last, eh?"

Gavin nodded and handed him a cut piece of leather to cover the patch. Rydar dipped the leather in the cooling pitch and pressed it against the hull. Then he coated the entire area with another layer of the pungent water-proof tar.

Rydar slowly unraveled his stiff legs. He stood crookedly in the low compartment. "You and Kristofer sop up this water. Get it good and dry. Well, as dry as you're able in this weather."

"Yes, sir." Gavin collected the tools that Rydar had been using.

"And keep a sharp eye out for any more leaks."

"Yes, sir."

"I'm going over to Rabbie's cottage and see if anything usable still remains there." Rydar climbed the ladder to the mid-deck. "What I can't find, I may need to purchase." Gavin handed up the tools and then followed him.

"Will we try her again tomorrow?" he asked.

"We must, Gavin. The next day is the wedding and I can't take her out then. And we plan to sail the day after that!" Rydar patted the tall fisherman's shoulder. "That's assuming she's done letting the sea come in for a visit!"

"Rydar!"

The voice from the pier floated up, disembodied. Rydar knew who called him, but he moved to the rail before answering. "Good day, Margoh."

She stood in the soft rain holding her shawl over her head. "Will you come down and talk with me?"

Rydar nodded and turned back to Gavin. "Have you thought of anything else we lack?"

"No, sir."

He patted the young man's shoulder again, then climbed down to the pier. Margoh tapped one leather-shod foot while she waited.

"I heard your boat leaks," she accused.

Rydar shrugged. "Not anymore."

"Is it safe?"

"Yes."

"Are you certain?"

"Yes."

Margoh narrowed her eyes. "What if you're wrong?"

"No one is forcing you to come on this voyage," he quipped.

Margoh coughed a spiteful laugh. "Why are you in such a hurry to leave, anyway? Has your little hostess run off with her lover?"

Rydar's composure ruptured. "Margoh!"

"Or didn't the knight want her after he used her?" she taunted.

His vision bloodied. He felt a rage heave through his soul, born of his own failure to claim Grier's heart. He stood resolute, fists clenching and ragged nails cutting into his palms, until he could manage to sound sane.

"You're welcome to stay behind."

He hoped she would choose to do so, regretting his promise to take her. She pressed one arm under her breasts, forcing their upper curves over the top of her gown. His eyes fell to the twin swells, but bounced away.

"I do not wish! I only want to be assured that I'm not sailing off to my death!" she spat.

"There were no promises. No guarantees," he reminded her cruelly.

Her gray eyes sparked like flint and steel. "I didn't think my safety fell under that condition."

Rydar leaned down close to Margoh, his face meeting hers under the shawl. "I sail on the morning tide the day after the wedding. Be here with your belongings packed if you still wish to go. I'm sailing with you, or without you."

She stared hard at him for a long minute. He didn't move, he didn't flinch.

"Fine." She whipped the shawl away, tossed him one last look, and stalked noisily along the pier toward the chyngell.

Then Rydar saw Grier.

Watching the exchange with Margoh. Too far away to hear them. But close enough to see his head dip under her shawl.

Skitt.

ᚱᚼ

Grier commanded her legs to move toward Rydar. And Margoh. There was only one path to the boat and the Old Aunt walked it between her and the Norseman. Grier's cheeks tensed in a smile-like grimace.

"Hello, Margoh." Why was he kissing her? "How are the wedding arrangements coming?" Is that what Rydar wanted to talk to me about? "Is Malise's gown finished?" Please God, give me strength!

"Hello, Grier." Margoh's eyes traveled over her and settled on the basket. "What have you there?" she asked, ignoring everything Grier said.

"Food." Grier nodded toward the boat. "For the men."

"Oh." Margoh glanced over her shoulder. "I thought you might be—never mind."

"Might be what?" Grier demanded.

Rydar approached and stood behind Margoh. Grier struggled to give him a real smile, hoping he was glad to see her. Lowered brows canopied his pale green eyes. His cheeks were splotched with red. He wasn't smiling back.

"You feel better?" he asked. His tone was cool, but the intensity of his gaze spoke of entirely different things.

"Yes. Thank you," Grier murmured, confused by his unfriendly demeanor. "How is the boat?"

He nodded. "Is no' leaking."

"Good. That's good."

Margoh made no move to leave. She seemed to be enjoying their awkwardness. A smirk curved her lips.

Grier handed Rydar the basket. "I'll see you at supper, then?"

"Aye. Wait! No." Rydar grabbed her arm. He looked like he was in pain. Grier glanced at his left leg out of habit, but he rested his full weight on it. "Logan and I eat in Durness with Malise's pappa and uncle. They tell me about Scottish wedding… um…" He asked Margoh a question in Norse.

"Customs," she said to Grier.

"Customs," he repeated. "On morrow I sail boat, next day is wedding. Ye ken?"

"Aye," Grier whispered. She struggled to keep her composure under the crushing weight of lost opportunity. Hope dribbled from her like sand. "We have run out of time."

Rydar tilted his head. "Out of time? How out of time?"

Grier stared hard at him. He truly had no idea that her heart was in pieces, her future tossed away, and her desires coldly murdered.

"Good luck with your boat, Rydar." She turned from him and hurried across the chyngell to Raven. She kicked the gelding to a gallop, spewing rain-dampened muck in all directions behind them.

July 19, 1354

Rydar avoided Grier, arriving at the keep late after supper yester eve and leaving early this morning. He set sail at dawn and he, Gavin, and Kristofer took turns looking for leaks in the hull. There were none.

The men sailed through the day, taking turns at the sail and rudder until all of them felt confident. Lars sat on the middle deck enjoying sporadic sunshine and the brisk sea breeze. Rydar was surprised when he first saw the boy; Lars had convinced Kristofer to shorten his splint so he could move with a bit more ease.

"And did you ask Lady Grier before you did so?" Rydar asked the brothers.

"No," Lars admitted.

"Does it hurt?"

"No more than before. Maybe even a little less." Lars grinned at him, reminding Rydar so much of himself and the way he mistreated his broken leg that he couldn't chastise the boy. He pointed one finger and tapped Lars' chest, his expression as grim as he could make it.

"If it hurts, don't do it. Do you understand me?"

"Yes, sir."

"I've been through this, haven't I?"

"Yes, sir."

"If you re-injure it, Lady Grier will not be around to save your arm again. You will lose your arm at the least and perhaps even your life." He leaned closer. "Do you understand that, Lars?"

Lars swallowed loudly, the grin gone. "Y-yes. Sir."

Rydar nodded. "Good."

Satisfied that he had frightened a modicum of sense into the boy, Rydar climbed to the top deck and stood overlooking the boat's pointed bow. The sun hovered over the edge of the North Sea. He watched as it slowly dissolved into the water. Only one more sunset—and Logan's wedding—remained before he sailed for home.

Rydar refused to allow the glorious orange sunlight that rippled across the summer sky like Grier's hair, nor the clear deep blue of the North Sea that soothed him like her eyes, to cause him to think of her at all.

Chapter
Twenty-Nine

T he day before the wedding placed so many demands on Grier
that she ate her noon meal—a thick slice of bread wrapped around a
chunk of cheese—as she stood in the courtyard watching two large
tents being erected. As soon as they were secured, castle tenants
began to arrange trestles, plank tops and benches under them.
Anywhere between one-hundred-and-fifty and two-hundred people
were expected, and the skittish Scottish weather made the protective
precaution necessary.

Grier moved from baker to butcher to brewer to chandler
assuring adequate breads, meats, ale, cider and candles. A brace of
young boys took turns cranking two spitted boars over carefully
tended fires. Wine casks were delivered and conveniently placed.
The grooms mucked out the stable and made room for additional
mounts. Moira and the triplets moved all the furniture in the keep to
sweep and mop; carpets were dragged outside, beaten, and
resituated.

The realization that Rydar would leave after tomorrow beat in
her head like a death knell.

Through all the preparations Grier doubted that anyone was
able to discern her devastation. She made her cheeks smile, made
her feet follow one another in stride, caused her hands to direct
others. But her heart was shriveling.

Rydar leaves after tomorrow. The repetitive din in her mind made it hard for her to concentrate on what her tenants informed or asked. Many times Grier requested that they repeat their words before she could comprehend them.

The Norseman would be in the wedding the next morning, standing tall beside Logan as his witness. He would partake in the celebration that followed; eating her food, drinking her wine, dancing in her courtyard. But it would not be hers any longer. Once the words were spoken in front of the priest, all of it would belong to Malise.

Panic squeezed Grier and she felt light-headed, her vision bordered by gnats. Cold sweat filmed her skin. She needed to be alone. Only one corner of the castle ground was devoid of quick, busy hands and scurrying bodies. She stumbled toward the graveyard.

Grier wove between the crowded, crooked markers until she reached Arne Jorgensen's grave. She fell on her knees beside his cairn. She rested until she could breathe more easily and the threat of fainting had passed.

"What will I do, Arne?" she whispered. "I love him with all my being. I can no' imagine my life here once he's gone. I can no' imagine how I'll do, and I never see him again."

In the silence of the yard, she felt he heard her. She closed her eyes and reached for her mother's crucifix. The metal was warmed by her body; it felt heavy and solid in her palm.

Unbidden, Lord Andrew's deep rumbling voice intruded in her thoughts. *Lady Grier, what holds ye here in Durness?*

Grier gasped and opened her eyes, certain he was standing beside her.

Of course he wasn't, but the question floated in front of her as real as anything. She grasped it in her other hand. She turned it over, inspecting it from all angles, and considered her reasons to stay. What did hold her in Durness?

Logan? He didn't need her after the morrow. He had a loving and eager bride.

The keep? 'Twas Logan's now and he would care for it as he saw fit.

Healing? Her skills went with her wherever she roamed.

Even to a foreign land.

"Oh my Father in Heaven!" she cried. "I can no' leave Scotland on my own! It's my home!"

But... She pulled a deep breath and waited. Somehow, Arne spoke to her heart.

The distance is no' what matters...

'Tis with whom that matters.

"Home is where one chooses it to be. Is that it, Arne?" Grier murmured to the pile of stones. "You sailed from the only home you ever knew to go with Rydar, because ye loved him. Ye loved him enough to die and ye brought him this far."

Grier felt her ravaged soul healing even before she mouthed the words that would craft her future. "Ye came this far and he was no' alone. Is it my turn now, Arne? Am I to go with him now, so he is no' alone?"

She rubbed her breastbone and pulled a deep breath, trying to ease the pressure of realization that pierced her there. She might get up the courage to ask Rydar to take her with him; but what would happen then, when they reached his home?

"I can manage," she stated. "I was very nearly the 'most sought-after healer in Scotland' after all!"

Where there are people, there will always be sickness and births and accidents. And she was certain Rydar would help her learn his language, after the help she gave him here.

Grier knew for certain that, if nothing else, she would rather be Rydar's friend and live in his town than let him sail out of her life forever.

July 20, 1354

The wedding was beautiful. Malise was beautiful. Logan was handsome and happy. But Grier could not command her eyes to follow any but Rydar. He wore the wool tunic she made for him with black hose and high black boots. The Norseman was the tallest man in the church, and now he towered over the other guests.

Yester eve she collapsed, exhausted to her bones. She had hoped to speak to Rydar about sailing to Norway but he returned too late and her rebellious eyes refused to stay open one minute longer. Tonight was her last chance and she would not let it pass. She could not.

Margoh was in attendance of course, dressed in a blue silk

gown. She wore a snood sewn with pearls, and a narrow strand of pearls slid between her breasts drawing the eye of every man she spoke to. The jillet sidled up to Rydar whenever the Viking stood still.

"It was a lovely wedding, was it not?" Margoh's voice dribbled over Grier's shoulder. She turned to face the older woman.

"Aye. Truly lovely," she concurred.

Margoh glanced toward the young couple. "They'll be happy together."

Grier nodded slowly, wondering what Margoh was about. "I'm certain of it."

"Well... I shall bid you farewell."

"So soon?" Grier considered the angle of the sun. "There are hours of celebration, yet."

Margoh laughed, her expression smug. "Of course there are! And I shall stay to enjoy them. I meant that I'm leaving Durness on the morrow."

That was unexpected. "Are ye?"

"I am. I'm sailing to Norway." Margoh tilted her head toward Rydar. "With him."

Grier whirled to face Rydar, no longer concerned with Margoh. She caught him staring at her. His expression was strained and he considered her with sadness and longing. When her shock-widened eyes met his, he frowned and his gaze shifted to Margoh.

She had seen Rydar angry before. Enraged even, when Drew challenged him after Lars' accident. But the cold hatred that now dilated his green eyes to black terrified her beyond reason. She had to get away. She had to run before that hatred might chance to turn against her.

Grier ran into the keep, up the stone staircase and slammed her chamber door, locking it. She slid her back down the far wall of her room until she was on the floor, her knees up and thighs pressed against her chest.

She didn't answer when someone beat on her door and tried her latch. The horrible truth thrummed through her veins and destroyed every hope she held.

Margoh was sailing to Norway.

Margoh was going with Rydar.

Now what would she do?

ᚱᚺ

The sky dimmed. Sounds of revelry faded. Grier emerged from her chamber, knowing she must play her role this one last night. Because after hours of silent agony she came to the conclusion that her adamant heart gave her no other choice. The reasons that brought her to this point were still compelling her, confirming her decision. Tonight she would ask Rydar to please take her on his journey.

Margoh could go straight to hell, for all she cared. Even if Rydar married the bitch.

Grier avoided Rydar as she thanked the wedding guests for joining the celebration. She skirted around Margoh while she gave instructions to the various servants. She stayed away from the dancing, and instead chatted with Malise's slightly plaistert father and weepy-eyed mother.

And after Logan and Malise were escorted to the master bedchamber amidst bawdy bellows, and all of the wine casks were emptied, and the last of the guests was tied onto his horse and slapped toward town, Grier went to make herself ready.

She stood before her mirror and scrutinized her reflection. This night, more than any other in her lifetime, she must be at her very best. Too much was at stake. She loosed her hair so it curled unencumbered to her waist. The summer sun had combed the red with gold, while underneath, winter's darkness gave it depth.

A woman's hair is her glory, her Da's words whispered from long past.

Sapphire eyes stared back at her. Dark, wide, frightened. She lifted her chin; there was her determination. *Keep your chin up.* There was no need to pinch her cheeks. They were flushed with embarrassment and would doubtless stay so.

Grier adjusted her gown and drew a resolute breath. "Get on with it, then. It'll no' get better with the keeping," she whispered.

In the hallway, she brushed her fingers along the wall to keep oriented. The rush of blood in her ears and the relentless pounding in her chest pulled her from reality. She was in a dream, lightheaded and lost. She knocked on Rydar's door, surprised when her knuckles made a sound.

"Grier!" Rydar's mouth worked, but he didn't seem to know

what else to say.

"A word?" Her voice seemed so distant.

"Aye. Come." He stepped back and opened the portal, his face a map of confusion and something else. Hope? She was vaguely aware that he was not fully dressed.

"I'm sorry to disturb your sleep."

"I'm not sleeping." In truth, candles lit the bedside table. A parchment waited there, the quill leaking ink over the words. He followed her gaze then hurried to set the quill aright. He folded the ruined document in half and tossed it into the banked fire. It flamed up, a burst of passion in the dull hearth, then curled, defeated, to gray ash. He came back to her, so close she could feel the heat of him against her cheeks

"What you want?" he whispered.

Her throat closed. She looked into his eyes, those impossibly green eyes, unable to speak.

His knuckles, cool and smooth, stroked her face. His voice bubbled softly from his chest. "Why you are crying?"

"Am I?" Grier gasped, and wiped away the offending moisture. She stepped deeper into the room, unable to be near to him and still coherently speak her mind. "I—I do no' know."

He turned to face her, his back to the fire. She could see the outline of his body through his linen nightshirt. Long, lean limbs, firmly muscled. Broad shoulders, narrow hips, strong buttocks. Heart rendering perfection.

"I've come to say—that is to ask—if I might… If you'll allow me to, um." Her words failed. How many times had she said it in her room? Practiced, until it rolled off her tongue, clear and confident? Where was that confidence now? Her fists clenched. "Shite."

"Grier?"

She lifted her chin. There was no other way around it but balls-on. "Might there be room on your boat for me?"

Rydar stared at her. "My boat? You come to Norway?"

She drew a deep breath and held it. "Aye."

Rydar felt behind him for the chair, his eyes never leaving hers. He dropped on its edge and slid back in the seat. His knuckles moved across his lip several times. He was obviously surprised by her request. Shocked perhaps. Could he not have known her heart after all?

"Why?"

Grier opened her mouth, then closed it again. She folded her arms over her waist and crossed to stand alongside the fireplace. She kent he must be able to hear her heart beating from across the room. She could hear nothing but.

"Logan has married Malise. She's mistress of the castle now. I'm supplanted," Grier's tone was unintentionally resentful. "That's how it goes, aye?"

"Aye." Rydar blinked slowly, his eyes shifted aside.

"The truth is I've no prospects here but to serve my cousin's fifteen-year old wife." Shame pushed her face toward the floor. "It's not the life I envisioned, nor is it the life I wish to lead."

Rydar was silent for a moment, his expression unreadable. "Is that only reason?"

Grier frowned. "I do no' understand."

He repeated the question with exaggerated patience. "Is only reason you wish for Norway? Because you have nothing here?"

Grier chewed her tongue. Nay, you foolish man! It's because I can no' live without you! She whirled to face the fire, afraid her true feelings would spill from her mouth and flood the room, drowning them both.

"Do ye need another reason, afore you'll agree to my passage?" she whispered. Part of her hoped he would say yes, forcing her to declare her love.

Rydar was quiet for so long, Grier wondered if he had fallen asleep in the chair. She looked over her shoulder and met an angry intensity that frightened her.

"I do no' need another reason…"

Something she couldn't name lurked in his tone. His beard rippled over his jaw muscles. He rubbed his face. Pushing up from his chair, he approached her once more.

Rydar stood over her, his vibrating masculinity just inches from her. She grasped the edges of her gown to keep herself from pulling him close and surrendering to him, uninvited. She lifted her face and stared into the depths of her own soul.

His eyes never wavered. He leaned down until his mouth hung over her lips and his unblinking green gaze held hers. She felt his breath caress her cheek.

"You come with me to Norway."

Did he speak? Or did she dream? Grier blinked. "Aye?"

One brow lifted. "Aye," he said sarcastically.

"Th-thank you." Grier backed away from him. She spun and ran to the door, needing to be gone before shame broke her beyond recovery.

"Grier!"

She halted and looked back at him. He swallowed audibly, his hands dangled awkwardly at his side.

"We leave on morning tide."

She nodded and pulled the door solidly closed behind her. Pressing her hand over her mouth, she struggled to hold back her sobs until she was behind her own door. Once there, she bawled into her pillow, her last night in Scotland spent in deeper misery than she could ever have imagined.

Chapter Thirty

July 21, 1354

Grier lifted her two laden leather satchels to Kristofer on the rope ladder, who in turn handed them up to Gavin on the middle deck. Next was her freshly stocked basket of healing supplies. In the false bottom alongside her sharpest dagger was a small leather pouch cradling fifteen gold coins, given to her in secret by her dying father.

"Tis all I have," he rasped with his last breaths. "Make your way with it."

"I never thought 'twould be this sort of way," she mumbled. Her tears finished and her determination unquenchable, Grier peered up at the vessel that was about to carry her on an unknown adventure to an unfamiliar country.

Kristofer climbed down the dangling rope ladder and helped her up. Gavin handed her onto the deck.

"Your cabin is here, Lady," he said leading her to one of two small doors tucked under the overhanging edge of the top rear deck.

"And the other?" she asked.

Gavin's face twisted a little. "Lady Margoh."

Startled, Grier realized she had put the young man out of his bed. "But where will you sleep?"

Gavin shrugged. "Kristofer and Lars and I sleep below. Sir Hansen sleeps in the forward cabin."

"I had no intention of putting you out!" Grier exclaimed. "I can sleep below."

A broad grin lightened Gavin's expression. "No, Lady Grier. It's bad for you but no' bad for us. It's only one week and we slept there all month. After Arendal, I get the cabin back, aye?"

"Arendal?"

"Sir Hansen's home."

"Oh." Grier hadn't thought of their destination as being other than the rather vague country of Norway. To have a place name— Arendal—made the voyage less intimidating. "He wasn't at the keep when I woke. Is he here?"

"He was. He'll be back. Then we sail." Gavin offered no further explanation. He bowed a little and then disappeared down the hole in the mid-deck.

Grier climbed the ladder to the top deck. She faced the northeastern sunrise and wondered what Nor—Arendal—would be like. The sun glowed through an orange bank of early morning clouds. A sea breeze blew against her back and pushed her hair forward. It was the same breeze that would push the boat forward.

Grier had wondered what Logan would think of the note she slipped under his door. She never expected him to throw the door open and grab her in the roughest hug of her life. He gripped her face with both hands and smacked a wet kiss on her forehead.

"Thank God, Grier! Thank God!" he cried.

"Are ye daft, Logan?" she gasped.

"Nay! But I've known ye loved Rydar for sae long! And he's admitted the same to you?"

Grier jumped back. "No! He has no'!"

Surprise washed Logan's countenance and left it assured. "And he will Grier. Have patience."

Grier shook her head. "He will no'… He's asked Margoh to go with him."

Logan's lips pressed to a thoughtful line and his eyes narrowed. "Still. He does no' feel for her what he feels for you."

"How can you know this?" Her heart thudded. "Has he said so?"

"No' with words."

Malise appeared beside her new husband, wrapped in a cloak. Her wide eyes were dark in the pre-dawn light. "Are ye leaving, Lady Grier?" There was panic in her voice.

Grier smiled at the young woman. "I am. I'm no' needed here

and you'll do fine as mistress."

Logan hugged his wife to his side. "We'll miss you, Grier. Godspeed."

"And I, you." Grier's throat tightened. "May God bless you with many strong sons."

"What are you doing here?"

Margoh's exclamation destroyed Grier's reverie. She turned to look down at the older woman, glad to know that Margoh had no idea she would be here. Anything that gave her an advantage over the Old Aunt was desirable as far as she was concerned.

Rydar tossed two satchels onto the deck then he sank below the railing. A large chest surged upward and tumbled end-over-end onto the boards.

Margoh shouted something in clipped Norse. Rydar reappeared and scowled at the woman. He barked a response. Gavin and Kristofer popped up from below and dragged the bulging objects into the cabin beside Grier's. Margoh and Rydar gazed up at her and neither looked particularly happy.

Was this a mistake?

She was suddenly quite eager to sail before she could think too hard on it.

ᚱᚾ

The linen sheet caught the wind and the boat galloped over the waves, her bow pointing toward the sun. Grier had never sailed beyond the bay before. As land moved farther from their little vessel she grew anxious. She stood on her toes, gripped the rail of the middle deck, and strained to keep Scotland in sight.

When it melted completely away, and the tiny craft was surrounded by nothing but endless waves and sky, panic nearly drowned her. Her breath came in uneven gasps and she fell to her knees. Sobs tore her throat and the wind chilled her tear-soaked cheeks.

"Rydar!" she screamed.

He was beside her in a blink. "What, Grier? What is amiss?"

"I can no' see Scotland!" she gasped. "I can no' see my home!"

Rydar straightened and his expression stilled like granite; his tone just as hard. "Ye want I take ye back?"

Grier looked up into his eyes, pale and intent. His cheeks twitched as the muscles under his sun-bronzed skin flexed. He was so beautiful. How could she leave him?

"No," she breathed.

"We sail and I can no' take ye back another day," he pressed.

She nodded slowly as her gaze moved to the endless water encompassing them. "I ken."

His tone eased. "All is good?"

"Are we going to die?" she squeaked, her throat constricted by fear.

"No. No' die! Why you ask me this?" He was clearly puzzled.

"The boat is sae wee. And the sea!"—she waved her arm in a frantic circle—"Is sae huge!"

"Aye. But you safe!"

"How can ye find your way?" she pressed. "There's no land!"

A smile lifted one corner of Rydar's mouth. His eyes glowed emerald in the cloud-filtered sunlight. "Come."

He clasped her elbow with strong fingers and led her into the forward cabin. The map of the North Sea that she pinned in his room was here, unrolled on a small table.

Rydar showed Grier the compass she gave him for his birthday and carefully explained in chopped English where they were, where they were going, and how they would know they were headed in the right direction.

"Norway is sae big." Rydar's fingertip traced the long, jagged coastline. "We sail to morning sun and we find it, aye?"

Looking at the map, that seemed likely. "Aye…" she conceded.

Rydar laughed. "We can no' miss it, Grier. Trust me."

She tilted her head back and gave him a wan smile. "I do trust you, Rydar. I've put my life in your hands, have I no'?"

His brow twitched and his smile faded. "Aye. Ye have."

An insistent knock on the door frame made Grier jump. Rydar leaned toward her and rested his palms on her shoulders.

"Do no' frighten," he murmured. He squinted and shook her a little. "I keep you safe."

Margoh's intrusive voice was loud in the small space. "*Jeg har alltid vært interessert i sjøreising!*"

Grier had to smile her rueful acknowledgement. In their contest for Rydar's heart, Margoh had gotten the better of her by speaking in Norse.

"One battle still does no' win a war," Grier whispered.

"What?" Rydar asked her.

"Nothing." Grier waved one hand toward the haughty widow. "Please show Margoh why she has no reason to fear the journey, will you?"

Grier crossed the cabin as gracefully as she could on the rocking craft and stood at the door until Margoh was forced to step back and allow her to leave. Then she lifted a brow and considered the older woman. "I found it quite fascinating."

Grier staggered to her cabin, trying desperately to walk the rolling deck with dignity. Unused to the constant movement, which was even more pronounced when she was closeted with Rydar in the airless forward cabin, she felt rather unwell. She wanted to lie down and close her eyes.

But that didn't help.

Nor did it help the next day.

And it didn't help the next day, either. Dizziness made her queasy and miserable every single moment she was awake. At the least, it kept her mind off the realization she would probably never see Scotland or Logan or little Durness Castle ever again. That was a mercy.

"You are good soon," Rydar assured her. He rubbed her back as she hung over the railing of the boat, but his words were hard to believe as the last of her noon meal became fish bait. Her spirits sank like the bits of food. Worse, she was humiliated in front of the Old Aunt who seemed unaffected by the unrelenting rise and fall of the horizon.

"How many more days?" Grier croaked.

"Four, I think." Rydar squeezed her shoulders. "If weather is good."

"You seem rather susceptible to stomach sickness, Lady Grier." One of Margoh's brows arched. "Might it be that you are with child?"

Incredulous, Grier rounded on the woman, dizziness be damned. "What!"

"You spent quite a lot of time with Lord Andrew... Alone."

"He was a royal guest! 'Twas our duty to serve him!" Grier gripped the slippery rail and pressed the back of one hand to her lips. A weakness passed through her and she wondered that her knees still held her.

Margoh looked overly concerned and her gaze hopped to Rydar then back to Grier. "But he was so handsome and charming… Was it a burden? Servicing him, I mean?"

"I've never lain with a man!" Grier snapped, her voice frustratingly thin. She spit into the water and tried to swallow past her sticky throat. Furious, she pinned her fiercest gaze on Margoh.

"And seeing as how I've no' been visited by an angel, a second virgin birth is highly unlikely!"

Rydar snorted then coughed, his face astonishingly ruddy. His eyes twinkled with amused appreciation. Grier stared at him, her anger throbbing past her nausea.

Then she began to chuckle.

Her chuckle turned into hysterical laughter, a ridiculous reaction to the dark apprehension that held her captive for so many weeks. She dropped onto her arse on the planks, legs sprawled improperly wide, unable to gain control. Tears streamed down her cheeks as tension from the past fortnight flowed out of her in the most unexpected and raucous way. The more she tried to stop laughing, the harder she laughed.

A hissing wheeze pulled her attention. Rydar sank to his knees beside her, his own face wet with tears. His hands gripped his stomach and he bent over. He leaned back, and a rushing gasp preceded the loudest roar of laughter Grier had ever heard from any human.

"Second! Virgin! Birth!" he shouted. His laughter went quiet again as he wheezed the last of his air. Another gasp. Another staccato roar.

Grier smacked the deck. "Stop!" she pleaded, unable to draw a breath against her own mirth. Her cheeks hurt. "Stop it! I can't breathe!"

"No angel!" he blubbered. "No angel! Å min Gud, Grier!"

"I don't see what's so funny!" Margoh spat.

Grier gaped at Rydar.

"Neither do I!" she whooped, then fell back onto the deck alongside the Norseman.

Margoh spun and stomped toward her cabin as the pair laughed themselves into belly-aching exhaustion.

July 24, 1354

Either the episode of hilarity, or the fact that she had finally been aboard the boat long enough, cured Grier's ailing stomach. On the fourth day she awoke feeling fine. It was such a relief that her spirit felt giddy, reborn. She gaily flung open the door of her cabin to greet the morning—and stepped into a world gone gray.

Gray clouds hung low in a cold gray sky. The gray water beneath them undulated in an endless multitude of oily gray swells speckled with tiny rain ripples. Even the sail looked like a limp, gray shroud.

The scent of food drew her to the forward cabin where the cooking fire burned in a large iron pot. Fresh fish sizzled on a grate resting over the fire. Rydar looked up from the meal. His expression brightened when he saw her.

"You look well!" he exclaimed.

"I feel well," she responded. But she shivered in the damp chill.

"The weather?" she asked.

Rydar pressed his lips into a grim smile. "Weather does no' look well."

"It's only raining a little," she offered.

"But, is thing says about weather: wind afore rain, sail fill again. Rain afore wind, your sail, ah, *overvær...*" He shrugged at the Norse word.

"What does that mean?"

"We have rain, not wind. Winds comes, and is bad."

Grier subdued her alarm as best she could, which in truth wasn't very well at all. "Are we safe?"

Rydar stared at her, his beautiful green eyes gone as gray as the day. "I do all I can, Grier."

By afternoon, their swirling world consisted of colorless shades of gloom from top to bottom. Wind pushed against the small craft from all directions, capriciously batting her like a cat toying with a mouse. Yowling through the mast and sail, she foretold their certain demise.

Grier staggered onto the deck. Even though the wind knocked her sideways, she could not bear to sit useless in her cabin where fear would drive her mad. The collision of wind and waves thundered in her ears and stole the men's words as they fought with sail and rudder to keep the boat afloat.

"Can I help?" she yelled to Rydar. "Show me what to do!"

Rydar let go of the spar and his expression shifted between irritation and admiration. Gavin's face showed only fear before he tugged the sail across the deck alone. It pushed him right back again. Grier battled to keep her footing as the storm tried to shake her off the boat.

"Margoh?" she shouted.

"Locked away!" Rydar answered. Then he said something else.

"What?" Grier shrieked. She shoved the already sodden locks from her eyes, though the north wind blew them back with a stinging slap. Rydar's mouth was moving, but she couldn't make out his words.

He closed the space between them. "Help hold rudder!" he bellowed. "Come!"

Grier followed, climbing to the upper deck. Rydar looped a rope around her waist and tied her to the iron ring that secured the sail. Kristofer was already there, straining without success to keep the massive paddle still by himself. Grier nodded and wrapped her arms around the rudder's smooth oak shaft. She braced her feet against the roof over the aft cabins.

"I—hold—spar!" Rydar shouted. He moved away from them.

The storm was so heavy it had substance. There was no way to determine where the sea ended and the clouds began. Violent movement in a featureless void buffeted her without mercy. Cold rain pelted her. Grier closed her eyes and concentrated on holding the pole still.

Her clothes and boots soaked through. Her hair clung to her face and neck like ivy on a stone statue. She licked moisture from her lips, sweet rain mixed with astringent salt.

At first her calves cramped and her thighs burned, their straining effort keeping her warm. But after an hour or more, they were numb. She couldn't feel her arms, and opened her eyes a slit to assure herself that she still held on.

Chapter
Thirty-One

Rydar and Gavin rode the spar, trying by their combined wills to keep the small craft's bow headed into the waves. They swung the sail to one side, then the other, in an elaborate dance with the wind. When they misjudged, water slapped onto the deck and tugged their feet out of rhythm.

Rydar's eyes stung from salt spray and his hands were bloodied. Tears of rage and frustration were disguised by rain and seawater. His chest spasmed with sobs of pain and exhaustion but, by God, he would see it through.

"You cannot have me!" Rydar roared at the storm. "Not this time!"

"What?" Gavin called back. His shirt was torn and sagged around his waist. His skin was blue with cold.

"We'll not go down!" Rydar screamed.

"Hell, no!" Gavin responded. He shoved the spar toward Rydar.

Time was inconsequential. Only the next swing of the spar, the next mouthful of seawater spat out, or the next resistance to movement counted. Eye the wave. Push the sail. Hold it. Don't slip. Don't let go. Once more. Once more.

Once more.

How long it lasted was unclear. All that mattered was that Rydar's enraged tenacity had lasted longer.

ᚱᚺ

"Grier?"

Rydar tugged at the unyielding arms circling the rudder's shaft.

Her eyes blinked open, reflecting a brief glint of moonlight. "What?"

"Is over. You can let go."

Confusion flickered over her features. "I can't."

"I help you." Rydar unwound her and helped her to stand.

"I can't feel my legs." A violent shiver shook through her.

Rydar lifted her and carried her down to the mid-deck. He set her in front of her cabin door, held her steady with one arm, and pounded on Margoh's door with the other.

That door creaked open and Margoh's pale face appeared. "Is it over?" she asked.

"Aye. Now I need you to help Grier undress and get into bed."

Margoh's gaze washed over the drenched woman. "Why?"

"She's a bit worn out from the storm." He adjusted his grip on Grier's waist. "She helped hold the rudder with Kristofer all this time."

"I don't need help," Grier protested, obviously discerning the word *hjelp* in the Norse exchange. She pushed Rydar's arm away and accomplished two uneven steps before she pitched forward. Rydar caught her. She was shaking.

"Stop being so stubborn, woman," he scolded in Norse. He kicked her door open and guided her inside. Her legs folded and she sat down hard on the bed.

Margoh followed him into the cabin. "Go on. I'll see to her," she grumbled.

Rydar gave her what he hoped was a grateful look and left the women alone. He made his way unsteadily across the sodden planks to his own cabin. Behind the closed door he dropped to his knees and rolled on his side, gasping. Deep pain pounded his left shin and spread from his ankle to his thigh. He prayed the bone wasn't broken again. His palms burned, raw with broken blisters soaked in sea salt. Shaken by the storm, he trembled in its aftermath.

While lying on the floor he stripped off his wet clothing, one laborious item at a time. Then he rested, cold and naked, until he trusted himself to stand. He dressed, relishing the feel of dry cloth against his saturated skin. He pulled on a pair of leather boots and wrapped his new woolen cloak around his shoulders.

Kristofer had reheated the pot of fish soup that they didn't have time to eat earlier. Rydar helped himself to a bowl, gulped it, and then refilled it. He took the second bowl to Grier.

Margoh sat on a low stool in Grier's cabin looking bored. "What else do you expect me to do?" she asked Rydar when he limped in, bent over. The cabin's ceiling was too low for him to stand upright.

He looked at the woman curled in the narrow bed, pale in the light of a single candle. "Has she eaten?"

"No." She pointed at the figure in the bed. "She's asleep!"

He swung his gaze to her. "Have you?"

"Yes."

Rydar swallowed the second bowl of soup. It filled his belly with warmth, though he was still hungry. "How is she?"

Margoh shrugged. "She said she was cold."

Rydar handed Margoh the empty soup bowl and knelt beside Grier's berth. Even by the flickering light of the cabin's lone candle he could see that her face was pale and her lips were blue. He laid the backs of his fingers against her cheeks; they felt like cold marble. Though she slept, her muscles twitched randomly in a shivering search for warmth.

"She's mortal cold." He stood and swung the cloak from his shoulders and laid it over the tufted blankets already covering her. "If she doesn't warm, she'll fall ill. Or worse."

He sat on the bed and pulled off his boots.

"What are you doing?" Margoh squeaked.

"Warming her."

"How?"

"How do you think?" He climbed over Grier, wincing when he put weight on his sore leg. He squeezed himself between her and the wall.

Margoh looked frantic. "That's not proper!" she cried.

Rydar snorted. "I'd rather save her life than her reputation; especially in the eyes of a trio of young fishermen she'll naught see again in her lifetime."

Margoh straightened on her stool. "What about in my eyes?"

"If it's that important to you, you may stay." He lifted the edge of the blankets and slid under them. "There's room on the floor."

Margoh jumped to her feet. "You go too far, sir!" she spat.

"Then might you close the door? The night air is not helpful."

Margoh slammed the cabin portal as hard as the wet leather hinges would allow. The puny candle flame wavered in her wake.

Rydar curved around Grier; she was so cold it felt like lying in snow. What warmth his body held left him as he absorbed her chill. He pressed his chest against her back. His thighs snugged under her arse and his knees bent behind her knees. He draped his arm over her and tucked his fist under her chin. Her wet hair was twisted above her head and splayed over the pillow. Rydar rested his face against the nape of her neck.

In increments, she warmed.

And as she thawed, she melted into him.

While Rydar had bedded plenty of women in his life, he'd never kept one overnight. Grier's soft form fit perfectly against his and filled him with such contentment as he had never known. This was so right; this was where she belonged. Grier's presence in his arms soothed his soul as it soothed his body. She healed him with her touch. He was safe, restored.

He must find a way to keep her here, whatever that required.

The first obstacle was already passed: Grier had left Durness.

All used up, Rydar finally allowed himself to sleep.

ᚱᚾ

Grier dreamt she was warm.

She stood on the bluff by Durness castle. There was no sound from the waves, no breeze teasing her hair. Intense summer sunshine wrapped around her shoulders and flowed down the back of her legs. The tension of being cold floated away from her and she relaxed. Her skin prickled. The heat was palpable, reassuring. Substantial.

And then, the heat snored.

With a startled cry, Grier churned through the blankets until she sat at the head of the berth, her back pressed flat against the wall. Her pulse pounded with shock. She didn't remember where she was.

"Grier?" Rydar's voice was coarse with sleep.

Oh, aye. Boat. Storm. "Rydar?"

The candle had guttered, but the night's endless sunset lightened the oiled skin that was stretched over the cabin roof's opening. In the pale glow, Grier could see the outline of Rydar's long frame under the blankets. He lay on his side, knees bent, facing her.

"Aye?" he croaked.

"What in God's good name have you done?" Grier gasped. She crossed her arms over her chest.

He propped himself on one elbow. "What?"

"Ye've bedded with me!" Her voice verged on hysteria.

He cleared his throat and coughed. "I sleep beside you. Is no' same."

"Rydar!" she barked, angry at his word play.

"You too cold, Grier! You shake and you sleep!" he chastised. Then he softened his tone. "You need me. I'm warm."

"But it's no' proper! And everyone must know!" She fought tears, prompted as much by her embarrassment at his presence in her bed as his admission of his care for her.

Rydar snorted. "You care what boys ken? When we are in Norway, they go far away."

"But... Margoh kens, does she no'?" Grier's face heated with anger and shame.

"Aye, she kens. I tell her what I do. And why." Rydar reached for her, fumbling through the covers until he grasped her hand. "I did no' mean you harm, Grier."

"What must she think of me?" she whispered. A sharp shiver shook her.

Rydar squeezed her hand. "I no' care! Now come. You too cold again." He pulled her toward him.

Grier hesitated, the very reason she wished to lie with him was the same reason she wished not to. Another strong shiver pushed her to inch back under the blankets, seeking his substantial warmth. She turned on her side away from him, tense and alert.

Rydar settled along her again. His head rested on one folded arm and he held her close with the other. He sighed deeply. His breath caught in her hair and warmed the nape of her neck. A blade of pleasure slid along her spine.

"Relax, Grier. I no' a 'ruffian' to you and you sleep."

Her pride riled, Grier inhaled sharply but swallowed her retort. Rydar was, after all, completely hers if only for this night's remaining hours. With a slight shift of her weight, she rested against him, easing into his solidity. Daring to take his hand, she laced her fingers with his and nestled them between her breasts.

Grier determined not to sleep; she wanted to feel every inch of his powerful body pressed against hers. Wrapped around hers. For as long as she could. She listened to him breathe, comforted by the slow, steady rhythm of his heart.

A tear rolled off the bridge of her nose and dripped onto her pillow.

July 25, 1354

Grier opened her eyes, angry that she had fallen asleep. She listened but heard nothing; sliding her foot to the other edge of the berth confirmed that she was alone. Had she dreamt Rydar into her bed? No. His cloak still covered her. The memory of his long, lean body pressed against her warmed her in ways that had nothing to do with temperature. She felt his absence as if a part of her was missing.

"Stop such thoughts," she whispered. She pulled his cloak to her face, unable not to. "He's no' interested in you. He slept a night at your side and did no' even kiss you."

Grier pushed the covers back and sat up. Her arms were stiff and ached with overuse. When she tried to stand, her abused muscles rebelled. She tottered around the tiny cabin, painfully pulling a dry kirtle over the chemise she slept in. Her leather boots were still wet, so she slid into a pair of wooden clogs.

Grier stumbled out into blinding sunshine. Rydar was high on the mast, retying the sail. She tilted her head back and considered him from under a cupped hand.

"Are you alive?" he called down, laughing.

"Aye. And why would I no' be?"

"You sleep so hard I must feel you are breathing." Rydar swung down from his task and stood before her on the deck. "You are hungry?"

He looked splendid. Alive. Strong. His light brown hair blew in the wind and his green eyes glowed in the morning sun. The lopsided grin and crooked tooth only made him more beautiful.

"What happened to your hands?" she asked.

Rydar lifted his palms, bound in strips of torn linen. "I do no' have the word."

She unwrapped one hand. "Blisters. And they must pain you something awful." She pointed a finger at him. "I have a salve. Stay here."

He spread his arms toward the endless water, still grinning. "Where else I go?"

Grier staggered to her cabin and returned with a small crock. By the time she did so, Rydar had unwrapped his other hand. She scooped a dollop with her fingers and rubbed it gently into his raw skin.

"Ach!" he grunted.

"Stings a bit. I ken. But it will help the healing and keep infection away."

Rydar sniffed his palm. "Smells like my bed?"

She nodded, still working the salve into the broken blisters. "It has oil of lavender. And beeswax."

"You put here?" He touched her shoulder where the sword sliced her.

Grier smiled a little. He had a good memory. "Aye."

Holding his hands like she was she could feel his pulse. She leaned a little closer and her ministrations slowed; she massaged his hands for longer than was necessary to work the salve into his skin.

"Give me the linen," she whispered. He did so, and she carefully re-wrapped the bandages. Only then did she allow her eyes to meet his. "Does that feel better?"

He watched her intently. The grin was gone. "Aye."

"You're changed," Grier said.

A series of indefinable expressions flicked across his handsome face. "How?"

"I do no' ken. But ye are."

Rydar shrugged. "Might be storm. It tried, but did no' take me this time."

"Might be." Grier could not stop staring at him.

He leaned close and murmured in her ear, "Or might be you heal me in night, too."

Grier believed her cheeks were literally set on fire. Snuffing the flames with cool fingers, she glanced around for unwelcome ears. "Rydar!" she snapped.

"What?" he teased. The grin was back.

"Ye're impossible!" Grier whirled away from him and lurched toward the front cabin—and breakfast—as gracefully as the rolling deck and her stiff, sore legs would allow.

Chapter
Thirty-Two

July 26, 1354

Rydar climbed the mast and looked hard, squinting at the east horizon. A fog bank billowed beneath the morning sun signaling land. His heart began to drum a victory beat against his ribs, harder and faster by the moment. He threw his head back and howled like a wolf sighting a dozen full moons.

"Do you see it?" Lars called up to him.

"Yes! I see it! I see Norway!" Rydar choked on the last word, an unexpected surge of emotion stealing his ability to talk.

"How far?" Lars shouted.

Rydar waved down at him. He couldn't speak past the strangling lump in his throat. He despaired of ever seeing his homeland again and now he was almost there. Almost back where he belonged.

He hugged the mast with both arms and stared at the apparition as Gavin aimed the boat toward the bank of mountains rising slowly from the sea.

For you, Arne. I could not have made it here without you. Rydar crossed himself and said a quick, silent prayer for his friend's soul.

They made landfall on the southernmost tip of Norway in mid-afternoon. Rydar consulted his map and estimated that they were about fifty or sixty miles from Arendal. He showed Gavin, Kristofer and Lars.

Gavin leaned close to the map. "All we need to do is sail with the land on our left until we get there!"

"We will be there by tomorrow morning!" Jubilant, Rydar almost slapped Lars' injured arm before he caught himself. He slapped Kristofer's shoulder instead. "How long will you boys stay before you set sail for Áslo?"

He was met with blank looks.

"Áslo?" Lars' glance bounced around the group. "Are we going to Áslo?"

"Didn't Lady Margoh make arrangements with you?" Rydar demanded.

"Lady Margoh? No..." Gavin said, his brow wrinkling. He turned to Kristofer. "Did she?"

Before Kristofer could answer, Rydar slammed his hand on the table, causing it to creak and wobble in protest. "That bitch!"

Three pair of startled eyes leaned away from him. Rydar glared at the retreating fishermen. "I'm not angry with you! I'm angry with her!"

"Why?" Kristofer ventured.

Rydar paced the confines of the cabin. "She asked for passage to Norway. She said she has family in Áslo. I said I was only going to Arendal. She said she would hire you. To take her there." His tone was as clipped as his sentences.

"Hire?" Gavin stepped forward. "She will pay us?"

Rydar stopped and considered the young man. "That's what she told me. That's why I agreed to bring her along."

"Paying us is a good thing, isn't it?" Lars posited.

"It is, if she will still agree to it," Rydar growled.

"Where is Áslo?" Kristofer asked. Four heads crowded over the map.

"It's almost a hundred and fifty miles..." Gavin looked at the other two. "If we agree to it, how much should we ask her for?"

Lars looked at Rydar. "How much is fair, Sir Hansen?"

Rydar scratched his head, then his beard. He might as well get what he could for the boys; his loyalty lay with them.

"In Scotland a laborer makes a penny a day. But you have to sail overnight, so you should get tippence a day. Each." Rydar grabbed a burnt stick from inside the fire pot and made six hash marks on his table top. "And it will take you at least three days to sail that distance." Rydar made two more sets of six marks. "How many is that?"

"Eighteen," Lars answered. The other two boys blinked at him, surprised. Lars grinned and shrugged the shoulder of his uninjured arm.

Rydar bit back his smile. "That's right. But I wouldn't do it for less than twenty-five."

"Twenty-five? We'll be rich!" Kristofer snickered.

"We could fish on the way!" Gavin suggested. "And sell our catch when we get there!"

"We'll be richer!" Kristofer hopped up and down. "Let's do it!"

"Are we agreed?" Gavin asked Lars.

Lars faced the floor. "It's not up to me. I'll be of no use to you."

Kristofer looped one arm lightly around his younger brother's neck. "But you're part of this, nonetheless. What do you say?"

Lars grinned sheepishly and nodded. "Then we're agreed."

"Good." Rydar moved to the door. "Lars, I'll let Lady Grier know we are nearly to Arendal so she might take the threads out of your arm today. And then I'll inform Lady Margoh that her travel arrangements are completed."

When Rydar asked her, Grier was happy to remove the stitches from Lars' arm. As she did, she gave the young fisherman explicit instructions for the weeks remaining with his splint. He thanked her and Rydar over and again for all of their respective help.

Margoh, on the other hand, was livid.

"How dare you take it upon yourself to hire those boys?" she ranted. "And twenty-five pence? That's usury!"

Rydar stooped crookedly in her cabin. He shrugged. "You may do as you wish, Margoh. I only sought to ease your way by securing your passage, since it slipped your mind to do so."

Margoh's mouth flapped impotently for a moment. "I—it was my intent to—to book passage when—we reached Arendal," she stammered.

"Fine. You are still free to do so."

Rydar turned and opened her cabin door. The wooden clog she lobbed at him clunked against the portal just inches from his head.

July 27, 1354
Arendal, Norway

Rydar recognized Arendal the moment he saw the town again. Tucked about a mile from the open water on an inside passage, the low spit of land was crowded with merchant shops and fishing boats. It appeared much the same as it had the day he watched it fade from sight amidst his mother's muffled sobs and his father's silent fury. His gaze traveled west and up. There was Hansen Hall, its ancient stone walls nestled atop a bluff against the hill's steep side.

"At least it's still there," he whispered. His emotions roared as he stared at his childhood home.

They tethered their little boat at the pier and the boys began to unload Grier's belongings. Rydar had only one bag and he carried it strapped across his shoulder. He climbed down the rope ladder and then assisted Grier's descent. She faced him expectantly.

"What now?" she asked.

What now, indeed. Rydar had plotted the next days with care, praying that his ambitious plans proceeded as he hoped. So much was dependent on the success of his anticipated string of events. He pressed down his anxiety, trusting it didn't show.

"First, lodging," he said.

Her brow quirked. "Lodging? Are you not going to your home?"

"No' first. I must barber and bath."

"Oh! Ye want to look respectable when you appear from the dead, aye?"

Rydar gave her an enigmatic smile. "Aye. Is most like that." He lifted one of her satchels and took her arm. "We go?"

She looked up at him, surprised. "I'm going with you?"

"Aye. I am only one you know here."

"What about Margoh?"

"Margoh no' come with us. She goes to Áslo." He grinned at the thought.

Confusion pinched her features. "Where is that?"

"One hundred and fifty miles away from Arendal."

Her mouth burst open. "How?"

"Boy fishermen take her. She pays them." Rydar shrugged and

tugged Grier's arm. "Does no' matter."

Grier refused to be moved. "But I thought you asked her to come to Norway with you!"

An incredulous laugh burst from him. "No! She ask me."

"But she said…" Grier's expression transformed from flustered to furious. "That bitch!"

Rydar nodded. "I say same!"

Grier glared up at Rydar from under lowered copper brows. "Do you expect me to come to your home with you?"

There was one piece of his plan. "I hope aye," he confessed. Before she could argue with him, he added, "Can you barber?"

"Barber?" That clearly took her by surprise. "Aye."

"Good." He tugged her arm again. "We go."

ᚱᚾ

Grier scraped the blade over Rydar's soapy chin and then wiped it on a towel. She tried to concentrate on the task at hand—and not risk the man's life—while the morning's surprising events played through her mind.

Rydar never asked Margoh to come with him to Norway.

Margoh was not here with Rydar, but she was.

Rydar wanted her to come to his home with him.

She wasn't left alone to fend for herself in this land where she couldn't understand anything that was said to her.

Yet.

And now they had two rooms at an inn. She was in his room. Shirtless, he wore only braies and hose while Grier stood between his long, warm thighs, held his chin, and shaved every hair from his sculpted cheeks and strong jaw. Rydar's eyes were fixed on hers, their green pools drowning her.

"Ye can no' keep staring at me like that, and ye wish me not to cut you!" she scolded.

With a slight wink, he lowered his gaze. She finished and handed Rydar a wet towel. He wiped his face clear of soap and examined his reflection in the mirror she held in front of him.

"Very good, Grier. What you think?" He grabbed his now shoulder-length locks. "Cut my hair?"

I think you're perfect just as you are. I think you're the most beautiful man I've ever met.

"It seems the men in the town wear their hair long," she said instead.

"What you like?" he pressed. "Long or short?"

"It's perfect," she breathed.

Rydar nodded, his gaze and smile slowly yielding. He seemed to be pondering something far away. "Hungry?" he asked.

"Aye."

While Grier put away the barbering things, Rydar pulled the tunic she made from his satchel and slipped it over his head. The last time he wore it was at Logan's wedding. A stab of homesickness twisted through her.

He raised his brows at her. "Good?"

"Perfect," she said again.

They ate downstairs at the inn and Rydar ordered their best meats and their best wine. He was unusually quiet and Grier wondered what thoughts bound his tongue.

But she kent she'd be a puddle of parritch if she faced such uncertainty as he. If she found herself returning to Durness after leaving on bad terms. If she couldn't know who of her family still lived—if anyone—following such widespread devastation as the Black Death.

After finishing the meal and the wine, Rydar stood and offered his hand. "I have a thing to talk with you," he said quietly. "We go to your room. For... alone."

Grier's knees quivered like the parritch she truly was. He was so withdrawn as they ate that whatever 'thing' he wanted to discuss must be bad. And he had just spoilt her with food and drink of the best quality to ease her mood in preparation. She realized that she had rejoiced in her situation far too quickly.

Rydar led her to her room without speaking while Grier tried to think of what she might do when he turned her out. She had money. She could pay for lodging, maybe with a family. She would ask for help with the language. Perhaps an assistant might be found who had English; then she could begin to practice healing while she learnt Norse. Certainly Rydar would help her in the search. He owed her that much.

When they reached her room, Rydar opened the door. He followed her inside and shut the door decisively. He gestured toward a chair and Grier sat, but only because her shaking legs refused to support her any longer. She prayed that her expensive dinner would stay put and not spill all over the floor.

Rydar stood in the center of the room, his hands gripped behind his back. He stared hard at Grier for several long, silent eternities. His face was flushed and his jaw muscles rippled under his newly shaven skin. When he spoke, his words came out in a rush.

"Marry me, Grier."

Chapter
Thirty-Three

Grier's eyes widened in shock and her surging pulse dulled her hearing. "What!"

"Marry me," he repeated.

She was not at all prepared for his words. "Why?"

Rydar grimaced. His fists swung out from his back, clenched. "I ken we are… same."

Grier sucked a breath through her teeth. She held it a moment, then let it out slowly. She kent she had to be honest with him, no matter how strongly she felt about the man. Though it might kill her, it was only right.

"You may think me daft, Rydar. And I would no' blame ye at all, considering where we are. But"—she swallowed a bit of the meal that climbed up the back of her throat—"I'll no' marry without love."

"I be sae good husband, Grier," he offered.

This was unbearably hard. Her one love stood before her and offered her heart's deepest desire. Grier longed to simply say yes and make the best of what might follow. Perhaps she should. Her chest tightened with unshed tears.

His pale green eyes searched hers. "Might be in time you start to love me?"

Grier frowned her confusion. "Love you?"

Rydar cleared his throat. "Is so hard?"

Grier stood, needing to make her point very, very clear. "No, Rydar! I spoke of you."

"Me?" Rydar's palm smacked his chest.

"Aye." Grier stepped closer. "I'll no' marry a man who does no' love me as I am."

Rydar fell back a pace, visibly shocked. Then he started to laugh. Hard.

"It's no' funny!" Grier cried.

"No! No is no'!" Rydar waved his hands. "I'm sorry, Grier! I've no' done this afore and I make a mess!"

With effort worthy of Robert the Bruce, Grier held together the scraps of her tattered emotions. "Un-mess it then, man! And quickly!" she demanded.

Rydar stopped laughing and rested his hands on his hips. He stared silently at the wood-grained floor, visibly gathering his composure. Then he faced Grier once again. His green eyes flamed.

"Grier MacInnes, I love ye with all my heart."

She disbelieved her ears. "What?"

Rydar stepped closer. "I love you."

"Aye?"

"Aye."

"Ye do?"

"I do."

"Oh… Aright, then," she said shakily. She was soupy parritch again. Was the chair close behind her?

Rydar reached for her hands. "You marry me, and now ye ken?"

Stunned, Grier met his gaze. "Do you no' care how I feel about you?" she blurted.

"You do no' love me now. Later you do, aye?"

"Rydar Hansen, you are a whappin fool."

Rydar bristled. "And what means that?"

Grier laid a hand against his flushed cheek. "I asked you to take me with you, did I no'?"

"Aye…"

"And do you believe that I would leave everything I ever kent for anything other than love?" Grier asked.

Understanding pulled all color from Rydar's face, then splashed it with joyous red. "You ask, and you love me?"

Grier nodded, her voice strangled.

"But I ask you!" Rydar exclaimed. "I ask you why!"

Grier's face heated with embarrassment. "Aye, you did."

"Why you did no' tell me?"

"I believed you loved Margoh."

"Margoh!" His face twisted. "Why?"

She spread her hands wide. "She said you asked her to sail with you."

Rydar scowled. "No…"

"And you spent so much time with her…"

"She teach me your talk!" he objected.

"She is beautiful…"

Rydar shrugged. "You sae more beautiful!"

Surprised, Grier flushed again. "But she wanted you…"

"I'm no' a thing she has without my say!" Rydar straightened. He towered over Grier. "I am strong man with my own plan!"

Grier jumped back as if stung, hands framing her face. His declamation had suddenly become real in her mind.

"Rydar! You love me!"

"Aye!" he barked. And then his countenance shifted to disbelief. "And you love me?"

"Aye," Grier breathed.

They stared at each other and the world was no longer the same.

"We marry, then?" Rydar asked.

Grier's hands drooped by her side. It was happening so fast. Nothing she expected, but everything she wanted. "Aye. We marry."

"When?"

Grier shrugged. "When do you wish?"

"This day. Before we go to my home."

Grier tried to think of a reason why they should wait but her mind wouldn't cooperate; the realization that Rydar loved her flooded its every corner with blinding light.

He lifted her hands to his lips. He kissed each of her knuckles without moving his consuming gaze from hers. He carefully repeated the English words they heard at Logan and Malise's wedding.

"Grier MacInnes, I pledge my troth. I take you for wife. From this day, you're mine and I'm yours."

Grier felt like she was in a dream. "Rydar Martin Petter-Edvard Hansen, I pledge to you my troth as well. I take you as my husband." Grier turned his hands over and gently kissed both of his rough, healing palms.

Rydar smiled at her with an intensity that gushed into her and warmed her from the inside out. "I go now and find priest for bless us. This night, you are my wife."

ᚱᚺ

Rydar remembered the church well. Constructed of heavy wooden staves and standing three stories tall, the two-hundred-year-old structure was in the center of Arendal. He spoke to the priest and gave the coins necessary for the cleric to prepare the papers that would legalize their marriage. Then he headed to the boat to ask Gavin to be his witness and hoped the boys were still there.

The boat remained tied to the pier, right where he left it. "Gavin!" he shouted.

The young man's face appeared over the edge and spilt in a wide grin. "Sir Hansen!" The rope ladder unrolled to meet him and Rydar climbed aboard.

"I was afraid you might have left for Áslo!" Rydar said, slapping Gavin's back.

"Not yet. Lady Margoh is trying to find a lower fee for the passage."

"Lower than twenty-five pence?"

Gavin snickered. "No, lower than thirty pence. Lars said that twenty-five didn't split into three equal portions, but thirty did. So that is what we asked for."

Rydar nodded his amused approval. "And what has Lady Margoh discovered thus far?"

Kristofer appeared through the hole in the deck. "Nothing below fifty pence!" he exclaimed, clambering to stand beside them. "No one wants to waste their time sailing so far."

"So, now we'll ask for forty-five," Gavin added. "Lars said fifty didn't split well either, but forty-five does. And then we're asking less than the others and she should be grateful."

Rydar tossed back his head and laughed. "Thank God for Lars!"

Lars opened one small cabin door and emerged. He had his good arm through the sleeve of his shirt; the broken arm was still tied to his side as Grier instructed. "What are you saying about me?"

"You figure numbers in your head very well, Lars," Rydar complimented. "You can keep these other two from becoming destitute!" Lars blushed and smiled. Rydar gripped Gavin's shoulder. "I've come to ask a rather unexpected favor."

"Anything," the young fisherman answered. "You have done so many favors for us already!"

"Will you be my witness, Gavin? I am marrying the Lady Grier."

Rydar wasn't prepared for the eruption of pure joy that followed his statement. All three boys jumped and hollered. Lars punched Kristofer who in turn punched Gavin.

"We were so afraid you might take the Lady Margoh!" Kristofer cried.

Gavin nodded, relief written on his countenance. "And the Lady Grier is completely besotted with you!"

"I knew you wouldn't, Sir!" Lars stated confidently. "I knew you wouldn't make such a foolish choice!"

Stunned, Rydar wondered if his own feelings had been so evident. "Well, then…"

"I'm honored, Sir. When will you marry?" Gavin asked.

"Now."

Their jaws dropped.

"Will you come?" Rydar teased. "Or shall I hire the innkeeper to stand beside me?"

In the rush for the ladder, Rydar was the last one off the boat.

When Grier opened the door to her room, she was dressed in the brown velvet gown, silver belt and silver-embroidered snood that she wore the day Lord Andrew arrived. Rydar ignored that particular memory.

"Å min Gud, Grier. You so beautiful!" Rydar murmured. He looked down at his own apparel, dismayed. "I'm not."

"But you're wearing the tunic I made for you, Rydar. The one you wore at Logan's wedding. The one that matches your eyes and your hair," she countered. "And I thought you were the most beautiful man attending that day."

Rydar was skeptical. "No. No' more 'beautiful' man than Logan."

Grier stepped forward and slid her hands around his waist. She lifted her smiling face to his. "Are you calling your bride a liar?" she challenged playfully. "You better kiss her quickly, then, and reassure her!"

ᚱᚺ

Grier pinched herself. Twice.

It was so hard to believe that she had truly left Durness and was here in Arendal, Norway. In this soaring, dark wooden church. With the Viking she was so completely in love with standing tall and straight by her side. Listening to the priest perform her wedding mass.

Both she and Rydar understood the Latin service. When the vows were spoken, his deep voice echoed in the large building and vibrated through her soul. Grier's heart was so overfull with joy she wondered that it could still beat.

Gavin stood beside Rydar and, when the sacrament was completed, he signed the papers witnessing their legal marriage. The brothers, Kristofer and Lars, stood behind them, shoving each other and grinning like madmen.

When everything was finished, Rydar pulled her close and kissed her very well. She kissed him very well in return, until the priest abruptly cleared his throat and slapped Rydar's shoulder with enough force to make his point clear.

"*Rikelig med gang for,*" he declared.

Grier looked to Rydar, the question clear in her expression.

"Much time for that," Rydar murmured in her ear.

"Oh!" Grier was horrified. And embarrassed. And surprisingly aroused.

The wedding party left the church and wound back through Arendal to the inn, where Rydar promised them all a celebratory supper. He held Grier close to him, as if she might dissolve were he to loosen his grasp. To the northwest, the sun hid behind distant coastal mountains that cast long purple shadows over the town. Glorious pink and orange streaks shot across a pale turquoise sky. Everything was so perfect.

Everything, except for the slim figure standing at the door to the inn, arms crossed over her breast and her mouth pursed under storm-gray eyes. Margoh blurted something in Norse. Her gaze flitted with disdain over the five celebrants.

Rydar gestured for the three boys to go on inside but his grip on Grier's waist tightened. She didn't attempt to move away. In truth, she was quite curious about the source of Margoh's extreme irritation.

"Alone!" Margoh added in English.

Rydar answered in kind. "What you say, Margoh, you say in front of my wife."

Grier startled to hear herself called a wife for the first time, especially in such a cold, cautionary tone. She daren't look to Rydar; instead she faced her foe, confident in this, her most decisive victory.

"Wife! Since when?" Margoh considered them more carefully then. Her gaze swept over Grier's velvet gown and silver trappings, Rydar's tunic worn at Logan's wedding. His arm tightly around her waist. Her triumphant smile. Grier watched Margoh's expression slide from anger to surprise to despair.

"When?" she cried.

"We come from church now," Rydar continued in English. Grier kent that was for her sake and she loved him for it. "What you need?"

Margoh spoke defiantly in rapid Norse, refusing to look at Grier.

He answered in English. "And no one here sails you for less. Only more."

She babbled again, and Rydar said, "Is what you say you do. I finish now."

Margoh pleaded with him then. Grier didn't need to know her words; she clearly understood the woman's tone. She looked older, suddenly. Worn out and desperate. Grier felt a little sorry for the Old Aunt.

Rydar interrupted her. "Margoh, you come for supper?"

Margoh stepped back as if struck. The color drained from her face leaving purple smudges under her blue-gray eyes.

"No. *Takk du*," she whispered.

Rydar dipped his chin in acknowledgement, and then faced

Grier. "Come, my love."

He pulled her into the building leaving Margoh alone on the stoop.

ᚱᚺ

Rydar stood outside Grier's door with his satchel. He paid for their wedding supper and this room with the last of his coins, after convincing the innkeeper that he was honestly mistaken when he asked for two rooms this morning. He ordered Grier a hot bath during supper. He expected she was experiencing that luxury right now.

He told himself there was no reason to delay. He had every right to enjoy his new wife's body while she bathed. He prayed that she agreed.

Rydar pushed the door open and stepped into Valhalla.

Grier lounged in the steaming tub beside the hearth, her russet curls tied on top of her head. A few strands straggled around her neck and pointed to the valley between her breasts. She smiled at him, a smile that was unlike any he had ever seen on her. It was sleepy, sultry, and seductive.

"Good eve, husband."

"Good eve, wife," he answered. He dropped the satchel where he stood. And he latched the door.

Her voice was husky. "How do I call you in Norse?"

"*Kone* is wife and *mann* is husband. *Du er min* means 'you are my'…"

"*Du er min mann*, Viking," Grier whispered.

"*Og du er min kone*," he replied.

Grier placed her hands on the edges of the tub and rose. Water sluiced off her pink skin in a multitude of tiny waterfalls. Light from the fire slid over her curves. Her narrow waist widened to luscious hips and a firm arse. Her breasts rounded from her chest in matching perfection and he imagined the taste of their deep auburn tips on his tongue.

"Hand me a towel?"

Rydar moved as in a dream. He could hardly comprehend that this magnificent woman was his wife. His gaze fell to the triangle of copper curls, the imagining of which had tormented so many of his nights. He gave her the towel.

Grier began to dry herself. She stepped from the tub without any discernable shyness. "Would ye care to use the water?" she asked. "It's still quite warm."

Rydar nodded and began to tug at his clothes. The pieces tumbled, forgotten, to the floor. When he pushed his braies down, he hesitated. He was fully erect and he didn't want to frighten her.

"Go on," she murmured. "I'm curious."

He looked up at her to determine whether her curiosity held any fear.

Her smile did tremble a little. "I saw men limp when I prepared them for burial during the Death," she said softly. "I understand that tonight I will experience something much more enticing."

Rydar grinned at her bravery and nodded. He pushed his braies over his feet and stepped away from them. Then he straightened and stood naked and rigid for her to inspect. Grier gasped. But there was no fear in her expression, only amazement. He closed the distance between them.

"Can I touch it?" she asked.

"I bath first, aye?" he suggested. He stepped into the bathwater before she could answer. He was so aroused by her eagerness, that one brush of her fingers and he might have erupted all over her hand.

Grier finished drying herself and she brought towels for him. She sat on a small stool beside the tub and combed her hair while he bathed.

"*Du er slik vakker, min kone*," he said.

"*Du er slik vakker, min mann*," she repeated.

Rydar chuckled. "Do you ken what you say?"

Grier's sapphire eyes glittered with laughter in the firelight. "You are 'something something' my husband."

He chuckled, and then translated, "So beautiful."

"Ah. And I was right, was I no'?" She put her comb down and leaned closer. "So, Viking, will you please come love me now?"

It was Rydar's turn to gasp. He stood and allowed Grier to dry him. Every inch of him. Her fingers explored his length and slid around the ridge of his tip. He struggled to keep control. His jaw clenched, and his muscles strained.

"What is amiss?" she asked, her brow puckered with concern.

"You touch more, I can no' stop," he groaned.

"Oh!" Grier jerked her hand away. She dropped the towel and moved to the tall bed. She pulled the covers all the way back. Climbing onto the mattress, she turned to look at him. Her cheeks were flushed and her eyes smoky.

Rydar followed and lay alongside her. He kissed her while his hand roamed over the curved landscape of her pale skin. She touched him in imitation, learning as he led. He wanted to be gentle this first time, but urgency quickened his pace. He rolled over and held himself above her, working one knee then the other between her legs.

"I try and no' hurt you," he rasped.

"I ken. Do no' worry." She spread her thighs. Her breaths came in quick bursts. "Let's do this quickly, so we may do it again later."

Å min Gud. His virgin bride was the most eager lover he had ever encountered. Rydar pressed his hardness against her.

"Help me," he whispered. "Put me right..."

Grier took hold and worked the tip of him into her. "There..."

She kept her hand on him until he pushed, easing himself into her slippery depth. Her entire body tensed for a moment. She winced and bit her lip when he began to move, pulling back gently and sliding in again. Then with a deep sigh, she relaxed.

When he stroked her again, she wrapped her legs around him. His movement gained rhythm, and his rhythm gained speed. Small grunts escaped her as she gave herself over to his welcomed intrusion. Before he would have counted it possible, her back arched, her grunts became gasping cries and her body twisted under him.

Rydar closed his eyes then, and let himself go, pushing deep and releasing inside her. He moaned as pulsating ripples tingled through him from the point of their joining out to the tips of his fingers and toes. He twitched and pressed hard against her, unable and unwilling to let this most astonishing coupling reach an end.

Chapter Thirty-Four

July 28, 1354

Grier opened her eyes to find that her dream was real. Rydar lay behind her, one hand loosely cupping her breast. He was hard against her bottom but she kent that was common for men in the morning. She rolled toward him and his eyes were open, pale green ponds that submerged her completely.

"*Jeg er din kone,*" she whispered. I am your wife.

"*Og jeg er din mann,*" he replied in kind. Then he kissed her with moist lips and a teasing tongue. She hummed a little moan of happiness.

Grier stretched long and lazily, and then re-curled against Rydar's warm, muscular length. Memories of their night's activities made her smile. The pleasure she found at Rydar's touch went far beyond her most imaginative expectations. All three times.

"I do no' wish to ever leave this room," she sighed. "Might we stay another night?"

Rydar combed his fingers through his hair and his smile evaporated.

She touched his cheek, tracing the thin pink scar that was again visible with his beard gone. "Rydar? What's amiss?"

He sighed. "You ken why I no' ask you to come with me?"

Grier tensed and her pulse quickened; why would he bring that up now? They were married and consummated. Thoroughly consummated.

She shook her head.

Rydar's cheeks seemed to fall inward and his gaze intensified. "I lost all and first boat sinks, aye?"

"Aye..."

"I hunt and get coins. I use coins for new boat, aye?"

Grier propped herself on one elbow, relieved at the direction of his explanation. "And ye do no' ken if you have family or money or position here. I kent that afore we sailed."

He flashed a rueful grin. "And ye—declined—Lord Andrew. He has all money and all power."

"I declined him because I was in love with you!" Grier exclaimed.

Rydar frowned. "But—but I ask Logan why you declined. And he say—"

"—That I was unwilling to leave Durness?" Grier interrupted. She smacked her forehead in realization. "That's the reason I gave him because I could no' tell him that I hoped for you! And you gave me sae little to hang those hopes on!"

Rydar's eyes widened. "You and I kent wrong things!"

That was an understatement in its extreme.

"Aye!" Grier gave a frustrated chuckle and stroked her hand across Rydar's chest, the curly light brown hairs tickling her palm. "I loved you when ye first looked at me. I do no' care how wealthy ye are, or how wealthy ye are not. I only wish to sleep beside you for the rest of my life."

Rydar lifted her chin and took her mouth. This kiss was slow and tender, with reminders of the past night and promise of more. Much more.

Grier pulled back and grinned at her husband. "So we can no' stay because you've no more coins?"

He nodded. "Aye."

Grier tossed the sheets aside and hopped on bare feet across the room to her basket, naked but for her cloak of waist-length curls. She fumbled for its false bottom and gripped the small leather pouch hidden there. She stood and turned slowly to face her husband. She dangled the pouch before her as she sauntered in her newly seductive fashion back to their bed.

"What that is?" he asked.

Grier tossed him the pouch and knelt on the mattress. "Open it."

Fifteen gold coins tumbled out, rattling in metallic chorus and gleefully catching the room's dim light. Rydar froze, stunned into confused silence.

Grier giggled. "Say something!"

His pale eyes lifted to hers. "Where you get this?"

"My da gave it to me afore he died. He said I should make my way with it." She laid her hand over his and squeezed. "We'll make our way with it together."

Rydar pressed his lips to a line and then considered Grier with narrowed eyes. "You trust me?"

"With my very life," Grier answered, her curiosity piqued. "What are ye thinking?"

Rydar leaned toward her. "I think this: we go to my father's house in good clothes. We look like we are right to be there. They will no' ken of us, aye?"

Grier saw the logic immediately. "So we present ourselves as worthy of the estate and the inheritance? As if your rights can no' be questioned?"

He nodded confidently.

"That will take some days, will it no'?" Grier pointed out. "And we might stay here, then?"

His hand slid up her leg to the forest at its apex. He smiled in a way that stole her breath as his long fingers wiggled deeper between her thighs.

"Aye. We go for clothes, then wait for them and they are finish. And we have food come up. So"—his lopsided grin charmed her—"you do no' need leave room for days."

"Promise?" Grier whispered. She wrapped her arms around Rydar's neck and eagerly gave herself over once again to his intoxicating touch.

August 2, 1354

After exchanging one of the gold coins with a moneychanger, and waiting five days for their new clothes, and selecting two fine horses with beautifully wrought tack to carry them, and energetically loving each other three times a day with an intensity and creativity that left both Rydar and Grier sweating and breathless and longing for more, it was time to emerge from the cozy room at the inn, with its very accommodating bed, and face their very uncertain future.

Rydar lay close to Grier and watched the sky slowly lighten. This day they would collect their expensive apparel. They would ride their matching mounts up the hill to Hansen Hall. And he would enter the home of his childhood for the first time since he was a boy.

That prospect submerged him into the despair of the dark days before he left Arendal. His father, scowling and silent. His mother, red-eyed and weepy. His two older sisters assuring him it would all work itself out, and then standing on the shore in white-faced shock when the ship carried their family away. Forever.

No. Not forever.

Rydar had come home.

He was eager to know if his sisters survived. Moving through Arendal these past days he could see what he saw in Durness: far too many empty houses and far too many crowded graveyards. Streets once filled with merchants pressing their wares on those who passed, now held more serene shop owners doing business in the bottom stories of some of the houses. The town was so much emptier than he remembered.

Well it would be, with more than half of the population gone.

Rydar determined he would search for his sisters soon. He would ask about them at Hansen Hall today; whoever remained there should know of them. Though he doubted they would recognize him, he thought he might know them. Astrid would be thirty-two, and Pernilla, the one who went into the service of the church, thirty-three. Or perhaps thirty-four.

Their ages don't matter. *All that matters is that I find what is mine, whatever that may be.*

"What are you pondering so fiercely, husband?" Grier's sleepy voice pierced his thoughts.

"*Du,*" he replied and hugged her. "*Alltid du.*" Since the day after their marriage, Rydar had taken to speaking to Grier in simple Norse, only translating when she was hopelessly lost.

"Always me?" Grier shifted her weight against him and grinned tiredly. "*Du er en* liar!"

Rydar chuckled.

"What is 'liar'?" she mumbled against his chest.

"*Liar*."

"Good. Since you are one, I'll know how to call you!" she teased.

Rydar tangled his fingers in her bed-tossed curls. The fierce color of her hair still fascinated him. "Do you think our children will have this hair?" he asked in Norse.

"*Ja*," she grunted, eyes closed.

"*Gjør deg forstår?*" Do you understand?

"*Ingen*." No.

Rydar slid his hands under her arms and pulled her on top of him. "What will I do with you?" he grumbled.

She understood that, apparently, because she snuggled her head under his chin and gripped his hips with her knees. "You will love me, husband," she sighed. "Now."

He did not hesitate.

The sun was fully up. Streaks of pink surged through the window, coloring Grier's skin and setting her wild hair aflame. She rode Rydar's hips as he bucked under her. His hands circled her waist to keep her from falling while he abandoned all control and pushed himself ever deeper inside her. She cried out when she peaked and might have tumbled backward if he hadn't held her against him. His grunts of release felt like they began in his toes and fought through his body to emerge loud and ecstatic. Grier collapsed against his chest, panting. Yet again, Rydar found it hard to believe that this beautiful woman was his forever.

And he almost left her behind in another country. A shudder shot through him.

Grier raised her head and rested her chin on her fist. "Husband?"

"I'm glad you asked to come with me," he said in slow Norse.

"I'm glad, too," she answered in the same language.

ᚱᚺ

Rydar reined in his mount. To his left was the glittering outlet to the North Sea. Over the cries of single-minded gulls, he could hear waves impaling themselves below the cliff. He wondered how far down the water actually was.

To his right was Hansen Hall. Dominated by a round tower built of rough stones, its turreted top stood three stories over the road. There were no windows in the tower, only the vertical slits which allowed archers to defend the inhabitants.

Viking archers.

Rydar felt their presence in the breeze that stroked his cheek. A thrill tingled up his spine and his belly clenched with recognition. He nodded his silent respect to those whose restless blood he shared.

Extending off one side of the tower was a two-story structure of gray quarried stone, built at the turn of this century. The addition had several glass windows, leaded in a multitude of small diamond-shaped panes. The front door was visible in an arched alcove beyond the gate of the tidy walled courtyard. Rydar turned to Grier.

His wife was stunning. Her glorious red hair was tamed under a snood of fine silver silk stitched with gold threads and seed pearls. Her gown was the blue of the sky, but it was shamed by the blue of her eyes. Her ermine-trimmed dark purple cloak fell back over her shoulders and was fastened across her breast by a gold and amethyst chain. She gave him a smile that set his soul ablaze.

"You look regal, Viking, especially with that long sword by your side," she declared. "Emeralds are your gem, sable is your fur, and burgundy is your color. No one who lays eyes on ye could ever doubt your place in this world."

Rydar pulled a bracing breath. "Now is our time, wife. You are ready?"

She nodded.

They rode across the bridge and into the courtyard. Rydar dismounted from his Arabian gelding and then lifted Grier from her matching mare. When no one appeared to take their horses, he blew a shrill whistle. A boy of about twelve or thirteen sprinted through a gateway, slid to a stop, gaped at the richly dressed pair, then approached them, bowing continuously.

"See to our horses, will you?" Rydar handed their reins to the lad.

"Yes, Sir!" he answered in a voice cracked by puberty. He led the animals back through the gate, glancing over his shoulder at the intentionally imposing couple.

Rydar took Grier's arm and they climbed the curved stone steps, already worn in the center from decades of shoes, until they faced the massive portal. The dark wooden door stood under a carved "H" which had, on either side, sculpted friezes: Thor on one side, and the Christ on the other. Rydar grabbed the round iron knocker and thrust it against the planks.

The door creaked open. A short man Rydar didn't know looked up his length to meet his eyes. "How may I assist you, sir?"

"I'm here to see the lord of the manor," Rydar answered.

The man's gaze flickered over Rydar's tall frame and paused on the daunting sword. When he glanced at Grier his brows arched appreciatively, annoying Rydar with his impudence.

He returned his attention to Rydar. "And you are?"

Rydar had debated when to give his name. If he gave it at the door, he might not be believed. Or worse, he might be believed and denied entry. But not giving a name would clearly raise suspicions. He figured he would know which to do when he reached this moment.

He didn't.

"Sir? Your name?" the short man pressed.

The answer came, then. It was simple and perfect. "Hansen."

"Hansen? Which Hansen?"

"That is for the lord of the manor. Please announce me, and my wife."

The man glared at the well-dressed couple, then stepped back allowing them into the manor's once opulent entryway. He led them to a parlor off to one side. The furnishings there were sparse but well matched.

"Wait here," he commanded before stomping out of sight.

Rydar hadn't noticed as a child, but inside the building the transition from the ninth century tower to the fourteenth century hall was not as disjointed as on the exterior. The manor appeared largely unchanged since his boyhood; only a bit worn and with far fewer servants rushing about. An avalanche of memories covered Rydar and threatened to suffocate him. He felt Grier's hand on his arm.

"Are ye well?" she whispered, alarm etched on her face.

He jerked a nod. "Aye."

A tall, slim figure approached, dressed in a jewel-embellished satin tunic over a silk shirt. His hose were finely knit and he wore soft, cuffed leather boots with wooden soles. His middle-aged face was vaguely familiar, but something about his appearance was out of place. What that was, Rydar couldn't yet name.

"Good day, travelers. How may I assist you?" he asked in a smooth tenor voice.

"Good day, sir. May I ask your name?" Rydar began.

"My name?" The man frowned. "Do you not know where you've come?"

"Hansen Hall," was Rydar's clipped response.

"Yes, of course." He smiled again, but offered no answer to the question.

Rydar glanced at Grier. She nodded slightly, but he couldn't know if she understood what was being said, or was merely encouraging him. He tried another tack.

"Who is lord of the manor since the Death?"

The man dipped his chin and crossed himself in overtly pious reverence. "I am."

This game of evasion could go on forever; Rydar decided to thrust more offensively. "Where is Lord Harald Martin Hansen?"

The man blinked. "Gone. In the plague, God save his soul. His two sons were taken as well." He crossed himself again and kissed his fingertips.

Rydar felt punched in the gut; he remembered his cousins fondly, though they were a decade older than he. Now they were dead and lost to him forever. With a nod of acknowledgement, Rydar pressed forward.

"And Harald's brother, Balder. Where is he?"

The man's eyes narrowed. "He remains in the priesthood, having foresworn all earthly goods. Who did you say you were?"

"What of Rolf?" Rydar parried, ignoring the man's query.

"Killed in the Crusades. Who are you?" The man frowned; his genteel façade was tumbling away.

His mouth gone dry with grief, Rydar straightened his stance. At six-and-a-half feet he dwarfed everyone in the room. This was the pivotal question and it needed to be asked with the proper air of authority.

"And Petter-Edvard? What became of him?"

The man stepped closer, squinting in his intense perusal of

Rydar. "What does he matter?"

"Let's say I'm... curious." Rydar bent over to put his eyes at the other man's level. "Tell me what became of Petter-Edvard Hansen!"

The man retreated and waved his hand dismissively. "Disowned. He fled the country decades ago."

"Did he have sons?" Rydar pressed.

Fear shot through the other man's countenance but vanished quickly. "One."

"And where is he now?"

The man sneered. "The father's destination was Grønnland. If the boy still lives, which I highly doubt, he's mucking out a life there."

Rydar nodded, seeming to be satisfied. He relaxed his stance hoping to lull the man into confidence. "And how did you come to be lord of the manor? Are you a Hansen?"

At that the man bowed. "My name is Jakob Sander Hansen. I am a cousin to Harald by marriage."

The name niggled at Rydar's memory. It was familiar, but not quite right, as was the man himself. "And you are the only remaining Hansen, then?"

"Sadly, I am."

"Have you a wife? Children?" Rydar prodded.

Sir Jakob shook his head and waved a chastising finger at Rydar before turning and walking to the other side of the parlor. "I don't believe you've introduced yourself sir, nor your beautiful wife who stands so silently by your side."

He faced Rydar again from across the room and clasped his hands behind his back, chin raised. He cocked one brow. "I'm waiting."

Rydar turned to Grier. "You ken what he say?" he asked her in English.

She dipped her chin and considered him from beneath her auburn lashes. Her carriage and expression were suitably solemn. "Aye. Most all. It's your turn now, is it no'?"

Then she winked at him.

Her sudden playfulness sent a silent chuckle through his gut. Unexpected, it fortified him in ways he never could have anticipated. No matter what happened next, this strong, stubborn

Scottish woman would endure it alongside him.

Rydar faced Jakob and mimicked his stance. "I beg your pardon, Sir Jakob. May I present the Lady Grier MacInnes Hansen of Durness Castle, Scotland?"

Grier gave him a dignified bow, appropriate for a married woman of her hoped-for station.

Confusion wrinkled Sir Jakob's brow. "My pleasure, my lady. Did you say Hansen?"

"And I am..." Rydar cleared his throat to keep the man in suspense, then waved his hand apologetically. "I beg your pardon. Road dust, you understand."

Sir Jakob reddened; a good host would have offered ale by now. A well-born host would not have forgotten. But before he could rectify the omission, Rydar spoke again, using the man's embarrassment as an opening for the thrust of his verbal blade.

"I am the Lord Rydar Martin Petter-Edvard Hansen, the last living heir to Hansen Hall."

Chapter
Thirty-Five

I mpossible!" Sir Jakob threw the word across the room, a verbal gauntlet that landed at Rydar's feet.

"And yet, here I stand," Rydar countered.

"You cannot be him!"

Rydar shrugged his lack of concern. "Why would you think not?"

"He's in Grønnland. At the settlement. If they even survived the journey, which I doubt!"

Lord Jakob's face turned a disturbing shade of red for a man of his age. His rapid breathing grew shallow and sweat sheened his skin. Grier crossed to him and took his arm.

"Sit, please," she said in Norse. "Rydar, bring wine."

"Madam, unhand me!" He jerked his arm from Grier.

"The Lady Grier is a skilled healer," Rydar declared. He looked around the parlor but the little man who let them in was already pouring a goblet. He scurried over to Jakob who gulped the liquid, spilling a little and staining his expensive tunic. Jakob was shaken, his distress visible in his darting glance and trembling hand.

"A cup for myself? And my wife?" Rydar asked the servant. With a disgusted glance at his employer, the man's head bobbed his assent. He moved to pour two more goblets, serving Grier first and then Rydar.

"My thanks. And your name?" Rydar inquired.

"Delling. Sir." He gave them each a small bow. Delling seemed to be rapidly re-evaluating his loyalties.

"The wine is excellent, Delling. Thank you," Rydar said smoothly. He turned to the older man. "Are you recovered, Lord Jakob? I'm afraid I have given you quite a shock."

Jakob glared at him. "Just because you come in here and claim to be Petter-Edvard's son doesn't prove a thing!"

True enough; it didn't. But Rydar hoped to be able to deflect that argument. He simply hadn't figured out exactly how thus far.

"And yet, I am," he said again.

"How did you get here?" Jakob demanded. "And when?"

"I sailed from Grønnland to Scotland in—" a smile tugged his mouth "—a very wee boat." Grier rubbed her knuckles over her lips to hide the grin that Rydar could still see. "I was injured when my boat was destroyed in a storm. Lady Grier and her cousin hauled me from the sea, and she tended my wounds until I was fully recovered."

"And then?" Sarcasm defined Lord Jakob's tone.

"And then I procured another boat, and we sailed here. We landed in Arendal a week ago."

"Why didn't you come here straight away? Why the delay? If your story is true, why would you not wish to lay your claim immediately?" Lord Jakob shouted.

Rydar looked at Grier and hoped she wouldn't understand his next words. "We were wed the day we arrived. Would you have me rush so soon from the bed of such a beautiful wife to charge headlong into this battle?"

Grier's eyes widened, but other than a pinkening of her cheeks she evinced no further reaction. At this revelation, Lord Jakob and Delling turned to consider her. She smiled at the two men and fluttered her lashes in a gut-twisting way that Rydar had never seen her do before.

She never trifled with me, he realized of a sudden.

If she had, he would have been married a month ago and still living in Scotland. He yanked his errant thoughts back into the room and to the situation at hand.

"And so, Lord Jakob, considering the circumstances we shall reside here. Will Delling be preparing our apartment? Or have we other staff that I must become acquainted with first?" Rydar arranged his features in as pleasant a manner as was possible. No need to further antagonize the man until he knew how he would go about proving himself.

Lord Jakob glared at Rydar. "I shall order rooms made ready."

"And the midday meal? Will it be served soon?" Rydar pressed.

Jakob's response ground through a clenched jaw in a ruddy face. "I shall let you know."

"Excellent. Now, I'm certain you won't mind if I show my wife around? I haven't seen the place since I was a boy and am very interested in what has—or hasn't—changed."

Rydar didn't wait for permission. He crossed the room and offered Grier his arm. She accepted with a smile and they exited the hall. He determined not to flinch, though had a dagger been pitched at his back he would not have been in the least bit surprised.

ᚱᚺ

Grier watched her husband carefully, reading his expressions and discerning his mood in order to help understand his words. He was patient with her when they were alone, speaking slowly and switching to Scots English when he needed to. She had that advantage at least. When he first washed up on her chyngell, he had no one who spoke Norse to help him.

But Rydar was so different here in Norway. She grew to know him when he was injured and unable to communicate. Now he was strong and healthy, and his language danced from his lips in long, lilting sentences. He teased, he informed, he debated, and he commanded. And her heart danced along with every exotic-sounding word he spoke.

Rydar led her down the hallway away from the blustering Lord Jakob, and stepped into each room along their path, ignoring the curious glances of servants sliding past them. An expansive formal meeting hall hung with large tapestries that depicted Viking longboats and pastoral mountain scenes. A banquet room was anchored by an enormous polished table. A second parlor held a vast writing desk littered with parchment and quills. When they reached the huge kitchen in the back, Rydar nodded to the half dozen women working over the fires and checked the larder. He frowned, gripped Grier's arm, and they retraced their steps.

When he led her up the stairway and no one was visible within earshot, Rydar tried to explain in simple Norse what had transpired with the very arrogant, very irritating man who seemed to be in charge of Hansen Hall.

"We will live here now," he began.

"Days? Months?" Grier asked in Norse. "How long?"

"I don't know. As long as we can."

Frustrated, she switched languages. "Does he ken ye are the son?"

"No. Does no' believe," Rydar responded. "But he will."

How, she wondered.

Rydar stepped into a sitting room and stilled. His face paled.

"Rydar?"

He didn't respond. As he moved through the room, his hands reached toward the bedroom door, the window, the hearth; but he didn't touch anything.

"Rydar!"

He whirled to face her, surprise chiseling the planes of his handsome face. "What?"

Delling stepped into the room. "Sir?"

His wide eyes shifted to the steward. "What?"

Grier caught the words "rooms, Lord Rydar" and "Lady Grier please come with me." Rydar reached for her arm and Grier let him take it again. Walking ahead of them, Delling grinned and babbled in rapid Norse, speaking far too quickly for her to follow. He opened a door further down the hall. Rydar nodded and thanked him.

Once inside, Grier considered the rooms they had been given. As in the other apartments, a public sitting room led to a private bed chamber. She passed through both and examined them closely. The rooms were a little neglected and they required a deep and thorough cleaning. Their mattress should be re-stuffed. At least the bedsheets were clean.

"What I do?" she asked, finally. "And we live here?"

Rydar smiled. He drew a breath and blew out his relief. "Love me."

"I do, Viking." She curled under his arm and leaned into his ribs. "What more?"

"Wait. Until I find the answer, it's all we can do."

ᚱᚺ

Rydar eased himself from Grier's side. She shifted in her sleep then resettled; her slow breathing attested to her continuing slumber. Rydar passed silently through their bedchamber into their sitting room, opened that door, listened, and slipped out into the darkened hall.

He padded barefooted along the row of apartments stopping outside his uncle Harald's rooms. Rydar assumed that Lord Jakob would have claimed these rooms, but the doors were ajar and the summer night's sky showed that no one rested there. Perhaps the man feared the shades of those men who died too young. A shudder twitched up his spine.

Something was written on the wall.

Rydar felt pulled into the room, recognizing the Norse runes. The wood floor, thickly dusted by abandonment, protested in a voice startlingly loud in the silent manse. As he approached the far wall the markings changed shape, undulating in the dim light. They whispered to him. *Come.*

He fell back, squinting. The runes had not been used for centuries and to find them here was a surprise. He stared at the esoteric shapes. The moon's path inched her light into the room, adding to the pale glow of the arctic summer. The shifting shapes held still.

He saw reid; 'riding' was the basis of his name. It was aptly linked to purs, the giant. Rydar's lips curved. Truly he was quite a tall man.

Next were kaun and ur.

Kaun is the children's scourge... and canker's seat.

Ur is the clouds' weeping, the hay's ruin and the shepherd's hate.

Prompted by the runes, the forgotten childhood poems now echoed strong in his memory. They seemed to define his life quite well up to now. Rydar stepped closer and the runes changed shape. Now he saw fe, wealth.

"What was that poem?" he muttered. "Wealth is kinsmen's contention... and the slitherer's track." He couldn't remember the middle part, but that seemed unimportant.

"The contention is clear. Who is the slitherer?" he asked.

Jakob Sander Hansen? Jakob Sander. Sander Jakob. Sandersen. Jakobsen.

Sander Jakobsen! That was the name of Harald's steward! That was why the man was familiar: he was steward when Rydar lived here as a boy! Recognition and realization tingled through his frame. The man was clearly a usurper.

He jumped back from the markings as they shifted again.

Ar. "Plenty is men's blessing, a good summer and a richly grown field," Rydar whispered. "Is that ever to be mine?"

Then the wall glowed with one large, pulsating symbol. Rydar could feel it beating with his heart, surging through his veins, thundering against his temples. The symbol—and its meaning— urged him to take his place here, and use whatever means that claim required.

It was yr.

A bent bow, brittle iron... and the giant's dart.

RN

Rydar jerked up in bed, covered in sweat. Grier slept peacefully next to him. Had he dreamt? Or had he truly been in his uncle's apartment? And if he was, had the runes spoken their truth to him?

He swung his feet to the ground and stood, stretching. He crossed to the open window and pulled back the heavy curtain. Water far below reflected the lavender sky and glittered with moonlight. He breathed deeply of the night air. In time, his heart slowed and his sweat evaporated.

Part of him wanted to walk down the hall and test his experience. But he was just as certain that the runes would still be there, as he was that they would not. It didn't matter. He remembered 'Lord' Jakob's true identity. And he planned to hoard that knowledge until the perfect moment.

"Husband?" Grier's sleep-husky voice reached out to him. He turned and looked at his wife in their bed, her hair spread in disarray and her eyes dark in the dim light. "Can't you sleep?"

He came back to her and slid between the sheets. "It's nothing," he murmured. "I'm sorry I woke you."

Grier's hand groped around under the covers until she found his yard. With a smile and a deep sigh, she squeezed it and sank into slumber once again.

He woke her up.

August 4, 1354

Rydar leaned on the mantle and gazed around his parents' bedroom. Some of the furniture was different. No doubt several occupants had moved through these rooms in the twenty years that passed, each with their own needs and preferences.

"My mother stood there," he pointed to the window. "My father stood here, by the fire."

"Where you?" Grier whispered.

"I held the post at the foot of their bed." Rydar wrapped his arms around an imaginary pole in front of him. "Like this."

"Sisters?"

"Crying into my mother's skirts." Rydar rubbed his eyes and pulled a deep sigh. "How am I going to accomplish this, Grier?"

She planted her feet and gazed up at him. "What you need?"

He pulled a face. "Only documents that no longer exist."

Grier shrugged and he recognized his own signal that the language was beyond her. He switched to English. "Papers. Like at church when we marry."

"Oh..." Grier's shoulders slumped. She returned to Norse. "You not have."

He tossed her a look of irritation. "No!"

Grier stepped back, away from him. "You know Jakob now?" she probed.

"I'm certain that I do. And I don't believe his story about being my uncle's cousin. If only I could prove... baugh!" Rydar jammed both hands through his hair.

Aggravation built inside him like lightning in a storm cloud. He loosed a thunderous roar and slammed his fists on the mantle, expressing his frustration in a consummately masculine manner. Angry, and feeling the weight of his continuing failure, he pounded the stones again, and again.

"Rydar!" Grier grabbed his arm. "Stop!"

Rydar jerked from her grasp and pummeled the carved fireplace with every agonized statement.

"I have no proof! It's my story and his story—and he has been here and he has moved into the role! And every trace of my father has been destroyed!" His fists stung, still tender with healing blisters, but he ignored the physical pain.

Grier pulled his hands toward her. "Stop it, Rydar!"

"Grier! Is no way to show!" he shouted in English.

"Ye need to stop, Viking!" she insisted. "This is no' going to help!"

Rydar's shook his head. "Tell me, then—what will?"

"I have no idea. But breaking your hands will no' and that's certain," she stated, still cradling his fists in her warmth. "And breaking the mantle with your bare hands is no' possible!"

She lifted his stinging fists to her lips, unfolded them and kissed his reddened palms. He watched her in the midst of his misery, and thanked God for giving her to him.

Then he began to shake.

"Are ye hurt?" Grier turned his hands over, searching for injury.

But Rydar didn't answer her. His gaze shot to the mantle. Was it possible? He tried to swallow but his throat was dry. He gulped air and tried to slow his heart.

"I need a hammer," he croaked. "And a chisel."

"What?"

He was back to Norse and he lost her. "Stay here!" he barked—in what language he didn't know—and he ran from the room. Down two flights of stairs, out the front door to the courtyard, across to the carpenter.

He was dripping sweat and winded when he returned to the chamber. Grier awaited him there, sitting on the bed, equal parts confusion and concern marring her features. She jumped to her feet when he appeared.

There was no possible way for him to explain to her what he was about to do. But it had to be done, even if they were thrown into the streets of Arendal in disgrace afterwards. He smiled a little, tossed Grier a shrug and turned to the fireplace.

"Rydar?"

He lifted the chisel and set it against the edge of the carved stone mantle.

"Rydar!" Grier moved to stop him.

He shook her off. "Grier. Trust me."

Her blue eyes darkened under rusty brows, but she stepped away. She crossed her arms over her chest and rested one trembling hand at the base of her throat. She nodded.

Rydar readied the hammer.

He drew a deep breath and held it.

He brought steel down against steel with a powerful singing ring.

And...

Nothing happened. Rydar snorted and tried again. This time a granite chip fell off. He leaned forward and searched for a seam, a crack, a weakness. There, closer to the wall. He wedged the chisel between plaster and stone. He hit it as hard as he could with the hammer. Again and again.

With each resounding clang, stone and wall separated in barely perceptible increments. And each resounding clang echoed throughout the manor, summoning Lord Jakob. The man strode into the room, anger pulsating from his tensed body.

"What in hell are you doing, Rydar?" he bellowed. He grabbed for the hammer and tried to wrestle it away.

"Leave me alone, Jakob!" Rydar shoved the older man aside.

"Have you lost your mind? I'll throw you out of here if you take one more swing!"

Rydar snarled and turned back to his task. He swung the hammer with all the desperation of his situation. This had to be the answer. Or there was none to be had.

He pulled back to swing again when a flash of fabric stopped him. Grier had her arms around Jakob and the pair tumbled to the ground. Grier clambered to her feet and faced Rydar. Her fierce expression resembled an arctic bear protecting its cub. She was furious and wild and glorious.

"Grier! What you—"

She straightened and held an unfamiliar dagger, aimed at the usurper. She glared at the man and uttered one guttural word.

"Jakob."

Rydar's jaw clenched and everything he saw turned red. Loosing a primal yell he ignored the chisel that clunked to the floor. With both hands wound around its shaft, he slammed the hammer into the mantle using every enraged muscle in his body.

Grier screamed and covered her ears.

A chunk of stone came loose, separating from the front piece. Rydar hit it again and again until it tumbled to the floor, shattering into scattered pieces. Sweating and panting, he stared at the empty space behind the mantle.

His breath came in raw, rough sobs. He knew his hopes were hung on a tenuous thread, an enigmatic phrase mumbled by a bitter and dying man. *My chamber behind the mantle.*

After the debacle of the destroyed hearth in Grønnland, he never really believed there was anything to it. He had even forgotten about it.

Until today.

Rydar's hands stung from the effort and new blisters rose on his palms. He knew he was crying, loud and ragged, but he didn't care. The hammer fell from his useless fingers. He looked at Grier. She was crying, too. Then he closed his eyes and reached into the hollow dusty space.

Too many hopes rested on what he did—or did not—find there. For a moment he paused. Then his shoulders slumped in stunned disbelief.

"*Å min Gud.*"

As he drew a ragged breath, Rydar gripped a leather-wrapped roll that had patiently waited in the dark for him all these years and pulled it into the light of day.

"What that?" Grier cried.

Lord Jakob clambered, wheezing, to his feet. "How did you—"

Rydar struggled to corral his erratic emotions. He faced the former steward and glared him into silence. The miraculous package in his hand secured his ability to prove himself. He worked to gain his composure. With a quick glance at Grier, he spoke.

"Because I am the Lord Rydar Martin Petter-Edvard Hansen, the last living heir to Hansen Hall!" he stated in a chilling tone. "And the documents here will prove it!"

The leather packet unfurled like a newly released butterfly. Inked on its wings was a complete family tree backing up five generations from Rydar and his sisters to their eleventh century forbearers.

A small pouch fell to the floor with a muted thud. Rydar bent down to retrieve it as baptism records and marriage records fluttered to the floor, yellowed with age but still legible. He handed the pouch to Grier to open, the leather packet pressed close to his chest.

She untied the bag and dumped its contents into her palm. A heavy Nordic-carved silver and gold ring, its recesses blackened with soot, rested in her hand.

"Oh my God," Jacob wheezed. "I believed it to be lost."

Grier looked at Ryder, her eyes wide. "What?"

"My father's ring. The chamberlain's ring." Rydar extended his hand and Grier slid the ring onto his finger. It was thick and solid and it fit like it was meant for him.

Overcome with a sense of his destiny, Rydar closed his eyes. He was finally here. And he belonged here. With a deep sigh, he blinked his eyes open and looked down at the packet in his arms.

Folded in the center was a letter addressed to him.

Rydar's heart rammed his ribs when he saw his father's strong, vertical script. He had no idea what to expect from the man who smoldered with bitterness until the day he died. Grier came to him and wrapped her arm around his waist, sliding her shoulder under his arm. He felt her warmth against his ribs.

He opened the letter.

Rydar ~

Here are the documents and ring that prove who you are. If you found this, then you have returned from the banishment that my foolish pride is now forcing on our family. Only God knows how it will be in Grønnland but I pray you might set things aright with your uncle and claim your rightful place at Hansen Hall.

Please forgive me.

Your father,

Petter-Edvard Hansen

May 29, 1333 Arendal Norway

Rydar handed the letter to Jakob. The man crumpled to the nearest chair and his lips moved silently with every word he read. He seemed to shrink and age before them as realization pushed him farther and farther down.

"So you see, Sander Jakobsen, I am who I am." Rydar waited until the man's stunned eyes rose and locked on his before he swung the final stroke.

"And you are, once again, who you always were."

Chapter Thirty-Six

June 3, 1355
Arendal, ten months later

Grier endured the intensifying pains quietly throughout the light summer's night. When the clock in their bedchamber showed seven in the morning, she eased her bulk from the bed and went in search of her maid. She found Astrid in the kitchen

"I'll need the midwife in a couple of hours," she told the girl. "After your breakfast, you will go and tell her?"

"Yes, my lady. Are you feeling well now?" Astrid had three children of her own and was unlikely to panic at the first signs of labor.

"I feel fine for nine minutes out of every ten!" Grier joked. "So you see, there is no hurry."

"First babes can be stubborn, and that's God's truth." Astrid laid her palm over Grier's belly and waited. "Does Lord Hansen know?"

Grier shook her head. "I tried not to disturb his sleep. I think he is unaware."

"Unaware of what, my love?" Rydar asked, smiling in the kitchen doorway. His gaze dropped to Grier's swollen abdomen before Astrid could pull her hand away. Color drained from his face. "Are you—is it—"

"Um-hmm," Grier grunted. She winced and tried to draw slow deep breaths while Astrid gripped her shoulders, offering support.

"What must be done?" Rydar demanded.

"Staying calm must be done!" Grier rasped. She couldn't speak again until the spasm passed. Then she straightened and glared at her anxious husband.

"I've delivered enough babes on my own to know what to do and when. You needn't shout."

"I'm sorry, Grier. But is your babe coming now?" A visibly panicked Rydar took her from Astrid and forced her to sit down.

"Today. But not right now," she assured him.

"But you have pains?"

"Yes. Since midnight," Grier confessed. "But first babies take some time."

Rydar's expression vacillated between fear and irritation. "All night you've had pains and you didn't tell me? Why?"

Grier laughed. "If you could see your own face right now, then you wouldn't need to ask!"

Rydar blushed. "It's only because I love you."

"I know, Viking. And I love you for it."

"What can I do for you?" he pressed.

Grier grinned and patted his bearded cheek. "Stay by my side and provide for my every need. Until the midwife banishes you, that is."

ᚱᚺ

Rydar sat on the floor outside his apartment door and leaned against the wall with his legs splayed and his feet wiggling nonstop. He listened to his wife as she strained and groaned her way through the birth pains, holding his breath with every contraction, as if his own intensity might give her strength.

"It's not long now," Astrid assured him as she went for fresh water.

She said that an hour ago. Rydar was thinking that by 'not long' she meant before the sun set. And being this close to the solstice, the sun never set. He shifted his bottom a little and listened for the next pain.

A brisk knock at the manor's door diverted his attention. He waited to be summoned if he was needed, unwilling to leave Grier's vicinity. But the familiar voices he heard below prompted him to clamber to his feet. He bolted down the stairs.

"Gavin? Kristofer?" Rydar called.

"And Lars!" the youngest fisherman cried.

The three young men swamped him like a litter of excited puppies, slapping his back and yelping in chaotic joy.

"You did it, Sir!"

"Guess where we've been?"

"You're lord of the manor!"

"My arm is fine!"

"Where is Lady Grier?"

"We went as far as the Holy Roman Empire!"

Rydar grinned broadly in amused silence until the boys realized he wasn't answering them.

"Sir?" Gavin paused for a breath. "Is anything amiss?"

"No, Gavin. Everything is wonderful. In fact, the Lady Grier is—"

An urgent call from the second floor knifed his gut. "Lord Hansen! Where are you?"

"I'm here!" he shouted. He whirled and took the stairs three at a time. "What has occurred?"

"Wait!" Astrid disappeared infuriatingly behind a solidly closed door. The three sailors tumbled up the stairs after him.

"What is it, Sir?" Kristofer asked.

Lars chimed in with, "Where is Lady Grier?"

"She's—" But Rydar was interrupted when Astrid's head popped through the doorway.

"Don't go away!" she ordered before evaporating again.

Gavin touched his arm. "Sir Hansen?"

A long straining groan pushed past the doorway and the four men froze. When it ended in abrupt silence, none of them moved. Or breathed.

"Was that—" Kristofer began. An indignant howl cut him off.

A loud, urgent, tiny, indignant howl that gasped in minuscule pauses and wailed again and again. Rydar found it hard to breathe and his legs were numb. He didn't remember sitting down, but he was splayed on the floor once more. Three frightened faces hovered over him.

"Sir Hansen! Are you well?"

The door to his apartment blew open and Astrid looked around the hall. Her face registered her surprise when she found him lying on the floor. "Sir Hansen? Are you well?"

"What is it?" he bellowed. All he could see were teeth. Lots of teeth. She must be smiling.

"You have a son!" she squealed. "A big healthy and beautiful boy!"

"I do?" Relief released him.

"You do?" the three visitors exclaimed in surprised unison.

"Can I see him?" Rydar ventured.

"In a few minutes. The midwife needs to finish up. Wait here." And Astrid was gone. The human puppies swarmed all over him again, laughing and poking and calling him 'pappa.'

ᚱᚺ

When Rydar was at last allowed to see Grier he felt all chewed up and spit out dry. He marched through his sitting room, eyes on the doorway. Firelight beckoned him through and he followed its undulating light. And there, in his bed, was his wonderful, amazing, magnificent wife.

She wore a soft cotton gown and a sheet pulled to her waist. Her ginger curls were tangled and dark hollows accented her blue eyes. An exhausted smile lifted her cheeks and pinched the corners of those same eyes.

And his son suckled at her breast.

"Grier," he whispered. He sat on the bed, careful not to jar her. "You did it."

"We did it together, Viking. We made a son." She rubbed the babe's hair, which was as orange as a carrot. He stopped sucking and turned away from his mother and peered at his father. His eyes were dark, murky blue.

"He has your colors," Rydar whispered again. He couldn't force his voice to be any louder.

"Right now he does. That might change. But he has your height." Grier un-swaddled the infant and he threw his arms and legs wide. Rydar was astounded at the length of the newborn boy's limbs.

"How did he fit inside you?" Rydar marveled.

Grier laughed. "How did he get out of me is the bigger question!"

Rydar stroked Grier's cheek. "Are you well? Have you survived, wife?"

"I have never been happier in my entire life!" Grier placed her hand over his. "What will you call your son?"

"If you've no objections, I'd like to call him Arne Rory Hansen, after Arne Jorgensen and your father. If it wasn't for Arne, I never would have met you. And," Rydar bit back his teasing smile, "if that ridiculous hair color sticks, he'll be aptly named."

June 4, 1355

The fishermen were allowed to see Grier and baby Arne the next day. Astrid brushed Grier's hair and helped her into a clean cotton gown and silk over-wrap in preparation. She was so excited to see all the boys again, but especially Lars. She yearned to examine his arm and see how it mended.

Rydar stood beside the bed when they entered, holding his son and oozing pride all over the room. After giving the trio enough time to examine the slumbering infant boy and say many nice things about him, Grier waved Lars to her side.

"Show me your arm," she begged.

Lars rolled up his sleeve and bared his arm to his shoulder. Grier felt the jagged pink scar, impressed with how well it had knitted. "Is it strong? Your arm?"

"Yes, Lady. I can do all the work I did before," he assured her.

"And do you have pain?"

Lars' expression turned apologetic at that, as if she would feel her skills lacking were he to admit to it.

"It's common in a mended bone," she continued. Then she leaned closer and whispered in a conspiratorial manner, "Sir Hansen's leg plagues him in the winter even still."

"Does it?" Lars answered in kind. "Can anything be done?"

Grier nodded. "I have a salve that helps. I'll give you some before you sail off."

"Thank you, Lady. And now I'll do a favor for you."

Grier leaned back against her pillow. "Thank you Lars, but

that's not needful."

"Oh, but it is! You've no idea where we've been! Or where we're going!" he exclaimed. He turned to his brother and cousin. "Have you told him?"

Rydar quirked his brow. "What have you been about, boys?"

"We sailed all the way to the Holy Roman Empire!" Kristofer exclaimed. "Lars' arm hurt in the cold, so after we left Lady Margoh in Áslo, we sailed south looking for warmth."

"We kept the land on our left and followed the coast. We fished and traded and just kept going." Gavin explained. "We saw so many places! It was amazing!"

"And then we wanted to come back to see what happened with the two of you, and if Sir Hansen got his land." Kristofer added.

"And now, we'll sail to Scotland. Back to Durness," Lars concluded. "So Lady, if you wish it, we'll carry a letter to your cousin. Then he might know how things have turned out for you and Sir Hansen."

Grier's throat tightened and she couldn't speak. All she could do was nod and grin like a lunatic.

ᚱᚺ

My dearest Logan and Malise ~

I never expected it, but these three wonderful sailors have offered to carry my letter to you. I hope you are both well and happy and that the castle, Durness and your Mercat Fair all continue to prosper. Afore I tell you about myself however, let me assure you that Margoh reached Áslo safely. She was given over to her husband's family by these same three men who hand you this paper.

The very same day we landed in Arendal, Rydar and I were married by a priest. His proposal was the greatest surprise of my life, and the greatest joy. We are well suited and very much in love, as you surmised.

Within a fortnight of our arrival, Rydar was able to claim his inheritance. The Black Plague was even more devastating here in Norway than it was in Scotland, and we soon discovered that Rydar was the last living member of his family (excepting his oldest sister secluded in a nunnery). We moved into Hansen Hall and I have spent the last months cleaning and setting the much neglected rooms to rights. We brought in new servants and are hoping to start a Mercat Fair here in Arendal later this summer.

Our son, Arne Rory Hansen, was born this very week. He is a fine, strong boy with his father's length and his mother's coloring. Rydar could not be more pleased with me or the boy.

I have, over time, become quite comfortable speaking in Norse, though I struggle still with the writing and defer to my husband. Norway is very beautiful but the winters here are quite harsh. Hansen Hall is built of strong stone with an abundance of hearths and plenty of wood so we are snug.

Dearest cousins, I could not be happier. I hope the same can be said for both of you. I send you my most faithful love and keep you always in my prayers. Please do the same for us.

Grier MacInnes Hansen
June 6, 1355 Arendal Norway

Following is an excerpt from:

Loving the Knight

by Kris Tualla

Goodnight Publishing
http://www.GoodnightPublishing.com

Chapter One

Castleton Village
Scottish Borderlands
December 1, 1354

Eryndal grabbed William, her fingers circling his scrawny arm. Though the nine-year-old tried to twist free she held tight.

"You are no' my mither!" he bellowed, stomping a foot. The clomp of his wooden soles echoed off the stone walls of the Great Hall. Young Liam was as indignant and red-faced as a boy his age could ever be.

"I'm not your mother, true. But since the Death, I'm all you've got!" Eryn bent her face to his. "And I'm all that stands between you and starvation—or a much worse fate. So I suggest you stop trying to destroy this estate afore it's yours!"

"He'll want a whipping," Geoffrey McDougal drawled from behind the boy.

Liam twisted his head to glare over his shoulder. "It's no' your concern!"

"Since I'm constable of Castleton now, your punishment is fully my concern, *William*." Geoffrey crossed muscular arms across his chest and gave Liam a stern look. "When ye open a gate and the sheep wander off it's akin to stealing then, isn't it?"

Eryn bit her lips between her teeth, damming any show of amusement. Friends since she was an adolescent, watching

Geoffrey in his new position of authority made her want to grin. Instead, she gave the boy a little shake and bolstered Geoff's point.

"Haven't the reivers done enough damage, Liam? Why do you do such things?"

The boy shrugged one skinny shoulder and shoved ragged hanks of red hair out of his eyes.

Geoffrey considered her from beneath gathered brows. "He'll want a whipping," he repeated with a bit more emphasis.

Eryn nodded reluctantly. She'd had her share of whippings from the nuns of Elstow Abbey for being as contrary as Liam was acting right now. Even so she still had trouble curbing her tongue, so she doubted a willow switch would do much for Liam. But it needed to be done.

Jamie, her newly elevated steward, stepped into the corner of her vision. "Lady?"

The summons pulled her attention from the pouting boy. "Yes?"

"The men are starting to arrive."

Eryn nodded and glanced out the window at the lowering gray sky. "Have them wait in the courtyard, but serve them something warm to drink while they're standing."

"Yes, m'lady."

"And William?" Geoffrey pressed.

"Will you do it, Constable?" she asked sternly. "I'll need to send some men to round up the sheep, and then meet with the tenants."

Geoff's gray eyes narrow slightly; long acquainted, he clearly discerned her reluctance. But one corner of his mouth lifted and he dipped a quick nod. "Of course."

She let go of William's arm and—to his credit—he didn't bolt. Instead, he lifted his chin in defiance. But it was wobbling.

"Come on, then." Geoffrey walked toward the kitchen and the back door. "Let's get on with it."

Liam followed with very small steps. Once they were gone, Eryn pulled a deep breath. At twenty-six, she could easily be mother of a nine-year-old son. But she wasn't. She wasn't even married.

And raising a sudden orphan that wasn't her child, living in a home that wasn't truly hers, and acting in a position that she assumed when none else was left to take it was harder than anything she could imagine; excepting, of course, those horrible years that the Black Death swept across Europe and left no town, no estate, no family untouched.

At least she was already an orphan. All she lost were employers.

Eryn sent two youths after the wandering flock and headed out to the courtyard to meet with her remaining tenants.

❈ ❈ ❈

Less than four dozen men stood in the courtyard, their feet stomping and their reddened hands wrapped around steaming wooden cups. Eryn lifted her chin and refused to look discouraged. She pulled her cloak tighter as if that action would hold the men here. Falling snow dusted all of their heads and frosted the ground.

Before the Death nearly a hundred and fifty men worked the Bell estate. Half of those had died. Now many were simply leaving, going in search of abandoned land to claim as their own. If Eryn couldn't find a way to keep them as tenants, young William and those still serving at his estate would starve.

"Gentlemen!" she shouted.

The crowd stilled. Gazes full of fear, hope and suspicion met hers. She gave them a smile and prayed that she exuded confidence. "Thank you for coming. We have been through a very rough patch, but I do believe we have turned a corner."

"What else is new, missy?" one man called out.

"New?" She lifted one brow. "How about this: I am prepared to let you earn your land." A rumble rose amidst a sea of wagging heads. "Do you want to hear more?"

"On whose authority?" another man asked.

This was the critical moment; her chance to take control.

"My own, of course." Half the crowd nodded, but the other half shook their heads. Eryn pressed on, "Since the death almost a year past of Henry le Bell, may God sain his soul"—Eryn crossed herself as did the assemblage—"I have been running this estate on behalf of young William Robert. I intend to continue, until he comes of an age to do so himself."

The head-shaking ceased, but the gazes were still suspicious.

"Explain yourself, then," the first man demanded.

Eryn stepped closer to the huddled bodies. "I am well aware

that many of our tenants have fled in hopes of better circumstances. But I ask you, what better circumstances are there to be had?" She spread her hands. "Your homes are here. Your families are here. You know this land well, do you not?"

Glances. Shrugs. Nods.

"Here is what I propose: the estate will be divided between those who wish to earn ownership of their own land, and those who wish to remain as serfs for William. For those men and women remaining as serfs, nothing will change; you will continue to work for, and be cared for by, the Bell estate."

"And the others?" a man in the back prodded.

"The others will work their own plots. Each year one tenth of what they produce must be given to the estate. In ten years, the land will be wholly theirs." Eryn chose one big man to lock eyes on.

"Why start with nothing?" she queried. She tossed her hood back, exposing her head to the icy elements. Snow melted in her hair and seeped to her scalp. "Why wander in hopes of finding empty, unworked fields? Tumbling plague houses? Broken fences? I am offering you fertile land, already tilled. Houses already built."

Another rumble rose, but this time the heads bobbed in affirmation.

"What abou' the livestock?" the big man asked.

"I'll sell them to you for a return of one animal per animal taken. You'll have three years to breed them and repay me. Repay William, that is." Eryn grinned to cover her slip. "All the rest are yours to keep."

A lanky redheaded young man pushed his way forward and pointed an accusing finger at Eryn. "What's in this for ye?" he demanded.

What indeed.

Not nearly enough.

"I will have a roof over my head, food on my table, and a little to set aside for the day when William takes his rightful place as lord of the Bell estate." She turned and stepped toward the manor, then faced the crowd again. "In the meantime, you shall address me as Lady Eryndal Bell and afford me all the rights and respect due the lady of an estate—because that is what I am. Have you any objections?"

For a moment, no one spoke. No one moved. All the men

seemed to be weighing the options before them, as well as her overt claim to the title. Eryn's hands fisted alongside her thighs. Her jaw clenched.

She earned this role, damn it.

She was head of the household staff when Lady Elspeth le Bell fell victim to the plague. For several months afterward, Eryn fulfilled every one of that worthy woman's roles, including the raising of William. When Henry le Bell's steward died, she assumed his authority over the rapidly diminishing staff as well. By the time Henry himself succumbed, there was nothing on the estate that she wasn't managing on her own. That was January seventh, the day after the feast of Epiphany, this same year.

She already proved herself capable. She only lacked the official designation. Now was the time to claim it.

The big man she had addressed directly straightened and dipped his chin. "No, my lady. I have no objections at all." He glared down at the younger redhead and nudged him with an elbow.

"Uh, no. Lady Bell," he squeaked.

She swept the crowd with an intense gaze, searching for reluctance or outright rebellion. There was none. "Good. Those of you wishing to earn your lands come back tomorrow at noon. Together we shall draw your boundaries on the map. If you do not appear, you will not be given the option again. Is that fair?"

Nods all around. Some smiles. Backs were being slapped. Hands were clasped and shaken. Eryn turned to her steward, Jamie.

"See that everyone gets another cup, will you? It's a cold day and the walk home will be thus eased."

He dipped his chin in grinning respect. "Of course, Lady Bell. As you wish."

⚜ ⚜ ⚜

Eryn's hands shook as she closed the door to the manor. She leaned her backside against it and blew a long sigh. A rivulet of cold sweat trickled down her backbone as melted snow dripped from her hair.

Her offer was accepted; her role wasn't challenged. The bastard orphan of Elstow Abbey, Bedford, England was now Lady Eryndal Smythe Bell of Castleton, Scotland. Foster mother of William Robert Bell, heir.

And still well-liked, so it seemed. Eryn crossed herself again and kissed the crucifix that hung from her belt. Its amber beads smiled dully in the candlelight, approving her success.

Thank you, Father. Be with me always.

Eryn straightened and made her way to the kitchen at the back of the huge manor. William was there, red-eyed and sniffling over a plate of toasted bread and honey. Geoffrey sat astride the bench beside the lad. He held a steaming goblet of his own.

"You're still alive I see," Geoff teased, though his eyes were unsmiling. "The peasants have accepted your elevated status, then?"

"They have. Tomorrow we shall see how many of them wish to earn their freedom." Eryn took the goblet from Geoffrey's hand and swallowed a large gulp of the warmed mead. She began to smooth Liam's russet hair but he jerked his head from her reach.

"Don't," he growled.

Eryn handed Geoff his goblet and sat beside Liam. "I know you're angry that your parents died, Liam. I have no intention of taking their place."

"Then leave."

"If I do, you'll starve. Don't you understand that?"

One shoulder moved a little and dropped back into place.

"Will you look at me Liam?" she whispered.

Brown eyes rimmed in red lifted to hers under a canopy of ginger. His lips were pressed in a hard line.

"Today I made arrangements that will keep the tenants here until you are grown. They will bring us food and animals and things that they make, so that we may always have a warm place to live and plenty of food. I'll make your clothes as I always have. I'll take care of you the way your mother wanted."

Tears bulged on the boy's lower lids but he swiped them away before they spilled. "You're no' my mither!" he snapped.

The litany was an old one and Eryn ignored it. "The thing is, Liam, every time you try to hurt me with your mischief, it's your own estate you harm."

"She's right, ye ken," Geoffrey added. He leaned closer. "And as Constable it's my task to keep peace and punish the wrongdoers, isn't it?"

William's mouth twisted and his chin trembled. He stood, grabbed the last of his toast in a grubby fist, and ran out of the kitchen. Eryn might have worried if she couldn't hear his boots thumping up the stairs. The slam of his chamber door assured her of his whereabouts.

Geoffrey took her hand. "He needs a man around, and ye ken it's true."

Eryn looked away. "Not now, Geoff, please. I'm done in after the meeting. Besides, I've got maps to study and—"

He rose to his feet of a sudden, stopping her words. He glanced over his shoulder at the women preparing the evening meal and then pulled Eryn to her feet. "Come."

"Where?"

"The Hall."

Eryn followed Geoff because he had firm hold of her hand. She didn't want to pull it away and upset him. If her intuition was correct, their pending conversation was going to be difficult enough as it was.

Geoff led her to a corner of the huge hearth and bade her to sit. He knelt in front of her. "Marry me, Eryn."

Her shoulders slumped. "Please don't ask me that, Geoff."

He shook his head and the grip on her hand tightened. "I've waited, as ye asked."

"I know."

"The Death is past. No one has died since Lord Henry. It's almost the year."

"True, but—"

"And the boy needs a father. Ye see it plain as day!" he pressed.

"And why do you ask me today?" she countered.

His brow furrowed. "What do you mean?

"Today I am the Lady Bell. Yesterday I was only Eryndal Smythe. Why not yesterday?"

Geoff's cheeks grew splotchy and darkened the gray of his eyes. "That's no' fair, and ye ken it well!"

She did. But his proposal made her feel like a rabbit in a trap. "It's only that, well, it seems as if… oh, I don't know." She pulled her hand from Geoffrey's.

"Do ye no' have a care for me, Eryndal Smythe?" he pleaded.

She laid her fingertips against his cheek. "Of course I do. You've been my steady friend since I arrived here, a maid of only fifteen years."

He laid his hand over hers and pressed her palm against his

bearded jaw. "I hoped for more than friendship."

"I know…" Her voice caught in her throat. How could she explain feelings she herself didn't fully understand?

"Is my hope foolishness, then?" he asked.

"No, Geoff. But I asked for a year, remember? A year with no deaths?"

He nodded slowly. "Aye. But it's been—"

"It's been ten and a half months."

His grip on her hand loosened. "Ye'll be a stickler then? Hold out to the end?"

Eryn leaned forward and kissed him softly on the lips. "Ask me again in a month and a half. Until then, give me peace and time to organize the changes. Will you?"

Geoff slid a large hand behind her head and pulled her into his more demanding kiss. He tasted of the mead and his warm breath grazed her cheek. She didn't resist; she didn't want to. When the kiss ended, he leaned his forehead against hers. "Aye, I'll do it. But don't hold me off forever."

"No," she lied.

She looked out the window. The snowfall was blowing harder.

Hermitage Castle
Scottish Borderlands
December 1, 1354

Lord Andrew Drummond wrapped a scarf around his throat and tucked the scrap of wool into the collar of his cloak. It formed a slight barrier to the snow that was beginning to fall harder and at a distinctly unfriendly angle. Hermitage Castle rose on the horizon, a formidable square of wood standing forty feet tall. Drew couldn't see any evidence of habitation; no activity around the structure, no smoke rising on this frigid afternoon.

"Shite. It appears deserted. This might very well be the longest and most miserable day of the past year," he grumbled to his vassal. Melted snowflakes ran into his eyes and snot dripped from his nose. He couldn't feel his toes.

Kennan steered his huge brown gelding closer to Drew's gray stallion. "If no one's there, we'll ride on, aye?"

"Aye. There's no reason to bide in that overgrown tomb

otherwise." He wiped his nose on the end of the scarf. "It's five miles to Castleton. If we push, we can be there in an hour."

"The horses are done in, I'm afraid," Kennan said.

"Hour and a half, then."

The castle was, indeed, uninhabited. Victim of both the endless border wars with England and the half decade of plague, no one—so it seemed—deemed this fortification important enough to winter here. They were on to Castleton, then.

Lord Andrew Drummond was done in as well. For a year and a half he and Kennan had traversed Scotland on behalf of King David II. Held in the Tower of London since 1346 as prisoner of England's King Edward III, Drew was his Scottish king's main connection with the country he reigned over. Frequent trips to London had been deferred until Drew could assess the condition of Scotland following the Black Death.

The news was grim at best, horrifying most often.

Bodies rotting in overfull graves. Villages devoid of any living being. Empty houses with fallen roofs. Animals, wandering and starving. Children's cries echoing in the night.

More than half of the Scottish countryside lay dead. England as well. And it was worse in the cities, where people lived in each other's pockets and disease scuttled without mercy.

After his visit to Castleton, it would fall to Lord Andrew Drummond to ride to London and explain all this to a king who witnessed none of it. To explain to his sovereign why Scotland was unable to raise a ransom to secure his freedom. Why the world he once knew was irrevocably altered. It was not a pleasant proposition. He shivered.

Drew truly was done in.

"There it is. And it's got people," Kennan said, rousing him from his lethargic contemplation.

Visible through the quickening snow, the sight of the lit manor, smoke leaning from her chimneys and bodies scurrying in her yard, sent waves of relieved exhaustion pulsing through Drew's tense body. His cheeks were stiff with cold and the scarf only served to act as a wick, dripping melted snow inside his cloak. Perhaps the time to quit his vocation was upon him.

"Thank God," he muttered. He pulled back on the reins as his warhorse strained forward, eager to reach shelter of his own. "Easy.

We mustn't charge in or they'll mistake our intent."

"Aye, sir." Kennan guided his mount behind Drew. "I'll follow ye."

⚷ ⚷ ⚷

"Riders are approaching, my lady."

Eryn looked up from her needle. "How many?"

"Only two," Jamie said.

"Have they a banner?"

"No."

She set aside the tunic she was making for William and followed her steward to the window. If there were just two of them, they were not likely to be reivers or thieves. But who would be out so late on such a violent day? The sun was buried behind thick gray clouds and her light was dying quickly.

Eryn leaned against the small window panes and tried to discern what sort of problem might be advancing toward her home. All she could make out were two enormous warhorses. The riders carried no colors that she could see, but then the snowfall turned everything into dark splotches on shifting white.

"Are they English or Scots, do ye think?" Jamie asked.

"It doesn't matter. If they come in peace, I'll shelter them." Eryn turned to her steward. They were the same height—five feet and nine inches—but his lean frame was deceptively strong. "Have the hands ride out to meet them. Watch for signs of aggression. If there are none, bring them inside and stable their horses. I'll meet them in the Hall."

"Yes, lady."

"And if they are suspect, kill them."

Jamie nodded and hurried to do her bidding.

Eryn looked back out the window. Ordering that men be put to death was not an act her conscience rested with, but at times it must be done even so. If she meant to hold her position, she had to give orders without fear. She had to do what was necessary to protect the estate, her serfs, and William.

Please, God, spare their lives, she prayed silently. *Let them be friends, not foes.*

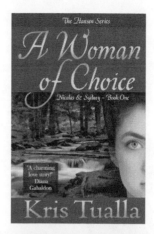

Don't miss:
Nicolas & Sydney
in
A Woman of Choice
A Prince of Norway
&
A Matter of Principle

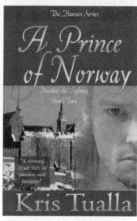

And the sequel to

Loving the Norseman:

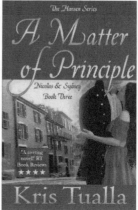

Kris Tualla, a dynamic award-winning and internationally published author of historical romances, writes with a fast-paced and succinct style. Her plots are full of twists, passion, and very satisfying outcomes! Kris started writing in 2006 with nothing but a nugget of a character in mind, and has created a dynasty - The Hansen Series.

Norway is the new Scotland!

For more information visit:
www.GoodnightPublishing.com

For inquiries about publication, contact:
info@GoodnightPublishing.com

http://www.KrisTualla.com
http://kristualla.wordpress.com
http://www.facebook.com/KrisTualla
http://www.youtube.com/user/ktualla
http://twitter.com/ktualla